I0589254

Seven Deadly Sins

Cynthia Hickey

Copyright © **2023 Cynthia Hickey**
Published by: Winged Publications

This book is a work of fiction. Names, characters, places, and incidents are the product of the author's imagination and are used fictitiously. Any resemblance to actual events, locales, or persons, living or dead, is coincidental.

No part of this book may be copied or distributed without the author's consent.

All rights reserved.

ISBN: 978-1-0879-6050-0

Contents

ACKNOWLEDGMENTS

Insert acknowledgments text here. Insert acknowledgments text here. Insert acknowledgments text here. Insert acknowledgments text here. Insert acknowledgments text here. Insert acknowledgments text here. Insert acknowledgments text here. Insert acknowledgments text here. Insert acknowledgments text here. Insert acknowledgments text here.

DEADLY PRIDE

Cynthia Hickey

Chapter One

"Let's play a game. Pride is one of the seven deadly sins; Beware of pride because you will be returning to the earth and your body will be eaten up by the worms."

It was the third such notice Harper Scranton had received in a week. What did it mean?

She felt as if the sender was building up to something, but what? She dropped the note into a paper sack with the others then snatched up her ringing phone. "Detective Scranton."

"We got a call that Lance Richardson was found dead in his penthouse. Foul play is suspected." Anna Crypton, one of the town's police officers sounded frantic'

"*The* Lance Richardson? The man who owns Lakeside Resort?"

"One and the same. I also heard the FBI is already headed over there. Something about ongoing messages."

Harper's blood ran cold. Her hand holding the phone shook. "I'll be there in fifteen." Could the FBI be receiving the same type of messages she was? Until today's note about playing a game, she hadn't taken the notes very seriously. More like chalked them up to a nutcase harassing the only woman detective in Oakdale.

She grabbed her jacket and holster then rushed to her jeep. Thirteen minutes later, she marched through the double glass doors of the Lakeside Resort apartments, made a beeline for the elevator and pressed the button for the penthouse.

Before entering the apartment, she slipped paper booties over her boots and snapped rubber gloves over her hands. The smell of death greeted her. Not recently deceased then. Enough time had passed for decay to begin.

"It's not pretty." A crime scene tech approached her. "Somebody really wanted to embarrass this guy."

"I prefer to make my own conclusions, but thanks." She didn't want anyone else's opinion to muddy her observations. She pulled a roll-on perfume from her bag and dotted her upper lip to help mask the odor and stepped into the bedroom.

A completely nude Richardson had been posed on his knees, tied to stay that way, in a posture of meekness. His throat had been slit so that he knelt in his own blood. On the wall in what looked like blood had been written Pride Goes Before the Fall.

Harper frowned. "What is it about pride?" She muttered.

"Detective Scranton? I'm FBI Special Agent Liam McConnell."

She glanced into a face too rugged to be drop dead gorgeous, but handsome nonetheless. Troubled hazel eyes stared down at her from under dark lashes. "Heard you've been getting messages." She motioned for him to follow her out of the room.

"Yes." His brow furrowed.

"So have I. Today's mentioned playing a game. Any idea what that means, and why is the FBI involved when we've had only one death?"

"I'm here because of having received several messages similar to the one you just mentioned." His deep voice rolled over her like thunder. "When Richardson's body was discovered, along with the message on the wall, I knew this was only the beginning to something."

Harper glanced through the bedroom door at the body. "He's been made to stay in a posture of humility. The opposite of pride, Agent."

"Call me Liam. We'll be working together."

She narrowed her eyes. "I prefer to keep things on a professional level, Agent."

Amusement flickered in his eyes. "I agree, but still call me Liam. Instinct tells me this guy won't be easy to catch, and we'll be spending a lot of time together. I'll call you Harper." He grinned.

Awesome. She forced a smile and turned back to the death scene to see whether she'd missed something. Not wanting to wait for crime scene photos, she started snapping pictures with her cell phone to pore over back at the station.

Being too close to the FBI agent with a slight Irish accent would make it hard to concentrate. She'd have to keep distance between them as much as possible. The past had taught her not to get involved with anyone during an active investigation.

"Why Richardson?" Liam stepped up behind her. "Tell me what you know about him?"

Without stopping what she was doing, she said, "Wealthy. A playboy. Respected but not necessarily liked within the community. Likes the limelight." The local and surrounding newspapers usually had some type of article on the man in each issue.

"Prideful?"

Her head snapped up. "You could say that. Why?"

He turned his cell phone to face her. "Got another message. The perp has my cell number. This one says, there are seven deadly sins, but many who are involved in each one. Mr. Richardson is only the beginning."

"He's targeting people he thinks are committing sins?" She widened her eyes. "That is…everyone."

"Makes our job harder. Let's head back to the station and start a case board." Without waiting for her to follow, he turned and left.

Harper's knees weakened. She knew the seven deadly sins and had committed more than a few of them herself. Was this why the perp chose to send the messages to her? Did he know her past?

~

Liam followed the pretty detective's royal-blue jeep to the police station. He'd noticed the fear shadow her dark eyes when he'd read the last message out loud. Was she the primary target?

He drummed his fingers on the steering wheel. At first, he'd thought maybe the perp could be someone with a grudge against Liam because he'd served justice on someone dear to them. Now, he wasn't so sure.

After the third message received early that morning suggested Liam head to Oakdale and telling him about a dead guy with a message painted on the wall in blood, he'd approached his director about heading to Oakdale to work with local law enforcement. He hadn't expected to discover the detective receiving messages also.

He frowned. Why bring Liam to Oakdale? Was there something connecting him to Harper? He shrugged. The pieces would all click together in time. The detective was correct, though. Most, if not everyone, committed at least one of the deadly sins on a regular basis, making it virtually impossible to narrow down the identity of the next victim. Liam hated feeling helpless.

The jeep pulled behind the one-story metal building and parked in back. A shapely leg, followed by a tall body with parts in all the right places, emerged from the vehicle. Liam had noticed Harper's beauty at the crime scene, but now he allowed himself a few minutes to appreciate the sight in front of him. Once he got out of his car, things would be strictly business between the two of them.

She glanced at him and jerked her head toward the building in a clear signal for him to get out and join her. Gladly. Leaving his jacket in the car, he got out and locked the door. "Hopefully, you've a desk I can use."

"There's an extra one in my office. The other detective retired recently. We haven't got a replacement yet." She didn't wait for Liam to hold the door open for her and entered ahead of him.

A middle-aged woman glanced up from the reception desk. "You've some messages on your desk, Detective."

"Thank you, Myrna. This is Special Agent, McConnell. He's working the Richardson case with me."

Liam smiled. "It's a pleasure, ma'am." He followed Harper through the bullpen and into a small office with a large glass window. Across from her office was one more, empty at the moment, home to the station's chief. "I knew your station was small, but had no idea it was this small."

"Which is why, despite my prickliness earlier, I'm grateful for your help." She removed her jacket, revealing a simple white, long-sleeved blouse. "Make yourself comfortable." She motioned to one of the desks. "I use this wall as my case board. It's convenient and easier than heading to the conference room where things might get moved around."

The only things taped there were three index cards. Liam stepped in front of them. "Not the original messages?" The writing looked feminine.

"No, those are bagged. I copied them." She sat at her desk. "I'll print off the photos I took, then we can tape them up. Maybe get a feel of what this guy is thinking."

Liam nodded, his attention on the messages. The last one she'd received mentioned playing a game. Murder wasn't a game he wanted to play.

The others merely talked about the dangers of a prideful heart. "We need to dig into Richardson's lifestyle, his background, find out if he's the trigger behind the perp's act. We need to know whether he's the first victim or if there are others we don't know about."

"We could visit one of the establishments he owns. Several bars in Harrington, a strip club, and he frequents the country club there a lot. At least according to the papers." She retrieved the printed photos from the printer and handed them to him. "I say the strip club might be a good place to start considering the removal of the victim's clothes."

Liam tapped a finger against one of the photos. The indentation of what could have been a buckle showed on the back of the man's neck. "Looks like he might have worn a collar."

"As in the S & M kind?" Her eyes widened. "Our perp might be female in that case."

"Would explain the reason there were no signs of a struggle." Liam heaved a sigh. "Could be a stripper, could be a high society woman. Could be the barista down the street for all we know."

"This all sounds more like lust than pride." She perched on the corner of her desk and crossed her arms, her gaze focused on the photos.

"I have a feeling we'll find out that Mr. Richardson fits all seven." He sat at the desk assigned to him and typed into his phone. "Lust, gluttony, greed, sloth, pride, envy, wrath."

Her lips twisted. "If not all, then most. But, again, I only know what I've read in the papers. I've never met the man." She returned to her desk and opened a laptop.

"Is there a hotel nearby? I didn't have time to find a room."

"Thirty minutes away on the outskirts of Harrington." She wrote something on an index card. "Why not go check in, then text me where you're staying? I'll pick you up tonight at nine to hit the strip club." She slid the index card across the desk. "My number."

Liam nodded and returned to his car. He searched hotels in his GPS, finding only two in the next town. One of them would have to do. He doubted he'd spend much time in his room anyway.

Not with a sadistic killer to find.

~

He watched the news unfold on his television. Watched the haughtiness on the face of Lance Richardson's sister. The diamond ring glittering on her finger as she waved it dramatically in front of the cameras, faking grief over her dear brother's violent death.

The woman wasn't capable of sadness. After the death of her parents five years earlier, now her brother, the woman couldn't spend her wealth in her lifetime.

He smiled, steepling his fingers. No, she wouldn't live long enough to spend even a portion of her inheritance.

He pressed a button on his phone. "Get me Sarah."

A few minutes later, a woman in a black skirt and white blouse, hair pulled into a severe ponytail, entered his office. A chameleon capable of beauty or melting into the background unnoticed. He'd used her beauty to lure Lance. This time he needed her ability to be invisible.

He pointed at the TV. "Your next target. I don't care how you get rid of her, only that it happens soon. The world will be a better place without such a prideful spirit. And cut off the finger sporting that ring. Leave it lying in the dirt next to her."

"Yes, sir." She bowed her head and backed from the room.

He'd surrounded himself with people of the same mindset as himself. Not as brilliant, but willing to make the world a better place. He dug his fingernails into the palm of his hands hard enough to draw blood in punishment for saying his followers weren't as brilliant as he was. Fighting the very things he wanted to rid the world of was a daily struggle.

Fifty years ago, his father had started the quest for a Utopian world. Cancer had stopped him before he could get his vision going, but Lance had spent hours listening to his father's dream and cursing the doctors who couldn't save him. Doctors that didn't care for the unwealthy, only concerned with patients who could help line their pockets.

Well, he'd taken care of them, and now he planned on finishing what his father had only dreamed of accomplishing. He'd worked hard to build an empire, make enough money to do what needed doing.

Imagine finding out that their only surviving family members were involved in law enforcement. He laughed, the sound ringing against the words. Now, he'd pit his wit against theirs in a game of who would be the victor.

His nails dug in deeper as pride once again started to rear its ugly head. He needed a distraction. He pressed the button on the desk phone again. "Send Lana to my room."

He had followers to satisfy his every whim. To kill, for sex, to do his shopping. Whatever he wanted, they'd do without question if it meant a world that had treated them unfairly would pay.

Once he'd fulfilled his father's dream, they'd all reap the benefits. He saw in their eyes the same drive, the same hunger for justice. He lived simply, requiring them to do the same. A few luxuries, but nothing extravagant, nothing to make the guilty take notice of them. No, they'd stay in the shadows until it was time to show their faces, to present their ideals to the world.

He got to his feet, wiped the blood from his palm on a cotton handkerchief, and marched from his office. He climbed the stairs to the room where Lana waited in a simple cotton gown. No need for trashy lingerie to create lust in his eyes. He didn't need anything more than the basic act between a man and a woman to regain his focus.

She looked up at him and smiled, her hand beckoning him forward. "My lord."

Chapter 2

Harper pulled in front of Liam's room at exactly nine p.m. Some people might think her obsession with punctuality a fault, but to her it was a virtue. She'd been told she was wound as tight as a watch spring before. Maybe, but she didn't think there was anything wrong with focusing on her career with everything she had. It wasn't as if she had family to spend time with.

Liam stepped out of his room on the bottom floor at five after nine when Harper laid on the horn. There would be problems if he ran late all the time.

He exited his hotel room and jogged toward the jeep. "Hold onto your hat," he said, sliding into the passenger seat. "I was finishing up." He frowned. "You look like law enforcement."

"I am." She eyed his jeans and polo shirt. "You don't."

"I thought it would be better if we blended in. You need to look like arm candy. A woman that might frequent a strip bar with her man. Not like someone getting ready to raid the place."

She rolled her eyes, untucked her blouse from her slacks, tied the ends high enough to expose her mid-section, and unbuttoned a couple of top buttons. "This is as good as it's going to get."

"Looks good to me." He winked.

For crying out loud. She shook her head and backed from the spot. "Try to focus on the job at hand. Have you received any more messages?"

"No. You?"

She shook her head. "I'm not expecting one before morning. He, or she, usually sends one a day."

"To make it easy, let's call the perp a he. Take your hair out of the ponytail."

The man was impossible. "Stick to the case." She pulled her hair free.

"I am." His gaze ran over her. "That should do it."

"Glad I meet with your approval."

Liam's room wasn't far from the seedy side of town and the strip club owned by Lance. She frowned at the neon sign depicting a pair of kicking legs in heels. The place was named The Gentleman's Club. Not very original, but the sign clearly stated what the plain white building held.

"Pretend you're my woman." Liam grinned. "Once we've scoped out the place, then we can start asking questions. When we do, you can be the bad cop. Too bad you aren't wearing makeup."

"I'll do my best to bat my eyelashes and giggle at every stupid thing you say until then." She shoved open her door, fluffed her hair, and waited for him to join her. When he did, he put his hand on the small of her back and guided her to the front door. His touch sent an electric current through her.

Loud music and flashing lights greeted them. A few heads turned, but most stayed focused on the mainly naked woman on the stage.

Liam found them a table for two in the corner, then motioned over a server wearing black lingerie. "Beer and a rum and diet coke."

"How did you know what I wanted?" Harper glared. "I don't like men ordering for me."

"It's my job to know people. You seem like a rum and coke kind of girl. Since you're thin, I figured diet." He didn't look the least bit ashamed. He faced the stage, his eyes narrowed.

Harper turned to see the woman stop dancing and drop to her knees, head bowed, hands clasped in front of her while another woman fastened a collar around her neck. The scene mimicked the death of Richardson to a T. If they performed the act regularly, it could be why his killer posed him that way.

"I'm going to need church and a shower after tonight," she said.

"Yeah, it's hard to see this side of life and not have it harden you."

"Why hasn't it?" She tilted her head, then remembering she's supposed to be enthralled with him, ran her fingers down his arm.

He cupped her head and pulled her close, his lips next to her ear. "Church and regular showers."

"Really?" She pulled back.

"What? You didn't take me for the type to go to church? I'm Irish. I attend mass when I can, and I drink. I do my best not to swear. My mom always boxed my ears when I did." He winked.

Heat rose up her neck.

The waitress set their drinks in front of them. Liam tucked a twenty under the strap of her top. "Do those two dancers perform that act regularly?"

"Every night." Her smile looked forced. "The clientele seem to love seeing--"

"Women in a subservient manner?" Harper arched a brow.

"Yes." She turned to leave.

Harper stopped her with a hand on her arm. "Can you tell us about Lance Richardson? We'll pay you to talk to us."

The woman stared for a moment, uncertainty flickering across her face, then nodded. "I get off at one a.m. Meet me in the parking lot. Cost for information is one hundred dollars." She marched away, head held high.

"I really don't want to stay here that long," Harper said. "Want to get a coffee somewhere?"

"Sure. I'm hungry. Let's find a place that is still serving food at this time of the night." He rose and offered Harper a hand.

She slipped hers in his and let him pull her to her feet. Outside, she immediately untied her shirt and retucked it into her pants, buttoning up the top buttons. She tied her hair back into its customary ponytail. There. She felt like herself again.

Liam laughed and opened her car door for her. "It won't work, you know?"

"What won't?"

"You can't hide your beauty." He closed the door before she could say anything. When he joined her back in the car, he faced her and smiled. "Bet that left you speechless."

"I dress professionally." She turned the key in the ignition, her hand shaking. A change of subject was in order, but yes, he'd knocked her speechless. "Start thinking about what questions you want to ask the server. I don't think we have much time before the killer strikes again."

~

Liam slid into a vinyl booth across from Harper. He'd rather liked her hair loose. Made her appear softer. No matter. They had a murder to solve and no time for anything else.

"What?" She narrowed her eyes.

"What kind of pie do you like?" He waved the waitress over rather than tell her where his mind had been.

"Possum." She laughed, the sound like music to his ears, as he shuddered and realized this is the first time her stern exterior had cracked. "Not the animal. It's a chocolate pie and absolutely delicious. Try it. I dare you."

"Alright. Two possum pies and two coffees." He arched a brow. "I rarely turn down a dare." The vinyl squeaked under his weight as he leaned against the back. "Do you think the club server will show?"

"Why wouldn't she?" Harper poured cream and sugar into the coffee set in front of her. "She'll make an easy hundred bucks."

"Something might scare her off."

She shrugged. "Maybe." Her features hardened at something she saw over his shoulder.

He turned and stared at a television screen depicting the front of a large, modern house. "Who's home?"

"Richardson's sister." She typed into her phone. "You'll have to try the possum pie later. We've got another dead body." She took a sip of coffee, slapped some money on the table, and rushed for the door.

He shouted an apology to the confused waitress and rushed after Harper. They had two hours until they were expected back at the club. He doubted they'd be there.

The waitress raced toward them, two Styrofoam boxes in her hand. "Here. Your pie." She thrust them into Liam's hand. He set them on the floor at his feet. "Thank you."

Harper sped from the diner parking lot as he clicked his seat belt into place. "Slow down. The victim won't return to life if we get there at the speed of light," he said.

"Sorry." She didn't slow down and took the next corner too

fast.

He grabbed the handle above his head. It wasn't that he didn't trust her not to get them killed, but rather he didn't trust anyone's driving but his own. He'd gone along with her so far, but no more. "I'm driving from now on."

She cut him a quick glance. "In what? That rented sedan?"

"Yes." He released the breath he'd been holding as she slowed and pulled into a curving drive leading to the house they'd seen on TV.

"There are booties and gloves in the glove compartment." Harper shoved her door open. "Get some for both of us."

"Yes, boss." He frowned. He had the authority, yet he felt like a rookie the way she barked commands. "I'm not one of your officers, Detective. We're working as partners on this case."

Her brow lowered. "Your point?"

"Stop playing boss." He handed her the gloves and booties.

She blinked, clearly taken back. "I'm sorry. I'm used to working alone."

"No worries. We're squared away now." He led the way up ten cement steps to a massive porch. He slipped on the booties, snapped the gloves over his hands, and motioned for Harper to move through the open front door ahead of him.

A woman wearing stark black, sitting in a wing-back chair in the corner of the foyer, wept into a tissue. She glanced up as Harper and Liam entered. "Finally, people with some authority. I'm Mrs. Blackwell. Miss Richardson's assistant."

"I'm sorry for your loss, ma'am. We'll be back to speak with you in a few minutes." Liam gave her a nod and headed up a sweeping staircase to where a uniformed officer waited.

"I'm Officer Crypton, first on the scene. The body has been placed exactly as Mr. Richardson's." She stepped aside so they could enter the bedroom.

A king-sized four-poster bed barely took up space in the large master bedroom. The lovely Miss Richardson knelt in her blood. A silk nightgown lay on the floor next to her as if she'd been in the process of getting ready for bed when someone killed her.

Liam squatted next to her. "She hasn't been dead long. Who called the authorities?"

"An anonymous caller. Electronic voice," Crypton said. "The

front door was open when I got here. I scared the bejesus out of the housekeeper when I called out that I was police. Woke her up."

"You sure she was asleep?" He straightened, reading the latest message on the wall. "Through pride the devil became the devil. Pride leads to every vice, it's the complete anti-God state of mind."

Harper stepped next to him. "Sounds like the perp will be moving onto other sins."

"Yep. Let's talk to the housekeeper. She's the primary suspect at this point. At least a person of interest." Her tears didn't mean anything. He'd met some very good actors during his career.

"I'll catch up to you. I want to snap some photos before the crime scene techs arrive."

Instead of heading downstairs, Liam took time to glance around the bathroom. Spotless, a towel neatly hanging on the rack. No cosmetics or toiletries littered the counter. A robe hung on a hook near a bathtub big enough for two.

The walk-in closet didn't reveal anything other than expensive name brand clothes and shoes. They had no more to go on than they did with the woman's brother.

He stopped at the top of the stairs and stared at the housekeeper. The woman didn't look strong enough to have taken down Lance Richardson. She had to be twenty years his senior which left Liam doubting she'd seduced him into submission.

No, the Richardsons' killer was planning his next move.

Chapter Three

Harper glanced at her watch. "We have five minutes to meet the waitress."

Liam said something to the housekeeper, then stepped back and nodded. "I think we're finished here."

"Get any information from Blackwell?" Harper asked as they marched to her jeep.

"Brother and sister didn't get along. Fought over the estate after the parents died. Sister didn't feel much grief over the passing of her brother." Liam stared over the top of the jeep. "Seemed happy to have it all to herself."

"Not just the sin of pride then. Greed, too." Harper opened her door and got behind the wheel. "Maybe that's why she was killed. Both posed in a humble position, though, which points back to pride."

"I think it's safe to assume we're dealing with all seven sins."

She drew a deep breath through her nose. Two deaths within twenty-four hours. "Why now? What triggered the killer to start killing?"

"That's what we need to find out."

Unfortunately, more people would die in the meantime. She drove back to the nightclub, arriving five minutes late.

The server paced the parking lot, one of the bouncers watching from the doorway. Good man. He knew the dangers of her being alone at that time of the night. "Hope you have a hundred dollars." Harper turned off the car and opened her door.

"What makes you think I do?" He got out and pulled his wallet from his pocket.

"You aren't the only one who can read people. Expensive suit, nice shoes...I figured you for someone who carried cash, especially when on a trip." She flashed a grin and headed toward the woman waiting. "Sorry we're late. I'm Detective Scranton, this is Special Agent McConnell."

"Amber. That's all I'm saying." She leaned against a beat up Volkswagon. "Money first, then I'll tell you anything you want to know about Lance."

"Alright, Amber?" The bouncer called.

"Yeah, go home, Mark." She kept her attention on Harper. "I knew you were cops the minute you entered the club. You both have that vibe."

So much for blending in. Harper pulled a small notepad from the inside pocket of her jacket as Liam handed Amber her payment. "Was Richardson well liked?"

"People couldn't stand him. Man thought he was better than everyone else. He snapped his fingers, and we all jumped. If we didn't, we found ourselves without a job." She crossed her arms. "Hate to speak ill of the dead."

"Any idea of who might want him dead?"

"The list is too long."

"What about his sister?" Her pen paused above the notepad.

"They fought a lot, but I don't think she'd kill him."

Amber hadn't heard about the sister's death. "That's the reason we're late. The sister was murdered in the same manner as her brother."

Amber sagged, her hand going to her mouth. "Why? What's going on?"

"That's what we're trying to find out. Here's my card. If you hear anything that will help us find out who killed them, please call." She handed over a business card. "Any strange people hanging around on the nights Lance stopped by?"

"It's a strip club, and not a fancy one. All we get are strange people." She tossed the business card through the car's open window. "I'm beat. Anything else?"

Harper shook her head. "Thank you for your time." She'd given them nothing. Maybe Mark, who watched from his car could fill in some blanks. She motioned her head toward the man.

"He's hanging around for a reason," he said. "Might as well find out why."

"Mind getting out of the car, sir?" Harper showed her badge.

"Amber in some kind of trouble?" The big man got out, his eyes wide and shining against his dark skin. "It isn't often people meet up with one of our girls in the parking lot. Not folks who mean well, anyway."

"We're here about the murder of Lance Richardson," Liam said. "Hear about that?"

"Yeah, I watch the news during my break."

"What time did your shift start?" Harper wrote on her notepad.

"I pulled a double shift today. Anyone can vouch for my whereabouts. Am I a suspect?"

She met his worried gaze. "Everyone is at this point." She pulled out another business card. "Any personal dealings with Mr. Richardson?"

"Nope. He signed my paycheck; I do my job. When he does show up, we nod. That's the extent of our contact."

"When he's here, what does he do?"

"Wanders around, making sure things are up to his expectations, then he sits at a table in the corner, has a couple of drinks, and watches the girls." He crossed his arms, biceps bulging. "He had a favorite. Jade."

"How would we contact her?"

"Show up here tomorrow night, eight o'clock. She's the star attraction."

"We'd rather visit her at her home." They could get a good feeling about a person in the comfort of their home. "Got an address?"

"I'll have to get it from the office." He jogged to the building.

"He's awfully helpful, isn't he?" Harper arched a brow.

"Guess the man doesn't want us to think he's guilty." Liam stared toward the club building. "Which makes me suspicious. I'm not used to people going out of their way to help."

"Neither am I." Not during a murder investigation anyway.

Mark returned and handed Harper a post-it note. "What now?"

"You go home. Don't leave town. We will be checking your alibi." Harper returned to her jeep.

She watched through the rearview mirror as Mark grew smaller and smaller. Her suspicion grew stronger. Oh, yeah, she'd be checking out his alibi as soon as the club opened again.

"What are you thinking?" Liam's question brought her attention off Mark and onto him.

"That the bouncer knows more than he told us. Why send us to talk to Jade? Why not tell us what we want to know?"

"I don't know, but I think we need to wake up Jade and ask some questions before someone tips her off that we're coming. We might want to check on Amber, too. Something doesn't feel right."

~

Jade lived on the fourth floor of an apartment complex that had seen better days. Plaster in bad need of painting looked as if someone tried to build with a Spanish theme. Liam eyed the rusting staircase, wondering if it would hold his weight.

"Why can't there be an elevator?" Harper groaned.

"Guess the star attraction doesn't make enough to afford a place with one." Liam motioned her to go ahead of him. "I also spotted Amber's car in the spot for 3A. We can check in on both of them." Then go get some rest.

They stopped first at Amber's. She was not happy to see them on her doorstep if the frown on her face was any indication.

"Did you follow me?" She glared.

"No, we're here to see someone else and saw your car." Liam smiled, trying to put her at ease. "We thought we'd make sure you made it home alright."

"You think I could be in danger?" Her eyes widened. "I don't have anything in common with the Richardsons. I live paycheck to paycheck."

Liam peered past her into her apartment. She might live cheaply, but the interior looked clean, everything in its place. A bookshelf full of paperbacks took up one wall.

"My guilty pleasure," she said.

"You could have worse ones. Goodnight, ma'am." He stepped back and followed Harper to the fourth floor.

"Do you think Amber could be in danger?" She glanced over her shoulder at him.

"Until we get a better idea of what makes our killer tick, it's safe to say anyone with any connection to the Richardsons could be." He knocked on the door to Jade's apartment. When no one answered, he knocked again, harder the second time.

A young woman with jet black hair and dark eyes answered

the door. "What?"

Liam introduced them. "We'd like to ask you some questions about Lance Richardson."

"Like what?"

"Were you aware he was killed?"

She paled. "No. I rarely watch the news and today was my day off work. I stayed home and caught up on cleaning." She raised a trembling hand to her throat.

"We were told the two of you were close." Not exactly those words.

"No. He liked to watch me dance. Bought me the occasional drink, but our relationship didn't go any further than that."

Since she didn't work that day, she wouldn't be an alibi for Mark. "Any idea who would wish him dead?"

"Probably every person he had business dealings with. This is a lot to take in. I need to sit down." Rather than invite them in, she sat on a plastic chair outside her door.

Harper shot him a curious look and peered into an apartment the exact opposite of Amber's. Where she was neat, Jade was anything but. Clothes lay scattered over every piece of furniture. Dirty dishes littered the coffee table.

"Excuse the mess," Jade said. "That's why I didn't ask you in. When I get home from work, I'm too tired to do anything but lay around. I had good intentions today, but…"

"Sloth," Harper mouthed.

He nodded. Of course, a person could probably assign any of the deadly sins to every living person in one way or another.

"I guess the club will be closing down." Jade hung her head. "With Lance...gone and no one to take it over..." she sighed. "I'd better start looking for another job. There's no shortage of strip clubs, fortunately."

Liam wanted to tell her she had other options, but maybe she didn't have any other skills besides dancing. Why hurt her feelings? "Be careful, ma'am. We aren't dismissing the notion that anyone who had connections with Richardson isn't in danger."

Something hit his cheek. He put his hand to his face, bringing his fingers away bloody as something popped, and another chunk of plaster fell from the wall. "Someone is shooting at us." He tackled Jade to the ground and rolled into her apartment with her.

"Stay down."

He pulled his weapon and moved to the window, keeping his back against the wall and peered through the blinds. A dark SUV idled in the parking lot.

"The shooter?" Harper asked.

"Maybe." Could be someone on foot. "I'm going out. Cover me."

Harper slid the window open and fired toward the SUV.

Liam took that opportunity to leave the apartment. Rather than take the front stairs as they had when they arrived, he took the back, hoping to surprise the shooter.

The only shots he could hear came from Harper. With his heart beating in his throat, he skirted the building. He rounded the corner in time to see the SUV, minus a tire, speed from the parking lot. He searched the surrounding area in case the shooter was still around. Not finding anyone, he thundered back to Jade's apartment.

Harper turned from the window. "That's not the same MO. Shooting doesn't leave the same message as Richardson's death. You're bleeding." She pointed to his face.

"Piece of plaster." He headed to the kitchen and tore a paper towel from the roll, wet it and dabbed at the cut.

Jade crawled from under the coffee table. "I think that was my ex."

"Excuse me?" Liam pressed the towel against his cheek.

"Dane Larson. He's been jealous of Richardson from the moment he caught us having a drink together. I couldn't take the suffocation and broke up with him last week."

"Does he drive a black SUV?" Harper asked.

"Yes."

Liam exhaled heavily. "We'll need his address." What they didn't need was a jealous ex-boyfriend complicating things.

Chapter Four

"I didn't shoot at you, I swear." Dane Larson held his hands up. "I thought you were visiting my girl, until I saw the detective with you. So, I ran."

"Why?" Harper narrowed her eyes. "Do you know me?"

He exhaled heavily and hung his head. "You arrested me a couple of years ago for breaking into a car and stealing a laptop. You weren't a detective then. Is Jade in some kind of trouble?"

"We hope not." Harper turned and headed back to the jeep. "If Larson wasn't the shooter, we lost the suspect by assuming he was." She leaned her forehead on the steering wheel. "We need rest. We aren't thinking clearly. I'll take you to your hotel and pick you up at nine." Which, if her mind shut off would allow her to get five hours of sleep. She'd worked on less.

Liam rubbed his hands down his face. "I agree. In our defense, we didn't see anyone but Larson."

Harper turned away from Larson's apartment as her cell phone buzzed. She put the phone on speaker. "Detective Scranton here."

"Officer Crypton. I responded to calls of shots fired. You need to get over here. We've got another body." She rattled off an address.

"That's Amber's apartment." Harper pressed the accelerator, dread weighing her down. Had they brought trouble to the woman by questioning her? How could the killer have known unless he watched their every move? If he did, how?

She cut a sideways glance at Liam. "Amber didn't seem prideful or anything like that to me."

"I agree. No noticeable deadly sins other than she worked at a strip club."

"Lust?" It had to be people connected to Richardson. Otherwise, it made no sense. Nothing was random here. Quite the contrary. The murders seemed very well planned out. The victims were not selected at random.

At the apartment complex, they thundered up the stairs to Amber's apartment where Officer Crypton waited outside the door. "She isn't posed like the others, but prepare yourself."

Harper took a deep breath, squared her shoulders, and entered another crime scene. Through the open bedroom door, she spotted a nude Amber, throat slit, arms tied with scarves to the bedposts. Harper's shoulders sagged. They'd failed to save her. This woman's death rested on her shoulders.

On the wall above her head were written the words, "She wanted what was not hers."

Harper pinched the bridge of her nose trying to ward off a threatening headache. "That doesn't make sense."

"Sure, it does. Come here," Liam called.

She stepped out of the bedroom and joined him at the bookcase. Every paperback depicted a man and woman in the throes of passion. Amber's guilty pleasure had been steamy romance. "Still doesn't say she had the sin of lust."

"No, but this does. Richardson spent a lot of time with Jade, right?" Liam arched a brow. "Spent time at the club with her. Look at this Christmas photo." He handed it to her. "See who Amber has eyes for?"

Harper studied the photo of the strip club decked out for the holidays. Lance Richardson had his arm around Jade's shoulders. Everyone smiled at the camera. Everyone except Amber. Her gaze rested on Lance. "Why didn't she tell us she cared for the man?"

"We didn't ask. We need to check on Jade." He led the way to her apartment.

A clearly not happy to see us again Jade answered the door. "I guess sleep is out of the question today."

"This is a safety call," Harper said. "Your coworker and neighbor, Amber, was found murdered in her apartment less than half an hour ago. Did you see or hear anyone?"

She gasped and sank into a chair. "Not Amber."

Harper sat in a chair next to her. "Were you aware Amber had feelings for Lance?"

"Yes. She'd laugh about it sometimes. I'd get mad and storm away. She was my friend, though." Tears welled in her eyes. "Why would someone want to kill her?"

"We think someone has targeted people connected with the Richardsons. Is there somewhere you can go? Someone you can stay with until this killer is caught?" Harper put a hand on her arm.

"No. I have no family. My only friends are at the club." She glanced from Harper to Liam. "Don't you have a safe house or something like in the movies? Or how about a bodyguard so I can still work? If I don't work, my bills don't get paid."

"If you're dead, they won't get paid either." Harper stood. Since they'd never had anything like this happen in Oakdale before, she wasn't sure how to proceed. "Agent?"

"I'll contact the field office. I'm sure we'll have somewhere she can stay. As for continuing to work, I don't advise it." He typed into his phone. "We have an officer downstairs who can stay with you until a place is found. Make it quick, though. We don't have a lot of officers at our disposal. Please lock your door behind us and don't open it unless you see an identification through the peephole. Your life could depend on it, ma'am."

Jade nodded, her eyes wide in a pale face. "I'll wait right here. I promise."

Harper moved to the door. The Richardson siblings and now Amber. Pride and Lust. What sin did Jade fall under? Would it be lust because of her profession? Did the killer consider her as guilty for causing lust as to having the emotion? Nothing made sense and the bodies kept piling up.

She stepped outside. Where are you? Who are you? Why did you bring this trouble to Oakdale?

~

So beautiful to be born of such evil. He peered through the binoculars at the detective. What sin does she hide behind those eyes?

Even if she were innocent, her grandfather had not been. She must pay for his sin. Her and the FBI agent whose relative had been just as guilty.

He watched as law enforcement and crime scene techs scurried around like ants. The latest kill had lusted after someone who belonged to another. Not that the pretty stripper was any better than the server had been. Her time would come. Uncareful planning of the deaths showed a lack of finesse, imagination.

She lowered the binoculars and drummed his fingers on the steering wheel of his car. Sarah had done well with her tasks, but it was time to implement someone else's skills. Time to really shake up the citizens of Oakdale and Harrington. He turned up the radio, blasting classical music through the open window, and pulled away from the curb as the Agent McConnell joined the detective on the apartment steps.

Fighting the urge to wave, he grinned and sped away. If he didn't have so much to do, he'd have enjoyed staying and watching as the two he wanted brought to their knees ran around like headless chickens. To them, none of what happened made sense. To him, it made all the sense in the world.

He drove back to his high-rise apartment in Knotsville. The gate opened automatically, the sensor picking up the card hanging from his rearview mirror. He parked in his space and whistled on his way to the elevator. He couldn't remember a time when he'd had this much fun. Who would have thought revenge really could be sweet?

When the elevator doors opened, he stepped out, nodding at the men and women milling around. His plastic surgery office wasn't the only business in the building, but his penthouse apartment was the only residence. He liked it that way. Once everyone else went home at five, the building became a silent abode broken only by another presence when he summoned them.

Tonight, he craved solitude in order to plan his next move. He stopped by the office and took note of the next day's consultations, before heading to the penthouse. There, he poured himself a glass of the finest Scotch and unrolled a blueprint of his target.

Unfortunately, there would be collateral damage, but were there any innocents who frequented such places? No, he'd feel little remorse at the act. Finding the perfect spot to cause the most damage, he reached for his phone.

"It's time. Put it under the stage. It needs to be done now, while you can sneak in and out unobserved." He listened as the man on the other end pointed out the fact there were still dancers, servers, and customers at this early hour. "Yes, but it can't be helped. If you wait until the busy time, you'll never succeed. Do it now." He hung up and moved to his window where he'd have a good view of the show.

He took a sip of his drink, feeling the smoothness as it slid down his throat and relaxed the tautness in his shoulders. He passed the time re-picturing the worried look on Detective Scranton's lovely face. What a waste when it was her time to face judgment. Maybe he should give her the chance at a new life first. A life righting the world's wrongs. A life at his side.

No, she was probably as deceitful as her grandfather had been. He grinned around the rim of his glass, remembering the shocked look on the old man's face during the last few seconds of his life.

The very look he'd someday see on Detective Scranton's face.

~

"Ah." Liam toed off his shoes and lay on his back on the bed, not bothering to undress. Finally, he could rest his weary body.

Despite ten years in the FBI, he'd never run across a case with as many dead ends as this one. Bodies were piling up, but they didn't even have a person of interest.

Finally, his body relaxed enough for him to fall asleep.

The pounding on his hotel room door woke him. No sunlight streamed through the curtains. He glanced at his watch. He'd gotten two hours.

"Liam!" Harper's voice rang out.

"I'm coming." He groaned and got up, padding to open the door. "What happened?"

"The strip club blew up." She pushed her way inside. "Get your shoes on."

"Casualties?" He slid his feet into his shoes and grabbed his weapon from the nightstand.

"Don't know how many. Some for sure, but it wasn't the busiest time of the night, thank God." She left his room and returned to her car, sliding into the driver's seat.

So much for Liam's declaration of driving from now on. He locked the door to his room and climbed into the passenger seat. "Did you manage to sleep at all?"

"No." She started the car and sped down the interstate. "I feel like I could sleep for a week."

"Why us at the club? Couldn't it be handled by other officers?"

She whipped her head toward me. "When was the last time you checked your phone?"

"Right before I fell asleep." He pulled it from his pocket. He had a text. One word. "Boom."

"The notification that I had a text is what woke me. I called the station and was told about the explosion. I came to get you as soon as possible."

Flames kissed the sky as they parked near the burning building. A flash of their badges allowed them past the police barricade crowded with onlookers.

"Who's in charge?" Harper asked.

"Right now, the fire chief." Officer Crypton jerked her thumb toward a man standing near the fire truck.

"Chief Langley, this is Special Agent McConnell," Harper introduced. "What can you tell us?"

"Not a lot. Fire's too hot for my men. We won't be able to see anything until the blaze is under control." He shook Liam's hand. "One survivor. A bouncer."

Liam glanced to where Mark sat holding a towel to his head. "Excuse me." He left the chief and leaned against the ambulance Mark sat in. "What happened?"

He shook his head. "I took out the garbage to make room for the nighttime crowd. I was headed back to the building when it blew up. The force slammed me against the dumpsters."

"Did you see anyone around that seemed suspicious?"

"Wasn't really paying attention."

"How many people were inside?"

"A couple of dancers, the bartender, maybe ten customers, the kitchen staff. Maybe thirty in all. They're all dead, aren't they?"

"Most likely. You're a very lucky man. Give us a call if something comes to you." Liam started to think the man too lucky, but since he'd received a head injury that looked like it would require stitches, he stopped his questioning and studied the crowd.

One of them had placed the bomb. Liam had seen enough explosions to recognize the aftermath. Why not wait until the club was full? Maximize the collateral damage? Unless the person responsible simply kept playing their evil game and not interested in body counts. Why involve Liam and Harper? Clearly the person responsible wanted them on the case.

"What's on your mind?" Harper joined him. Exhaustion creased her pretty face. If the two of them didn't get some sleep, they'd be no good to anyone.

He explained his thoughts. "My brain is fuzzy from lack of sleep."

"Mine, too. The fire department won't know anything for a few hours yet. If you don't mind me crashing on the other bed in your room, we can grab some sleep. The chief will call me when he knows something."

"That's the best thing I've heard all day. I've got to warn you, though. The bed is hard."

"I could sleep on a rock at this point. Let's run past my place, grab a change of clothes, then sleep." He waited in the car while she ran into her house, returning a few minutes later with an overnight bag.

At the hotel, he changed into a pair of shorts to sleep in while Harper ducked into the bathroom. He widened his eyes when she came back out in an oversized tee-shirt that looked as if she had nothing on underneath. Nothing but shapely legs that seemed to go on forever.

He cleared his throat and climbed into his bed, covering with only a thin sheet. "Good night."

She turned the air down, professing that she slept better in a cold room, then burrowed under the blankets in the other bed. "Good night."

He lay awake for a while wondering if she had anything on under that shirt until weariness overtook his brain and his eyes drifted closed.

Chapter Five

He watched as the heavy woman devoured a glazed doughnut in four bites. His nose wrinkled in disgust. Gluttony. He shuddered and tossed his napkin onto his half-finished breakfast, his appetite ruined. How could such a fine establishment let in such a creature?

It didn't matter that the purse at her feet cost as much as his Italian leather shoes or that the designer dress that strained to cover her bulk cost more than most people's weekly salary. Something needed to be done.

Pride was supposed to be his focus right now, but the other sins kept raising their ugly heads and pulling him off track.

He waved over a server and ordered a dozen assorted pastries. Since the woman had ruined his breakfast, he'd take care of her himself. He drummed his fingers on the table as he waited, trying not to watch her eat. His gaze kept drifting that way as if he watched a fascinating animal behind bars at the zoo.

What he really wanted to do was let the news of the previous evening's devastation entertain him. The detective and the FBI agent would be scurrying around trying to gather clues they wouldn't find. Another thing this woman ruined. Instead, he sat there waiting to pass judgment.

"Your order, sir." The server sat a white box on the table.

"Thank you." He pulled a vial from the inside pocket of his suit jacket, dribbled a liberal amount on the doughnuts, and slid a card under the treats on which he'd written, Glutton. Then, he called the server back over and asked that the box be given to the woman in the yellow dress.

He marched from the restaurant and grabbed a newspaper. A

padded chair near a silk plant would provide a good place for him to watch from. He snapped open the paper and peered over the top. How many would she eat before keeling over?

The server sat the box on her table and pointed to the table that now sat vacant. The woman smiled, patted her hair, and glanced around the room.

Did she really think the doughnuts were from an admirer? The delusions of people never ceased to amaze him.

She opened the box. Her red lips made an O resembling the hole in the doughnuts. She clutched one with scarlet talons and took a big bite. The second doughnut had her clutching her stomach. She dropped it on the pristine tablecloth, groaned, and landed face first in the box.

He folded his paper, dropped it in a nearby trashcan, and strolled from the building. Cries of alarm followed him. His morning seemed a little brighter now.

In his office, he turned on the television, surprised not to see the detective or the agent at the scene. The naughty two must have slept in. Didn't they care that the sheep they tried to protect needed them or were they like their grandfathers and fathers who cared only for themselves? The two were the poster children for greed.

The building still smoldered. Firemen milled about. Some curious onlookers huddled across the street. The obedient servant he'd sent to set the bomb watched over a woman's shoulder. Why was he still there? Everyone knew the perpetrator stayed behind to see the results of their handiwork. Any camera footage would show his face. He'd be located and questioned.

He pressed numbers into his phone. "Get out of there you imbecile." He hung up as his servant stepped backward and marched down the sidewalk.

Shaking his head, he pressed the intercom on his desk phone and called for Sarah. She would clean up the situation.

"Yes, sir."

"Get rid of David. I don't care how, but make sure he's never found. Erase all evidence the man ever existed. He's an idiot."

~

Harper had taken a long time to fall asleep. Hearing the soft snores from Liam in the other bed made her realize how long it had been since she'd been interested in a man. Not that she was interested, not during an active investigation, but the man did have what it took. Brains, handsome, kind, and an accent that fluttered her stomach.

Sighing she flung off the thin sheet she'd covered herself with and checked her phone. "Liam, there's been another death."

He groaned and sat up. "I didn't hear my phone."

"Neither did I. We both overslept." That's what lack of sleep did. Once you did lie down, you were dead to the world. "I'll hit the shower first, then you. Do you mind letting them know we'll be there in thirty minutes?"

She stood under the shower's spray, letting the water clear her mind of things that didn't belong...like dwelling on Liam. Once this case was over, he'd be gone. She'd do well to remember that and keep things professional.

Showered, she donned her usual uniform of a dark suit and blouse, the blouse pink this time, and put her hair into a ponytail. "All yours." Her eyes widened as she stepped out to see him standing there in nothing but a pair of cotton shorts. So much for professionalism. Her mouth dried up.

"Excuse me." He brushed past her and into the bathroom.

She occupied herself by checking her phone again, then checking her weapon and making sure she had her badge. By the time he returned in pants, shirt, and tie, she'd regained her composure. "Ready?"

"Yes, ma'am." He tucked his badge in his pocket, his gun in his shoulder holster, and waved her on ahead of him. "I'm driving this time, so hand over the keys. I fear you'll get us killed the way you drive."

"What's wrong with the way I drive?" She narrowed her eyes.

"You take corners too fast and weave in and out of traffic. You aren't a race car driver, Detective." He held out his hand and wiggled his fingers.

"Fine." She fished the keys from her pocket and dropped them into his hand. "You'd better not drive like an old man."

He laughed and opened the passenger side door for her. "Unfortunately, the victim is already deceased. Breaking speed records won't bring him or her back. When I need to speed, I will."

Ten minutes later they pulled in front of an upscale restaurant Harper could never afford on her salary. Side-by-side they headed for an area closed off by crime scene tape. Slumped over a table, a box of doughnuts in front of her, was the body of a woman in a bright yellow dress.

"We suspect the doughnuts, a gift from another patron, were poisoned," the officer said.

"Description of the gifter?" Harper asked.

He jerked his head toward a server. "Working on that now."

Harper marched toward the pale faced young man. "You saw the person who purchased the doughnuts?"

He nodded. "A man in a fancy suit. Dark hair combed back from his face. Dark eyes. Handsome, I think women would say. Seemed nice enough. The...woman kept smiling his way, flirting, you know? I thought maybe he liked bigger women. Anyway, she fell over and he got up and left. Creepy thing? He was smiling."

Harper glanced up at Liam's stern face. "Want to ask around and see whether anyone here knows the man?"

He nodded. "I doubt anyone who did is still here, but we can check."

How did this man keep slipping through their fingers?

~

Liam studied the shocked faces of those in the restaurant. Not everyone was still there that would have seen the suspect. The manager stood at the register gathering the nights room service tickets and credit card charges. It would be like looking for a needle in a haystack.

"He paid with cash," the server said. "I remember that because he left me a big tip."

"Was he a regular?"

"No. First time I've seen him, anyway."

Great. They'd be lucky to get an accurate description.

He sighed, pulled a notepad from the pocket inside his jacket, and approached a couple sitting at a table near where the suspect had. "I'm Special Agent McConnell. I'd like to ask you a few questions about the victim."

"She ate a lot," the woman said. "Poor thing didn't seem to mind her size and got giddy when that man bought her doughnuts."

"Can you describe him?"

"Handsome. Looked as if he worked out. Dark eyes. He

didn't look like a killer."

"Most of them don't ma'am." Her description was the same as the server's. "Please stick around and speak with our sketch artist."

He glanced to where Harper questioned a woman and moved to the opposite side of the room. A couple of teenagers huddled in a corner booth. Pale faces, wide eyes. They'd have nightmares for weeks. He introduced himself and asked the same question as before, adding, "Where are your parents?"

"In the room. We wanted to stay for dessert," the boy said. "Man." He rubbed his hands briskly down his face. "She just...fell face first in the box of doughnuts."

Fast-acting poison. "Anything else you can tell me?"

"The dude smiled on his way out the door. Who does that after killing someone?" He clutched his sister's hand. "My parents are over there. Can we go to them?"

"I'm sorry, no. But, they can join you here until we're finished." He waved them over, introduced himself, handed the parents a business card, then moved on. He'd get no more from the kids. Not right away at least.

Several hours into the night, he joined Harper. "Anything?"

She shook her head. "All descriptions match. He dropped cash on the table and walked out smiling as soon as she keeled over. The freak stayed to watch her die. He's like sand, Liam, slipping through our fingers and leaving a trail of death in his wake." Forehead creased, she raised worried eyes. "How many more are going to die before we catch him?"

Liam wanted to soothe the flicker of fear that crossed her eyes. Instead, he dropped his gaze to the pad in his hand. "More than we want."

"Why us? He hasn't sent a text in a while."

"That's a question that will be answered when we catch him." Realizing he gritted his teeth, he moved his jaw back and forth releasing the tension before a headache formed.

"I've never felt so inadequate in my life." She plopped into a chair at an empty table. "What do we do now? Wait until someone else dies as he leads us along in this macabre game he's playing?"

"We have a sketch now. We'll post it over the media. Somebody knows him."

"If they do, they won't say anything. They'll be too afraid."

"How do you know?"

"I feel it. He'll have some kind of control over anyone he comes into contact with. Call it instinct. We're looking for a powerful man. Not your everyday Joe."

Liam had the same feeling and had prayed he was wrong. They were looking for someone influential in the community. A sociopath who would destroy anyone that got between him and his goal. His goal seemed to be fixated on the seven deadly sins, but that would turn out to be nothing more than a facade.

Chapter Six

Officer Crypton rushed toward Harper, her steps slapping the floor of the restaurant, drawing attention from those being questioned. "A body washed up in the river. It's the bouncer from the nightclub."

"Can you finish up here?" Harper closed her notepad and stuck it in the pocket of her jacket. There weren't enough hours in the day with this mad man. "Did you find Jade somewhere to stay?"

"Yes to both. Almost everyone has been questioned. I'll meet you at the river later if you need me. Jade called an old friend from high school and took the bus to Little Rock."

"Liam and I can handle the bouncer's death." She caught his gaze and jerked her head toward the door.

Once they were in the car, Liam in the driver's seat despite her protests, he showed her his phone. "Looks like it's going to be envy this time."

She glanced at the phone's screen. "Envy is thin because it bites but never eats." She stared his way. "But who is the target?"

"I doubt we find out in time." He turned the key in the ignition. His shoulders slumped. "We're running in circles with nuggets tossed at us."

"Have you ever been on a case like this one?"

"I've brought down some very bad people, but this one is the worst." He drove to the interstate. "What really has me stumped is why he insisted on pairing the two of us together. This wasn't a coincidence."

She made a noise in her throat and stared out the window. That fact bothered her, too. As far as she knew, she and Liam had never made contact before. There had never been a reason for the FBI to be called to any case in Oakdale since she'd turned detective. Her family hadn't known any McConnells. If they had, they'd never mentioned them.

A crowd had gathered outside the crime scene tape by the river. A body bag lay on the shore.

Harper shoved open her car door and marched to the scene. Ducking under the tape, she approached the body. His throat had been slashed. One pant leg had ridden up, revealing what looked like marks from a rope.

"I don't think this is our envy victim." She hunkered next to the man. "His body wasn't supposed to be recovered. Look at his ankles. He'd been tied to something."

Liam glanced where she pointed, then ordered for someone to see if her theory was true. A man in scuba gear dove into the river.

"Who found the body?" Harper asked a nearby officer.

"A couple out jogging. Their dog went off the trail and started barking."

Harper looked over to where a young couple with a Labrador huddled under an oak tree. Planting her hands on her thighs, she pushed to her feet. More questions that wouldn't result in answers to resolve this case. "I'll take their statement if you want to handle things here."

"Sure." Liam nodded. "Hopefully, the diver will return with something."

Harper approached the couple. Tears filled the young woman's eyes. "You found the body?"

They nodded in unison. "It's awful." The woman buried her face in the man's chest."

"My wife and I jog here every morning," he said. "It's a peaceful trail. This is a good town. What's happening here?"

"That's what we're trying to find out, sir." Harper asked the same type of questions she'd asked the last few days and received basically the same answers. Except for at the restaurant, no one saw anything suspicious. A simple jog that had turned into a nightmare. Harper handed him her business card. "Please call me if you remember seeing anything that might help."

She returned to Liam's side as the diver emerged from the

water pulling a cement block attached to a rope. Harper exhaled sharply. "Old style gangster stuff. I thought our killer was smarter than this."

"Doesn't seem his MO." Liam pressed his lips together. "What if the man at the restaurant isn't doing the killings?"

"He was seen ordering the doughnuts."

"No, I mean the other ones. What if he's hiring someone?"

Her mouth fell open. Could he be right? Multiple killers? Was this man hiring a professional? "The deed at the restaurant seemed as if he'd known what he was doing?"

"Yes, but it was smooth and in the open. These other killings have been committed in secret." Liam took her arm and led her off to the side. "It's an avenue we need to explore. I'll get a list of hired killers in the state. It's a starting point."

~

It didn't take long after Liam's request to have a list of killers for hire in Arkansas and neighboring states for it to show up in his inbox. He copied the email to Harper. They could discuss their next step at lunch, which by the way his stomach complained, was way overdue.

He approached Harper who leaned against the bumper of her car. "Ready to eat?"

"Yes, I'm starving. Do you like sushi?" She didn't look up from her notepad.

"No. What's so interesting? Someone have something to tell you?"

"Don't look, but there's a woman who's been tying her shoes for half an hour. She arrived shortly after we did."

He glanced over his shoulder. A woman in jogging gear messed with her shoes, one foot propped on a bench. "The pretty dark-haired one?"

"I told you not to look. Yes, her. She seems overly interested in what's happening here." She snapped her notepad closed.

"Want me to go question her?" Why hadn't Harper already done so as soon as she grew suspicious?

The instant he took a step toward the woman, she jogged away from them. Instinct honed over the length of his career alerted him to the fact she wasn't merely a curious onlooker. "Let's try to catch up with her. Get in the car." He sprinted for the driver's door, Harper getting in the passenger side.

He had the car started and moving before her seat belt clicked into place. "We make a good team, detective."

"How so?" Her brow furrowed.

"We don't have to explain too much when something needs doing." He tossed her a wink, enjoyed the subtle pink tinging her cheek, and sped down the road next to the jogging trail. He passed the woman they pursued and stopped the vehicle in her path.

Her eyes widened, and she whirled to race into the trees. Harper shoved open her door and gave chase, Liam right behind her.

The woman dove into thick brush. A second later, a gunshot exploded from her hiding place.

Liam tackled Harper to the ground. "Are you hit?"

"Have a hole in my suit jacket. I spun."

Which likely saved her life. Liam pulled her behind a thick bush. He tossed a rock across the path, eliciting another gunshot.

Harper returned fire. "I think we found one of, if not the killer."

"We need to get around her. Come in from the back. Follow me." Keeping low, he led her horizontal to where the shooter hid, then turned again to where he thought they would be behind her.

"Get up nice and slow," he said. "Drop the gun and put your hands on your head."

She turned and raised her weapon.

Harper fired, striking the woman in the shoulder. The shooter spun like a puppet before falling to the ground.

Liam rushed forward and pinned her gun hand under his foot. When her grip loosened, he snatched the gun. "Come on, lady." He handed the weapon to Harper and hauled the woman to her feet.

Her features remained passive despite the fact he knew she had to be in a lot of pain. He unclipped handcuffs from his belt and cuffed her hands behind her. As uncomfortable as that was, she didn't whimper. He read her rights.

"Why'd you kill the bartender?" He led her in the direction of the car.

No answer.

"Who hired you? Did you set the bomb at the club? Did

Mark see you?" He rattled off questions trying to get a response. "You really should start talking. I'm not in a good mood. I haven't eaten in hours, and that makes me angry. Not to mention you shot at me and the detective."

She grinned, showing a capsule between her teeth. She bit down and swallowed. Seconds later, she writhed on the ground.

"No." Liam pried her mouth open, trying to get her to vomit up the poison.

Too quickly, she was dead.

~

Sarah's tracker stopped beeping on his computer screen. Cursing, he swept everything from his desk onto the floor. She'd been the best. Now, he'd have to find someone else he could trust whose heart was as cold as the Titanic iceberg.

He pulled up a list and chose another woman, Lucy Maine. They followed orders better than a man, he'd discovered. No testosterone getting in the way. He punched in the number listed. "This is Carl Landry. You should know who I am. I have a proposition for you. If interested, be at this address in less than an hour." He texted the address.

"I'm in Texas, but I'm definitely interested. I'll be there by nine a.m. tomorrow." Click.

Laughter burst from him. The woman had spunk, he'd give her that. "I'm going to enjoy taming you." He had no doubt that she'd show. Having no idea what she looked like, he could barely contain his excitement over this new development. He'd miss Sarah, but new blood was always nice.

He turned on the television and watched as his two targets stood in the woods behind crime scene tape. Their time was coming, but Carl was in no hurry. Why cut his fun short?

Some made-up, hair-sprayed Barbie doll spoke into a microphone about a woman's body in the woods, a shootout, and further law enforcement investigation. She went on to say the authorities had spotted a person of interest while on another crime scene and given chase.

Foolish of Sarah to have let herself be seen. Carl had thought her smarter than that. He got up and pour himself a small amount of whiskey, then returned to watching the news.

Not finding anything more of interest, he stood at his penthouse window and stared at the darkening skyline. He thought about calling for female companionship, any of his employees would come at his call, but decided to enjoy the evening alone. A few drinks, a few minutes reflecting on what Lucy would be like, sometimes a quiet evening was just what a man needed.

The detective's voice on the television drew him back to the screen. Harper, beautiful even after time in the woods, stared into the camera.

"This is for the person responsible the killings. Two more are dead today. How many more before you've had enough? I challenge you to come out and face me. Stop playing childish games." She turned, back straight, and marched to a waiting car.

"Oh, I will, my dear. And when I do, I'll be the one walking away. You and the agent don't know what is coming." He turned off the television and went to bed.

The next morning, he opened the door to room service and settled at the table by the window to wait for his new hired hitwoman. He shook open a newspaper, being old fashioned enough to still enjoy holding one in his hands and sipped his coffee. So engrossed was he in the headlines, he didn't realize someone stood next to him until they cleared their throat.

Assuming it to be the server, he waved a dismissive hand without looking up. "I've no further need, thank you."

"Strange, since you called me."

He jerked, spilling some of the hot coffee on his hand, and stared into the homely face of a pudgy woman in a housedress, her hair streaked with gray. "Lucy Maine?" Uglier than a burnt piece of toast.

Her lip curled. "The very one." She sat across from him and snatched a piece of toast off his plate. "I'm guessing you suspected someone like your pretty former killer. Let me tell you, I can get in and out of places unnoticed looking like this."

Since she'd managed to sneak up on him, he suspected she was very much correct. He met her steely gaze and smiled as he wondered how in the world had she gotten into his room.

Chapter Seven

Carl turned on the television to watch the morning news while Lucy played a game on her phone and waited for his order. Crossing his ankles, he propped his feet on the coffee table as a lovely brunette in a red suit smiled for the camera.

"Lucy, I'd like to explain to you what I'm doing. How I'm trying to make the world a better place."

"Not interested. All I want is to be paid for my job." She cast dark eyes on him. "No friendships, no boss and employee, no calling you sir; simply an assassin doing what she's getting paid for. If I do need to use your name, it's Carl." She wagged her finger between them. "Even."

He frowned, not liking her attitude, and turned back to the television. He was the boss. He was the one who paid a ridiculous amount of money to have the jobs done. The news reporter's smile never faded as she blathered on.

"This is Brittney Burnes, award-winning reporter from AZZK, your local network coming to you live in front of the strip club where the person who's been killing sinners caused multiple deaths." She turned dramatically to the pile of rubble that had once been a den of inequity.

A trace of excitement laced her words as she went on to inform the public that the Seven Sins Killer had done the unthinkable in killing so many people at one time. "We're coming for you, sir." Her smiled widened. "I've met your kind before and brought you down. Every killer falls at some point."

"She sure likes to embellish, doesn't she?" Lucy set her phone on the sofa beside her.

"She's prideful." He rubbed his bald head and glanced at the cupboard that held a myriad of wigs, different colors of contacts, and other items to disguise his identity.

People who furthered themselves on the disasters of others didn't belong in the Utopia he wanted to create. That's why he'd become a plastic surgeon. To make the world more beautiful. His fingers itched to do something to Lucy's face and body. "I want her taken care of before I return home this evening."

"Consider it done."

~

Harper sat at her desk, feet propped on top of it, and stared at the case board. A lot of death without a lot of answers.

"Coffee?" Liam handed her a Styrofoam cup from the local coffee shop. "It's not the sludge in the breakroom."

"Thank God for that." She accepted the cup and continued staring at the board. "We got nothing."

"We will. The perp will make a mistake sooner or later." He perched on the corner of her desk.

"But we don't know where or when he'll strike again. We also don't know how many people he has working for him, killing for him." Her phone buzzed at the same time as Liam's. She glanced at the text and read, "Pride goes before a fall, as the lovely lady in red will soon find out." She stared into Liam's face. "Lady in red?"

He bit the inside of his cheek. "The morning news reporter wore a red suit. She kind of taunted the killer on television."

Harper leaped to her feet and reached for the phone. "We need to call the station." She dialed the number, identified herself, and then asked to speak to Brittney Burnes.

"She hasn't returned to the office yet," the receptionist said. "Would you like to leave a message?"

"Do you know where she is?"

"No, Detective. After the news cast this morning, she may have gone to question witnesses. She is an investigative reporter, you know."

"Thank you." Harper hung up. "Let's go to the explosion site. Brittney may still be there."

Liam snatched the keys off her desk, then motioned her forward. "After you."

Taking her coffee with her, Harper practically ran to her jeep and slid into the passenger seat. "Make it quick. A woman's life might be at stake." She slapped the red light on top of the vehicle.

"Yes, ma'am." Liam backed up and spun the jeep toward the road. "Buckle your seatbelt." He yanked on hers to tighten it and took off like a race car driver.

"So, you do know how to drive fast." She arched a brow.

"Yes, when the situation warrants. Trying to keep a woman alive is a need for speed." He squealed tires going around a corner. Horns blared as he came close to crossing the yellow line into oncoming traffic.

A few people milled around on the sidewalk when they arrived at the night club. The news van sat at one end of the parking lot. A cameraman loaded equipment in the back. No sign of Brittney.

Harper shoved her door open before Liam had the jeep in park and hurried to the van. "Where's Brittney?"

The man shrugged. "Went off to talk to people and hasn't returned."

"How long?"

"Maybe half an hour. Is she in trouble?" He crossed his arms.

"It's quite possible. If you have a way of contacting her, please do and ask her to come back here right away." An icy fist clenched Harper's heart. The morning's coffee ate at the lining of her stomach.

The cameraman placed the call. "It went straight to voice mail."

"Which way did she go?"

Harper and Liam sprinted in the direction he pointed, ignoring his shouted questions. They'd explain later.

Their feet pounded in unison as they ran down the sidewalk dodging curious onlookers. "Have you seen Brittney Burnes?" Harper asked a man.

"She went that way with some woman." He pointed to a path across the road.

Harper glanced at Liam. "I would've thought Brittney too smart to go into the woods with a stranger."

"Maybe the other woman promised her answers to the bombing. A woman might not seem as threatening as a man." Looking both ways, he darted across the street, Harper on his heels.

The overgrown path went into the thick foliage and blocked most of the light from the sun. Again, Harper couldn't help but wonder why Brittney would follow a stranger. Especially, if they went into the dark woods.

There weren't many buildings around the nightclub. The town of Oakdale wouldn't allow the place within its borders, so it had been built between Oakdale and Harrington. While the towns were spreading toward each other, there was still a lot of woods between the two.

The further they ran, the more it looked as if they were on a wild goose chase. Until she spotted the red pump from under a bush. "Liam."

He peered under the bush. "No body."

They continued down the dark path until reaching a slow-moving creek. Lying half in the water and half out was Brittney. Her suit made a sharp contrast against the dirt of the creek bank.

"We were too late." Harper leaned against a tree.

"We tried." Liam turned the body over.

Lifeless eyes stared heavenward. Blood soaked the white blouse and red jacket she wore.

Nausea rose, burning Harper's esophagus. "Did the killer cut out her tongue?"

~

"Looks that way." Liam straightened. "The slit across the throat is what killed her." He studied the area for the tongue, finding it on a flat rock near the water's edge. "The tongue has been washed."

"Why?" Harper's brow furrowed.

"To wash the lies from her mouth?"

"Makes as much sense as anything. I'll call the crime scene techs."

Which had to come from Harrington and would take about fifteen minutes. The hair on the back of his neck stood on end. They were being watched. "Harper, mind standing closer to me?"

"What's wrong?" She stared into the trees.

"Over here, please."

A puzzled look on her face, she went to stand next to him.

"I don't think we're alone," he said softly. "We can't leave the scene until the techs arrive. I want you close."

"Let's at least find something to stand behind." She headed for the trunk of a thick oak.

It wasn't much, but it was better than nothing. He stood in front of her, shielding her with his body. Just in case.

The scent of gardenia wafted to his nose. "You smell nice." His mouth twitched. "Like something feminine."

She pushed against him and rolled her eyes. "Now is not the time for flirting."

"Just stating a fact." He grinned down at her, her eyes dark pools he could drown in. He knew she downplayed her beauty to get respect from coworkers and the citizens of Oakdale.

A twig snapped, pulling his attention back to where it belonged. He took her hand in his and put a finger to his lips. Maybe they could circle around and get behind the person. He pulled his gun and pulled Harper deeper into the shadows.

Birds twittered from the trees. No more twig snaps. The faint roar of an engine. Whoever had killed Brittney had gotten away.

"It's the closest we've gotten other than the assassin who killed herself." He put his gun away. They'd catch the person responsible, because no matter how long it took, Liam wouldn't stop.

Harper exhaled heavily and marched back to the body. She stood over a sheet of paper that wasn't there before. "It says that the game is only going to get more exciting, and that the reason will be made clear soon."

"Great." He sat on a large rock. "Might as well sit."

She lowered herself next to him. "I hate this rushing out to body after body with no clues as to who is doing this."

"Because the main perp isn't doing this." He leaned against a tree trunk. "He's got others to do his dirty work. I've been working down the list of known assassins. There's quite a few. I'm sure there are some that aren't on the list. I'm crossing off the ones in prison or deceased."

"How many does that leave?"

"About twenty." He crossed his arms.

"I had no idea we had twenty in the states."

"This one could have come from overseas." It was like the proverbial needle in a haystack. "Or it could not be an assassin at all, but simply a partner.”

“Thanks for the encouragement.” She stood when two men and a woman all wearing CSI vests approached.

Liam pointed out the shoe further up the trail and the tongue. By now, people were starting to drift down the trail out of curiosity. “We need to secure the scene.”

“I’ve tape in my car.” Harper fetched the yellow roll and strung it between two trees in order to keep the crowd back.

One of them trying to see what was going on was the camera man. Liam shook his head and approached the man. “Mind stepping over here for a minute?”

“Is it Brittney?”

“Please. Just over here.” Liam led him away from the crowd.

“Does Brittney have family?”

“No.” He tried peering around Liam. “She’s a workaholic. Not many friends. I’ve been her cameraman for five years.”

“I regret to inform you that, yes, Brittney Burnes has been murdered.”

“By the Seven Sins Killer?”

Liam pressed his eyes closed. He hated the names the media came up with for killers. In his opinion, it only fed into their ego. “We don’t know at this time.”

“I need to tell the office. They’ll want another reporter out here.” He hurried and rushed away.

Liam rubbed his hands roughly down his face. Who would be next?

It seemed as if the killer stayed on the sin of pride. How long until he moved to another alleged sin?

His gaze landed on Harper. Again, why put the two of them together?

Chapter Eight

Carl handed a large envelope to the man standing in front of his desk. A man he'd done a great job of restructuring his face so he'd never be caught and trialed for murder. Unless he left fingerprints. "Wear gloves. In there are clues, think scavenger hunt, only there's no prize." He laughed. "You'll figure out where to leave them. I'll text the players the first clue. You have one hour to put those where they belong."

"I could've done that." Lucy plopped into a chair.

"You are used for different things. I've no one to kill today."

"Pity." She cleaned her fingernails with a small knife.

Carl sneered and turned away from her. The woman needed some lessons in acting like a lady. "Have you considered better clothes? Makeup? Manners?"

"Don't need them in my line of work."

With a sigh, he turned back to his follower. A man he knew would do his bidding. "Understand?"

"Yes, sir. I'll have it done quickly." He nodded and backed from the room.

Lucy narrowed her eyes. "Look at me in disgust again, and I'll carve out your eyes. I've killed the one signing the checks before."

"I should've done a better job of vetting you." He stood and stood in front of the office window overlooking the parking lot.

His next appointment, a woman wanting bags removed from under her eyes, strolled toward the door. Time to beautify another. He picked up his phone and sent another text, then turned to Lucy. "Find something to leave at the last clue sight. Something that has nothing to do with pride."

"Anything?" Her eyes widened. "What about something related to the last clue. What is it?"

He bent down and whispered in her ear.

~

Harper scowled at her phone. "I hope you're wearing your walking shoes."

Liam glanced up. "What?"

"The text." She held up her phone. "Didn't you get one?"

"I've got my sound turned down." He stared at his screen. "This is a weird one. I imagine we'll get another soon explaining what this one means."

A few minutes later, the next one came through. "What lies behind the red door? A clue perhaps? You have twenty minutes before it disappears."

Red door?

"You know this place better than I do. Where do we go?" Liam grabbed his suit jacket.

"I don't know if he means Oakdale, Harrington, or some other place." She grabbed her weapon, knocking her phone off her desk and onto the floor. She snatched it and slid it into her pocket. "But, since we have so little time, I'm assuming Oakdale. Only one place has a red door, and that is the Chinese buffet."

She really hoped it wasn't a dead end. She'd follow any clue the perp left if it gave her hope of a conclusion to all this. The longer he played the game, the more chances of him making a mistake.

As they drove, Liam cut her a sideways glance. "Have you been thinking on why we were thrown together?"

"Not really. More concerned about the deaths that are piling up." She frowned. "Why?"

"There has to be a reason. I'm positive I've never met you before this. We've never worked on a case together before."

No, they hadn't. "What kind of work did your father do?" If in law enforcement, maybe that was the connection, except she was the first in law enforcement in her family.

"Physician. Yours?"

"Both my father and grandfather were oncologists. It seems far-fetched that could be the connection." Her frown deepened.

"Do you agree?"

"I don't see how that could be it." He pulled into the parking lot of the Chinese buffet and sat staring out the front window without turning off the ignition. "Maybe we should get patient lists and compare them. We don't have anything else to do on."

"Okay. My father isn't practicing anymore, but he should be able to get his and my grandfather's. Did your father practice in the states?"

"For a few years." He turned off the jeep. "Let's find out about this clue."

She glanced at her watch. They had ten minutes to spare. Inside, she approached the hostess stand and introduced herself. "Do you have anything for me?"

"An envelope." She pulled a white envelope from under the podium.

"Who gave this to you?" Harper used the corner of her jacket to take the envelope.

"Some guy in a motorcycle helmet."

That didn't give them much to go on. When they returned to the jeep, she snapped rubber gloves over her hands and read the note inside. "Water crashes when there's been a lot of rain. Unfortunately, we're in a drought. You have ten minutes." She smiled. "That's easy. The spillway by the dam."

"How far?"

"Hit the gas. We'll barely make it."

The next clue sent them to the Dairy Queen, the next one to the elementary school. Both said the notes were left by a man in a motorcycle helmet. One said he rode a Harley, one said it was a Yamaha. The only consistent fact was he wore a black motorcycle helmet and riding leathers.

Harper groaned. "We're getting nowhere. I think we're being distracted from something."

"I agree. We have to finish this, though."

What were they being distracted from? It had to be something big. Something Harper and Liam could stop. Her throat seized. If they didn't stop whatever, people would die. She felt it deep in her bones.

Liam remained silent as they went to their next stop. A rock held the note to the top of a picnic table. Liam picked it up and read, "Having fun yet? The last clue will be a doozy and will take you where you need to be."

"This isn't going to be good." Harper studied the area around them. "We need help on this case, Liam."

"I agree. I'll call in some of my fellow agents." He marched back to the jeep.

Harper tried to get peace from the sun on the lake. The duck family swimming past. Nothing calmed the racing of her heart, the fear of the unknown. She turned to gaze where Liam waited by the jeep, somehow knowing she needed a moment alone.

Why him of all the law enforcement people in the world? Why an Irish man with a brogue? An FBI agent? Why not Officer Crypton who already worked for Oakdale?

No, the reason they were together was a big one. Hopefully, they'd find out soon and put an end to the Seven Deadly Sins Killer.

She rejoined Liam and slid in the passenger side.

"You okay?" His brow furrowed.

"No. But, someday, if we're lucky, I will be."

~

Liam wanted to punch something. The next clue simply said to take a lunch break at the food truck near the grocery store. How many senseless clues were left?

"I guess this guy believes we can't think on an empty stomach." Harper approached the window and ordered a grilled cheeseburger on Texas toast with fries and a diet soda. "It's awfully nice of him to give us thirty minutes to eat."

Liam ordered a mushroom burger meal. "It'll be interesting to see how he'll deliver the next clue."

"I sent my father a text requesting patient records. He said there are quite a lot, but he'll get them to me as soon as possible." She sat at a round table with an umbrella.

"I'll do that now." He texted his father, although he couldn't see how this could be the missing piece in why they'd been paired together.

Their food arrived. In the bag was an envelope with a note telling them their next clue was in Harrington and they would have thirty minutes from the time their lunch was over to get there. His shoulders sagged. Each time frame became more and more difficult. Before unwrapping his burger, he texted the agency and requested backup.

He jerked his attention to the road as a Harley roared by driven by a rider in all black. Could that be their guy? If so, they'd never catch him. Why the continuous taunting?

"That can't be the only rider in black on a Harley in town," Harper said, her thoughts mirroring his.

"I hope not because he just got away."

The instant their time was up, they sped toward Harrington and the library. The librarian handed them a book with a bookmark saving a page. Liam flipped the book open.

"You just missed the man who asked me to give you that book," she said. "Not two minutes ago."

Liam heaved a sigh. The book was by one of the world's most popular authors. "Isn't there a movie playing at the theater based on this book?"

"Yes." Harper's eyes widened. "That's where the next clue will be."

"Oh, a scavenger hunt. How fun." The librarian clapped her hands together.

"I don't think you'd enjoy playing this one, ma'am." Liam handed her back the book and marched back to the jeep. They only had five minutes this time. At this rate, they'd receive a clue they wouldn't have time to get to. Maybe that was the point. They wouldn't make it in time, would waste an entire day, and someone else would pay the price.

At the movie theater, they were given another clue. This one took them back to the Oakdale Police station. "There's no way we can make it back there in fifteen minutes." He shook his head.

"We're meant to fail." Harper raced for the jeep.

He followed close behind. Seconds later, they were speeding toward the police station. How would a clue get there? "Call ahead and see whether the note has been delivered. If not, then alert them to restrain the deliverer."

Harper did as he instructed. "No clue yet. They'll be on the lookout." She turned to face him. "I can't see the motorcycle dude leaving a clue at the station. That is way gutsy, even for a sadistic killer."

"We're just following the clues." Doing what they were told

like puppets.

They arrived at the station to no sign of an envelope being left at the reception desk. At a loss, they headed to the bull pen and sat at Harper's desk. "Now what?"

As if they'd been listened to, both their phones buzzed. He glanced at the screen. *Don't expect this one to be easy. You'll have to look for it.* He met Harper's confused gaze. "Okay." He pushed to his feet. "We start looking."

"Do you think it'll be close by?"

"He did send us here." He put his hand on the small of his back. It fit perfectly as if the curve of her waist into her bottom were made for that purpose.

They checked with everyone at the station, even those in handcuffs. No one had seen the man in black. Liam bit the inside of his cheek as he thought. If the clue hadn't been given to anyone inside, it had to be waiting for them outside.

He led Harper outside where they searched the area around the building. "Let's go around back." He glanced at each vehicle in the lot searching for an envelope, card, anything.

"Do you think it was just a ploy to make us run in a big circle? To keep us out of the office?" Harper stepped around the corner of the building. "I'm not seeing anything."

"Look everywhere. Something is here. This man doesn't do anything for no reason." Liam approached the dumpster behind the building. The hair on his arms stood on end.

Heart in his throat, he peered around the edge. A middle-aged woman wearing a white clinical coat lay propped against the dumpster, her hands bound in a praying gesture.

"Harper? Come take a look."

She joined him. "That's Mavin Jones, the pharmacist." Her gaze rose and clashed with his. "We're supposed to go to the drugstore."

Chapter Nine

News vans from Oakdale, Harrington, and any other city where they could arrive on Main Street quickly sat behind crime scene blockades before Harper and Liam arrived. Something big, something bad, had happened while she and Liam ran out around like headless chickens.

A crowd had gathered behind the vans and squad cars, watching the drugstore as if they were at a holiday parade. One man had his toddler on his shoulders. Where was the chief?

Harper glanced around, then made a beeline for the chief, recently returned from vacation. "Just in time, sir. Welcome back."

"What in tarnation have you gotten involved in?"

"You haven't heard the news?"

"Of course, I have. Why you?" Chief Donnelly glowered. "What's the FBI doing here?"

"It's all related, sir. What's happening here?" She could fill the chief in on all the other details later.

His frown deepened. "Where have you been that you don't know some mad man is holding those inside the store hostage?"

She cut a quick look at Liam. "Following clues left by the killer. Mavis Jones is dead behind the station, sir. She was the final clue. He wanted Agent McConnell and me occupied while he put this plan in place. Any contact?"

"Not yet." He crossed his arms across a burly chest. "Why do these things happen when a man goes on a fishing trip? Mavis was a good woman."

Knowing the question to be rhetorical, she kept quiet and stepped to Liam's side. "No demands yet."

"Introduce me to the chief."

Idiot. She should've done that first thing. "Chief Donnelly, Special Agent Liam McConnell. He's been receiving the same text messages I have and came to Oakdale to help us."

"Text messages?"

"We have a lot to fill you in on, sir." She turned as a SWAT team arrived. "How long has the drugstore been held hostage?" It would've taken the team an hour to arrive.

He glanced at his watch. "A couple of hours."

"Why didn't anyone call me?"

"We tried. Your phone went straight to voice mail."

She pulled her phone and scrolled through recent calls. The chief had tried five times to get a hold of her. Why hadn't her phone rang? Could the perp have a way of blocking her phone?

"Check the volume. Sometimes, when a phone is dropped, it shuts off the volume," Liam told her. "No one could tap into your phone."

Sure enough, the volume had been turned off. "I'm sorry, sir."

"You're here now. Maybe the man inside will make his demands now."

"Any sight of him?"

"Wears black leather. Hasn't removed his helmet. Haven't seen hide nor hair of him in the last hour."

Officer Crypton handed the chief a phone. "It's the man inside."

"This is Chief Donnelly. What do you want? Yes, they're here." He sighed and set the phone on top of his car. "Just checking to see whether the two of you have arrived."

That was it? What game was he playing now? Was the motorcycle man the Seven Deadly Sins Killer? Seemed too easy. Her skin prickled. Things were going to go downhill fast. She moved closer to Liam, relying on his solid strength.

His arm snaked around her waist. "We've got this."

"Whatever this is."

The phone rang again. This time the man inside wanted to speak to Harper.

"This is Detective Scranton."

"Good job on following all the clues to lead you here. Today is not your lucky day, Detective," the man said. "But, the game is not over. A sacrifice will be made in the name of pride." He hung up.

Her voice shook as she repeated the short conversation.

"What in the hell does that mean?" The chief's face darkened. "I want details now."

Liam filled him in on everything that had transpired since the time he'd arrived. The big things, like the deaths and the club explosion, the chief knew about. The texts he had not.

"Are you telling me, this guy has a personal vendetta against the two of you?"

"It appears that way, sir." Harper knew it sounded hard to believe. "Why else bring Agent McConnell here? Why thrust us together? The only connection we can find is that both of our fathers were in the medical field. We've requested files to compare patients."

"Good." He turned his attention back to the store. "What is this guy waiting for?"

"Instructions." Liam crossed his arms making him and the chief look like matching bookends. "I don't believe this is the man behind the killings. He uses other people to do the actual deed."

The chief cursed. "What are we doing to find the person responsible?"

"Whatever he tells us to do," Harper muttered. "We have no actual clues to his identity. Not yet, anyway."

"I saw the case board. The two of you need to step this up. Find this man."

"It's not going to be easy or short, sir." Liam kept his gaze straight ahead. "I believe he is working his way through the seven sins. He's on pride right now. Hopefully, today's event, however this ends, will start the next sin. The sooner we get through all seven of them, the sooner this is over, and the perp locked away."

Harper didn't like the sound of that. Having this drag on meant the possibility of many more deaths. They had to stop him before he got through all seven.

The chief ordered the SWAT team into position. "If you get the chance, take the shot."

Ten men in armor skirted around the drugstore.

Harper tossed up a quick prayer for a safe ending to the day.

~

Carl smiled as the detective and agent arrived on the scene. With all the news vans around, he wouldn't miss any of the excitement. When the SWAT team surrounded the building, he picked up his phone and dialed the man inside.

"Stay away from the windows. SWAT team will be looking for their shot. You aren't to die at their hands."

"Understood, sir. What's my next move?"

"How many people do you have inside?"

"Six. A pharmacy tech, a mother and two children, and an elderly couple."

"Anyone showing signs of pride?"

"No, sir. All humble and frightened."

"Good. Let's let those outside stew a bit." He hung up and grinned at Lucy. "Isn't this fun?"

"I prefer things done quickly." She never looked up from whatever game she played on her phone.

He sighed. Sarah had been much more enjoyable as company. Beautiful, willing to carry on a conversation…among other things. This woman in front of him was nothing more than what he'd hired her for, and a bit of a disappointment.

Shrugging, he poured himself a glass of fine whiskey and settled back to enjoy the show on TV. Were the detective and agent starting to figure out why he'd chosen them?

"Why the seven sins?" Lucy piped up, finally putting her phone down.

"I thought you weren't interested."

"I changed my mind."

"I'm working on making the world a better place. That's why I became a plastic surgeon. To make people more beautiful. I could do wonders with you, if you'd let me."

"No, thanks. So, you're playing God. Deciding who lives and who dies. Everyone sins, Carl. Even you."

Was he playing God? He supposed so. "The only sin I've committed is murder, and that in a roundabout way. I can live with that."

She laughed. "You're the epitome of pride, thinking you can change the world. Heck, I'm prideful knowing how good of an assassin I am. Is that really such a bad thing?"

His hand squeezed the whiskey glass as he pretended the glass was her neck. "Some carry it to extreme."

"So?" She laughed again. "I'm enjoying this way more than I should. I can't wait to see what you do next, my Lord." She got up and poured herself a glass of whiskey and raised her hand in a toast.

He'd never hated anyone more. He picked up the phone again and gave the next order.

~

The chief's phone rang. He snatched it off the car, listened, and hung up. "He wants the two of you to approach the building. When the door opens, you're to go inside. Once you do, he'll release the other hostages. Leave your weapons with me."

Liam didn't move or speak for a second. His hold around Harper's waist tightened. "Did he say why?"

"Nope. I want the two of you wired. I need to know what goes on in there." He snapped his fingers and ushered over someone to put a wire on them as they set their guns on the hood of his car.

Liam averted his gaze as Harper unbuttoned her blouse so they could attach a wire to her bra. While one woman worked on her, a man worked on him. Within five minutes, they both wore a wire and an earpiece.

"If things start going south," the chief said, "SWAT team will storm in. Try not to get yourselves killed."

"I don't think it's time for him to kill us, sir." Liam took Harper's hand. "Ready?"

"Not really." She gave a shaky laugh. "But, here goes. On to see what's next in this diabolical game."

"I mean it, Harper. Don't die." The sheriff's words choked off.

"Definitely won't, Chief." Her hold tightened on Liam's hand. "I sure hope you're right about it not being our time."

"He'll want to meet us face-to-face. Tell us why he chose us. No, sweetheart, this is only the beginning." A thought that left him very cold inside.

In his career, he'd seen a lot of bad things, but nothing as insane as this. He hated feeling helpless, with no clear plan on moving forward. This perp pulled all the strings and knew he did.

As they approached the front door, it swung open. Taking a deep breath, Liam entered first.

The man in black still hadn't removed his helmet. He stood in the back corner, an automatic rifle trained on the front door. "Everyone else out. The two of you stand in front of the window. Make it quick."

The hostages shoved past, pushing each other out the door. Liam moved to the window, Harper next to him. The other man stepped forward.

"Now that the two of you are effectively keeping me from being shot, I'll introduce myself. Call me Billy. Not my real name, but it won't matter in a while." He grabbed a soda from a cooler and popped the tab. "Thirsty?"

"No, thanks." Liam sent a quick glance around the store. "Why are we here?"

"You'll find out soon enough." He leaned against the counter.

"Who are you working for?" Harper asked.

"A man intent on making this a more perfect world." He set the can on the counter next to a cell phone without taking a drink. Drinking would require removing his helmet and, the man seemed reluctant for them to know his identity. "It's needed, don't you think?"

"By committing murder of a lot of people?" She shook her head. "No, I don't think that's needed."

"You aren't as enlightened as the one I serve."

A cult? Liam frowned. "So enlighten us."

"I've said all I need to."

"Tell me about the sins."

"There are seven deadly sins. Surely, you know that. You don't take me as a stupid man, Agent."

Liam felt as if the man smiled behind his helmet, laughing at them. "What now?"

"I wait for further orders."

"How long?" Harper glanced over her shoulder out the window.

"For however long it takes. Please keep your gaze directed on me."

"Get the fool to tell you more." The chief's voice came through Liam's earpiece. "Act interested in his beliefs."

"I really would like to know what the man you serve believes." Liam pasted on a smile. "How do you get followers?"

"Law enforcement isn't allowed in our ranks."

"Why not?" His smile faded.

"Because you are some of the most prideful."

"How can that be when we serve the public and rid the streets of thieves and killers?"

"That's the exact reason. You don't allow man free will. You place orders and rules that keep mankind penned in."

"Like the man you serve does you."

The man stiffened. "No. It's different."

"How?" Liam tilted his head. "He tells you what to do, and you do it without question. I doubt you have the choice whether to do what he says or not. I'm sure the consequences are severe if you deny an order or disobey."

"Don't push him too far," the chief said in his earpiece. "We don't want him shooting you. I mean it. You're not to provoke him, only to get information about who sent him."

The phone on the counter rang.

Chapter Ten

The man in the helmet picked up the phone, listened, nodded, and hung up. "We're leaving."

"Excuse me?" Harper glanced again over her shoulder. "How do you propose to get past the SWAT team?" Where were they going?

"It won't be difficult." He grabbed a plastic picnic tablecloth off a shelf. "Time to get cozy." He stepped out of sight of the window and motioned them forward.

He couldn't be serious.

"Agent, please take off your pants. You'll be switching with me."

Clever man, but not too clever. If they weren't wired…

As Liam went to do as he was told, the man shook his head, putting a finger to his helmet where his mouth was. Ah. He suspected they wore a wire.

She cut Liam a sharp glance. If they shot, they'd hit him. She opened her mouth to say something only to find the barrel of the man's rifle aimed at her gut. He shook his head again.

A muscle ticked in Liam's jaw. Without speaking, he moved to stand next to their captor.

Harper took a deep breath and did the same.

The man, Billy, covered their heads with the tablecloth which fell to their waists. "We'll go out the back. Any funny moves and someone gets shot."

Hopefully, Billy. Light filtered through the red tablecloth. She hoped enough light got through that the SWAT team could tell the difference between Billy and Liam. "Where are we going?"

"Shh." Billy hushed her. "It's the next step."

She didn't like the sound of that at all.

Liam reached over and gave her hand a squeeze.

"Detective, please reach out and open the van door," Billy said. "Then, we'll all crawl inside together."

She reached from under the cloth and felt around the smooth panel of the van until she located the handle. The door swung open easily, and the three got inside.

"Now, Detective, please zip tie the agent's hands behind his back." He tossed the cloth to the floor.

The van was an old 1970s model complete with shag carpet and curtains. Through the dim light, she located the zip ties. "Sorry, Liam."

"No worries."

She tightened the tie. "Now, what?"

"Remove the wire on you and on him and give them to me."

"Do as he says," the chief spoke through her earpiece. "We'll find you."

She nodded and stuck her hand down Liam's shirt. Her hand brushed against the warmth of a toned chest. A scattering of chest hairs tickled her palm. Her eyes locked with his. A slight quirk on his lips helped diffuse the tension.

She smiled and pulled the wire from his chest, taking care not to rip the tape too hard, before removing his earpiece. She did the same to herself and handed it all over to Billy.

"Wonderful. Now, sit in the passenger seat and open the curtain." He slid into the driver's seat and opened that window and the one over the front windshield before slamming his foot on the gas pedal and rocketing them away from the police, news reporters, and curious crowd.

Hopefully, that meant any danger to innocent people had been lessened. Not having direct contact with the chief anymore left her palms clammy. It took several tries before the seatbelt would click into place around her.

She turned to check on Liam who sat with his back against the wall behind Billy. He gave her a nod, then flicked his gaze to Billy. She nodded back. She'd take the first opportunity to yank the wheel away from him. "Be careful," she mouthed to Liam. He wouldn't have a seatbelt to save him.

"Now that you've tossed the wires out the window, what's the next step, Billy?"

She had to repeat the name, affirming that wasn't his real name.

"We'll find out when we reach our destination."

"How far is that?"

"Not too far." He glanced in the rearview mirror and slowed the van's speed. "We'll be told what's next then."

She wouldn't let them get that far. He still drove too fast for safety. She'd have to wait until he slowed more or Liam could be severely injured upon impact. The only one she didn't want left standing at the end of the day was Billy.

"Unbelief was the first sin, and pride was the first-born of it...." Billy said.

"What does that mean?" Were they going to be forced to join this, what she was quickly starting to believe was a cult?

He cut her a sideways glance. "You do not believe. That causes you to be sinful with pride."

"Sometimes people don't believe because they haven't been introduced."

He laughed, the sound strange under his helmet. "You are a worthy adversary of my..."

"You're what?" Employer? Friend? Relative?

"Lord." He whipped the van to the right taking a dirt road that would take them to the lake.

He had to slow again, but the trees crowded the van too close for her to be able to get much of an impact. Not enough to knock the man unconscious at least. She caught a glimpse of the lake up ahead.

Saying a quick prayer, she reached over and pressed the man's foot harder onto the accelerator. "Hold on, Liam!"

They shot for the water. The van took a slight incline, went airborne, and splashed into the lake before slowly starting to sink.

She then rammed Billy's head against the steering wheel until the face shield on his helmet cracked and stopped moving. She fought with her seatbelt as cold water seeped into the vehicle.

~

Liam tried to find something to stop him being thrown around the back of the van as soon as he realized what Harper expected to do. Nothing. With his hands bound, he was helpless.

When they hit the water, he slammed against the back of Billy's seat, knocking the breath from him. His head whipped to the side, striking the wall. Things went dark for a moment.

"Liam!" Harper slammed her feet against the passenger side window. "Once I break this, you'll have to come to me. I'll pull you to the surface."

"You'll never be able to get me to the shore. Not with my hands tied." His heart sank as he realized this could be the end for him.

"I won't leave you." The window drifted from the van. Harper reached toward him and grabbed the collar of his shirt, yanking him between the two front seats. "Take a deep breath, we're going under." She took one and dove, keeping a hold of him.

One foot caught him under the chin, and he bit his tongue. The metallic taste of blood filled his mouth. She moved her hold from his shirt collar to his arm and kicked for the surface.

They broke the surface, both gasping for air.

"Relax and lay back." She rolled over and cradled him against her as a mother otter would her offspring. She kicked her legs slowly, taking them closer to the shore.

Billy shot to the surface. With long strokes, he swam toward them.

If Harper let go of Liam to fight the man off, Liam would sink, unless he could kick hard enough to keep himself above water. "Let go of me."

"No."

"Harper, you can't hold onto me and protect yourself. I'll make it to shore." He wouldn't dare leave her to fight the man alone.

A shot rang out. A hole appeared in Billy's helmet. The man sank below the water's surface.

"Help has arrived," Harper said. "How did the chief know our location?"

"He slipped a tracker in my pants pocket while wiring me." He kicked along with her to make her burden easier. "Thank you for staying with me."

"Hey, we're partners. That's what we do. It's going to take both of us to stop this mad man."

Yes, it would.

Hands reached down and pulled them from the water. The chief cut the tie from Liam's wrist.

"You've got a text," he said, handing Liam and Harper their phones.

Liam glanced at the screen. "Covetousness teaches people to be cruel and crafty, industrious and evil, full of care and malice; and after all this, it is for no good to itself, for it dares not spend those heaps of treasure which it has snatched." He glanced at Harper. "Round two."

DEADLY COVET

Cynthia Hickey

Covetousness teaches people to be cruel and crafty, industrious and evil, full of care and malice; and after all this, it is for no good to itself, for it dares not spend those heaps of treasure which it has snatched.

Chapter One

Carl Landry, wearing a slicked back black wig and dark contacts, studied his menu in an upscale restaurant, one he frequented quite often under one disguise or another. After all, he deserved the finer things in life, especially since his life goal was to make the world a more beautiful place.

A man trailed his fingers across a woman's back as he passed, then gave her hand a quick squeeze before joining a different woman at a table. A few seconds later, another man exited the men's room and joined the first woman. Then, the two joined the other two.

Carl raised his menu a bit. What did he have here? Blonde woman belonged to dark-haired man, yet she'd been touched by the brown-haired man. The brunette at the table barely looked up when her companion seated himself next to her, setting her menu aside as the others joined them.

Clearly, the four were friends judging by the smiles and air kisses. He never could understand why people spent money to go to the theater when watching people in public never failed to entertain.

"What can I get for you, sir?" A pretty, young waitress stood between him and the other table.

Carl forced a smile. "The filet, medium rare, blue cheese crust, baked potato, fully loaded, and asparagus. Oh, and a glass of red wine."

"Yes, sir." She gave him a nod and rushed away, leaving his view of the other table clear again.

Dark-haired man lifted his glass of water as the blond woman slipped her foot from her shoe and ran it up and down his leg all while continuing with the group conversation. There were two sins being played out in front of him. Which would prove to be the stronger?

After losing a man to the lake during the game of pride, Carl had laid low for a week and concentrated on his plastic surgery practice. But now, boredom threatened. Time to get the detective and special agent playing again.

The blond woman stood and headed for the ladies' room. The brown-haired man's gaze locked on her and never wavered.

Carl smiled. Covet it was.

Now, how to find out who the man is and how to make him pay without harming the wife who appeared to be innocent and blind to her husband's faults. The man walked outside to have a cigarette. Carl's smile widened. He could take care of this one himself. No need to get Lucy to do it. He might actually enjoy the task.

~

Detective Harper Scranton plopped into her office chair and stared at the case board that still hadn't been cleared. Why should she take it all down? Just because they hadn't heard from the Seven Deadly Sins Killer in over a week didn't mean it was all over. The man the chief shot at the lake wasn't the man they sought, was he?

When he'd taken the drugstore hostage, he'd clearly been following orders from someone else. So, why hadn't he made contact again? Out of the country?

"I can see the steam coming out your ears." Liam handed her a cup of coffee.

"Why be gung-ho about ridding the world of pride, then go silent? Thanks." She took a sip of the coffee. She hissed as it burned her tongue.

"Maybe he's trying to decide on which sin to work on next." He sat at his desk. "If he doesn't act soon, I'll be called back to Little Rock, then possibly somewhere else."

Her heart stuttered. She'd gotten used to working with him each day at their small precinct. Thinking of him leaving left her feeling empty. She returned her attention to the case board, so he wouldn't see how the thought of him leaving left her.

"We've got a hit and run outside a restaurant in Harrington." Liam leaped up from his desk. "Want to go take a look before we call it a day?"

"How does that affect us here in Oakdale?"

"The victim is holding your business card, so we've been asked by HPD to come take a look."

She'd handed out quite a lot of business cards since making detective, but since they didn't have much else going on, she nodded. "Always willing to lend a helping hand." Staying busy would keep her from dwelling on Liam's comment about being called back to his FBI office.

Tossing him the keys to her jeep, she grabbed her jacket and service weapon before following him outside. Night had fallen, cooling the late summer air. Stars winked in a clear sky. Sitting out on her patio, a glass of wine in one hand and Liam sitting next to her with a beer sounded like the perfect way to end out the day.

Where had that vision come from? The man stayed at the local motel, not in her guest room. What had happened to focusing on her career with no plans on getting involved with anyone?

She yanked open the passenger side door and slid into her seat. "Do you know the way?"

"GPS." He slipped his phone into a holder on the dash. "Twenty minutes, fifteen if we speed."

She laughed and put the revolving light on the roof of her jeep. "Have at it."

He pulled into the parking lot of the restaurant in fourteen minutes. Once, he'd complain about Harper's need for speed, now he seemed to enjoy it as much as she did.

Side-by-side, they approached where a man in a nice suit lay crumbled against a Jaguar. His open hand held Harper's business card. A brunette sniffed and dabbed her eyes from near the building's door, while a blond sobbed on the chest of a dark-haired man.

"Did anyone see anything?" Harper asked the police officer standing next to the body.

"Nobody saw anything. Two couples out to dinner. One stepped outside to smoke. When he'd been gone too long, his buddy went to check on him and found him here. Best I can tell, a car rammed him against the Jaguar, then sped away. Man's name is David Alexander. The brunette is his wife."

"Hmm." Harper studied the ground. No sign of skid marks.

No sign that someone had tried to stop before running the man down.

She eyed the large glass windows along the front of the building. A popular restaurant and no one saw anything? She knelt next to the body. The corner of a pamphlet stuck out from under him. She pulled a rubber glove from the pocket of her jacket and pulled it over her hand before slipping the pamphlet free.

She stared at the word Cancer written in bold red letters on a black background. The subtitle read, *You've got it, now what? What's the next step?*

Straightening, she handed it to Liam. "Might be related, might not. Doesn't look as if it's been out here long. It rained earlier today which would have ruined the pamphlet."

Liam slid it into a paper sack and handed it to the other officer. "I'm not noticing a different color of paint on the Jaguar's dent. Whatever hit him had to be the same color. Want to speak to the wife, or shall I?"

"We'll both go." Although, she doubted they'd get anything from them.

They approached the three standing next to the restaurant. "Mrs. Alexander?" Harper stopped in front of the brunette. "Mind if we ask you a few questions?"

"I've already told the officer we didn't see anything." Her voice broke. "We were celebrating tonight."

"What's the occasion?"

"We sold off a significant property for a large sum of money." The other man gave a heavy exhale. "I'm Stan Reynolds, David's partner."

"Any hard feelings about the sale?" People had killed for less than business.

"No. We hadn't made a formal announcement yet."

The blond woman's wails increased. A bit overkill for someone not the man's wife in Harper's opinion. The wife barely sniffled in comparison.

Harper motioned her head for Liam to follow her. "Nothing more we can do here. This isn't our crime."

He slid into the driver's seat. "Get the feeling blondie and the victim might have been close? The wife could've figured it out and hired someone to off her husband."

"That's quite the stretch." Harper tilted her head. "But it's up to HPD to figure this one out."

"I'm beat. I'm sure we'll have our own dealings soon enough. Why your business card, though, and what's up with the pamphlet on cancer?" He turned the jeep toward Oakdale.

"That's the question, isn't it?" She stared out the passenger window. Her gut told her they'd be getting involved in solving the man's death. Her head told her it didn't make sense to get involved without more reasons. But" she'd learned a long time ago to trust her instincts. Now, they waited for the reason.

Liam stopped in front of his hotel. "Good night."

"Good night." She got into the driver's seat. "See you tomorrow." She watched him enter the room on the second floor before driving home.

Guilt ate at her that she actually hoped for the Seven Deadly Sins Killer to pop up again so Liam wouldn't leave. She hadn't realized how lonely she'd gotten until working with him every day for the last few weeks.

She pulled her vehicle into the garage, cut the engine, and entered her house. She punched in the security code before the alarm could sound and set her keys and weapon on the kitchen island.

As was her usual routine, she went through the house checking doors and windows. Confident her home was secure, she kicked off her shoes, discarded her jacket, and then poured herself a glass of wine before padding to her bedroom to get into something more comfortable.

A few minutes later, dressed in baggy cotton pants and an oversized tee-shirt, she curled up on the sofa and turned on the television. She groaned as her phone buzzed. A glance at the screen chilled her blood.

Covetousness teaches people to be cruel and crafty, industrious and evil, full of care and malice; and after all this, it is for no good to itself, for it dares not spend those heaps of treasure which it has snatched.

Then another. *No matter what the statistics say, there is always a way.*

Statistics about what? She dialed Liam's number. "Did you get them?"

"Just now. Looks like we know what the next sin is."

She closed her eyes and leaned her head against the back of the sofa. The feeling of guilt increased. She'd gotten her wish. Liam wouldn't be leaving any time soon.

The killer had returned.

Chapter Two

Carl woke and stared into the dead eyes of Lucy. The woman really was a phantom. "What?" He sat up and rubbed his eyes.

"You're doing your own killing now?" She crossed her arms.

"What are you talking about?" He hung his legs over the side of the bed.

"David Alexander. The man you hit with the car."

"Ah. Was that his name? Opportunity knocked, my dear." He padded naked to the bathroom and turned on the shower. "Never fear. You'll have plenty of killing opportunities."

"You took money out of my pocket."

He peered around the door. "Are you in need of funds?"

"No."

"Then what is the problem?" He shook his head, adjusted the water temperature, and got into the shower. He'd never understand women.

It had been a while since he'd had one in his bed. With Lucy hovering all the time, the opportunity rarely presented itself. He needed to set some boundaries. No more of this sneaking around. How did she manage to get into his house? He had the best security. He thought.

"What's next?" Lucy stood right outside the bathroom door. "I don't do well with inactivity."

He scowled, wrapping a towel around his waist. "I'm headed to work. At this point, I don't have a plan other than I'm focusing on the sin of covetousness."

"Everyone wants something they don't have." She plopped into a chair.

"Even you?" He arched a brow.

"Of course. Right now, I'm envious of the fact you rid the world of Alexander."

He rolled his eyes and stepped into his walk-in closet. The woman really had no idea how his vision for a better world worked.

He glanced her way, noting the serious expression and shark eyes. He shuddered, doubting he was man enough to teach her anything.

"You need to wreck your car to hide the damage caused by running over Alexander." Lucy stared at her phone screen. "If you take it to a mechanic as is, you run the chance of being discovered."

The woman was brilliant.

When he arrived at work, he made a turn too sharp and clipped a concrete barrier. Then, he stormed into work pretending to be angry over his mistake.

~

Harper tapped a pencil on her desk. Why the cancer pamphlet?

Her gaze fell on the large envelope delivered that morning. Medical records. Her father hadn't asked why she needed them, only sent them as quick as he could. A similar envelope waited on Liam's desk.

"Since we dealing with covetousness…" He handed her the morning's coffee. "I think it's safe to assume that Mr. Alexander was killed because he had his eye on his partner's wife. You know, thou shall not covet thy neighbor's wife?"

"One of the commandments." She reached for the envelope. "I'm going to spend the morning going over these medical records."

"HPD is requesting our help with Alexander since we received those text messages."

She nodded. "Alright. We'll head out in a bit if that's okay."

"Let's take these to the conference room. We can spread out and see whether the same names show up."

She gathered the pages and her coffee and followed him to the larger room. She gave a head nod to the chief as they passed his office. He spoke on the phone, reciprocated with a nod, and kept talking.

He hadn't been happy to hear they were back dealing with the Seven Deadly Sins Killer. At least this time, the chief wasn't on vacation.

In the conference room, she flipped through the stack of pages and called out names for Liam to compare to his list. It was tedious, mind-numbing work. After two hours, they had three names of people who had used Liam's grandfather as their primary physician, and Harper's as their oncologist.

"I'll give these to Officer Crypton to see what she can find out about these people."

"Sounds good. That leaves us free to head to Harrington and dig into Alexander's life and work. Maybe question his wife some more. Try and find out why he was targeted."

"Because he was in the wrong place at the wrong time with someone playing God." She shoved the papers back into the envelope and stood. What could possibly be the motive if one of the three men's names she was giving to Annie turned out to be their guy?

She located Annie in the breakroom. "Call me as soon as you turn up anything."

"Will do." Annie added sugar to the coffee in front of her. "I want this over."

"We're only on the second sin." Harper patted her on the shoulder. "Good luck."

"Thanks for being so upbeat." The officer gave her a shaky smile. "Maybe we'll catch this guy before he goes through too many more of these sins."

"We can always hope." Harper joined Liam in their office and grabbed what she needed for the day.

"Hear me out." Liam glanced over the top of the jeep. "What if this is about revenge?"

"For what?" She frowned.

"What if…one of those three men didn't make it? What if our grandfather's failed them?"

She gave a sarcastic laugh. "That's a stretch, Liam."

"But what if? I've been doing this for seven years. My gut tells me I'm on to something. It could be why the two of us were thrust together."

She got into the vehicle. She'd heard crazier things in her life. A lot of people killed in the name of revenge. "Why the games? Why not come after us?"

"A deranged mind doesn't always make sense."

Less than half an hour later, they pulled up in front of a sprawling modern mansion of concrete, steel, and glass. Harper figured the buying and selling of businesses paid very well. "I think I'm in the wrong line of work."

Liam laughed. "I'd bet my favorite pair of boots that this guy was handed the rich life from his daddy and his daddy before him. This kind of money gets passed down."

Maybe. She shoved her door open and marched for the front porch. She pressed a bell that sent Westminster chimes throughout the house.

After a couple of minutes, Mrs. Alexander, dressed in flowing pants and blouse, answered the door. A well made-up face barely disguised the redness of her eyes. "May I help you?"

"We'd like to ask you a few questions if you've the time." Harper gave a slight smile. "It won't take long."

The woman gave a suffering sigh and stepped back to allow them entrance. "We'll have to make it quick. I've funeral arrangements to attend to."

"They've released the body?" Harper arched a brow.

"Not yet, but they will eventually. I don't like waiting until the last minute." She led them to a living room of white leather furniture, fuzzy throw pillows, and accents in red and yellow. She perched on the edge of the sofa. "What do you want to know?"

~

Liam sat across from her, leaving Harper to study the room. "We believe your husband may be a victim of the Seven Deadly Sins Killer." He fought back a wince at using the title.

"Why him?" She pulled a tissue from a nearby box. Her gaze flicked to where Harper studied photos on the mantel over the fireplace.

"Is it possible your husband wanted something he didn't have? His partner's wife, perhaps?" He kept his features stoic as she flinched.

"Don't be ridiculous. We're all friends. We have been for years."

"You take vacations together?" Harper held up a photo of the four of them on a tropical beach. "Your husband and Mrs. Reynolds seem cozy here. He's holding her closer to him than he is you." She set the photo back. "Sometimes, the wife is the last to know."

"You think the killer ran over him because he looked too long at Sylvia?" She shook her head. "I refuse to believe it. I'm sure when you speak to her, you'll realize I'm right."

"I hope so, ma'am." Liam stood. "If you should think of anything that would help us catch your husband's killer, please let us know."

"Perhaps, I'll take a vacation and visit my parents in Europe until they release David's body."

"I wouldn't advise you leaving town, ma'am." Liam gave her a stern look, then followed Harper from the house.

Outside, Harper faced him. "If he wasn't having an affair with Mrs. Reynolds, then he sure wanted to. Mrs. Alexander may not want to believe her husband's infatuation, but photos don't lie. In everyone with the four of them, David Alexander looks as if he wants to gobble up his partner's wife."

"All this line of questioning is doing is confirming that Alexander is the first victim of the second sin. We need to find out who the next victim will be and try to prevent their death." A near impossible task.

Back in the jeep, he sat without starting the engine. "I have no idea where to go from here. So what if Alexander wanted Sylvia Reynolds? That doesn't get us any closer to who killed him. Confirmation is not a clue."

His fingers curled. He fought off the urge to punch the steering wheel. Losing his temper wouldn't solve anything.

"Let's go to the station. See what HPD knows." She put a hand on his arm. "We'll catch this guy. It'll take time, that's all."

And deaths. Possibly many of them. He started the jeep and drove to the station where the same officer from the accident site led them to a case board.

"As you can see, we don't know anything other than the texts the two of you received and that we have a dead guy." Officer Perez crossed his arms. "But we don't have another body, so that's good."

Yet. They had nothing to do but wait. "Tell me the local gossip. Who's cheating with whom? Who's fighting over property, anything that could be construed as coveting."

"How much time to you have?" Perez shook his head. "We're dealing with the human race here. Sin is rampant, but I'll get someone on that and try to have some idea by the end of the day."

"Thanks. We can at least warn some people."

"My chief has been talking to the detective's chiefs. They're both going to hold a press conference this afternoon warning the public. If the danger escalates, they'll enforce a curfew." He shrugged. "People will balk, but it might save some lives."

Liam regretted that things had come to enforcing curfew. He sighed and followed Harper back to the jeep. "Hungry?"

"I could eat." She sounded as down as he felt. "Do you really think you can figure out the next victim off rumors?"

"If they're in the public eye, maybe. We don't have anything else to go on. Where's the best place to grab a quick bite?"

She gave directions to a fast-food chicken place as her phone buzzed. Liam waited, expecting to receive a text. When he didn't, he realized it wasn't from the killer.

"Annie has addresses to the three men on the list. I'm going to have her check those who died next. Our man has something to do with one of those lists."

"Finally, something that might pan out." He considered himself a good judge of character and reading of body language. If one of those men had something against him, Harper or both, he'd sense it.

Chapter Three

Harper bit into her chicken sandwich and caught the amused glance of a dowdy woman a couple of tables over. She smiled around her bite and averted her gaze. Maybe she'd committed some kind of bad table manner rule.

"The first address isn't too far, but one is over an hour away." She took a big drink of her soda. "It'll be a long day if we question all three today."

"I say we do. Something else might come up tomorrow." Liam dipped a fry into ketchup. "There will come a time when the perp has us running at full speed instead of toying with us."

True. She caught the other woman's gaze again. "That woman keeps staring at me."

"She probably recognizes you from the news." He wadded up his garbage. "Ready?"

With another glance at the woman she now considered rude, she nodded and got to her feet. She tossed their garbage in a nearby trash can. By now, the woman had a full grin on her round face.

Harper frowned. Was she supposed to know her from somewhere?

"Come on." Liam put a hand at her waist and steered her to the jeep.

The back of her neck prickled as she got in. When she glanced back again, the woman was gone. She shook off the notion she should know who she was and put her mind back on the task in front of them.

"First name on the list is Larry Moore. Prostate cancer thirty years ago. Resides in an assisted living home now." Hopefully, he was of sound enough mind to answer their questions.

When they reached the facility, a receptionist guided them to the dining room. "He never misses a meal. You'll find him over there at the table in the corner. He's the one wearing the tie."

Harper arched a brow at the sight of the old man in a button up shirt, tie, and coordinating sweater. "Mr. Moore, I'm Detective Scranton. This is Special Agent Liam McConnell. May we ask you a few questions?"

He wiped his mouth with a napkin. "Please. Sit."

"We can wait until you've finished with your meal."

"No, I'm done." He smiled. "I'm always willing to help the authorities. Used to be a cop myself back in the day."

They sat. Harper folded her hands on top of the table. "We're questioning patients of two doctors. Doctor McConnell and Doctor Scranton. Do you remember them?"

"Same name as you two. Sure, I remember. It isn't every day a man gets diagnosed with cancer. Those two saved my life."

This man had no reason to hate the former doctors. "Do you know of anyone who had been dissatisfied with their services?"

"I doubt those who died were very happy." He laughed at his joke. "What's this about?"

Liam leaned forward. "Have you heard of the killings in Oakdale?"

"Of course. Got yourselves a serial killer, kind of."

"What do you mean?" Liam's brow furrowed.

"Seems like hired killings to me. At least that's what my cop instinct says."

Harper raised her brows. The man was good. "You are correct, sir." She grinned. "But, that is not common knowledge."

"I won't say anything." He pretended to lock his lips. "What's this got to do with my doctors?"

"It's a long shot, but we think the man responsible for the killings has a grievance against my grandfather and the agent's father. That's why he's brought us together." Harper straightened in her seat expecting Mr. Moore to tell her she chased the wrong thread.

Instead, he folded his arms and studied her face. "Someone who lost someone important to them to cancer and wants the two of you to pay for his loss. Seems to me you should be looking through the files of those who died."

Harper smiled. "That's why we're asking the questions. We have someone working on that list." In fact, she'd be willing to bet her grandfather hadn't forgotten the names of a single patient he lost. She'd ask her dad if he'd left anything behind with that information. "Anyone come to mind?"

"There were a few that passed away while I underwent treatment." He waved over an orderly. "Could you bring me a pen and paper, please?"

"Right away." She patted his shoulder and hurried away. She returned a few seconds later with a small spiral notebook and a pen.

"Alrighty then." Mr. Moore's mouth twisted. "Let's get this old brain to work." He wrote, then tore out the sheet. "Five names during the time I was there. Hope the one you're looking for is on there. Otherwise, I'm of no help."

"You've been a huge help." She noticed the orderly bringing a wheelchair. "Are you doing alright, sir?"

"Ah." He waved a hand in dismissal as the orderly helped him into the chair. "Cancer's returned and settled in my back. My time is almost finished on this earth. Hope you catch this guy while I'm still alive to watch the drama unfold."

She cleared her throat. "I'll personally make sure you're kept up to date, Mr. Moore." She stood and thrust out her hand. "Again, we thank you."

As she left the building with Liam, she couldn't help but wish the old man would beat the cancer again. She glanced back toward the building before getting in the jeep.

Her eyes narrowed at the sight of a woman in nursing scrubs standing next to a dark sedan. The woman turned. It was the same woman who had stared at Harper at the chicken place.

"Liam." She darted after the woman who whirled and disappeared around the building.

~

"Harper, wait. Ugh." Liam slammed the jeep door and pulled his weapon as he took off after the women. Didn't she know better than to take off after someone alone? Obviously not.

He lost sight of them and stopped around the corner. A startled nurse stared at him through a locked glass door, then pointed across the garden.

He gave chase in that direction. Crashing through the brush, then the blaring of a car horn, alerted him he ran in the right direction. He burst through some foliage and skidded to a halt on the edge of the highway. Across the traffic, Harper still chased the woman in scrubs. They disappeared into the trees.

If he got hit by a semi, he'd throttle Harper. Liam dashed across, dodging cars and waving apologies as drivers laid on their horns.

He found Harper standing on the edge of a ditch. "Are you crazy?"

"It's obvious that woman is following us. I lost her. She jumped where I wasn't willing to go. I'm surprised she didn't break an ankle."

Liam glanced at the rocky bottom of the ditch. A good six-foot jump. "Don't run off like that again. You could've been killed."

She shot him a look he couldn't decipher and made her way back across the highway, him on her heels. On the other side, she faced him. "Why do you think she's following us? Crazed fan of this game we're involved in or the assassin?"

"She doesn't look like the other assassin, but let's not rule her out. Either way, we'll see her again." He hoped it wasn't by staring down the barrel of her gun or up in the woman's face after being shot.

"Sorry, I lost her. She could've led us to the killer." Harper continued to the jeep.

"Or swallowed a poison pill like the last one." He slid into the driver's seat. "Where to next?"

"I doubt we'll get as much information as we received from Mr. Moore, but let's take the one that's an hour away and work our way back." She punched the address into his GPS.

With a glance in his rearview mirror, Liam drove away from the assisted living facility and toward their next destination. A few miles down the road, he spotted a dark sedan he thought followed them until it got off at the next exit. A few miles further on, he spotted it again, staying two cars back.

"I think our friend is back."

Harper turned in her seat. "What's she up to?"

"I'm sure we'll find out when she's ready. What I don't like is if she is the assassin and is following us, she'll always be two steps ahead." He increased their speed, then whipped down an exit ramp. The sedan continued past.

He got back on the Interstate at the next exit. Soon after, the dark sedan pulled in behind them. "She isn't even trying to hide now." He wasn't sure he wanted to lead her to the man they were going to speak to. When he expressed his concern, Harper agreed.

"Head back to the station. She's put an effective halt to our day."

When they returned to the station, the woman drove past giving a couple of toots on her horn.

Annie met them at the door. "Here are the names of those who died under the care of Doctor Scranton."

Liam glanced at the list. "Only ten? That's impressive."

"My grandfather was good at what he did." Harper took the sheet. "Get a copy of the CTV camera of this facility. You'll see a woman in dark blue scrubs. Run her through facial recognition, please."

"Will do." Annie headed out the door.

"Where have the two of you been?" The chief exited his office. "From now on, you tell me where you're going."

"Did something happen?" Harper widened her eyes.

"No, but it could have."

Liam didn't think it the time to let the chief know they'd been followed. "We're pretty well able to confirm that the killer has a grudge against my father and Harper's grandfather because he lost someone to cancer. Someone they were caring for. We're going to work down the list of those who died in hopes of finding the killer's identity."

"Good work. The public is clamoring for an end to all this. I'm going to do a press conference this evening to try and soothe some ruffled feathers. Get me something to tell the reporters." He closed his office door.

"He's not asking for anything easy." Harper sighed and headed for the office they shared.

~

Carl entered his home after work to see Lucy staring at her phone and laughing. "What's so funny?"

She set the phone down. "Since you haven't given me a job

recently, I created my own fun. I followed the detective and the agent around, put a tracker on the detective's jeep, and made a nuisance of myself."

"Good. Make their job harder. I did come up with a plan at work today." He shed his suit jacket and hung it in the closet. "I could use one of my faithful followers, I do have a meeting tonight and could speak with them, but since you aren't enlightened, you're expendable if something should go wrong."

"Gee thanks. You sure know how to sweet talk a girl."

Ignoring her sarcasm, he continued. "I like leaving clues for the detective and agent to follow. This time, I want to leave a trail they must follow in time to save someone. Of course, they won't be able to save them, because I've already chosen to rid the world of this person."

"I'm listening."

"I hope so because I don't want this messed up. It will have to be timed just right. You'll leave a trail of breadcrumbs and kill the target right before the detective and agent get there. It has to be planned perfectly."

"The tracker I planted will help with that. What are the clues? I can also track their phones."

"I'll have them for you by morning." He grabbed a long-sleeved black shirt from the closet and replaced the white one he wore. "You can work on them, too, while I'm at my meeting, unless you want to come along."

"No, thanks." She gave an exaggerated shudder. "Finding myself surrounded by a bunch of freaks doesn't sound like a fun evening."

He gritted his teeth so hard his jaw ached. Someday, he'd put Lucy in her place. He couldn't wait for that day.

"But, before the game begins again, I do have someone I want you to kill." The other surgeon in the building had snapped after finding out that Carl had taken a few of the woman's clients as his own.

She'd always wanted what he had, ever since they rented space in the same building.

Chapter Four

Harper woke the next morning to her cell phone buzzing around her nightstand. She grabbed it and glanced at the screen. A body had been found in the city park. Another text told her Liam was waiting and where was she?

Eight a.m.? She jumped out of bed, tangling her legs in the blankets and tumbling to the floor. She landed on her elbow and knocked the breath out of her. Now, she lay gasping like a stranded fish. How could she have overslept?

Untangling herself, she dashed to the closet and quickly dressed. She splashed water on her face, tied back her hair in a ponytail and sprinted out the door to her jeep. Five minutes later, she pulled up in front of Liam's hotel.

He shook his head as he strolled toward her. "I never thought I'd see the day you overslept."

"Me either." She laughed. "I really needed the sleep, though. What do we have?"

"Body of a woman in a very unflattering pose on a park bench."

She frowned. "Our killer?"

He shrugged. "The former assassin liked to pose the victims in humble poses. Maybe this one is doing something similar. If, it's our killer. We don't know that yet."

True. By the time they arrived, the area had been taped off, news vans and reporters crowded the area, and onlookers crowded as close as they could get without crossing the line. Harper skirted the area and ignored the microphones and questions thrust at her."

"Is it the Seven Deadly Sins Killer?"

"Is the chief going to enforce a curfew?"

"Wait. Just one question."

She held up a hand to get the reporters to step back, then followed Liam across the park.

"Fifty-year-old, white female." Annie approached them. "Susan Davis. Plastic surgeon."

She sighed glancing at the nude woman posed in a lewd position. Her only adornment was the stethoscope around her neck. From the marks on her skin, it was also the murder weapon.

"Look." She bent and studied the scars left behind from breast surgery. From the perfect nose, Harper would bet the woman had other work done on her face and body. The fifty-year-old looked like a thirty-year-old. "Disgruntled patient, maybe, but I'm going with our guy."

Heat rose to her cheeks. Enough was enough. She marched to the closest reporter. "I have a statement."

The others crowded around.

"I'm Detective Scranton of OPD and I have a message for the Seven Deadly Sins Killer." She squared her shoulders and cut Liam a quick glance. The man stood with a grave face. Maybe what she was doing would accomplish something good or something bad, but Harper was tired of the death and games. She didn't care what the woman on that bench had done. The way she'd been posed was purely to humiliate.

"We are going to hunt you down and make sure you never play a game again. You can count on this. Soon, I will stand face-to-face with you and come out the victor. Let's make that real soon."

The chief scowled at her from the sidelines. The lecture she'd get would be worth blowing off steam. She marched back to the crime scene.

"What was that about, Scranton?" Chief Donnelly blocked her path. "Your act could have driven the perp underground."

"I believe the contrary, sir. I've challenged him. He'll rise to the challenge, and we'll arrest him." Or shoot him, whichever opportunity presented itself.

His dark eyes bored into her. "This could get you killed."

"That is always a possibility. Excuse me, sir." She whirled and joined Liam. "I guess you'll lecture me, too?"

"No. You surprised me, is all." He snapped photos of the

body and surrounding area. "I realize you acted on impulse."

"Do you think it will work?" She put her hands on her hips.

He lowered his phone. "I'm sure it will increase his game."

"More people will die."

"That would happen whether you taunted him or not."

"But you don't approve."

"No, I don't. I'm not saying taunting him was wrong. What is wrong is that you acted without thinking first." He returned to the scene. "That is how mistakes are made. Sometimes deadly ones."

He was right. She'd let her temper get the better of her.

~

Ah, the detective issued him a challenge. Carl rubbed his hands together and turned off the television in his office. He'd gladly accept her challenge. Things had just gotten a lot more fun.

He glanced at the list of clues he'd come up with for Lucy. A childish scavenger hunt that would get the detective closer to her desire of meeting him face-to-face.

This latest game would cost him a fortune. Lucy charged a set fee for murder, but for running around keeping tabs on Oakdale's finest required an hourly rate. He could've gotten one of his followers to do the deed, but they didn't seem to live long when he got them involved. If they kept having to kill themselves, he'd have no one left to rule with once he'd accomplished his mission.

He left the office, locking the door behind him to consult with a prospective new client and do some Botox injections. When he returned, he stood at his office window. Three stories down, Agent McConnell and Detective Scranton marched toward the front door.

Time to play the shocked and grieving colleague. It would be very difficult not to let the pretty detective know she'd already gotten her wish. She didn't know how soon it had happened.

~

Liam and Harper followed a woman with bleached hair and a too-tight dress to the elevators. "You'll find Doctor Landry in suite 301. Please check out at the desk when you're finished." She sashayed away.

"I'm surprised the poor thing can breathe in that dress,"

Harper said.

"Hmmhmm." Liam tore his eyes away from her swaying bottom.

"Oh, please." Harper slapped his arm and pressed the button for the elevator. "If that's what you like."

"What do you mean?" The type of woman?

"That. All fake and made up. I can't tell how old she is. She could be twenty or she could be sixty."

He seriously doubted she was sixty. "She works in a plastic surgery office. She's bound to get some perks from her job." The elevator doors opened, and they got in.

"So, is that kind of woman attractive to you?"

"Not really, but I'm not adverse to looking." He grinned. "I prefer women to look more natural." Like her. Beautiful without trying. Brave and impetuous. Yeah, he wasn't looking forward to the day he had to return to Little Rock.

The suite they sought was to their right when they stepped off the elevator. Liam reached around Harper to open the door and got a faint whiff of her shampoo as the door blew her hair in his face. Something soft and sweet with a scent of coconut.

Another made up woman greeted them. She smiled as they presented their credentials. "I'll let Doctor Landry know you're here. I do believe he's had his last appointment for the day." She spoke into an intercom. "Go on back. Last door on the left."

A knock on that door got them an invite in.

Doctor Landry's office of cherry wood bookcases and desk, a black leather sofa, and large window let Liam know the man did very well for himself. He introduced him and Harper, then sat in the offered seats across from the doctor as the man covered up the papers in front of him with a binder. An overhead light shined off his shiny bald head.

Landry arched a brow. "I'm wondering why you're here, Agent McConnell."

"It's about Susan Davis."

"What about her?"

"She's been murdered, Doctor." Liam watched for signs of grief, but the man's face remained impassive. Maybe he had too much Botox to show emotion. "Were you close?"

"That's awful. We weren't any closer than two doctors

sharing the same building. We had a friendly rivalry going on about getting and/or taking away each other's clients. I can't believe someone would want to kill a respected doctor such as Susan."

"When was the last time you saw her?"

The man tapped his right forefinger against his lips. "I'd have to say around two o'clock yesterday. She didn't come to work today. Oh, I guess she couldn't. What a horrible thing for me to say."

The man's words spoke of caring, but Liam got the feeling he wouldn't miss the other doctor much. No more competing for clients.

"You can't think of any clients unhappy with her work?"

"No, as I said, she was very respected professionally."

"Outside of work? A disgruntled boyfriend or ex-husband?"

"Not that I know of. Her secretary might know more." He tilted his head. "I'm very sorry I can't help more, but Susan and I weren't friends outside of work and rarely spoke of anything personal."

Liam stood. "Thank you for your time. Please call if you think of anything that might help us find out who killed Ms. Davis." He dropped a business card on the desk.

Since Ms. Davis's receptionist had the day off, they headed for the jeep. Back inside, he frowned. "The good doctor showed very little emotion to the news."

"He's got alibis according to his receptionist. He was already in the office when she arrived, and the chief texted that Susan Davis had been killed around six a.m. this morning. She hadn't been dead long when we arrived, and the receptionist was in the office by six-thirty. For Landry to have done this he'd have to be a magician. What would be the motive for Landry? He doesn't seem to be hurting for business."

"No, he doesn't. I'm grasping at straws. Where to now?"

"Ms. Davis's receptionist, a Mary Excell lives half a mile from here. She might know something."

Probably not, but they still needed to talk to her. He followed the directions on her GPS and pulled up to four-unit apartment complex.

The woman who opened the door had pufferfish lips and a

perpetually surprised look on the rest of her face. He pasted on a smile and introduced them.

"She's dead?" The woman's fingers fluttered around the neckline of her blouse. "Murdered?"

Liam nodded. "Any idea who might want her dead?"

"No one other than Doctor Landry. I overheard them arguing about clients yesterday. Ms. Davis was very well-liked otherwise."

Unfortunately, Landry had an alibi. "Thank you for your time." He exhaled heavily in the car. "We don't have any more answers for this murder than we do for the Seven Deadly Sins Killer."

"Would save time if they were connected. We're already stretched thin."

Liam glanced up to see Landry watching them from his office window. "Is there a Landry on the list of family members who died while under your grandfather's care?"

She scrolled through her phone. "No." She followed his gaze. "What are you thinking?"

"Nothing." He looked for a suspect where there wasn't one. He drove to Mary Excell's house.

Harper knocked on the door of the house belonging to Mary Excell. The door swung open. She put her hand on the weapon at her hip. "Anyone home? Ms. Excell?"

Liam held out his arm. "Let me go first."

Scowling, she stepped back. "We're equal, Liam."

"Yes, but I'm still going first." He entered the house and let his eyes adjust to the gloom. "Ms. Excell?" The hair on his arms rose. Something wasn't right.

Chapter Five

Harper followed Liam inside. The house was eerily quiet as if death resided inside.

"I'll take the back of the house." With slow steps, she made her way down a short hallway.

Rather than search the front of the house, Liam followed close behind and ducked into the bathroom. "Clear."

Her hand shook as she reached for the doorknob of what she guessed would be a bedroom. The door squeaked as she pushed it open. Her heart dropped.

Sitting in a posture of prayer next to the bed was a woman, naked except for the doily on top of her head. Her folded hands rested on a sheet of paper.

"Liam." Harper moved toward the bed. She peered over the woman's shoulder. "It's instructions for what seems like a scavenger hunt."

"Follow the clues. Take no one other than the agent and the detective. If you follow the clues successfully, you'll find another clue. Fail and another dies. Time is ticking. You have twenty-four hours. Your clue is here."

Harper frowned. "I don't see it."

"The body. We need to go to a church."

"But which one?" She stared at the body. "One where they wear head coverings? There's only one that I know of. The catholic church in Oakdale. Some of the women there cover their heads during mass. What did Mary Excell covet? Do you think it relevant?"

Liam moved to the room next door. "Home office."

She joined him and flipped through the woman's calendar.

"She was scheduled to have her nose fixed. Coveting beauty?"

"Right along with the others who worked with her." He thumbed through a stack of mail. "A few bills, mostly junk. Let's go. We'll let the chief know what's going on. I think the twenty-four hours is for the whole game, not just the next clue."

She agreed, wondering whether the killer had already taken his next victim. Whose fate rested in her and Liam's hands? How did the killer pick his victims? Her shoulders slumped as she followed Liam from the house.

In the jeep, she called the chief and filled him in on the latest. She held the phone away from her ear as he shouted curses. When he slowed, she said, "We couldn't stay at the crime scene. Not if we're going to find whoever it is he's going to kill in twenty-four hours."

"I understand that. I'm not blaming you. We'll take care of it. Don't get yourself killed." He hung up.

She stuck the revolving light on the roof as Liam peeled away from the curb. If the killer took them from town to town, it would be difficult to solve all the clues. He wasn't going to make it easy. He wanted them to fail.

At the church, they stepped into an empty sanctuary. Harper approached the podium while Liam searched the pews. A sheet of paper lay on top of a bible. *Sins require confession.*

She eyed the confessional. With heavy steps she went inside and closed the door. She could just make out a shadowy figure on the other side. "I'm Detective Scranton."

"I'm to give you a message." The priest's voice trembled. "But first we have to play a game. If I don't win two out of three, then the knife close to my head will stab me."

Her mouth filled with cotton. "What kind of game?"

"Rock, paper, scissors."

Oh, God. This was a game she wanted to lose. "If I lose?"

"I'm alive to give you the next clue."

"On three. One, two, three." She waited a split second before choosing scissors to what she thought looked like his rock through the screen. "I have scissors."

"I have rock." His voice shook harder. "I won that one."

"Harper?"

"I'll be out in a minute, Liam. It's part of the game. One, two, three." She did scissors again, thinking she'd tie with the priest. Unfortunately, he did paper. She blinked eyes growing weary from straining to see through the screen. She had one more shot. She did scissors a third time praying the priest had got onto her plan. He had. Harper wanted to shout when he did a rock.

"The clue is…" He cleared his throat. "I'm full of stories, some true, some not."

The library. Harper smiled. "We'll get you out of there, Father." She opened the door to the confessional, then removed the stick holding the priest's door closed. "Are you okay?"

The priest nodded.

"Can you tell us what happened?" She helped him to a pew. "But quickly, please. We don't have much time."

"A woman came into the confessional. She told me to cooperate,' or she'd set the confessional on fire with me inside. So, I sat while she rigged the booby trap of the knife, then told me to give the detective a message. I'm sorry, but I didn't get a look at her. She did seem to be having a very good time if her laughter was an indication. I'm grateful to be alive."

Lucky to have survived a close encounter with the killer's assassin. Harper thanked him again and raced back to the jeep, praying the library was the one in the same city they were in. So far, the killer kept his clues in Oakdale. But, for how long?

~

Liam held the door to the library open for Harper, then approached the front desk. "Do you have a message for either Agent McConnell or Detective Scranton?"

"No."

"Maybe an email?"

"Okay." Her brow furrowed. "Oh. Yes, here's one."

Liam moved to her side of the desk as she opened the email. Her screen went black, then what looked like viruses bounced around the screen.

"That email had a virus attached to it." She immediately shut down her computer.

Liam glanced up and met Harper's gaze. "The hospital?"

"Or the clinic. It's closer. We'll check there first."

He noted the time on the clock on the wall. "Almost two hours gone."

"Did the Seven Deadly Sins Killer do this?" The librarian's eyes widened, her penciled on brows disappearing under thick bangs.

"We're not at liberty to say, ma'am." He took Harper by the arm and rushed from the building. "If it's not the clinic, how far is the hospital?"

"It's in Harrington."

He exhaled slowly. "Let's hope it's the clinic."

It wasn't. After questioning the nurses, doctors, and patients for almost an hour, they sped to the Harrington hospital where they met the same fate.

"Where then?" Liam growled, rubbing his hands roughly over his face.

"Text." Harper held up her phone and read, "'Use your GPS to travel 1.3 miles from your starting place and check-in at the city's most famous landmark.' Liam, he's tracking us. How else would he know to text us from this location?"

"Which direction?"

Harper pulled up her GPS. "The courthouse is west. That's the only building of any significance in that distance."

"Let's go." His stomach growled reminding him how long it had been since he'd eaten. Did they have time? "Any fast-food restaurants between here and there?"

"There's a taco place. That should be fast, but hard to eat while you're driving. How about chicken tenders and fries?"

"Perfect." Luck was on their side. No other cars sat in the drive-thru. Food in hand, Liam continued toward the courthouse.

Before they got out of the car, Harper received another text. "Type in this address. Go there, then take 10 steps in any direction. Look to your left. What do you see?" She shrugged. "I'm guessing the address of the courthouse. We're going to have to split up and each take two directions."

He agreed but didn't like the idea. I'll take east and south." How big of steps? His size or Harper's? He went east. Was the object of interest the mailbox or cement pot full of flowers? Maybe the streetlight? In the other direction, he spotted a print shop. Wouldn't hurt to try.

His phone dinged as he stepped into the street. "You're getting cold." Thanks for the tip. "You should stay with the detective. She's hotter. New game."

Liam jogged to Harper's side and showed her the texts. "Have you seen anything?"

"There's a small park over there. Should we check it out?"

"I think we're going to be led where we're to go." He took several steps that way. Another text. "Getting hotter."

They played the hot and cold game across the playground, down another street, and into a coffee shop where another text told them to sit and have coffee for twenty minutes. They'd become the assassin's puppets and had no choice but to do what she told them. He tried sending a reply text and got an error that that number couldn't receive texts.

"We're several blocks from the jeep." Harper ordered a small coffee with room for cream and sugar. "If we need to drive again, we'll have to make the trip back. She's stalling us."

"At least we aren't finding any more bodies." Yet. He carried his coffee to a table. They still had thirteen minutes. "I guess the coffee is to keep us going during the twenty-four hours. This won't be over until suppertime tomorrow."

She nodded, staring into her cup. "What if we don't find whoever she's taken? Will we even know?" She stood. "I'm taking this to go. Want a lid?"

"Yes." He stared out the shop window. Was she watching them right now or simply tracking their phones? To do that, she'd have to be tech savvy.

"Got another one." Harper set her phone in front of him along with a lid.

Step outside. Turn right. Keep walking until I say stop.

They walked out of the section of busy shops and down a road flanked by industrial buildings most of which sat empty. A few men who looked like gang members stared with hate-filled eyes as they passed.

Enter the building to your left. The one with the faded green door.

Feeling very much as if they were walking into a trap, Liam led the way across the street. The door screeched as he opened it.

Go through the building and into the alley. There you will find a small shed. Go inside.

"I'd be a fool not to be scared spitless right now." Harper

stepped closer to his side.

"I know the feeling. I've never run across anything like this in my career." He hoped he never would again. He'd dealt with sick psychos before, but this one won first place.

Steps faltering, Harper pulled back as they approached the shed. "I don't want to go in there."

"We don't have a choice. Someone will die if we don't play this game to the end." He pushed the door open.

Steps led underground. Nope. Not liking this at all. "Leave the door open."

"No problem there." Harper pulled a small flashlight from her belt and shined it down the stairs. "I sure hope this isn't our grave."

Liam pulled his weapon and started down. The air grew noticeably cooler as they traversed the twenty cement steps. The door at the top of the stairs slammed shut, but not before he heard a woman's laughter.

His phone dinged.

Another game.

Chapter Six

Carl entered his apartment and glared at Lucy who cackled on the sofa, the TV remote in her hand. "What's so funny?"

"Doing the job you hired me to do. Leaving clues and such. I added a new element. Sit and be entertained."

Intrigued, he tossed his car keys in the bowl on a credenza and sat next to Lucy. The dark screen flared to life. The agent and the detective stood in a concrete room. Balloons hung on one wall. Throughout the room were tables with items and furniture with drawers. "What is this?"

"An escape room." Lucy laughed shrilly. "It'll slow them down big time."

"Where did you get the clues?"

"Online."

"Have you chosen the person they are supposed to save?"

"Of course." She sighed. "The girl is tied up, gagged, and waiting in a hotel room. I gave her something to make her sleep. If she does wake within the twenty-four hours, no one will hear her."

"Who is it?"

"A cheerleader who wants to be head cheerleader, but that spot is already taken. She's the daughter of a prominent businessman. She won't be missed until she doesn't show up for cheer practice in less than an hour." She wiggled her eyebrows. "I thought I should continue with your theme of coveting. Now, hush. Watch the show."

One of these days, he would rid his life of this bossy woman.

~

"What is this?" Liam glanced around the room. "A child's party?"

"I don't know." Harper studied items on a table. One table held scissors with a padlock holding the handle together. Another a sheet of paper and watercolor paint. Another had blocks made with Legos. She turned and moved to the wall of balloons. "These have something inside them."

She faced him. "I think this is an escape room."

"I hate those."

"I love them. Let's get busy. I have no idea how long this will take us. Since everything looks childish, it shouldn't stump us too bad." The killer toyed with them, wasting their time. Well, Harper was good at puzzles. "Start popping these balloons."

"Okay." Liam pulled a pocketknife from his pocket and started popping. Pieces of balloons, graffiti, paper, and plastic numbers fell to the floor.

Harper picked up the three numbers and set them on an empty table. "Let's put all the clues we find here. Then we can decipher them."

"Why a kid's escape room?"

"To slow us down." Harper moved to the scissors. "See if you can arrange those three numbers to open this lock." She headed to the piece of paper and watercolor paint. Picking up the paper, she held it to the light. Something faintly glistened.

She dipped the brush into the paint and swiped it across the paper. "Look in the blue drawer." Okay. She opened the blue drawer across the room. Inside was a small, locked metal box. She'd need a key for this one. She set the box on the table Liam worked at. "Any luck?"

"Almost…there." The lock fell off the scissors. "What am I supposed to cut?"

"I don't know yet."

She handed him a bunch of popsicle sticks. "Work on this puzzle. Shouldn't take but a couple of seconds."

Before she'd reached the new clue, Liam told her it said to pull the string by the door. She glanced back to the door they'd entered through. No string. A string hung from the ceiling on the wall opposite the door. Upon closer inspection, she realized a door was inserted there. A door that blended in perfectly. She reached up and pulled the string.

A large cardboard arrow fell and pointed to a small hole in the door. Heart beating so hard she could hear it, Harper peeked through the hole. "Liam, there's a girl in here!"

He joined her and peered through. "A mannequin wearing a cheerleading costume. But there is something pinned to her shirt. I can't read it from here." He straightened. "Want to bet it's the name of the person we're trying to save?"

"You're probably right." She stared at the keyhole in the door. "It looks like a regular key like you'd use in your house."

"Here's a glass jar with a key inside, but it says not to shake it and the lid won't open, but it does have a hole in the lid."

Harper rummaged through a box of odds and ends. She smiled at seeing a magnet. The clues really were juvenile. She tossed the magnet to Liam. It wasn't the key that would open the door, but it might open the blue drawer.

"Here you go." Liam dropped the wet key into her palm. "I'll go try and decipher the Legos."

Harper picked up a very grainy photograph. What in the world was it a picture of? She turned and stared around the room, finally realizing it might be the wood of a small box in the corner of the room. Something she confirmed once she held the photo next to it.

She opened the box.

Something struck her.

She screamed and fell backward as a snake slithered from the box.

Liam darted over and slammed a heavy iron bar on the reptile's head. "Are you bit?"

"No." Her arms and legs trembled as she got to her feet. The snake's mouth opened and closed, revealing the stark white inside. A cottonmouth.

Liam cut off its head with his pocketknife. "That isn't kid's play."

"No, it isn't." She narrowed her eyes at the red light high in the corner of the room. She'd noticed it when she'd landed on her backside. "We're being watched." At least they didn't have the satisfaction of watching her die, at the least get very ill, from a poisonous snake bite. "Let's find our way out of here." And put an end to their fun. She returned to the box and pulled out a cardboard box secured with tape. "Here's what the scissors are for."

~

Liam continued to stare at the Legos. That one has one hump. Is that what they called the parts that weren't flat? Another square had nine. He stepped back and closed his eyes, then opened them and stepped forward. "They're the letters of the alphabet. It spells out something."

"I think it goes with this clue." She handed him a sheet of paper that looked like gibberish. "We have to figure out the code."

"Find something to write with."

Harper returned a few seconds later with the stub of a pencil. A few minutes later, Liam had deciphered the code. "Marble run. We need a marble."

"I've looked in every box in this room. There isn't a marble."

Liam glanced at the snake carcass. At first, he'd thought the lump halfway down its body had been its recent meal, now he wasn't so sure. With a shudder, he pulled his knife again and cut into the reptile's belly. A green marble rolled out. "The snake had been a clue after all."

"I've got the blue drawer open. There's another box inside with a number lock." She set it on the table.

Liam dropped the marble into the top cardboard roll of several mounted to the wall. The marble rolled from one tube to the next until landing in one. "Try 589."

"It worked." She held up a laptop before setting it on the table and lifting the lid. A message scrolled across the screen. "Ashley Stevenson is waiting." She met Liam's gaze. "The name of who we're looking for?"

"That's my guess. Ring any bells?"

She nodded. "Her father owns a lot of land outside Oakdale. They're probably our wealthiest family. How does knowing her identity help us get out of here?"

"To give us a sense of urgency."

"I'd move as quickly as possible no matter who the person was." She closed the laptop. "We're missing something."

And time was ticking away. "Bring anything that moves to

the table." He shoved aside the items they'd already used and started adding things from one side of the room while Harper did the other.

His foot nudged a toy truck. It started to move across the room, but not in a straight line. Someone operated it by remote control. He followed the truck to a chair where it stopped. Liam moved the chair and revealed a round hole cut in the wall big enough for his fist to fit through. He grabbed the iron bar he'd held the snake down with and inserted it into the hole.

Two blades snapped around the bar. This was no longer a childish game. He could've lost his hand. At his feet lay a plastic easter egg. His hand trembled as he picked up. Something rattled inside. He opened the egg to reveal a door key. "We're out of here." He glanced at his cell phone. It had taken two hours.

He unlocked the door and approached the mannequin. The note pinned to her shirt looked like GPS coordinates. "Harper, punch these into your phone."

"It's a location two hours away." Her gaze locked with his. "We'll never make it in time."

"I don't think we were ever expected to." He shoved open another door and stepped into the night. They still had to get back to the jeep.

He took Harper's hand and started running. The group of gang members they'd passed earlier had grown. The boys tossed out threats and taunts, finally giving chase.

Liam whirled and drew his weapon. "You do not want to start anything. We are not interested in you."

The boys took a step back and held up their hands. "No worries, dude," one of them said. "We don't like cops around here."

Liam shook his head and continued to run alongside Harper until they reached the jeep. Thank God, the tires were still there. He'd been afraid the vehicle might have been stripped.

Harper shouted out directions as he sped from the city. "The map shows an old motel at these coordinates. The place has changed owners more time than one can count."

"If the manager hasn't seen Ashley, which I doubt, the killer wouldn't have had her with him when he placed her in a room, we'll have to search every room."

"Let's hope there aren't many."

They arrived at the motel with fifteen minutes to spare. The manager hadn't seen Ashley but did recall a woman renting a room.

"We need to check all rooms unless you know for a fact there's no one in them." Liam explained their urgency. They'd never find her in time.

"I saw that the girl was missing on the news. You want to check all twenty?" The manager shook his head. "We'll have to split up." He handed Liam keys to one end and Harper the other. "How much time did you say we had?" The man paled.

"Less than fifteen minutes. You stay here and call the police. Tell them who we are and what we're searching for." Liam whirled and thundered toward the rooms he held the keys for.

He startled a family in the first room. He called out an apology and kept moving. Four doors later, he burst into a room where a young girl sat up, eyes wide over the gag in her mouth. She shrieked and shrank away from him. Thank you, God.

"I'm Agent McConnell. I'm here to get you out of here. Come on, sweetheart. We don't have much time." He glanced at his watch. Three minutes. He scooped her into his arms and sprinted from the room, expecting a booby trap.

When one didn't come, some of the tension left his shoulders. He removed Ashley's gag and cut the zip ties holding her hands and feet. "Are you okay? Are you hurt?"

"I'm okay. I don't know what happened. I was on my way to practice when this woman asked me for directions. The next thing I knew, you barged into the room. Where are my parents?"

He handed her his cell phone and waved Harper over. He didn't have much experience with traumatized young girls. "We need to get her to a sketch artist."

When ten minutes past the twenty-four-hour mark arrived, he entered the room again. On the dresser holding the TV was a note that said, "I don't kill children. I've my eye on someone else. Someone more important."

Chapter Seven

So, the assassin had a conscience. Carl shrugged, twirling the amber-colored whiskey in his glass. "Who do you have your eye on? I must know that they deserve to die. That this person is coveting something they can't or shouldn't have." He didn't like her calling the shots. When had he lost his grip on his mission?

It had also been too long since he'd had a meeting with his followers. He would remedy that and set up a time for the next evening. He needed to get someone else involved. Lucy had too much power.

"You're pouting, Carl."

He scowled. "I'm the one who makes the decisions. I'm the one who chooses who deserves to die. I don't fault you for the child you chose. After all, she'll be fine. But she isn't the one I told you to take."

"I have something far grander planned for her. You'll enjoy it. What do you have against the Stevenson family?"

"My father and his father were business partners. Stevenson stole a large amount of money from the company." Carl wasn't one to forgive or forget.

"Make sure to watch the evening news." She grinned and left his apartment, closing the door firmly behind her.

He drained his glass and went for a refill. Who cared that it wasn't even nine a.m.? It occurred to him he might be losing his mind.

He supposed he could have saved the target for the sin of lust, but after Lucy took the girl, he'd decided to go ahead with his original plan. He could say one thing about Lucy. She was very creative when disposing of a target.

But it was time for him to regain control. He sent Lucy a text to let him know where and when the deed was done. After all, he needed to let the agent and detective know where to find the next victim they failed to save.

~

Harper paused in the doorway of the living room. Since they'd been closer to her place than the hotel Liam was staying in, he'd crashed on her couch. He lay sprawled out, one leg hanging off the sofa, and one arm over his head. Soft snores emanated from his mouth.

He might not be book cover handsome, but he turned heads. His lean body reminded her of a jungle cat. He moved with a slow, determined purpose. Lips a little too full, a square jaw, hazel eyes that could look right though a person, and inky hair. Yes, the man was handsome enough. She sighed and headed for the kitchen to start the coffee.

While she might not want him to leave, she didn't want a relationship either. Relationships complicated things.

Seconds after the coffee percolated, Liam entered the kitchen. "Now, that's the way a man likes to wake up. Well, second best way." He tossed her a wink. "You look cute with your hair all mussed from sleep." He poured a cup and leaned against the counter. "Has anyone told you that you look far too young and innocent to be a detective?"

"All the time." And she hated being reminded she didn't look her age or look tough enough to bring down a bad guy. She could do the job as well, if not better, than a man. She might not look like a detective, but Liam looked every bit an FBI agent.

"You did good in that escape room. I know it started off as geared toward a child's birthday party, but if we hadn't figured things out, one or both of us might not be standing here."

She nodded. "And the girl is safe. That doesn't seem like his MO, does it?"

"Not really, but I think the escape room was set up by the assassin. The man behind her doesn't seem to be calling the shots anymore. The escape room isn't something he'd do."

"I agree. Before, the people were killed and humiliated in death." She poured creamer into her coffee. "Do you think the assassin is taking over? Could she have the same vision?"

He shrugged. "I don't know. Sure wish I did. Thanks for letting me crash here last night."

"I have a guest room, Liam. There's no need for you to stay at the hotel. No need for us to waste time with me picking you up." What was she thinking? She'd wake up to him every morning.

"That's great. Thanks. We can stop by and get my things before heading to the office." He saluted her with his coffee. "Will be more comfortable than sleeping in the clothes I wore all day."

"Let me get dressed, and we'll go by the hotel so you can shower and get your things." She carried her coffee with her to her room and donned one of her suits. Hair back, minimal makeup, gun, handcuffs, and taser completed the look.

She stared at her reflection. Liam was right. She didn't look like a detective, but she was one, and a very good one, too.

Liam jumped up from his seat at the kitchen table when she set her cup in the sink. "Thanks again for the offer."

"No problem. It only makes sense. We don't know how long this is going to go on." They were only on the second sin as far as they knew. Five more could stretch on for quite a while.

At Liam's hotel room, she glanced around as he showered. He kept the room neat. Clothes hung in the tiny closet or folded in drawers. A paperback crime novel on the nightstand next to a tube of ChapStick. Deodorant, cologne, toothpaste, and a toothbrush lined up on the counter outside the small room containing the shower and toilet.

She smiled. The chief's office looked like a disaster zone compared to this room.

A shirtless Liam exited the bathroom and headed for the closet. Muscles rippled as he reached for a shirt.

She tore her gaze away. "I'll be outside." She rushed from the room and took deep breaths to steady herself. Seeing him half-clothed didn't do much for her resolve of not getting involved.

~

"I'm ready." Liam stepped outside and stared at Harper's red face. "You feeling okay?"

"Just fine." She climbed into the passenger side of the jeep. "Now what?"

"We add to the case board and wait for a message." He hated that they knew nothing more than a man with a grudge against them because of their fathers and grandfathers, and that the man had enough money to hire an assassin. He most likely had followers, similar to a cult. The question was…how many?

He doubted it had anything to do with religion, so meetings wouldn't be held in anything resembling a church. Something more like an AA meeting? "Where would people hold meetings outside of a church or fellowship hall?"

"The library has rooms. Some of the hotels do. The country club in Harrington…" Her blue eyes widened. "Since we're dealing with someone with money, it stands to reason that he would be a member of the country club. It shouldn't be too hard to get a list of members."

"Looks like we have our plan for the day." He turned the vehicle toward the Interstate.

"Not so fast. I just got a text." She lit up the screen. "It's an address in Harrington." She typed into her phone. "Liam, it's the Stevenson house."

"Change of plans. Does it say anything else?"

"No. Just the address."

Not good. Chances was the target was already dead. "How far are we?"

"Thirty-five minutes. Their place is on the opposite side of the city in a ritzy neighborhood. We'll need to get past the gate keeper."

Who won't have seen a thing. Liam pressed the gas pedal, rocketing them down the Interstate. Construction set them back, making the drive forty-five minutes long.

He pulled up to the gate and showed his credentials. "Do you know whether the Stevenson family is home?"

"Mr. Stevenson has gone to work, sir. Miss Ashley is at school. I believe his wife is home." He pressed the button to open the gate. "Please check out when you leave."

"Has there been any other visitors this morning? People who don't live in the community?"

"Not that I've seen, sir. Have a good day."

Dismissed, Liam drove through the open gate. The road curved around, taking them past houses that could only be called mansions. He shook his head. If he had this kind of money, he wouldn't sink it into a house or fancy cars. He'd travel the world. They arrived at the Stevenson address, and he drove up the flagstone driveway.

A whistle escaped his lips. The glass and metal house took up an acre, not counting the size of the plot. Expansive lawn stretched on all sides of the house.

"Some people have too much." Harper shoved her door open and got out.

Liam's phone buzzed. He glanced at the screen. *Sometimes the sin of covetousness and lust entwine.* "He's moved on to lust. He's combining them."

"I'm wondering what happens when he reaches the seventh sin." She marched beside him as they moved toward the house. "I think the seventh sin is anger."

"That's when he comes directly after us." The thought chilled his blood.

He knocked on the massive double door, then pressed the doorbell, sending a melodic tone throughout the house. When no one answered, he jerked his head to the corner. "Let's check around back." They had every reason to enter without permission after receiving the texts, but he wanted to make sure no one was out back first.

They found no one, which he thought strange for a house that size. Where was the staff? Gardening, maid, housekeeper? He walked up the steps to a deck and drew his weapon before reaching for the door handle. The door swung open easily at his touch.

He stepped into a massive white and stainless-steel kitchen the size of most studio apartments. He stopped and listened for signs of life. When something curled around his leg, he almost jumped out of his skin.

"Just a cat." Harper gave a whispered laugh, then cut it off short. "It's leaving bloody footprints."

He glanced down at the furry white feline who definitely left bloody footprints across the tile. "Stay behind me."

"No, we'll split up. I doubt anyone is waiting in hiding to jump out and slash us. I'll take downstairs, you take up."

"Yes, boss." He grinned and walked as quietly up the

wooden staircase as was possible. She was right. They most likely wouldn't find anyone. Not alive anyway.

He passed multiple bedrooms, all with their own baths, plus a guest bathroom, a game room, and a media room. How could anyone possibly use all these rooms?

Something banged downstairs. He froze.

"Cat jumped on the counter and knocked a rolling pin off." Harper's voice drifted up the stairs.

He took a deep breath and pushed open a set of double doors. His heart sank. Lying in the middle of the four-poster bed, their throats cut were two naked people. Both had their hands folded over their stomachs as a corpse in a coffin did. "Up here, Harper."

Within seconds, she stood at his side. "That is Mrs. Stevenson, but that is not Mr. Stevenson with her. I'll call HPD." She stepped into the hall, leaving him to case the room.

If the man wasn't the woman's husband, then the killer had most likely caught them in an adulterous act. Which, yes, would go with covet and lust. But why take the daughter yesterday? Would she have been killed if they hadn't found her in time? The assassin had said she didn't kill children, but what if they hadn't gotten there in time? Surely, the killer wouldn't cast judgment on a child?

He stood next to the bed. Both wore wedding rings, which meant two spouses were going to find out their spouse cheated and was also murdered. Not a good way for anyone's day to start.

His gaze roamed down their bodies. Where were their wedding ring fingers? He pulled gloves from his pocket and pulled them over his hands before opening the woman's mouth and removing the man's finger. It didn't take much to figure out her finger was most likely in his mouth. He set the appendage next to her and joined Harper in the hall.

"Things are escalating. Body parts are being removed now."

Chapter Eight

Harper marched up the brick path to the Harrington Country Club with Liam at her side. He'd been quiet after finding Mrs. Stevenson's body. She didn't blame him. The mounting number of deaths was getting to her, too. How many more before the killer came to them as he tried to rid the world of anger? Except…wasn't he the one with that particular sin?

Since they didn't have a name, finding the person they sought would be near impossible. She stepped aside as Liam reached around her to open the door. Despite his stoic expression, she knew he tired of the game. So was she.

She led the way to a tall desk such as a concierge desk in a hotel and flashed her badge. "We need to see a member list, please."

"Do you have a warrant?" The diminutive man arched a brow.

She tilted her head. "Do we need one? You have watched the news, right?"

His eyes widened. "No such person would be allowed to join this club."

Idiot. "He wouldn't exactly tell you, now, would he?"

Liam slapped the podium. "Look, man. I've had it up to here." He put a flat hand by his nose. "Stop messing around and get us that list."

"Yes, sir. It will take a few minutes." The man scurried away.

"That's the first time I've seen you lose your cool." Harper peered up at him. "Are you losing it?"

"Of course not. I'm just ready to find this guy." He went and sat on a black leather sofa. "And I'm acting like petulant child."

His mouth twitched.

"After that stupid escape room, I'm ready to turn in my badge." She sat and leaned forward, hanging her folded hands between her knees. She straightened as a man entered. "There's Doctor Landry."

The man did not look happy to see them but forced a smile and came over when Harper motioned him to. "Agent. Detective. Fancy seeing the two of you here."

"Just checking the place out." Liam grinned. "Thinking of applying for membership."

"No offense, but I doubt you have sufficient income. Is there something I can do for you? I have a meeting to attend to."

"What kind of meeting?" Harper pasted a smile on her face.

"Business." He seemed to force the word through clenched teeth. He glanced at the smart watch on his wrist. "I must be going. Have a good day." He rushed away from them and down a hall.

"I didn't think of the club having meeting rooms."

Liam shrugged. "I think people could congregate almost anywhere. Unless we catch one of the killer's followers and they talk, I doubt we'll find their meeting place."

"Don't be a Debby Downer." It might take a while, but they *would* catch this guy. "You need a vacation when this is all over."

"So will you. Maybe we can take one together. I'll take you to Ireland. Ever been?"

"No." Her heart jumped at the thought of traveling with him. Her attention was diverted by the return of the unfriendly little man.

He handed her a jump drive. "I copied names, just the names, on here. You're capable of finding their addresses yourself. I don't want the members any more upset with me than they will be."

"They won't find out unless you tell them. Thank you." She pocketed the drive. "We're going to stroll the grounds for a few minutes. We'll let you know when we leave."

He sighed. "Very well."

Harper didn't know what she hoped to find. From the suspicious looks of those enjoying a meal on the patio, they'd be lucky to get anyone to speak to them. Since the murders started recently, she hoped the killer was a new member.

"The kitchen staff might not be as unfriendly." Liam opened

a small door on the patio.

It was worth a try, anyway. She kept a smile in place and entered the kitchen. She identified them both. "Who has been working here the longest?"

"I am." A man in a chef's hand approached them, wiping his hands on a white towel. "Can I help you?"

"Is there somewhere we can speak privately? Somewhere with a computer? This won't take long."

He nodded, then ordered the staff to continue without him. "Follow me." He led them out of the kitchen, across the common area, and into a small conference type room. A laptop sat in the middle of the oval table. He sat in one of the chairs. "There's a laptop in every conference room in case someone forgets theirs. What do you need to know?"

Harper sat next to him and opened the laptop, then inserted the drive. "We have a list of all the members. Can you write down the names of those who joined in the last three months?"

He shot her a quick look. "May I ask why?"

"It's part of a police investigation."

~

Carl found it hard to concentrate during his meeting. He stood at the front of the room as he usually did and asked the ten people in front of him, all club members, whether they had recently run across someone committing the sin of covetousness. He tried to listen without wondering why the agent and detective were there.

"I know someone deep into the sin of greed."

"My neighbor blew up at his wife in a fit of anger."

"I drove past a hoarder's house the other day."

The naming of sins bombarded him. Didn't the men in front of him realize they were most likely the guiltiest of them all? From the smug looks as they pointed out the sin in others let him know they didn't.

Carl didn't blame them. He had his own sins. What the men in this room had that others didn't was the desire to be better, to make the world a better place.

"You know what to do. Write down the information and mail it to my office." He had plenty to target on the countdown to getting to the agent and detective.

His eyes almost bugged out of his head as he spotted those very two walking past with the chef. The detective glanced his way and nodded. He didn't think it possible, but his eyes widened even farther when Lucy entered.

The frumpy assassin stuck out like an oil stain on wet pants. She stood and cased the room. When she saw him through the glass, she waved, before ignoring Arnie who ran the front desk, and heading for the outdoor restaurant.

Less than a minute later, Arnie entered the conference room. "There's a…" his nose curled, "Lady who says she knows you and has come for supper. Her name is Lucy."

Fire crept up his neck. "Yes, she works for me. Let her know I'll be right out." His fingers curled around the edge of the table. He ended the meeting with the promise of the entire group meeting soon. The rich weren't his only followers.

Blood still boiling, he joined Lucy outside and glared at the housedress she wore that was too sizes too large. "What are you doing here?"

"Eating. I've already ordered shrimp and steak for us." She took a deep breath as she glanced around the patio. "Very nice place. Get me a membership. You know I make enough money." She laughed.

"You don't fit in."

"Sure, I do, from one killer to another." Her laugh grew louder, then stopped abruptly. She leaned closer to him. "Get. Me. A membership. I want to look respectable."

"Then start dressing better."

She laughed again and reached for her wine glass. "You are a funny man, Carl Landry."

"We shouldn't be seen together. McConnell and Scranton are here."

"So? They don't know what I do for a living. I mean, they might have caught a glimpse of me, but they can't prove anything. If it means so much to you, I'll wear makeup next time." She rolled her eyes.

He cursed under his breath as the agent and detective strolled toward the front doors. He got to his feet and out of sight. "Let me know when they're gone."

"They're gone." She took another swig of her wine. "You're

on the skittish, dumb side of things. How have you not been caught yet?"

At the next table, two stylish women talked about a third who had just bought a newer, bigger house and a Mercedes. "Who does she think she is?" One asked. "A movie star? Did you see the pink color of the outside? Hideous."

"I might not like the house," the other added. "But I would like the money she threw at the place."

Lucy's gaze met Carl's smiling face.

~

They had five names of people who had joined the club in the last three months. One of them being the good doctor, Carl Landry. Liam's earlier suspicions returned. The man had money. He'd done some research on Landry. Proving that he was behind the murders would be difficult. Their best bet was finding his assassin. The woman or someone else? The woman had been following them.

"Do you think the sketch artist got anything from Ashley Stevenson?" He glanced at Harper.

"Let's go see. It'll be nice to have a face to go by."

He drove them to the police station. The sketch artist handed them the drawing. Liam looked at it then at Harper. "It's the woman who had followed us."

"I need a press conference. I want her face plastered all over the news." Harper picked up the desk phone and arranged a press conference outside in an hour.

While they waited, they both took some of the names of new members and got some background on them. All men. All wealthy. Variety of careers. Liam's gaze kept returning to Landry.

The thing that kept throwing him was the fact Landry was a plastic surgeon. He dealt with the so-called sins every day. People either coveted a better face, which meant they envied something or someone. Then, their new look could cause pride or greed. Since his patients weren't dead, Landry didn't seem the likely suspect.

So, why couldn't Liam get the idea that the man is their perp out of his head?

"None of these men have ever been arrested. Nothing so much as a restraining order." Harper crossed her arms. "They're all squeaky clean."

Even Landry. "I still think one of these men is our killer. If we put enough pressure on them, one of them might crack."

"Or file a complaint against the department."

"I'm willing to take that risk. Let's hit their places of work."

"Okay, but the chief's head will explode if anyone complains. He likes to keep the peace, literally, and prides himself on very few complaints against those who work under him."

"I'll explain it to him. I'm also calling in a few more agents. Let's really put the pressure on this city. The man we're looking for is bound to crack eventually." A cornered animal always strikes back.

Chapter Nine

Carl marched into his apartment. Where was Lucy? She'd said she'd be waiting here for him. He hated waiting and made a beeline for the whiskey decanter. He'd poured himself a glass when the front door opened.

He turned and dropped the glass. A vision of loveliness, all curves and fashion, a sly smile on painted lips. "Do I know you?"

"It's not that much of a transformation, surely." Lucy stepped around the shattered glass. "Do I fit the country club now?"

He nodded, unable to speak around the cotton in his mouth. When he could, he took a deep breath. "If you can look like this, why look like…before?"

"This look is unforgettable. I prefer to go unnoticed. But, since my face is now plastered all over the news, thanks to our lovely detective, I needed to change things up. No one will think this," she motioned at her body, "Is the same woman going around killing people at your request. So, for now, we pretend to be lovers."

For the first time since meeting Lucy, he didn't want to pretend. Still in shock, he retrieved a broom and dustpan from the kitchen closet and cleaned up the mess. When he'd finished, Lucy handed him another glass.

"To our success." She raised her glass in a toast. "Once we're finished, you'll have the world you dream of, and I'll be the world's most sought-after assassin."

"To us."

They clinked their glasses. Lucy downed her's in one gulp. "I've got to get to the club and meet our two jealous ladies."

~

Their first stop slammed the door in their face. "Mr. Moore, we will get a warrant if we have to." Harper rapped her knuckles on the door again. "We only want to ask you a few questions about the Harrington Country Club." Why was the man so against speaking to them unless he was guilty. But she couldn't see their killer refusing to talk to them. Instead, he'd play innocent and enjoy the act.

The door opened again. "What about the country club?"

"We heard you're a new member. I'm sure you've heard the news. It's quite possible the Seven Deadly Sins Killer is also a member. We're hoping you may have noticed someone acting strange? Overly interested in the case?"

"Nope." Something flickered in his eyes before he slammed the door closed again.

Harper sighed. "I don't think he's our guy."

"I agree." Liam put his hand on the small of her back as if he made the gesture all the time.

A jolt of electricity rippled through her skin despite the suit jacket and blouse she wore. She cleared her throat and glanced back at the house. A curtain twitched in a window. The man might not be the one they sought, but she'd bet her badge he knew something about the killer. A follower?

In the car she opened her phone and punched the next address into the GPS. "I feel as if this is all a waste of time."

"Most likely, but at least we'll have checked them out. Those that won't talk to us, we'll come back tomorrow and the next day until either the chief tells us to stop, or we find out something. If the killer is a member of the club, one of these men will have seen or suspected something."

"Maybe the club has a strict no-talk policy. A contract they signed. If they talk about the other members, they're kicked out."

Liam turned the key in the ignition and chuckled. "I wouldn't doubt it. I've met a lot of wealthy people with big secrets."

She sighed. No one would want to rat out another. "You'd think they'd want the killing to stop."

"Depends on how loyal they all are to each other. Birds of a feather flocking together and all that."

At the next house, a woman dressed in tennis clothes stepped off the porch and headed for her car. Liam blocked the driveway.

Harper led the way and gave her spiel. "We're hoping you can help us, Mrs. Weston."

The woman's arched brows drew together. "Yes, my husband and I are new members, but he really doesn't talk to me about his male friends. We have our own interests and usually go our separate ways once there. I'm sorry, but I can't help you."

"Is your husband home?"

She shook her head. "I just left the club to change and am returning now. I have a last-minute opportunity for a tennis game. My husband was still there when I left. Sorry, but I must hurry." She got into her car and backed up, stopping a few inches from the jeep.

Harper and Liam got in the jeep and drove to the next house. Because they all lived in the same ritzy neighborhood, each stop only took minutes to arrive at.

Each house had the same response. If the husband answered the door, he refused to talk. If the wife was home, she knew nothing. "We wasted our afternoon."

"Not necessarily."

"What do you mean?" She shifted in her seat.

"We know that these five new members are connected by a vow of secrecy."

"Followers?"

"Perhaps."

"Which means one of them is our killer."

He nodded. "That's what I'm leaning on. My biggest suspect is Carl Landry."

"Why?"

He gave her a quick glance. "The opportunity to find people he deems as sinners, the meeting today which I'd be willing to guess these other men attended. We know they were all at the club today by either their mouth, the club roster, or their wife's lips."

Harper rubbed her temples. Proving any of them to be the person who used assassins would be near impossible. They'd have to catch them in the act. Even more impossible since the person stayed behind the scenes.

Her phone buzzed. "The chief wants us back at the station."

~

For a lecture no doubt. "I'll contact my buddies when we

arrive." He made two calls before he and Harper joined the chief. One to his FBI buddies, and another to men who were once active agents and were now for hire for just about anything. The FBI would arrive within three days. The others would start digging immediately.

Chief Donnelly wasn't happy about anything they told them. "I didn't authorize the FBI."

"We're getting nowhere on our own." Liam crossed his arms.

"I'm also getting complaints from Harrington's most upstanding citizens about you two harassing them. It'll only get worse when the FBI starts pounding on their doors. HPD is not happy."

"Making people happy during a serial killer's rampage isn't a big concern of mine."

"Instead of bothering people, you should be out looking for the woman who kidnapped Ashley Stevenson. She's our killer." The chief's face darkened.

"But she's only the assassin. We need the one who has hired her." Liam refused to back down. He was right. All he needed to do was prove it.

"Heed my warning, Agent McConnell, or I'll contact your supervisor." The chief waved a hand dismissing them.

Harper glared over her shoulder at the chief's door. "How can he be so unreasonable?"

"Stress from the pressure of ending all this." He didn't fault the man, but he also wouldn't be deterred.

Back in the office he shared with Harper, he booted up his computer to dig deeper into the backgrounds of the men they'd visited today. Landry's background seemed too clean. Parts of his life seemed to be missing. Not married, no children, attended Harvard, successful plastic surgeon. Nothing more. No social media, no news articles or press releases. It was as if the man's past had been scrubbed. Was what Liam found real or was Carl Landry an alias?

There were no Landry's on the list of those who died under the care of Harper's grandfather. "What do you think about the idea that Landry isn't the doctor's real name?"

She turned from the case board. "A new identity?"

"Yeah."

"That would mean he'd been planning this for a very long time."

"I'd say from the day he lost someone he cared about."

She leaned against her desk. "Without DNA, he's a ghost. The chief is right. We need to focus on the assassin. Draw her into a trap and prevent her from killing herself like the other one did. Force her to talk."

"This isn't the CIA. We can't torture people and make them talk."

"I bet you know people who can." She tilted her head. "Am I right? I heard the two phone calls you made."?

He laughed. "Alright, Miss Smarty Pants. Yes, I have a team working on this case. They will keep us updated."

"Why didn't you tell me?" A flicker of pain crossed her face.

"I didn't want you involved in case it went all wrong." He kept his gaze on her sad one.

"I don't need you to protect me, Liam. I was doing just fine before you showed up."

"Yes, you were, but this perp wants us working together. I'm sorry for veering away from that." He got to his feet. "Let's go home. We can pick up something to eat on the way."

"Where are you two going?" The chief stopped them. "You're needed at that country club. We've got two women who were supposed to play tennis missing."

They sprinted for the jeep and sped back to Harrington. Police vehicles filled the parking lot. Two officers blocked the door to keep anyone from leaving.

Liam flashed his badge and entered the building, Harper right behind him. "What do we have?" He approached an officer who looked to be in control.

"Two women missing."

"How long?"

"About three hours." He shook his head. "They missed their tennis game, but no one thought anything of it. The court was given to someone else. When they didn't join their husbands for the evening meal, the men got worried. Another hour after that, they called us. At least that's what they said."

If this was their perp, why hadn't Liam or Harper received a text? "So, a lot of people have come and gone since then."

"Unfortunately. We've shut the place down now, but I'm sure it's too late."

"Anyone check the women's bathroom?" Harper asked.

The officer nodded. "Yes, and the women's lockers are still locked, which means their things are still inside. I'm waiting for permission to cut the locks."

"What's the holdup?"

He shrugged. "No one seems to be in a hurry."

After half an hour passed, Liam took matters into his own hands and hunted down the club's maintenance man. "I need you to cut a couple of locks."

The man glanced at the club's owner who paced the common room. "Go ahead. How can this have happened here? We have top-notch security."

"Because you have a killer in your midst." Liam followed the maintenance man to the women's restroom. Harper entered a few seconds later.

The man cut both locks and stepped back. Liam opened one, Harper the other.

An expensive handbag rested inside. On top of the bag was a folded sheet of paper. Liam pulled gloves from his pocket and pulled them on before reaching for the paper. He unfolded it and read, "You have two hours to find these women who are not content with what they have. I enjoyed the last game so much and liked that the two of you succeeded in saving the child. Let's try again."

He glanced at Harper. "No instructions, though."

"I have those." She handed him the paper from the other locker. "There's a bomb icon at the end of the message."

An icy fist clenched his heart. "Where are those coordinates?"

She punched them into her phone. "A campground two hours away."

Liam shoved the paper into his pocket and dashed from the club. They had no time to waste.

Chapter Ten

Lights flashing and siren blaring, the jeep rocketed down the Interstate. "There will be quite the climb on a twisting mountain road." Harper tried not to gasp as Liam swerved to switch lanes, barely missing the bumper of a car in front of them. "It'll slow us down."

"I'll try to make up time on the flat Interstate." His focus remained straight ahead, an intense look in his eyes. His knuckles were white from a tight grip.

She had plenty of tension of her own. By all accounts, they wouldn't reach the women in time. But they had saved Ashley Stevenson, so she had hope they could get to these two in time to.

She phoned the chief and told him where they were headed. He promised to try and get a chopper in the air, but Liam and Harper would probably get there first. "Send a bomb squad, sir."

His shout caused her to hold the phone away from her ear. "I can't let you and Agent McConnell risk yourselves in that way."

"What? Sir? We're breaking up." She pressed the off button. There'd be hell to pay when she returned to the station.

"I take it he didn't like the news."

"You'd be right. We'd better not get blown up or folks in the next county will hear his tirade." She smiled. It warmed her heart that the chief cared so much. Sure, he treated her and Annie differently than the men who had once worked with them, but she felt she could handle him.

At the first opportunity though, she was going to request another officer or two be hired. After the string of deaths, surely those handling the funds could see the need. "Take the next exit."

Liam followed directions taking them to a two-lane highway.

"This will slow us down a lot. How much time has passed?"

"Forty-five minutes. We're making good time. Keep it up."

Construction loomed ahead. Liam groaned but didn't slow. Instead, he took them speeding down the shoulder past the cones and work trucks.

"I've been wondering something." Liam steered back to the road. "You're an Oakdale detective, yet HPD doesn't seem to mind working with you. They don't seem in competition."

"Because we aren't. I'm being targeted by a mad man. We all have the same goal. To lock him behind bars. Most of his victims are residents of Harrington, but since he sends us the texts, we have to leave Oakdale and help HPD. They'd do the same if the circumstances were reversed." She narrowed her eyes. "Is there a lot of competition in the FBI?"

"Not as much as most police precincts. Each jurisdiction seems to stay to their own."

"Take a right. I don't think I could do this job if all law enforcement didn't want to work together."

He jerked the wheel to the right. "A little more warning next time. We were almost driving on two tires."

"Sorry." Maybe talking wasn't such a good idea at that time. "How much farther?"

She glanced at the GPS. "Ten miles up the mountain. Thirty minutes. That gives us twenty to find the women and get them out." They'd never make it. Liam had driven like a pro, but they still didn't have enough time.

The jeep roared up the mountain, skidding around corners. Harper wanted to close her eyes and brace for impact but couldn't do anything more than stare wide-eyed at the trees rushing past. "Don't kill us."

"Have faith, sweetheart." He let up on the gas as they rounded another turn, but increased speed again until the next turn.

"The campgrounds are coming up. No buildings other than the bathrooms."

"Then that's where we check. How many?"

"Two. One at each end." Her phone buzzed. *Covetousness is the greatest of monsters, as well as the root of all evil. – William Penn.* It had been a while since the perp had sent a quote. Why now? Was he trying to tell them the women were already dead?

"Our guy?" Liam shoved his door open.

"Yeah. Doesn't say much other than calling covetousness a monster."

"He's the monster. I'll take the men's room."

Harper darted inside. One stalls and two showers stood empty. She shoved on the other stall.

"Hey. I'm in here."

"Are you okay?"

"Why wouldn't I be?" The woman muttered something about a weirdo.

"My apologies." Harper rushed back to the jeep where Liam drove them to the opposite end of the campground to the other restrooms.

"There's a lock on the women's door." Harper glanced at her watch. "We have five minutes, Liam." Her heart thudded so hard she thought he could hear it.

He picked up a rock the size of his fist and started pounding on the lock. Harper counted the seconds with each whack. "Hurry."

On the tenth hit, the lock opened and fell to the concrete with a thud. Liam had his pocketknife out before he opened the door.

Harper drew her weapon and entered right behind him. A woman, clad only in her underwear, what there was of it, sat in each stall. Their hands had been zip-tied to the toilet tank. Both were gagged with their ankles tied. On the wall, a timer counted down. "We have two minutes!"

She didn't carry a knife. How was she going to free this woman in time?

~

Liam quickly sliced through the woman's bindings. "Harper, take her outside. I'll cut the other one loose." He glanced at the time. One minute. "Hurry."

She grabbed the woman by the arm and dragged her from the building.

"Hold still. I don't want to cut you." He sliced the tie around her wrists.

She squealed behind her gag and bounced on the toilet seat.

Thirty seconds. Liam cut the tie around her ankles.

The woman tried to stand and fell. "My legs are asleep."

He put his arm around her waist and dashed for the door. Harper peered at him from behind the jeep, her eyes wide in a pale face. Time was up.

The explosion slammed him into the side of the vehicle. Stars swam in front of his eyes before darkness claimed him.

He came to as sirens wailed. He struggled to a sitting position and groaned.

"Stay still. The ambulance is here." Harper smoothed the hair away from his face.

"The women?"

"The one you helped is injured. A broken arm from the concussion, I think. What about you?"

"I don't think anything is broken, but I've got one heck of a headache." He put his hand to the back of his head and brought his fingers away sticky. His stomach rolled as he blinked into the angry face of Chief Donnelly.

The man's fists were planted on his hips. "When are the two of you going to start calling for backup before doing something stupid."

"We saved the two women, sir. Barely. If we'd waited for help, they'd be dead." Liam used the car to get to his feet. A pang of regret pierced him at the damage he'd caused to the driver's side door when he'd been slammed into it.

Harper's gaze followed his. "The door can be fixed. Don't worry."

The chief shook his head and marched to the burning bathroom.

"When I saw you flying through the air…then hit the car and go limp…" Harper's choked back a sob. "I thought the worst."

He cupped her face. "I'm far too mean to die that easily, sweetheart." He smiled through the pain of his headache.

"But people can die days later from head trauma." Tears streaked down her cheeks. "I don't want you to die."

He leaned his forehead against hers. "I'm in agreement with you." With his forefinger, he tilted her face to his and planted a soft kiss on her lips. "We still have work to do."

She smiled through her tears. "Yes, we do." She stepped back as her phone buzzed, then showed him the screen.

Of all the worldly passions, lust is the most intense. All other

worldly passions seem to follow in its train. – Buddha.
Without any break, they'd be headed off to the next clue or death scene.

DEADLY LUST

Cynthia Hickey

Conscience will sleep a while when lust is awakened.

Chapter One

Harper would try not to shoot the Seven Deadly Sins Killer when they came face-to-face, or his assassin, but if she had to, she'd have to repent about feeling good about it. She stared at the latest text message. *Of the seven deadly sins, only envy is no fun at all.* She didn't know what that meant.

She shrugged. "I guess envy takes too much out of a person." She booted up her computer and searched the newsfeed for any murders that might be related to their case. So far nothing. Again, the killer and his assassin had chosen to lay low.

After a week of no activity, Liam had been called back to his office and no other agents sent to Oakdale. Harper leaned back in her chair. Why would the killer stop before finishing the seven deadly sins? It didn't make sense.

To have them lower their guard perhaps? The text she'd received let her know the man still lived.

She glanced at Liam's empty desk, missing him more than she had a right to. Maybe she could call him. See how he was, what he was working on. As she reached for her phone, Annie stepped into her office.

"We've got a call of shots fired on Monroe St."

"Coming." Calling Liam would have to wait. She grabbed her jacket and weapon and followed Annie grateful for something to do other than think about Liam. She slid into the passenger side of Annie's squad car. "What do we know?"

"Not much. Multiple shots fired. It's a residential area. No idea of casualties."

Hopefully none, but that was rarely the case when shots were fired in a residential area. "Backup?"

"Called, but they won't be here for twenty minutes." She turned on the lights and siren and sped from the parking lot.

When they arrived, neighbors reported hearing five gunshots, then the squealing of tires. "Any sign of the shooter?" She glanced at the house they'd been called to.

"No, ma'am. Things like this don't usually happen in this neighborhood."

"Thank you for your help. Please return to your home. We'll handle things here." She marched to the front door and pressed the bell as Annie strung crime scene tape around the yard. The officer had already sufficiently blocked the road with the car.

"I count four casings," she called out.

Harper glanced at the house, spotting four holes in the walls. She turned and glanced at the porch roof. There was the fifth hole. She'd bet her jeep the fifth bullet was lodged up there.

The door opened and she stepped back. "I'm Detective Scranton."

"Thank God. Please come in. I'm Susan Knell." The middle-aged woman moved aside. "I have a name for you."

Harper did her best to keep her cop face on. "A name?"

"Yes. When we woke up to someone was shooting at the house, we were awakened by a picture falling off the wall. You'll see the bullet hole. Anyway, I asked my teenage son who would be shooting at us. He had a name within five minutes."

"I would like to speak with your son, please." Some of the tension left her shoulders as she realized the morning's proceedings most likely had nothing to do with The Seven Deadly Sins Killer.

"He's sitting at the kitchen table."

"Anyone else home?"

"My husband is with my son. Do you mind if I step outside for a smoke?"

"Go ahead. Stay out there until I call for you." A minute later, Harper had the son at the kitchen table and the husband in the TV room. Separated, they couldn't compare stories. "You're awfully calm, ma'am."

"If you think chain smoking and shaky hands is calm, then I guess I am." She opened blinds covering an arcadia door and stepped outside.

Harper sat across from the table. Annie entered the room. "There's a neighbor kid who says he wants to talk to you."

"Tell him to wait on the porch." She folded her hands on the tabletop and pierced the nervous teen in front of her with her sternest stare. "So, who's the shooter?"

"Ryan Jones. But he wasn't supposed to shoot our house. It was supposed to be Jose's two doors down. Something about drugs."

A bust gone wrong? "How do you know this?"

"Because Ryan took his brother's gun and his car. Him and his friends had been drinking. When they got home, his older brother hit the roof. He had a friend over who started spreading the word."

Thankfully for law enforcement, there was no honor among thieves. "We'll check out your story."

Further questioning of the Knell family resulted in no further information. Harper went to interview the neighbor kid. Sure enough, he'd gone to sell pot at the park, was short the amount, and targeted. Thankfully, no one was hurt.

She left the boy to be cuffed by Annie. Not exactly a normal day in the life of Oakdale law enforcement, but it sure beat the days trying to catch up with The Seven Deadly Sins Killer. If only every case could be this simple.

~

Carl slowed as two people exited an adult bookstore a few miles outside Harrington. A place like that shouldn't be allowed to remain standing. Like the nightclub, a bomb would do the city a favor.

The couple hung on each other, stopping every few seconds to kiss. He'd bet a dime to a dollar one of them was married to someone other than the one they kissed. Using his cell phone, he snapped a few photos. Lucy would be able to find out their identity. Then, they'd pay for their lustfulness and the games would continue.

He coughed, not completely over the virus that had kept him and Lucy locked up for almost two weeks. He'd had everything they needed delivered but started to go stir crazy. Not to mention that he needed to continue his quest of making the world a better place.

Sending the text to the detective that morning had helped make his day a bit better. He couldn't help but wonder what her and the agent had done while he'd been down. They must be wondering the same about him.

"What are you looking at?!" The man with his arm around the woman flipped him off.

Carl snapped out of his thoughts and drove home. In a few more days, he'd be back in the office, and things would return to normal.

He sent the photos to Lucy from the parking garage, then used the elevator to get to his apartment. "Find out who they are."

"Hello, to you, too." She scowled. "How did you know I'd even received the photos this fast?" She hooked her phone to a laptop and started typing. "Don't start getting all bossy again, Carl. I mean it."

"Don't forget who pays you large sums of money to do what I say." He plopped onto the sofa. "Can you find out who they are?"

"Of course, I can. Relax. When I do, am I supposed to dispose of them?"

"Yes. They've committed the sin of lust."

"You and your sins." She shook her head. Ten minutes later, she had their names. "Rob Jackson and Josephine Whitley. Both married to other people. He owns Jackson construction. She's his secretary. Totally cliché. Want their addresses?"

"I won't need them. You do. Then, blow up the adult bookstore outside Harrington."

"Ask one of your goons. I don't do that particular type of job."

Back to dressing frumpy, at least when they weren't out of the apartment, she grabbed a black bag from the closet. "Ciao!"

~

Liam's phone buzzed. He smiled at seeing a text from Harper, but his smile faded as he read. *Got a double murder. Looks like our guy and his right hand are back. Coming?* She'd included a photograph of a man and a woman in a skanky motel room.

Both were nude, their limbs entwined, throats cut, but no blood pooled under the bodies. Definitely seemed like their killer's MO.

He replied that he would be there later that evening, then

marched to his boss Cruz's, office. "Sir?" He showed the man the photo. "I'd like to take a couple of agents with me, this time."

Cruz sighed. "I was hoping the man had died in a car crash or something. Take Macey and Harris. They don't have a lot of experience, but they've got good heads on their shoulders. Use them however you see fit. They're finishing something up. They'll be in Oakdale tomorrow."

"Yes, sir." He hurried home to pack, more pleased that he'd be seeing Harper in a few hours than he should be.

Since he kept a to-go bag packed at all times in case he had to leave in a hurry, it didn't take long before he was ready to go. Toss in a few more items, call for a ride to the airport, and voila. He sent Harper a text asking that someone pick him up from the airport, hoping it would be her. He then called his friend who owned a small plane and requested a ride, eager to get back to work stopping the crazed perp responsible for the rising number of deaths.

Harper leaned against her jeep, arms and ankles folded, when Liam stepped from the plane. She smiled and opened the passenger side door for him. "It's good to have you back."

"It's good to be back." He placed an impulsive kiss on her cheek. "Fill me in on the way to the hotel."

"You can stay in my guestroom. It saves time."

"Thanks." He'd like seeing her first thing in the morning and last thing at night.

As they drove, she talked, giving him the victim's names first. "We've cased the scene the best we could. Friends say the two were having an affair. That fits in with the lust scenario, don't you think?"

"Absolutely. Any message left?"

"Nothing other than the bodies. No witnesses. They weren't killed at the motel. We haven't located where they were killed yet."

"I thought that might be the case from the lack of blood on the bed." He rubbed his chin. "We're fairly certain the assassin is a woman. It would take a strong one to move two dead bodies without being seen."

"Unless the manager is lying to us, and he knew all along she would bring them here." She yanked the wheel to the right, taking an exit. "I think we need to put some pressure on the motel manager."

"You think he might be a follower of the perp?" He liked the way her mind worked.

"Sure do. There's no explanation otherwise. Whoever put the bodies in that room had to have help. Someone would have seen. The manager's office faces the motel room doors." She stopped in front of the motel.

They rushed inside and skid to a halt.

The manager lay on the floor.

Liam felt for a pulse. "He's dead." He glanced around for a murder weapon. No gunshot wound, no knife cuts. "I think he poisoned himself."

"Take me to church."

"For salvation?" He arched a brow. "Or for peace."

"Peace."

Chapter Two

Once they'd taken care of the crime scene, Liam drove Harper to a Catholic church. "It doesn't matter if you're Catholic or not. You'll find the peace you seek inside. I'll wait for you at the back of the sanctuary."

She nodded and sat in the front row and stared at the carved man hanging on the wooden cross. She supposed if he could get through what he had to, she could too. Closing her eyes, she let the quiet and peace of the place wash over her.

She ignored the buzzing of the cell phone in her pocket and the soft cough of someone who entered the building. A whiff of perfume tickled her nose before the woman turned to sit on the other side of the aisle.

After allowing herself fifteen minutes to just be, Harper smiled at the wooden Christ and got to her feet. She shot a quick glance at the other woman who sat with her head bowed. Something about her seemed familiar, but Harper didn't know anyone who could afford the purse and shoes the woman had.

Liam stood when she reached him and put his hand on the small of her back. "Better?"

"Much. I feel as if I can think clearly now. Thank you." She smiled up at him.

"Church always helps me." In the car, he faced her. "The two agents who will be helping us are at the office."

"Tell me about them." She clicked her seatbelt into place. The more people they had working this case, the sooner they'd get it solved.

"Agent Macey is a big man. Think wrestler. Bald head, dark eyes, all business. Agent Harris is as opposite as anyone could get." He pulled from the parking lot and headed in the direction of the office. "Petite, blonde, takes herself seriously, but always ready to crack a smile."

Hopefully, they'd all get along. It helped that one of the agents was a woman. In the past, Harper had taken a second seat to male agents.

Their receptionist sent them to the conference room where she said the chief and the two agents waited. "Chief Donnelly isn't happy to be kept waiting."

Harper shrugged. "We're working. The agents could've spent their time studying the case board." She marched into the conference room, nodding at the two new arrivals. "Welcome to Oakdale."

Agent Macey thrust out his hand. "Hope we can help bring this guy to his knees. I'm Agent Macey, this is Agent Harris. We've worked serial killer cases before." He motioned his head to the case board. "A whole lot of nothing. Are you leaning toward one suspect over another?"

"We are." Liam shook the man's hand after Harper did. "My gut tells me it's a plastic surgeon by the name of Carl Landry. I can't prove it, but we're trying."

"Don't focus too much on one person." The chief waved for them to sit. "You don't want to wear blinders and miss a stronger suspect."

Harper folded her hands on the table. "Landry is a strong suspect, but whoever the perp is hires assassins to the killing and uses his followers to do the other dirty work. From what we can gather from his text messages, the perp thinks he's making the world a better place by getting rid of undesirables."

"People committing the seven deadly sins," Harris said.

"Exactly."

"Then, we've got a long road ahead of us." Macey shook his head. "There isn't a person alive, except for babies and small children, who aren't guilty of at least one of those sins."

"The Seven Deadly Sins Killer has brought Liam and I together because our grandfathers failed to save someone they love from cancer." Harper pushed the stack of medical records across the table. "That's our theory anyway. It's the closest thing that makes sense at this point."

"Mind if we take these and study them as time allows?" He tilted his head.

"Not at all."

"Let's start divvying up tasks." The chief leaned forward. "Harper and Liam will continue following the trail this creep leaves via text messages and disasters. You two go behind them picking up the pieces and digging through the proverbial debris to see what got missed. Eventually, something will be found to help lock this guy and his assassin behind bars. Any comments?"

Four heads shook negative. For the first time since she'd received her first text, Harper started to feel a bit of hope that they'd catch the guy.

~

It hadn't been difficult to find someone willing to blow up an adult bookstore. Carl's followers saw the need to cleanse the country, starting with their hometown. But, it galled him that Lucy refused direct orders when she didn't want to do something. Beautiful or not, when she cleaned up, she was merely hired help.

Carl lifted his binoculars when the one he'd chosen for the job ducked around the corner of the building. From the amount of cars in the parking lot, collateral damage would be great. No matter. Those people shouldn't be in such a place. Their deaths were on them.

First the nightclub, now this. Things were happening on a regular basis. When he returned home, he'd make a list of other places to rid Oakdale and Harrington of.

His man darted from behind the building and to his waiting car. As he sped off, the building exploded into flames sending debris into the air. Carl got out of his car and melted into the crowd of onlookers gathering across from the building. He wanted to watch as the detective and agent arrived on scene not knowing that he was there.

The fire department arrived first, then an ambulance, not that either would do any good. Then, after what seemed like a long time, the familiar jeep stopped on the other side of the police barricade and the two he wanted got out and marched down the sidewalk.

They studied the crowd he stood in. He didn't care. They wouldn't see past his disguise. He pasted on a concerned look and turned his gaze to the burning building.

~

Liam felt watched. The perp was there somewhere. He knew it but saw no sign of Landry. Could he be that wrong about who they searched for?

He turned from the inferno in front of him to the crowd watching, taking mental snapshots of everyone there. Where are you?

One man, pudgy face under a graying beard with a paunch that hung over his belt, met Liam's stare before taking a few steps back. When Liam continued to watch him, the man turned and sprinted down the sidewalk away from the crowd.

"Harper!" Liam raced across the chase and barged through the crowd after the man. His speed belied the middle-aged look. Whoever he was, the man was fit.

Glancing over his shoulder, he spotted Harper following and increased his speed after the suspect. He pulled his radio from his belt and called for backup, describing the man he chased.

The man darted into a bookstore. Screams followed when Liam drew his weapon and ordered shoppers out of his way.

A back door slammed. Liam shoved it open and exited into an alley. He skidded to a halt, glancing both ways before spotting the man turning left onto a nearby street.

"Who is it?" Harper caught up with him.

"Someone acting suspicious." He continued the chase, Harper at his side. When he turned the corner, the man was nowhere to be seen. His shoulders sagged as he replaced his weapon. "I think he's wearing a disguise. A man the age he appeared to be would not be able to run that fast."

"Landry?"

"Maybe. This guy's the right height." He led her back to the building.

Firemen shot streams of water on the fire. Liam approached the fire chief. "Any chance of survivors?"

"Nope. I don't think there will be enough body parts to identify the victims. You'll have to go by the license plates. This fire is hot enough to burn bone. The arsonist was no amateur."

Liam turned to face Macey and Harris. "Thanks for coming. Unfortunately, I lost the guy in the alley." He gave them a description, adding that he believes it to be a disguise. "When we're finished here, Harper and I will pay Doctor Landry another visit. See if his schedule is the same as the length of time we didn't receive text messages or have any deaths in the MO of his assassin."

"It's a long shot," Macey said.

"It's all we've got." He'd never felt so helpless in his life. Because of his incompetence catching this guy, people were dying. More people would die. They were only on the third sin.

Harper stepped in front of him, her blue eyes focused on his. "What's wrong?"

"What if I don't have what it takes?" He kept his gaze locked on hers, searching for anything to prove him wrong. "What if we never bring this guy down?" What if he kills Harper? Liam was pretty certain that would happen with the seventh sin. The man would come for them.

She put a hand on his cheek. "You're one of the most dedicated people I've ever met. We will catch this guy. Have you ever missed bringing justice?"

He shook his head. "There's always a first time."

"No. This will not be the first time you fail. We're a good team, Special Agent McConnell." She gave his cheek a pat. "Now pull out of your pit of despair. We've work to do."

His phone vibrated. He pulled it from his pocket and glanced at the screen. *Whew, that was close. LOL.*

His fingers clenched around the phone, imagining them wrapped around the man's throat. Instead, he showed it to Harper.

"Well, at least you were close."

He frowned, then burst into laughter. "Yeah. At least I was close."

Grinning, she started taking photos of the license plates belonging to the cars in the parking lot. "Some of them are damaged, but I think we can see enough to find out who these vehicles belong to."

There would be a lot of mourning families once they did. Most likely some mixed with horror and embarrassment. He and Harper would be busy doling out the bad news, something he deeply regretted having to do.

Chapter Three

Harper divvied the license plates up between her, Liam, and Annie. By late afternoon, they had the names and addresses of those at the bookstore. "Since it's crowding five o'clock, we should probably hit Landry's office first."

"Agreed. I really want to see if something in his schedule coincides with the fact our perp laid low for a couple of weeks." He stood from his desk. "Ready? We've got a long, unpleasant, evening ahead of us."

"All your suspicions about Landry are circumstantial." She followed him to the jeep.

"Listening to my gut has saved my life on multiple occasions, helped me solve cases, I don't dispute it." He opened the passenger side door for her before moving to the driver's seat. "Besides, we can't find a current address on the man. That alone makes him suspicious."

"If he is our guy, I doubt we'll get much info from his staff. I figure he hires loyal followers. The man we're looking for wouldn't take any chances on an outsider keeping their mouth shut." She thought it too easy for Landry to be their man but did have her own small inkling that Liam could be right.

They parked in front of the office building and marched inside side-by-side. They must have achieved the formidable look Harper had hoped for if the pale face and wide eyes of the receptionist was any indication.

"We need to speak to Doctor Landry." Harper flashed her badge.

"He's been out sick for two weeks."

"Any idea when he plans on returning to the office?"

She shook her head. "He'll be in when he can. I don't have any surgeries listed for another couple of weeks."

Harper shot Liam a glance. The doctor's schedule fit the time of no texts and no deaths. She handed the receptionist a business card. "Please have him call us when he returns to the office. You wouldn't happen to have his home address, would you?"

"I'm afraid I'm not at liberty to give that out."

"Of course not." Harper forced a smile, then turned and exited the building. Without a warrant, they couldn't force the woman to talk. "I'm starting to think you're right about him. Let's say he is our guy. What now?"

"We try to find him."

Not an easy task. The killer was like a phantom, hiring out his dirty work and sitting back to watch the show. "Let the other agents know. We need all the help we can get to find him and the woman assassin." Hopefully, with Landry behind bars, his followers would disperse. The thought of them continuing what he'd started was too horrible to contemplate.

Harper spent the ride to the first house lost in her thoughts. She might have dispelled Liam's insecurities earlier, but she had plenty of her own. She hadn't been a detective more than a year and was very close to losing her first big case. Maybe she should've stayed a street cop.

But then, she wouldn't be working with Liam every day. She wouldn't have a chance to prove herself to the chief. She drew on the peace she'd felt earlier in the church, reminding herself she was exactly where she should be.

By the time Liam parked in front of the first house, she'd regained some of her confidence. She stared at the white wood house with wraparound porch, dreading the task ahead of them. With a heavy sigh, she shoved open her door and stepped onto a freshly moved lawn.

She knocked on the front door and stepped back, glancing at the list in her hand. She put on her cop face and squared her shoulders.

Liam reached over and gave her hand a squeeze when a woman answered the door.

"Mrs. Connor?"

"Yes." The young woman's brow furrowed. An infant cried in the room behind her.

Harper introduced them. "May we come in?"

"Is this about Mark? What happened?"

"Please, ma'am. Inside?" Liam moved forward.

She stepped back, allowing them entrance, then scooped her baby from a blanket on the floor. "I'm ready."

"Please sit down, Mrs. Connor." Liam motioned to the sofa.

When she sat, Harper cleared her throat. "Were you aware that your husband was at the adult bookstore on I40?"

She shook her head. "I assumed he was at work."

"Were you aware of the explosion this morning?"

"No." She gasped. "Are you telling me Mark is dead?"

"Presumably so, ma'am. I regret to inform you that we can't identify any of the bodies and are going by the vehicles in the lot."

A smile lit her face. "Let me make a call. Mark said he was going to lend a coworker his car so the man could run some errands." She muttered a "please God" under her breath and snatched a cell phone from the coffee table. A few seconds later, she nodded. "Mark is at work. His coworker's name is Ben Ally."

Harper made a note on her list. "You're positive?"

"I just spoke to him. My husband is a bit shocked to say the least. Said he heard about the explosion on the news and was about to call and let me know he was fine." A shadow crossed her features. "Ben just got married a month ago."

"Thank you, ma'am. I'm glad it wasn't your husband. You may send someone to pick up the vehicle. It's minus a back window."

Outside, Harper sagged against the porch railing. "One relieved wife, several other loved ones to still pay a visit to."

"Come on." Liam put his arm around her waist. "Let's get this over with."

~

Carl listened to the woman on the other end of the line. "Thank you. I'm taking a lengthy absence. Cancel all appointments until further notice." He hung up and turned to Lucy. "I think the detective and agent may have figured out that I'm the one responsible for the cleansings."

"So?" She never looked up from her phone. "They'll never

figure out your real identity until you want them to."

"How do you know I'm not who I say I am?" He narrowed his eyes.

She shook her head and set her phone in her lap before turning a pitying look on him. "Darling, you aren't as bright as you think you are. If you were really Carl Landry, you'd have been caught by now. The detective and the handsome agent will figure that part out, but not the fact that you are Robert Thompson."

His blood chilled. "How did you discover that?"

"DNA." She grinned.

"What do you do on that phone of yours?"

"Research. Searching for hits that pay well. You aren't the only one paying me money. When I'm not busy on a task of yours, I'm taking other jobs. Someday, I plan on retiring from this line of business and want to make sure my lifestyle doesn't change when I do. Relax, Bob. I've got your back." She turned her attention back to her phone. "Oh, and you shouldn't always try to hide the fact you have one blue eye and one green. It's kind of cool."

Someday, Carl would take great pleasure in putting the woman in her place. He poured himself a glass of whiskey and went to stand on the apartment balcony. Now what? How would he fill his days without work?

Sure, he could make further plans for the remaining sins, but that wouldn't take more than a day or two to lay out. Another few to implement.

He downed the drink in one gulp. He needed to keep things rolling so he could reach the final sin and the end of Detective Scranton and Special Agent McConnell.

"I'll be back later. I need to get some things from my father's house."

"Take your time. I've got a job. I won't be back until tomorrow morning." She grabbed a large bag from beside the sofa. "If I'm not back, hire a new assassin."

~

They weren't as lucky at Ben Ally's home. His wife, shocked at his location, then shattered at the news he was most likely dead.

With tear-filled eyes, she dropped to the sofa. "He promised me he'd left all that behind when we got engaged."

"Some things are hard for some people to shake." Liam kept his voice soft and soothing. "Is there anyone we can call?"

"No. He was all I had. I grew up in the foster system. No parents to speak of. A few friends, but not really anyone I can lean on."

He handed her a card. "This is a counselor's office. Someone there can help you. Why did your husband need to borrow a car?"

"Because I had to work today, and we only have one vehicle." She leaned her head against the back of the sofa and fixed her gaze on the ceiling. "See yourselves out, please. I'll be fine."

"I hate these kinds of calls." He marched with heavy steps back to the jeep. "And we still have a lot to get through."

"We could've given the list to Annie or the other agents, but since we're the ones doing the footwork on this case, I felt it should be us." She met his gaze over the hood of the jeep. "I'm sorry."

"No need to be. I agree." He slid into the driver's seat. "The case is becoming personal. It should be us."

They stopped informing families at nine p.m. just in time for the local nightly news. Liam had hoped they could let the families know before they heard the names of the victims on television. They'd accomplished something they'd set out to do at least.

"Back to your place or do you want to grab something to eat?" He turned the jeep toward home.

"After today, I don't have much of an appetite. Leftover pizza and a glass of wine is fine by me." She leaned her head against the seat and closed her eyes. "I don't want to think about this case again until morning. I'm going to curl up on the sofa with a good book until I fall asleep."

"Which sounds amazing to me." He pressed the button on the garage door opener and drove the jeep inside.

While Harper changed into something more comfortable and warmed up the pizza before pouring them both a glass of wine, Liam turned on the news. He wanted to know what was being said about the explosion. Nothing new to report, at least nothing he and

Harper didn't already know.

The faces and names of the victims scrolled across the screen, making him doubly glad they'd managed to notify the next of kin before the broadcast. When Harper entered the room, he clicked the TV off.

"Thanks." He accepted the food and drink and stretched out on the opposite end of the sofa from Harper.

Weariness lined her pretty face as she stared into her wine glass. The paper plate with two slices of warmed up pizza threatened to topple from her lap.

Liam set the plate on the coffee table. She'd said she didn't want to talk about the case, and he respected that, but had no idea what to say. Was their friendship based only on the case? He'd hoped for something more. More than friends someday, if he were honest. Harper had come to mean a lot to him.

She finished her wine without eating. She never did open the pages of the book on the end table. Instead, she watched him over the rim of her glass while he kept his gaze locked with hers.

No words were spoken, but her eyes said a lot as a myriad of emotions flickered through them. Sadness, determination, strength, and what he thought might be caring for him.

"Did you realize that everything you think is seen on your face?" He leaned forward. "Even the fact that you know I want to do this?" He pulled her close and kissed her, softly, tenderly.

"It's a curse," she whispered, her eyes drifting closed. "Kiss me until I forget all this, even if for a little while."

He was more than happy to oblige.

Chapter Four

Harper stared into Macey's face. "How can you not believe, at least a little, that Landry is our man? He was gone from the office, supposedly sick, during the time we heard nothing from the perp." She'd been reluctant to believe the man was right under their nose too, but the overwhelming evidence changed her mind. "I don't believe in coincidences, *Agent*."

"We have no solid evidence, *Detective*. Until we do, we are not going to focus all our time on one man."

"I didn't say we should. What I said was that we need to focus on him more than we have." She crossed her arms and glared at the chief. "What do you think?"

"I think we continue as we are. Do you and Liam have any leads?"

She glanced at Liam. "No. We're waiting for him to make contact again. We'll dig deeper into our grandfathers' medical files."

"There's no Landry listed." Agent Harris slid the files across the table. "You think he's using an alias."

"Absolutely." The perp wouldn't make his true identity known until it suited his plan. She opened the file on top and started reading for the third time since she'd received them.

Liam took the bottom file and did the same as the other three filed out of the room. "Sorry, they don't see it as we do."

"When this is all over, they'll realize we were right all along. I'm sorry I didn't agree with you sooner. If I had, maybe Landry would be behind bars."

"No, your believing wouldn't have changed anything." He placed a kiss on her cheek and turned his attention back to the task in front of him.

After two hours of poring through the files, she realized going through them again also didn't change anything. She widened her eyes. "Do we have a photo of Landry? Maybe we can get one online. Then, we can question anyone still alive from these files. They might recognize him and be able to give us a real name."

"Smart and beautiful." Liam opened his laptop. "Here's his photo on his office website." He printed off several copies. "We'll give one to the chief. Maybe he'll have the news broadcast him as a person of interest. Somebody, somewhere, will have to have seen Landry recently."

Photos in hand, they dropped one on the chief's desk with a note explaining their theory, handed another to the unbelieving Macey, then set off to question the two survivors from Harper's grandfather's practice. One woman and one man both living in a nursing home. Hopefully, they were in their right mind enough to answer questions clearly. Luckily there was only one nursing home in Oakdale, and they were both residents.

When they arrived, they showed their identification to the receptionist and were given room numbers. "Neither of them are in a single room. If you'd like to speak in private, we can bring them to you. We have a small conference room."

"That would be wonderful. Thank you." Harper smiled. "The less questions from others the better."

"I'll have Mrs. Wilson brought to you straightaway." She reached for the phone on her desk. "Head down that hall. Second room on the right. You can't miss it. Large window."

"Thank you." With his hand on her back, Liam guided her down the hall. "Let's pray this helps."

She couldn't agree more. She stepped into a room with an oval table and six chairs. Not large, but suitable for their purpose. When she spotted an elderly woman being wheeled their way, she moved one of the chairs out of the way so the woman could be close to the table.

The orderly smiled and put Mrs. Wilson in place. "Water, tea, or coffee?"

"Coffee," Harper and Liam said in unison.

"Make that three." Mrs. Wilson patted the man's hand. "I

like mine black, you know."

"Yes, I do." He left with promises to return in a couple of minutes.

"Now, what can I do for you?" The old woman's shrewd blue-eyed gaze locked on them. "It isn't often I'm visited by law enforcement. Has my past finally caught up with me?" She laughed.

"No, ma'am." Liam smiled and slid a photo of Landry to her. "Do you recognize this man?"

She pursed her lips. "Vaguely, but there's something off about him. Why do you want to know?"

"You were a patient of my grandfather's. An oncologist. Doctor Scranton? Your primary care physician was Dr. McConnell. Do you remember?" Harper folded her hands on the table.

"Of course, I remember. That was a difficult time in my life. How could I forget?" She squared her shoulders. "But, I survived to live a ripe old age. Not everyone receives that gift."

"We believe this man had a loved one who was also treated by these two doctors. Someone who didn't survive. Perhaps you had treatment with them?"

"Oh, dear, people came and went through that cancer treatment center with terrifying regularity. Let me think. Have you spoken to Harold Fox? He's also a survivor. We talk about those days a lot."

"Would you mind if we had him brought here while we speak to you?" Harper straightened as the orderly returned with their coffees.

"Billy, go get Harold, would you? We need him in this pow wow." When the man left, she turned back to Harper. "Harold isn't quite as sharp in the head as he once was, but he remembers enough. Perhaps with the two of us bouncing ideas off each other, we can help you."

Harper really hoped so. The running in circles the perp had them doing started to make her dizzy.

~

Billy was quick. It didn't take long for him to wheel Mr. Fox, the old man clutching a coffee cup between wrinkled hands, into the room. The man's eyes lit up when he spotted Mrs. Wilson.

"Hello, Mary."

"Hello, Harold." She held out a hand to him.

He set his cup on the table and took her hand. "What's this about?"

"These nice people want to ask some questions about our dark days. Are you up to it?"

"As long as we're finished before lunch. That's in half an hour. I don't like to miss my meals."

"We'll make sure of it." Liam smiled and went through the same spiel Harper had with Mrs. Wilson.

Mr. Fox studied the photo for a few minutes. "This man had a son with two different colored eyes."

Liam shot Harper a glance, then turned back to the old man. "This man is the son."

"No, no, no. His eyes are wrong." He peered closer at the photo. "Chin is a little less pointy, too, but this is definitely Richard Thompson. His son fell in the center once and broke his nose. It's not crooked anymore, but there is still a hint of a scar. Son's name is Robert. I'm positive. I sat next to the man most times I had treatment. Don't you remember, Mary?"

The man jumped from father to son in every sentence, but Liam got the jest of what he meant.

"I do now that you mention him. His son came with him most of the time. The two were very close even if the boy was undisciplined in my opinion. Poor Richard didn't get better like Harold and I did. His liver cancer had progressed too far before detection. Was in his bones and blood, but he still insisted on getting treatment. Swore he'd beat the cancer." Mary clicked her tongue.

Since Landry was a plastic surgeon, he most likely knew several others in the profession. One of them could have worked on his chin, straightened his nose. Another long list for him and Harper to go through. "Mr. Thompson waited too long to see a doctor?"

The other two nodded. "Nice man, a bit strange minded, and very stubborn."

"Strange how?" Harper set her cup on the table.

"Wanted to fix the world. Said he couldn't die because he had too much work to do and didn't want to leave the burden on his son." Mr. Fox shook his head. "Oh, we debated over the fate of the world many times. I missed him when he died. It's been twenty years now. That would make his son about thirty, I think."

At least they now had a name. All they had to do was find Robert Thompson. Since Landry continued to elude their grasp, it wouldn't be easy.

"Was Thompson married?" Harper tilted her head.

"Wife left him years ago," Mrs. Wilson said. "Died of complications from the flu a few years after that."

Liam stood. "Thank you both so much for your help."

"You think he's the Seven Deadly Sins Killer, don't you?" Mrs. Wilson tilted her head. "I saw the boy pull the wings off a fly once that got in his soda. That's true serial killer behavior. I saw it on a movie once."

Liam chuckled. "I can't divulge that information but the two of you have helped us immensely. If either of you remember anything that might help us find this man, then please give us a call." He handed them each a business card.

"Have you tried his house?" Mr. Fox stared at the card. "His father lived in a mansion, so he said. Somewhere outside Harrington on twenty acres. I doubt the boy's there, but you might find out something."

Liam thanked him again and left the room with Harper. "It should be easy enough to find the Thompson place." He called the office and put in the request for both an address and a warrant. "We should know something by the time we've finished lunch."

"Feel like Mexican food?" Harper slid into the jeep.

"I never turn down Mexican food."

Ten minutes later, a young woman led them to a booth and handed them menus. A man brought them chips and salsa.

Liam's phone buzzed. "We've got an address."

Harper started to slide from the booth.

"We might as well eat. Thompson won't be stupid enough to stay in his childhood home, and we don't have a warrant yet."

She shrugged. "If he's arrogant enough to think we'd never find out his real identity, he might."

"That would be easy for us, and nothing has been easy so far." He chose a chimichanga.

Harper ordered flautas. "This could be our big break."

"That's what I'm praying for." He dipped a chip into the salsa and popped it into his mouth. "Got a bit of spice to it."

By the time their order arrived, the warrant had been approved. Since Harper wolfed her lunch down and stared at him while he finished, Liam sighed, tossed money onto the table, and slid from the booth. "Come on, Miss Impatient."

"I don't want to miss him if he's there."

"He won't be."

"Ugh." She marched to the jeep. "Are you ever wrong?"

He chuckled. "Rarely."

"Show off." She smiled and got into the vehicle.

When he joined her, he grasped her hand. "I am wrong sometimes. But I'm not wrong about this or about how I feel about you." He pulled her close for a kiss.

"I feel the same, but let's keep this from the chief and Macey and Harris, okay? I don't want them to think our feelings for each other will cloud our judgement."

The only thing that might send him off course was if something happened to Harper. If she was injured or missing. Then, Liam would turn vigilante. It wouldn't be pretty.

Chapter Five

Falling for Liam wasn't smart in any sense of the word. Harper stifled a sigh and stared out the passenger side window as they drove to the Thompson residence. Emotions clouded a person's judgment. People made mistakes. She needed her mind fully focused on the case, not on the handsome Irishman.

"You're awfully quiet." Liam pulled onto a gravel drive. "Anything you want to talk about?"

"No, just running things through my mind."

The drive wound through lines of crepe myrtle trees before stopping in front of a house that looked so out of place. Even in Harrington.

A large dolphin fountain, long gone dry, took up prominence in a lawn full of weeds. Bushes in need of trimming lined the porch that circled around half of the monstrosity, because there was no other name for the place in Harper's mind. The huge steel, glass, and stucco building looked as far from being a home as it could get.

"It doesn't look as if anyone has been here in a long time." She shoved her door open. Where had the young Thompson gone after his father's death? Had the man immediately set off on his quest for revenge toward the living relatives of his father's doctors?

Their feet crunched across gravel as they made their way across the lawn toward the double doors painted an inky black. When no one answered the doorbell or Harper's knock, she stepped back.

Liam turned the knob. The door opened with the squeak of unused hinges. Dimness greeted them. Dust motes floated on what light did manage to get through broken blinds on the windows.

Rat pellets littered the floor. Harper shuddered. The place must be crawling with rodents.

A curving staircase rose to the second floor.

"I don't think anyone is here."

Liam nodded. "I agree, but maybe something was left behind that would give us an idea of where the son might have gone. Do you want upstairs or down?"

Neither. The thought of roaming the large empty place full of rats chilled her blood. "Down."

She turned left into a dining room with a table large enough to seat twenty. Why hadn't Thompson sold the place? The furnishings alone would bring him a good amount of money. Did he have plans on returning here once he completed his quest?

Her gaze rose to the twenty-foot ceiling. Despite the dirt and evidence that four-legged things lived there, the place was in amazingly good condition for having been vacant for so many years.

Continuing, she entered a kitchen any chef would dream of owning. Commercial grade everything. Who needed a place this big?

Muffled footsteps sounded overhead, then stopped. Wood floor to carpet? She shrugged and opened the back door of the kitchen. An expansive lawn full of more untrimmed bushes stretched to a thick grove of trees. The place was definitely private. She turned and headed across the foyer into a living room.

One photo adorned the mantel. She peered through the gloom at the face of a ten-year-old boy. No smile, only a sad look in his eyes. One blue, and one green. Striking and definitely not something anyone would forget. This had not been a happy home, she guessed. No other photos. Not one of a wife and mother. Very few knickknacks and decorations. Very clinical with its sheet-covered furniture.

Dusty books lined a bookshelf. She reached for a thick volume titled The Seven Deadly Sins. As she went to remove it from the shelf, something clicked. She stepped back as the bookcase swung open.

"Liam!" She unhooked a small flashlight from her belt and shined it into a dark room. Not wanting the case to shut on her, leaving her trapped in darkness, she shoved a chair between the case and the opening. This way, Liam could easily find her if something happened.

She gasped as her light shined on the very things Robert Thompson tried to stop. A stack of porn magazines, shelves full of Cuban cigars, expensive clothes tossed in a corner as if they meant nothing. The room had been turned into a shrine of everything the son hated.

Were these his father's things? Had he locked them away as part of his quest.

She swung the light toward a desk. No computer sat on the desk blotter. She moved closer. The blotter was actually a calendar from ten years ago. The last recorded date had been for a cancer treatment. The father's office then.

She flipped through the pages, noting the notations on the dates. The last thing not related to the man's cancer, had been a charity ball in Little Rock for a children's hospital. She stepped back and shined the light on the opposite wall.

A stack of newspapers sat on a side table. On the first page of the top paper was an article about philanthropist Richard Thompson's sad announcement of his disease.

"Whoa." Liam stepped into the room, his light joining Harper's. "The rest of the house is so sparse compared to this."

"I think Robert brought all his father's things here. Look." She picked up a framed photo from next to the papers. "The wife." A pretty brunette with her hair swept up out of her face with a barrette. "She had the same two different colored eyes as her son."

"Let's step back outside. I didn't find anything upstairs. Anything personal is in this room. We need to get a crime scene in here to bag this stuff up. There's bound to be a clue."

With one final sweep of her flashlight, she followed him onto the porch. "Robert is a very troubled man. His mother left him, his father, despite the things he was into, did try to change the world, but in a far different way than his son is."

Liam put his hands on her shoulders, his gaze boring into hers. "Don't let your empathy cloud the fact that Robert Thompson is a very evil man."

"I won't." Her phone buzzed, and she read, *I don't believe in love at first sight. You fall in lust with what your eyes see, and in love with what your heart sees.*

What did he mean?

~

Look at them. Robert glared through the binoculars. When Lucy had given him the heads up that they were headed to his family home. Ah. Family home was definitely not what he could call the place. Home meant happy, and he had not been a happy child.

When she had alerted him as to where the detective and agent were headed, he took the back roads and arrived shortly after they did. His blood boiled to see that the den of iniquity that contained all the sordid parts of his father, had been discovered.

As he had gone through the house as an adult and seen the things he hadn't noticed as a child, he'd realized how misguided his father's quest had been and designed his own. Robert's would truly rid the world of all depravity.

Now, the two people he toyed with until the time came, looked at each other with lust. Everything in him wanted to order Lucy to get rid of them, but the time wasn't right. He needed them to be the final sin. The one to erase the sin of anger he felt. The only way to do that was to end their lives.

After glancing at the phone in the detective's hand, the agent whirled and scanned the tree line.

~

"He's watching us." Liam strained his eyes to see movement in the trees.

"How could he know where we are?" She glanced at her phone. "Is it possible to get phones that can't be traced?"

"I think so. We also need to have the jeep swept." He pulled her to where the bushes hid them from anyone's view. His main consolation was that Thompson wouldn't strike until the seventh sin. They had to find him before then. "He won't be happy that we discovered that room."

"It explains a lot, though." She slid her phone into her pocket. "We can't get new phones. He wouldn't have our number, couldn't communicate with us. We'll have to let him follow us and hope he makes a mistake."

Liam agreed, but he didn't like the idea. "I want a light in there so we can go over every corner of that room. If it's a hiding place for his father's sins, maybe Robert left a piece of himself in there, too."

He placed the call to the office and got the confirmation that a team would arrive within forty-five minutes. As he hung up, his phone vibrated. "Got another text. *It bothers me that two law-enforcement officers would be foolish enough to gaze on each other with lust in their eyes. What will your chief say?*"

Harper paled. "He thinks we're guilty of the sin of lust. Do you think he'll change his plans of when he comes for us?"

"No. It's another part of his game." At least, he hoped so. A deranged mind would continue to unravel and make Thompson unpredictable. His fear was that the man would think he no longer needed both of them to play the game with.

They moved back inside and waited for help to arrive. While Liam placed calls and paced the room, he'd pause and peer through the blinds for a glimpse of Thompson. So far, nothing. Not that Liam expected him to look like his picture. Unless he didn't always leave wherever he was hiding in a disguise.

A woman answered his call. After asking his question, she responded. "The power has been shut off for the last five years."

"Can you tell me whether anyone lived here during the ten years before that?"

"No, only that the power was turned on under the name of a Richard Thompson."

"Thank you." It was quite possible someone, a nanny perhaps, maybe a relative they had yet to find. had raised Robert until he turned eighteen. He sent an email to the chief asking that he have someone dig into the Thompson family for relatives that might have stepped in to raise the man's young son.

"Found something of Robert's," Harper called from inside.

He joined her, frowning at the ratty teddy bear in her hand. "That isn't sinful."

"No, but rather the disappearance of innocence. Look at this photo. It looks like it came from a security camera." She held it so he could see with his light.

It showed the senior Thompson cutting open the back of the bear and inserting a small bag of white powder. The man hid his drugs in his child's toy when he was bound to have more than one safe in the house. "Why? It doesn't make sense."

"This helps." She handed him another photo. This one of a party.

In the middle of a dining table were a variety of stuff animals, each labeled with a number. Smiling people held up matching numbers. "Wanna bet they got what was inside the toy with the corresponding number?"

"Wow." They'd discovered that Richard had two sides to him, but this went over the top. No wonder his son went nuts. What kind of sickos used their children's toys to indulge in their fetishes? Liam felt a bit sorry for Robert Thompson.

Chapter Six

By the time the crime scene people arrived, and lamps set up around the house, specifically the hidden room, Harper's stomach growled in protest. Now that things were in the hands of others, she motioned her head toward the jeep. "I'm starving."

"We can't leave yet. I want to go through that room now that we have a light." Liam shook his head. "I happen to know that Carla always carries granola bars in the truck. I'll get you one."

"How do you know that?" She'd worked with the woman several times and didn't know.

"I watch." He flashed a grin and approached the leader of the crime scene team. Minutes later, he tossed Harper a bar.

"Thanks." She wanted to go through the room again with lights, but knew once her stomach started its loud rumbling, she couldn't concentrate." While she ate and waited to be allowed back inside, she studied the darkening tree line. Was Thompson still out there?

Where was the man hiding? He wouldn't be foolish enough to return to his office building. By now, she hoped his photo had been plastered across all the news stations. Someone might see through his disguise and alert the police department.

Hunger satiated, she again entered the front door of the house and made a beeline for the room behind the bookcase. She blinked against the harsh lights that brought all of the senior Thompson's sins out of the shadows.

Despite what he had grown up to become, she wanted to give the hurting child Robert a hug. Orphaned at ten, then having cleaned out the house once grown, only to discover all this. She shook her head. Some people shouldn't have children.

Her phone rang. "Detective Scranton."

"It's Annie. I've got the information you wanted on the Thompson nanny. I'll text you the number."

"Thanks. You're a marvel." Smiling, Harper waited for the text to come through, then stepped outside to place the call.

She asked the woman who answered about the nanny for a Robert Thompson. "Yes, that was Nancy Moore. I'm sure she'll answer any questions you might have. I'll give her your number and have her call you."

"Thank you." Harper rejoined Liam inside. "We might have gotten a break. Annie located Robert's nanny."

"Still alive?"

She nodded. "Let's pray the woman isn't one of his followers. If she is, she won't talk, and she'll alert him. Anything new here?"

"Only that Robert Thompson was a very wealthy man before becoming a plastic surgeon." He pointed out a laptop that had been removed from somewhere. "The techs cracked a safe hidden behind those shelves. Found the laptop, financial records, birth certificate, etc. What most would put in a safe. This room is also fireproof."

"Really?" She arched a brow. "Why, I wonder?"

"Any reason, I suspect. Without the senior Thompson here to ask, we probably won't know."

"So, it's a panic room."

"Yes. There's food, water, blankets, and the entire house can be watched from this laptop."

Why would the man need a panic room? "What's he afraid of?"

"Someone coming for his money, I'd think. There is still several hundred thousand dollars in that safe."

"Robert hasn't needed to come for it." Must be awful to live in fear of someone coming to take what you'd worked so hard for. Made her glad she didn't have millions in the bank.

"Not yet anyway."

Her phone rang. "Detective Scranton." Harper again stepped outside away from the noise of the crime scene.

"This is Nancy Moore. I'm more than happy to answer any question you have. I still live in Oakdale. Can you come now?"

Harper glanced at the time on her phone screen. Close to eight p.m. "Absolutely. Please text your address to this number." As the text came through, she fetched Liam. "She's only fifteen minutes away." Excitement leaped in her chest. "We're going to get something to move us forward, I feel it."

"I sure hope you're right."

Following her directions, Liam drove them to a modest residential area on the south side of Oakdale. Small red brick houses with white wood trim lined the streets. Ms. Moore's house was at the end, on a cul de sac. A basketball goal stood on one side of the driveway. A welcome sign was propped near the front door. A porch light lit our way.

Nancy, a still very pretty woman around forty-years-old opened the door before she could press the doorbell. "Come in. I saw Robby's photo on the news. He's had some work done, but I recognized him. I cannot believe he's…oh, yes, I can." She drew breath sharply through her nose. "Sit. I'll tell you all about Robert Thompson and his father. Anything to stop these killings."

They sat on a plaid sofa in different shades of brown and tan. A coffee pot with four cups and cream and sugar rested on the coffee table.

"I didn't know how many there would be." She poured them all a cup.

A cup of coffee sounded wonderful. "Thank you." Harper added flavored vanilla cream to hers, then glanced up. "Tell us everything you can."

~

Liam lifted his coffee to his lips and rested against the back of the sofa. Hoping, praying, the former nanny could help them find Thompson.

"I got hired at the age of twenty. Robbie had just turned ten. An unhappy, surly kid, but I couldn't blame him. His father was always gone even when at home. The child would be locked upstairs during one of his father's parties." She made quote marks with her fingers. "I, unfortunately, wasn't so lucky."

"Please explain." His heart clenched at what he might hear.

"Well, I was young, impressionable, and he paid me a lot of money to attend those parties." She clenched her hands in her lap. "I refused the drugs but participated in pretty much everything else. I felt desirable and like I actually had the life of the rich." She gave a sardonic chuckle. "How stupid of me. I lived that life for a year before Richard died."

"Then, everything fell apart. Oh, I was still the nanny even when Richard's cousin, the only living next of kin, moved in with his wife, except now I became little more than a slave. The boy was ignored by the adults in the house, and I did everything from schooling him to cleaning that monstrosity. I breathed a sigh of relief when Robbie went off to college, and I quit my job."

"Why didn't you quit before?" Harper set her cup on the table.

"The poor child would've had no one if I did." She shook her head. "I couldn't do that to him."

A good woman. Liam cleared his throat. "That's a sad story, but can you help us find where Robert might be holing up?"

"Right." She jumped to her feet. "His cousin, Larry Thompson, had a penthouse at this address the last I heard. I guess the mansion is too far from the nightlife to his liking." She handed Liam an index card with an address. "The uncle passed away last year. That would make Robbie his only relative."

Why hadn't the department discovered this information the second they knew Thompson's real name? This kind of incompetence could prevent them from ever bringing justice to this man.

Unless, someone in the department, someone working on the case even if remotely, was one of Thompson's followers. He shook the thought off. The man couldn't have eyes everywhere, could he?

He stood. "Thank you, ma'am. This is very helpful."

"I really hope so. Despite his anger, I did, do care for Robbie. It breaks my heart that he has come to this."

"One more question. Were you aware that Robert is trying to better the world by cleansing it of sin? I'm sure you were aware of his father's attempts at the same thing, albeit in a different way. Is there a property somewhere that might be a meeting place for a group of people who follow him in his mission?"

She put a hand to her throat. "A cult?"

"No one else has this information, ma'am. I'm asking you to keep it that way. If the news leaks, we'll know it had to come from you." He hated threatening her since she was so willing to help, but he couldn't have her talking.

"I've kept plenty of secrets related to this family." Her brow furrowed. "I can't think of anything. The Thompson family is very wealthy. It's quite possible they simply never mentioned such a thing in front of me. Or, Robbie could have purchased something himself."

Which should show up if they had someone dig into property sales. He handed the woman a business card. "You have been very helpful. Please call if you think of anything else that might help us."

Once they were back in the privacy of the jeep, Liam turned to Harper. "What if someone working on this case is a follower of Thompson's? Don't you think law enforcement should have dug up some of this information? A man as wealthy as Robert Thompson, his cousin even, would have very little privacy. Everything they did would be news."

Her eyes widened. "We should appoint something, no matter how small, to every single arm of local law enforcement. Whoever doesn't come up with important information would have to be our mole."

"We'd better start digging for work to hand out then because all I got is someone digging in property sales." He turned the key in the ignition and backed from the drive. "That and a penthouse to visit first thing in the morning."

~

So, they'd visited Nancy. He sighed. She'd been the only adult nice to him when he'd been a hurting child. Now, she'd betrayed him. But he couldn't send Lucy after her. He didn't have the heart.

She'd only been doing what she thought was right. His nanny would've done anything if she thought it would help him. Even if helping him meant locking him up.

He grinned and downed the last drop of whiskey from the glass he held. The room behind him, filled with every luxury a man could want, was empty of companionship. Lucy, bored, had accepted another job and wouldn't be back for a few days. He could've called any woman that followed him, but none of them compared to the enigmatic Lucy.

The plain, often beautiful woman, who held him at arm's length. Rather than set him off, her aloofness only made him desire her more.

Below, the headlights of cars created waves of color on the road as a drizzle turned to rain. Not many people strolled the sidewalks at nine p.m., but those who did bustled along, heads down against the rain.

Larry had done well spending the money on this place. It suited Robert much better than the big house. He didn't seem to rattle around as much in the thirty-five-hundred square foot space rather than obscene amount of the house his father had built.

He set the glass he held on a side table for the maid. He didn't fear her turning him in; she thought he walked on water. One more glance out the window, before turning into bed. In the morning, he planned on visiting the big house to see exactly what the detective and agent had dug up.

Chapter Seven

The apartment building that housed Thompson's penthouse stood ten stories high. Not big by New York standards, but grand for those parts.

Harper and Liam, accompanied by the apartment building's manager, rode the elevator to the tenth floor. The manager glanced at them. Liam nodded and the man unlocked the door.

"Please wait out here," Harper said. They didn't think Thompson or his hitwoman were inside, but she didn't want to risk an innocent civilian.

Weapon drawn, she stood on one side of the door while Liam stood on the other. He knocked. "FBI. Open the door." When no one answered, he asked the manager to turn the knob.

No gunshots, no shouts. Harper stepped inside.

Immaculate. As stark and modern as the Thompson mansion but a fraction of the size.

Liam motioned that he would head to the back of the apartment, leaving her to search the great room. She nodded and snapped rubber gloves over her hands, then closed the front door against the manager's curious looks.

The nightstands in the room revealed nothing to even prove Thompson lived there. One held odds and ends for a man, the other for a woman. It surprised her that it appeared his hired assassin shared his bed. She'd thought he'd go for a less frumpy woman. Arm candy.

She checked every box and container in the freezer. Empty. No credit cards like her grandmother had done. Of course, a man as wealthy as Thompson wouldn't have to worry about credit limits.

The apartment looked staged as if an open house would happen soon. Nothing personal. No photos, no books, although an expensive whiskey decanter sat on a sideboard. She moved to the bathroom.

The room was as large as her bedroom. No prescriptions in the medicine cabinet. A vanity drawer held expensive makeup.

Harper scrunched her mouth. The woman she'd seen, the one believed to be the assassin, didn't seem the type. Maybe another woman lived here with Thompson. They'd only assumed it would be the one he hired.

She went in search of Liam. "Makeup in the bathroom."

"A variety of women's clothing in the closet." He frowned. "Cheap department store clothes and not-so cheap designer labels. Two women?"

"One. A woman who can change her appearance as well as Thompson can." Another stumbling block in front of them. "We need to get a sketch artist to do the plain woman's face with makeup and a nice hairdo. Give us something else to look for." But they did have another potential piece to the puzzle.

She studied the clothes hanging in the closet. "Either our assassin is a chameleon or you're right, and Thompson has two women in his life. Maybe he keeps the nice clothes for a special woman in his following?"

"Maybe. He probably needed someone on occasion to attend functions with him." Liam felt around the wall behind the clothes.

"What are you looking for?"

"Another hidden passage." His voice sounded muffled behind the clothes.

Harper suspected it would be harder than a wall panel. She studied the wall of shoes and started lifting them one at a time. When she lifted the Louis Vuitton's on the top right shelf, something clicked. "Found it."

Hair mussed, Liam emerged from the hanging garments. "The built-in dresser swung open." He withdrew his gun and stepped inside.

Harper followed. Definitely a safe room. She backed out and used a boot to hold the door open before rejoining Liam.

Crates of food and water. A queen-sized bed, sofa…a safe

room the size of a studio apartment with all the luxuries they'd seen in the main part of the apartment. "Hiding here wouldn't be much of a hardship."

Liam grinned. "No, it wouldn't." He returned his gun to its holster. "Wonder where Thompson is this fine morning."

"Looking for his next sinner, I suppose." She stepped in front of a wall of monitors. Every room, the street, and the apartment building's front door were being recorded. No one would be able to sneak up on Thompson if he was home.

"I say we wait here a bit. We'll see him coming."

~

So, they knew everything. Robert stood in the entrance to his father's hidden room. The room that had held all the man's secrets. The room Robert had one day intended to burn. Ridding the world of his father's things, the agent and the detective would have been his final cleansing. The fulfillment of his father's quest for a better world.

If he hadn't been so deep into the sinful things of the wealthy, his father wouldn't have needed the oncologist. Without the liquor and indulgent foods, he might not have caught liver cancer. It pained his heart to know that his father had been as much responsible for leaving Robert alone as the doctors had been.

Nancy had done the best she could after Cousin Lloyd took over, but the man's indifference, often cruel way of dealing with his young cousin and cut to the quick. No matter. Robert had made sure the man paid. Now, he owned everything. He had to be careful about his pride. He didn't want to fall into the same trap of sin as the others in his family had.

That's why Robert lived off what he made as a surgeon, leaving his father's wealth untouched in offshore bank accounts. He only wanted to use money he'd earned himself.

He closed the door to the hidden room, aware that he also closed the door on a chapter of his life. As he walked out the front door of the house, he removed a lighter from his pocket, lit it and dropped it in the trail of gasoline he'd left.

~

Liam straightened. The two front legs of the chair he waited in slammed to the floor. "That's Thompson. He's not bothering with a disguise."

"Which means the manager is one of his people." She punched a button on the keyboard and pulled up a view of the lobby. "See? The manager said something to him. He's leaving. So much for waiting in the hall." She bolted from the room.

"Hold up." Liam gave chase. "Take the stairs. We'll cut him off outside." He placed a call to the office requesting backup.

Their feet thundered down the empty stairwell. Liam held out a hand to stop Harper when the click of a door echoed. He put a finger to his lips and peered over the railing.

A well-dressed woman with dark hair had entered the stairwell. On stilettos, she made her way slowly to the next floor. When she did glance up, dark eyes widened at the sight of him and Harper. Recognition flashed.

"The assassin," Harper whispered.

The woman whirled and ducked out of sight. A gunshot rang out, kicking a piece of plaster from the wall.

"Who are you?" Liam returned fire.

"Your worst nightmare." Stilettos flew over the railing and to the floor below her. She fired again and dashed down the stairs.

Liam and Harper gave chase. So much for catching Thompson. They'd have to make do with his hired killer.

The stairwell door slammed.

Liam yanked it open and barged out, almost knocking over a cleaning woman and her cart. "Sorry." He continued his mad dash down a hall.

Swinging doors told him the direction the woman had gone. He glanced over his shoulder to make sure Harper still followed, then entered the kitchen.

Work stopped. Mouths flew open. A young man pointed to the back door.

The door led to a storage room. A door sat open at the other end, framing the alley behind the hotel.

Liam peered outside in time to see the woman climb onto a dumpster and vault over a fence, the dress she wore hiked up to her thighs. Admiration for her athletic skill washed over him until he reminded himself that she was a cold-blooded killer who needed to be in good physical health.

Harper sprinted past him, also seeming to fly over the dumpster and the fence. Liam grinned. This woman he could freely admire.

As he dropped to the ground on the other side of the fence, a shot rang out. His gaze searched the area for Harper. Another shot rang out, and he increased his speed until he found her hunkered down behind a pony wall surrounding a smoker's area behind a restaurant.

"I can't see where she's hiding," she told him.

Where was their backup? Liam risked a peek over the wall.

A bullet kicked up dust near his face. "I couldn't see her either." The woman definitely had the upper hand. He placed another call to the office. "Where's our backup?"

"Stuck on the highway. Multiple car pileup," the receptionist said. "They're trying to clear a way to get through. You'll have to hang tight."

"We're being shot at!" He shoved his phone back into his pocket. "We're on our own for a while."

He glanced around them. "If we stay low, weaving in and out of the few cars out here, we might be able to get around her." It was risky, but they couldn't stay down and allow her to escape. This woman could get them Thompson. "Follow me. Nice vault over the wall by the way."

"Thanks. If she could do it in a dress, I definitely could in pants." She grinned.

They dashed to the nearest car. Another gunshot. Something repeated each time they went from one shield to another.

"She doesn't want to kill us." Liam stopped, back against a delivery van. "Thompson hasn't given the order." He stood and stepped into the open.

"What are you doing?" Harper reached for him.

"Trust me." He held up his hands. "Why don't you come out and talk to us? I have to admit that in my years of service, I've never met someone quite as skilled as you."

"You flatter me, Agent." A soft, seductive voice drifted from in front of him and slightly to his right.

"Then, at least give Thompson a message."

"Which is?"

"That we're tiring of this game and coming for him."

Laughter erupted. "Such arrogance, Agent McConnell. My boss might not be the brain I am, but he's too smart to be captured by the likes of you. No, only someone like me could take him down, and before you get any ideas, I am nothing more than a hired hand. I do not follow his beliefs that this world will ever be what he dreams of it being."

"You're only in it for the money."

"Absolutely. Ciao."

No amount of calling for her would bring her back. He lowered his hands and returned to Harper. "Thompson might be the one telling her what to do, but that woman won't be caught by us. I get the feeling that someday, the tables will turn, and this woman will have all that Thompson possesses." Once that happened, she'd disappear with his riches and never be seen again.

Sirens wailed from one street over. The cavalry had arrived too late.

Liam heaved a sigh and helped Harper to her feet. "Let the games begin."

They met the other officers in front of the hotel. Annie rushed toward him. "The Thompson mansion is burning. Has been for at least an hour. There's no saving the place."

"Arson?"

"Suspected. Several gas cans were located in the bushes. The shooter you were after?"

"The hired assassin. She got away. Good news is the sketch artist will be able to do a good drawing. We saw her face clearly."

Chapter Eight

Lucy threw a zebra print pillow at the TV. "How could you let them get inside? How could the apartment manager have let them in?"

Robert frowned. "They flashed their badges. It couldn't be helped. Besides, you weren't due back until tomorrow."

"They've seen my other face!" She threw another pillow, this time at his head. "You're an imbecile. How you manage to get those fools who follow you to do your dirty work is beyond me."

Robert's blood chilled. He'd never seen Lucy angry before, and the sight scared him spitless. An angry killer was not a good thing. His hand shook as he brought his drink to his mouth. His mind whirled trying to come up with something to say that would calm her down.

"Do you realize that if I hadn't been seen in the stairwell that you would've walked into your apartment where they waited? Now, we're here, in my house, my private space. I ought to kick you out right now."

"I can leave." The ice clinked against the glass as his hand shook.

"No, Robert, you can't. You know where I live now. We're stuck together until I find a new place." She fell back onto the white sofa and pressed a button on the remote. Seconds later, a drawing of both versions of Lucy were on the screen. She cursed. "I need a disguise."

"Surgical?" Hope leaped. That could be his chance to get rid of her before she turned on him.

"Heavens no. I'm not allowing you to cut on me." She

pursed her lips. "A wig, prosthetic makeup, that should do for now. I think I could pass for a college kid, don't you?"

"Absolutely." No. The hard glint in her eyes made her exactly what she was. A thirty-something killer. One that was escalating out of control.

"Fabulous. Find me another job to do before I get bored. Look. The detective is going to say something."

"It's hard to find sinners when I'm locked in this house." He, too, needed new disguises.

~

Harper stared over the sea of reporters, then at the camera. "We have a person of interest in the Seven Deadly Sins Killer case. We believe the man responsible is Surgeon Carl Landry. His real name is Robert Thompson. He is considered extremely dangerous. He is most likely with a female paid assassin. We will put her face on the screen again at the end of this press conference. Anyone with news of either Mr. Thompson or this woman is asked to call the department or the DBI."

A reporter's hand went up. "Detective, can you tell us who was involved with you in the shootout yesterday?"

"The woman we suspect is with Mr. Thompson." Harper pointed at someone else.

"Is it true that Thompson set fire to his mansion?"

"We believe so."

Another reporter's hand shot up. "What about the penthouse?"

"Considered a crime scene."

"What's the next step, Detective?"

Harper smiled. "You know I can't divulge that information." Especially since she had no idea. At this point, they were waiting for Thompson or his hired killer to make another move. "No further questions." She gave the camera a sharp look, hoping Thompson was watching, then marched into the police station.

Liam, who had waited by the door, now opened it for her and followed her inside. "You did good."

"I wanted to challenge Thompson."

"I know you did. Good thing you held back. We want as few innocent people to die as possible."

"Right. Far too many are dying as it is." She sat at her desk and stared at the composite of the assassin. "She'll change her look."

"Yep." Liam sat at his desk across from her.

"Any ideas what to do?"

"Nope. I'm going to browse the internet and study everything I can on Thompson's family and career. Hopefully, something will pop up."

"Haven't the other agents been doing that?"

"Supposedly, but since you and I suspect one of Thompson's followers to be in our midst, I don't trust the information getting to us."

She sighed. "More work for us. Any ideas of the jobs you want to divvy out to try and ferret the mole out of hiding?"

"Working on it."

Harper tapped a pencil on her desk. They had the forensic lab in Harrington, their own small crime scene, Annie, the two other FBI agents, and IT. She didn't count the chief. He couldn't be, could he? She mentally added him to her list, not wanting to put anything into writing that could be found by someone.

"The tapping makes it hard to concentrate." Liam glanced up from his computer.

"Sorry." She gave an apologetic smile. It was easy. All they had to do was ask them to look up something they already knew the answer to and see what happened. Annie would never betray the department. The rookie street cop worked hard. She'd been visibly shaken at the crime scenes. The crime scene techs and forensics would be harder. Especially the techs as they were at every scene.

"We need to go over the bagged evidence from all the sites to see if anything was left behind. Something that's missing."

He straightened. "That's a great idea. Can you get us in?"

"Of course." She dangled my lanyard. "I'm completely trusted. Top of the food chain, so to speak. Small police departments give everyone dual roles. Come on."

"You check everything in?"

"No. James does that, but I am his supervisor. Not that he needs one…" She should add James to the list of alleged moles.

"A man with opportunity."

"Yes." She pressed her keycard to the slot. A loud click sounded, and they entered. "Good afternoon, James. We'll be studying evidence for the next hour or so."

"Sounds good, Harper." The middle-aged man as he waved them through.

The five-hundred-square-foot room had shelves from floor to ceiling on all four walls and more standing shelves making rows down the middle. Harper headed to where the latest boxes should be.

They weren't where they should be.

~

"What's wrong?" Liam peered over her shoulder.

"This is where the files should be. See? Everything is chronological. They should be between the murder we had last year and the domestic violence Annie handled last week." She turned and studied the other shelves. "Sometimes things are misfiled. There are several boxes, so they shouldn't be too hard to find." She gave him the number that would be on each box.

They split up. Liam found one box on a high shelf, another on a low shelf. It seemed done on purpose. He took each of them and set them on a table at the front of the room. Harper found three more and added them to the pile.

"One is missing." She counted them again. "I'll keep looking. You start digging."

"Yes, boss." He grinned at her bossiness and opened the box marked one and laid the items found at the murder of Lance Richardson. Not much. A tie, some carpet fibers, hair from the assassin who had offed herself with poison. Not a lot left behind when the victims were murdered in the nude.

He pulled up the photos from the scene Harper had taken and sent to him, comparing the photos to what lay in front of him. Everything seemed to be in place. He opened the second box.

"Here is the last one." Harper placed the box on the table. "It's from the bookstore explosion. Not much in there. Photos mostly. I'll go through them."

He nodded absently counting the photos on his phone with what was in the second box. "We're missing the reports on the poisoned doughnuts and the clothing of the first assassin." He understood the clothing. Often, a lot could be traced from them, but poisoned doughnuts?"

"There are at least two license plate photos missing from this box." She showed him the screen of her phone. "Someone is definitely tampering with the evidence." She glanced at the door.

He followed her gaze. James stared in at them.

Something slid across the door. He turned and left.

Liam turned the knob and pulled. The door wouldn't budge. "He's blocked us in."

Smoke drifted under the door.

Harper's eyes widened. "If a fire gets in here, we're goners. The whole place is cardboard and paper."

He looked around for something to shove under the door to keep the smoke and flames outside until somebody found them. Someone would find them. Someone would smell the smoke.

Coughing, he removed his shirt, having left his jacket on his chair, and shoved it between the door and the floor. It didn't stop the smoke completely but helped. "Let's get to the far side of the room. Do you have phone service?"

He glanced at his phone screen. "I don't."

"No, this basement room isn't great for that." She headed for the back of the room. "James is the only one who knows we're down here."

"When Annie returns from wherever she is, she'll notice our jackets. She'll come." He slid to the floor, the metal of the shelf behind him cold on his bare skin. "Come." He held out his arm for Harper to snuggle under. "We'll be fine."

"Why, though? Why would James lock us in here? Sure, it'll destroy whatever evidence is left behind, but it's all been logged into the system. Someone would have to go in and remove it all. Getting rid of us won't do anything in stopping that."

He shrugged. "I don't know." What he did know is that he did not want to die in here. He stared through the small window at the flames licking the metal door. "I'm going to break out the window and try to reach the door handle. Find something to shove in the window in case my plan fails."

"You'll be burned."

"I'd rather suffer a burn on my arm, than on my entire body. Death by fire is not the way I want to go." He removed his arm from around her shoulders and got to his feet. Another fit of coughing wracked his body.

"Here." She shoved a bloody blanket into his hands. "We are now burning evidence."

"Can't be helped. Cold case?"

She nodded. "The oldest one I could find."

He wrapped the blanket around his fist and broke out the glass, then cleared the area of shards. The fire singed the hair on his arms as he reached through the small opening. The handle seared his palm. He hissed and felt the door. His fingers gripped the red-hot bar thrust through the handle.

A scream escaped him as the fire burned his forearm, drowning out the sound of the bar falling to the floor. He withdrew his arm, cradling it against him.

Harper used the hem of her blouse to open the door. "Hurry, Liam." With her arm over her face, she leaped over the three-foot flames.

Taking a deep breath, he followed, grateful the fire hadn't grown larger. If it had, he'd be seriously burned rather than what he thought would be minor blisters.

They rushed past James's empty glass-enclosed office and up the stairs to the main part of the station.

The chief's eyes widened at the sight of a shirtless Liam. "What's going on?" His gaze flicked to Liam's cradled arm. "You okay?"

"James locked us inside the evidence room, then set it on fire." Harper grabbed a fire extinguisher from the wall. "Someone grab the one in the breakroom. We can't let it spread."

Liam took the one from the breakroom and followed her while the chief barked orders for someone to call the fire department, then clear the building. A couple of minutes later, he joined them, also armed with an extinguisher.

Since the door was metal, nothing had burned inside the room. The fire had started to eat away at the walls, spreading to James's cubicle.

"McConnell, get to the hospital and have that armed looked at. Harper, you go with him. I'm sending the other two FBI agents to James's address." The chief set his extinguisher on the floor. "Find me when you get back. I'm ready to hear you out."

Something good had come out of the day then.

Chapter Nine

Robert hung up his phone and faced Lucy. "I've got a job for you. It's a simple one, so only half the money. Take it or leave it." What a fool James had been. How dare he step outside the plan?

"Well, well, aren't you an angry hornet." She moved to the bedroom, returning half an hour later looking like a young black-haired beauty around twenty-years-old.

"How do you do it? I thought I was a master of disguise."

"Talent, baby." She patted his cheek. "Text the target's address. Any sin I should think of?"

"Not the one we're currently working on. Only disobedience."

"Boring. Okay, I'll be back in a flash." She waltzed from the room with a bounce in her step making her look even more like a young woman.

Strange that he didn't find himself physically attracted to her. Perhaps it was her bossy attitude toward him. He liked women to be submissive to him, and it had been a long time since he'd had one to care for his needs.

No, he needed to focus on the task at hand. He paced the living room of Lucy's modest house. Like her, the outside didn't match the inside. Expensive furnishings and stylish décor hidden behind the red brick of a home built in the late 70s.

What to do, what to do. He wanted something big to end lust and propel them all into the sin of gluttony. A sin not so different from lust when you think about it. A lust for the physical things, or a desire for excess. He'd need a disguise, too. One he hadn't used before.

A visit to the country club with Lucy on his arm would give him his next target. One that would fit both sins.

He wanted this to end. Once he'd worked his way through the seven sins and rid the world of the last descendants of the men responsible for his father's death, Robert could widen his place for a sin free world.

He'd gain more and more followers. Devoted men and women who would do his bidding without question.

He would become their god.

~

After recounting every single step of the case to the chief and agents again, them finally agreeing to focus their energy on Thompson, Harper had spent the most restful night she'd spent in a very long time. She stretched and tossed aside the sheet.

She sniffed, capturing the aroma of coffee and…something sweet, yeasty, buttery. Her stomach growled.

"Good morning." Liam turned from the stove when she entered the kitchen.

"Are those cinnamon rolls?" She sniffed the air again. "From scratch?"

"Is there any other kind?" He set one on a plate and handed it to her. "Sit. I'll pour you a cup of coffee."

"Thanks." The roll was still warm and gooey when she took a bite out of it. Laughing, she reached for a fork, wishing she were five again so she could eat it as messy as she wanted.

"You've frosting on your lip." Liam wiped it away with his thumb. He lingered, brushing his thumb across her lips. Then, he gave a slow smile and set her coffee on the table.

She told her racing heart to slow back to normal and cleared her throat. "What's the occasion?"

"The fact we'll finally get somewhere. The office agrees with us now. Macey and Harris are going to focus on the mule, leaving us to find Thompson." He sat across from her and cut into a roll. "What bothers me right now is the fact the man hasn't sent a text in a while. They didn't seem to this few and far between before."

"When we hadn't heard from him in two weeks, I had hoped he'd died." She shrugged. "Not the right thing to want, but he needs to be stopped."

"If he'd died, we might not ever have known his identity."

True. She'd have wondered her whole life what had turned this man into a monster.

She jerked as her phone buzzed. She half-expected a text from Robert. Instead, it was a call to work. A neighbor had found the body of James in his home. Another sip of coffee, a big bite of the roll, and she stood. "We've got a body. James."

"The man who tried to burn us to death?" He wolfed down the rest of his roll, then wiped his mouth with a napkin. "Want me to wrap these up to eat later? You barely got any."

"Yes to both." She rushed to her room and quickly dressed in the usual. Dark pants, light-colored blouse, dark jacket. All she switched up was the color of her blouse. A detective didn't need a fancy wardrobe to get the job done.

She tied her hair into a ponytail, clipped her tools to her belt, grabbed her shoulder holster, and then joined Liam in the living room. "I'm guessing James wasn't supposed to try and kill us."

"I'm thinking the same thing. The man paid for that mistake with his life."

James hadn't lived far from her. Same subdivision, which made her nervous. His killer had been two blocks away. Harper shuddered and marched toward the open door where crime scene techs milled around.

Annie greeted them. "Next door neighbor found him when he left for work. Since the front door was open, he stopped and went inside to make sure Mr. Miller was alright. He found him in front of the television, a gun in his hand. Appears to be suicide."

That came as a surprise. She shot Liam a surprised look. "Staged?"

"We'll see." He slipped the paper shoes over his, then gloves on his hands while Harper did the same.

She'd done the same thing so many times, she did it on autopilot. She followed him to the living room.

Blood splatter and brain matter on the back of a recliner and the wall behind James. His finger looped through the trigger kept the gun from falling to the floor.

"Definitely staged." She hunkered down for a closer look. "Someone hung the gun like this. Otherwise, it would have fallen. James died instantly." She straightened. The killer would have left a message. She liked them to know she'd killed again.

She studied the room. Sofa, recliner, end table, entertainment center. A few books lay on a shelf. She studied the titles. All but one had a layer of dust on them. James wasn't much of a housecleaner. She picked up the clean book. "The benefits of Discipline. Liam, I think I found the clue." She flipped through the pages, pulling out a letter written in a sweeping hand and read,

"Unfortunately, disobedience has a price. This man stepped out to do what he wanted rather than his master's. The price of disobedience is death. Ciao." Had to be from the assassin. Harper doubted Robert would end the note in such a flippant way. He took his mission more seriously.

Liam joined her. "It's almost as if he's trying to warn us against disobedience. We don't owe him allegiance. Do you think he wants the note read on the news as a warning, not to us, but to his followers?"

"I think that's exactly what he wants us to do." She bagged the book and the note, undecided whether she would do what he wanted. "I don't like being treated as someone's puppet."

"By not doing what he wants, you might make him angry. Angry people make mistakes. I say hold onto it for now."

She nodded. "He's working toward the sin of anger, anyway: let's help him." She stuck the bagged item inside her jacket pocket. She'd log it at the station, then check it out. If she didn't follow protocol, the chief would have her head.

"Laptop is on a desk in the second bedroom. I'll take it with us and see what we can find out about his beliefs. Maybe something that will lead us to Thompson. He has to have a way of communicating with his followers."

"If you can't get in, do you have a hacker you trust? We don't want to use anyone in the department for anything this serious."

"I have someone." He grinned.

~

Liam didn't need help. James Miller obviously didn't expect anyone to dig through his computer files. In a Word document, he found the man's website logins. One of them was to a social media account that required a person to log in every time.

He leaned back and drummed his fingers on his desk.

Should he? If he did, whoever monitored the account would know it couldn't be James. Dead men didn't need social media.

"I'm in." He glanced over at Harper. "Not sure how far in I should go, though."

She got up and perched on the corner of his desk. "It's no secret that we're looking for Thompson. I say log in. We might see something useful before we're kicked out and blocked. Print out that document. We can search everything of James's."

Liam sent the document to the printer, then logged into the social media account. "No recent meetings. Must be because we're breathing down Thompson's neck."

"No, but he's told his people that he hasn't gone. To stand strong and wait for his word." Her eyes widened. "I don't like the sound of that."

"Neither do I." The man was planning something big. They needed to stop him before he could implement his plan. Easier said than done.

Liam had never felt so incompetent as an agent before. Robert Thompson stayed two steps ahead. He glanced around the bull pen. This small, police department was no way equipped to handle this case. Not even with three FBI agents. "Why hasn't the chief called in help from Harrington or other neighboring towns?"

"That's a very good question." She glanced toward Donnelly's office. "He dragged his feet for a long time regarding Thompson being our guy. Do you think he's a mole?"

"I hate to say it, but we need to consider the possibility."

"How do we work this without giving him updates on the case? Macey and Harris will tell him everything they discover."

"We'll have to pick and choose what to pass on. Whoa." He held his hands up.

The computer screen flickered, then a swirling vortex of color appeared on the screen. Seconds later, the screen went black. "That's it. We won't get anything else."

Harper retrieved the paper from the printer. "Let's start visiting all these before they're shut down. One of them looks like it might be his bank account."

The man's account showed he lived modestly and had no debt outside his mortgage payment. Liam stared at the account with a thousand in checking and five thousand in savings. Did

Thompson expect his followers to not conform to the world's need for things? To be buried in debt?

While Liam strongly suspected that to be the case, they couldn't know for certain without studying the finances of other followers. He logged out of the account and doubted he'd be able to get in again. Instinct told him the man's records would probably be expunged. Within a day or two, there'd be very little to show James Miller had ever been alive.

"Got something." Harper waved him over. "These are the coordinates to their last meeting place. The country club." She narrowed her eyes. "They were having a meeting the day we were there. Tell me you'd recognize some of the faces in that glassed-in room if you saw them again?"

"Absolutely." He felt pretty certain she would be able to. Harper didn't miss much. "Shall we go?"

She shook her head. "We may be working every day right now, but the club is closed on Mondays. They open in the morning at eleven."

"Guess we know where we're having lunch. I'll get us reservations and a membership."

"You can get us a membership? Won't our badges do?"

He grinned. "We're going incognito. No agent and detective, and yes, I can. I have connections. My hacker friend will have us in the country club's system before the end of today. It'll look as if we've been members for a few years. How do you feel about being Mrs. Maureen O'Ryan for a day? I'm your husband, Sean."

"Won't they recognize us?"

"I doubt it. You won't be wearing a suit. Your hair will be down or in a stylish do. Do you own a dress?" She nodded. "Good. I'll be dressy casual. We'll blend right in."

"If you say so." She resumed to typing on her keyboard, muttering something that sounded like, "Of course, I own a dress."

"For funerals and weddings?"

Spots of dark pink colored her cheeks. "Yes."

"You'll need something girly. Like a sundress. We'll stop on the way home tonight. I've seen a women's boutique in this town."

She crossed her arms. "Are you finished bossing me

around?"

"Am I?" He turned his chair to face her. "I'm sorry. I thought we were making plans."

"You're making plans."

"Okay. What would you like to change?"

"Nothing." She gave a one-shoulder shrug. "I'd like to be asked rather than told, that's all."

He chuckled. "Do you mind if we stop after work so you can buy a girly dress?"

"I don't like girly clothes."

"You'll need to fit in. No stern woman detective tomorrow."

"Fine." She sighed and returned her attention to the computer screen in front of her.

He'd never understand women. Shaking his head, he searched the database for the member's list and started looking for photographs. If they've been "member" for a few years, he'd need to know some names.

Chapter Ten

Harper could not believe she'd let Liam talk her into the white sundress with blue flowers that matched her eyes. She felt alien in her own skin. Add kitten heels and she felt like she clomped around like a drunken cow.

"Relax." Liam put his hand on the small of her back. "You look beautiful. You'll fit right in."

Taking a deep breath, she entered the club, doing her best to look as if she'd been there many times. She smiled and nodded at people strolling past until a hostess in black led her and Liam to a table, then handed them each a menu.

"Now what?" Harper asked from behind the laminated list of expensive foods.

"We watch and wait for one of those men who met with Robert."

"Did you notice there weren't any women in that meeting?" She peered over the menu. "And he seems to prefer women assassins." At least, that's all they'd seen working for him.

From behind her menu, she studied those at the other tables. A middle-aged man with his daughter, a few couples, none who looked familiar. No, not the man's daughter. Not the way she reached across the table and placed her hand on his. She shrugged. None of her business. Yet…she couldn't stop glancing in their direction. Something seemed familiar about the two.

"What's wrong? Wait. There's one of them." He jerked his head toward the entrance.

"How are you going to strike up a conversation?"

"Easy. That's Steven Maysup. I recognize him from a newspaper article when he donated money to the hospital." He grinned. "We're old friends."

"Right." She smiled back. "Go say hello." She set her menu down, planning on having the cobb salad.

The young woman in skinny jeans and a baggie shirt stood and headed for the women's restroom. The man stared at something on his phone. Harper got up and followed the woman. If she could get a glimpse of her face, she might be able to place her.

The woman had entered one of the stalls. Harper washed her hands and fiddled with her hair. Isn't that what girly-girls did?

The stall opened.

Harper stared at the reflection of the assassin. "You." She whirled.

The other woman raised a handgun and brought the butt down on Harper's head.

The world went black as she crumbled to the floor.

~

"Yep, she recognized me." Lucy slid into the seat across from Robert. "I knocked her out, but we should really get out of here. If the FBI realizes who we are, then the gig is up."

Robert cursed under his breath. "I had plans for today. Big plans to usher in the sin of gluttony. You leave."

"Fine." She got back to her feet. "I'll be in the car, changing into a different disguise. How do you like a woman in uniform?

"A cop?"

"No, silly. A server." She grinned and flounced out of the building.

He shook his head. The woman was a great actress, he'd give her that. He set his menu on the table. Lucy wasn't the only one who needed to change their looks.

He shot Steven a sharp look as he passed the man and the agent on his way to the men's room. Robert wasn't a fool. He kept a disguise behind a wall panel for such a time as this. One more warning glance to Steven, and he pushed the door open.

When he exited, his hair now fully gray and sporting a beard to match, he scanned the dining room for his next target. A server strolled around the table and refilled coffee. When she turned, she tossed Robert a wink. Ah, Lucy. Good. He'd let her know who to kill next.

His gaze landed on a heavyset man clearly already having had too much to drink and the woman half his age who giggled at something the man said. Robert jerked his head toward them.

Lucy nodded.

~

"It's nice to see you again, Steven." Liam thrust out his hand. "It's been a while. My wife and I were touring Europe. A second honeymoon."

The man frowned but accepted the handshake. "Welcome back, uh."

"Liam."

"Right." He turned to leave.

"So, what have you and the missus been up to? Still going to church?" He doubted that's what Robert called it, but maybe Maysup will let something slip.

"We don't go to church."

"Oh, my mistake. I thought you had mentioned meetings, and, well, I assumed." Liam plastered an apologetic grin on his face.

"I have no idea what you're talking about." He took a step away. "If you'll excuse me, I have someone I need to see." He turned and rushed away.

Definitely skittish but hadn't revealed anything useful. Liam rolled his shoulders, then headed back to the table. Since Harper's phone sat on the table, he expected her back within a few minutes. After ten, a tickle of worry crawled up his spine.

After fifteen minutes, he grabbed her phone and headed for the women's restroom. He opened it a couple of inches. "You in there, Harper?" When no one responded, he opened the door further.

Harper lay on the floor. A knot showed through her hair.

Liam knelt next to her and patted her cheek. "Wake up, sweetheart."

Her eyes fluttered open. "The woman assassin is here. I recognized her. She's dressed like a young woman in skinny jeans and baggy shirt. She's at a table with a middle-aged man that has to be Robert."

With his arms around her, he slowly helped her to her feet. "Come show me. Maybe we can still catch them."

"Okay." She put a hand to her head. "She got me good."

"We'll need to get you checked out by a doctor."

"Not until we find out whether they're still here." The tone of her voice left no room for argument.

The couple no longer sat at a table in the dining room. In fact, Liam didn't see them anywhere. His gaze lingered on each person there. No one who resembled the assassin or Robert in the slightest.

The front window shattered.

A large man fell face forward onto the table.

His companion screamed a split second before she, too, fell.

Pandemonium broke out as people fought to get out of the building.

Liam rushed for the table where the couple slumped. Both were dead from a gunshot to the head. He faced the window. A sniper.

He squared his shoulders. The shooter wouldn't take him out. It wasn't time yet.

Rather than hide, he tried to determine where the shots had come from. The glint from a scope from the window of parked car.

Fire ripped through Liam's arm, spinning him like a top. He dropped to the floor and scuttled to the safety of the hostess stand.

"You're shot." Harper crawled toward him.

"That's what I get for taunting the shooter." He glanced at his arm. "Just a flesh wound. Nothing a few stitches won't fix."

"Looks like we both need to see a doctor." She pulled her phone from her pocket and held it so he could see the screen. *O lust, thou infernal fire, whose fuel is gluttony; ...*

"I guess we're moving on." With a groan, he got to his feet. With his good arm, he pulled Harper up as sirens wailed from the parking lot. The shooter would be long gone.

DEADLY GLUTTON

Cynthia Hickey

Chapter One

Harper sat in a chair while a paramedic looked at the knot on her head and shined a flashlight in her eyes. "My partner needs attention more than I do."

"He's receiving it but will most likely be sent to the clinic for stitches." The man straightened. "You've got a minor concussion. Take it easy for a few days."

She didn't have a few days. Robert had started on another sin. More people would die. "Thanks." She pushed to her feet, gripping the table when a wave of dizziness washed over her. Once she steadied, she made her way to Liam.

"I need stitches." He twisted his lips. "Mind making a pit stop?"

For him? She absolutely didn't mind. "Sure. We need to figure out our next step anyway. I'll drive."

"No, ma'am." The paramedic who tended to her shook his head. "Not with a concussion."

She should've kept her mouth shut. If she could walk, she could drive. She stared at him without responding, until he shrugged and strolled away.

"I can drive with one arm." Liam slipped his arm into the sling he wore.

"I'm fine." She sighed, torn between staying and helping case the scene or get Liam to the clinic for stitches. She chose the clinic. "Come on. The other agents can handle this." She cast one last glance at the two bodies still slumped over the table, then at the shocked faces of those being held in the dining room. She spotted the man Liam had questioned.

He looked resolved rather than shocked. She nudged Liam

and continued to search the faces in the room, finding two more men who looked unsurprised. None of them seem concerned about the dead man and woman. "We need to question those three. I'll get Macey and Harris to have them brought to the station."

"Good idea." Liam gave her a smile of approval and waited near the door for her.

"Sure," Agent Macey said. "We'll take them ourselves, so they don't have a chance to run."

Or kill themselves. "Thank you. We should be there shortly after the rest of you." It would take them a while to finish at the club.

Outside, she glanced for signs of the sniper.

"They shot from a vehicle." Liam stepped to the passenger side of the jeep. "The shooter is gone."

"The assassin?"

"Since she was here, that's a good assumption." He frowned over the hood. "Dark sedan. A Chevy, I think. I couldn't see the license plate. I was too busy trying to duck." He gave a short laugh. "Guess I wasn't fast enough."

She smiled. "Neither of us were." She got into the driver's seat as it started to sprinkle. A peer through the front windshield revealed rapidly darkening clouds. "We're about to get hammered."

"Hopefully not until after we get back to the station."

"What's the next step?" Harper drove from the parking lot.

"I don't think it will be too long before we hear from Robert again. Things are speeding up the closer we get to the sin of anger. After gluttony, we only have three left."

Then things would get really dicey for her and Liam. Robert's anger would only be directed toward them. "I think we need more help on this case."

"The chief is working on it, but since a lot of the deaths are also in Harrington, the precinct there can't spare anyone."

She cut him a sharp sideways glance. "They aren't solving any of the deaths. It's all been pretty much left to us, and we haven't done very well either."

"It will all fall into place." He reached over and patted her shoulder. "We keep moving forward until we get him."

She hated that being their only choice.

~

Robert sat in a leather chair with a zebra throw blanket over the back and drummed the fingers of one hand on the arm while the other hand held a glass of whiskey. It grew tiresome that the agent and detective were harassing his people. They weren't as strong as him. Sooner or later, one of them would cave under the pressure. Not all of them had the fortitude to follow through with being a martyr.

The two needed to be stopped. "Lucy, I have an ongoing job for you. Something for you to do in-between killings."

She set down her phone. "I'm listening."

"I need you to do everything in your power to keep the lovely detective and the Irish agent busy, so they aren't bothering my followers."

"Define power." She arched a brow.

"Anything short of killing or maiming. I'm going to need them eventually. Can you restrain yourself?"

"I'll do my best." She rubbed her hands together. "I'll start immediately. They're at the clinic, and there's a storm coming." She rushed to her bedroom, returning a moment later draped in a black raincoat.

~

Finally, a job that would prevent boredom. Not to mention the fact Lucy would be paid handsomely for it. An ongoing assignment would cost Robert a fortune. Possibly the amount she needed to feel secure about retiring in Europe.

Another glance at her phone showed the two were still at the clinic. It wouldn't take long for her to get there. She'd park out front and wait for them to come out.

Not that she needed to physically follow them, not with the trackers, but she was an opportunist. She couldn't take advantage of an opportunity unless she was there.

Mindful of the increasing storm, she drove carefully to the clinic and backed into a spot as far from the detective's jeep as she could. Now, she waited. Lucy was very good at waiting. She slumped down in her seat and watched the front door.

~

Liam paused as Harper stopped suddenly right inside the clinic doors.

"She's coming for you," she read. "Why? We haven't reached the last sin."

He shrugged. "I don't know, but I don't like it."

The rain came down, and according to the weather on the waiting room television, it wasn't stopping anytime soon. "We'd best make a run for it." He eyed Harper's shoes. "Can you run in those?"

"Maybe not a sprint, but we're going to be soaked no matter how quick we are." She pulled open the door and darted out, splashing her way through the parking lot.

By the time Liam reached the jeep, his feet sloshed in his shoes, and his pants were wet to the knee. There would be no saving the Italian leather shoes he'd splurged on.

Harper leaned forward, peering out the front windshield. "Those clouds look wicked. We aren't under a tornado watch, are we?"

"Not that I know of." He pulled up a weather app on his phone. "A slight chance. High chance of heavy rain and high wind gusts. We need to get to the station ASAP. It says here that it's a fast-moving storm, but I still don't like being out in it." He hoped she could drive in this type of weather. He couldn't. Not with one arm in a sling.

She turned the windshield wipers to high and pulled from the parking spot. "Hold on to your horses. This might be a wild ride."

Tension set in his shoulders the instant they emerged onto the highway, although he preferred to slower speed limit as compared to the interstate. He closed his eyes, said a short prayer for protection, then popped them back open as a blast of thunder boomed.

After ten minutes, Harper pulled over to the side of the road. "It's too dangerous to continue driving. I'll put the flashers on, and we'll wait it out."

He didn't mind some quiet time with Harper. He unhooked his seatbelt and shifted in his seat so he could see her better. "Does the weather act like this a lot in Arkansas?"

"This time of year, it does." Her eyes widened. "Who is that?"

He narrowed his eyes to try and see better. A person in a

dark raincoat stood in the middle of the highway. What kind of idiot did that in the middle of a storm? "Maybe they've had an accident."

"My gut tells me they aren't friendly. The assassin?" She pulled her gun from the glove compartment and set it on the dashboard in easy reach.

Liam did the same as the person came closer. "We can always hope a logging truck comes along and mows her down."

A laugh escaped Harper. "That's awful, but yeah, we can always hope. If it's her. What is she doing?"

"She's trying to intimidate us."

"It might be working…a little."

He had to agree and hated sitting there while she contemplated who knows what. The person took a few more steps closer. He peered harder through the rain. "What's in her hand?"

"A board?"

"With spikes?"

It was the assassin. She stopped and peered through the window. No makeup on her face. Amazing how changed her looks were without it. She grinned and held up two boards, both with spikes.

Liam reached for his gun.

The woman ducked. Was she putting the spikes in front of the tires?

She straightened, appearing next to the passenger door. With a wiggle of her fingers, she strolled back down the highway, until the rain engulfed her.

Harper's phone buzzed with a text. "Enjoy the thorn in your side. Great. We'll be running into her a lot." She reached for her door handle. "I won't be able to get us back onto the highway without puncturing tires. I have to remove those boards."

"You can't go out there. Not until we're sure she's gone."

"If she'd wanted to kill us, she would have. We were sitting ducks. Stupid ducks that didn't shoot her when we had the chance. She's only playing with us. I'm already wet, so it won't matter." She opened the door and stepped into the rain.

Not wanting her to be out alone, Liam stepped out and removed the back spikes while she did the front. Harper opened the back and they both dropped the boards inside.

She peered up at him, her hair plastered to her face. Their gazes locked.

Before he could change his mind, he moved the hair out of her face and claimed her lips in a kiss. If the assassin made a move at that moment, he'd die a happy man.

"I've always wanted to do that." Harper smiled.

"Kiss me?"

"Kiss in the rain." She wrapped her arms around his neck and kissed him.

Chapter Two

Gluttony was more than just eating too much. This particular sin encompassed so many things. While most associated it with overeating to the point of excess, not eating to live, but living to eat, it also stood for greed.

Robert's father had been a prime example on his constant search for wealth and depravity. So much so that he'd not been around much to raise his only son.

He stared out the back window as the clouds opened and dumped a torrent of rain. He'd like to know what Lucy was doing to make the agent and detective's lives miserable but knew she wouldn't allow him to tag along when she worked.

So, here he was, bored to tears, unable to go to the office. His disguises no longer made him feel as safe as they once had. Still, he wouldn't stay locked up until his quest was finished. He needed to find those who were destined to leave this world. To do that, he had to go out.

But, where? Where would be the best place to find the next target? He smiled. The Harrington mall would be the perfect place.

Once the rain eased, he dressed as an elderly man, complete with suspenders and a sweater, and headed for the mall. He shuffled across the parking lot, not making eye contact with anyone, and entered the building at the food court.

People filled the place, shoulder-to-shoulder. Long lines stretched from a variety of food choices. A baby wailed from a stroller while the mother pushed it to and fro in vain.

Robert scanned the place, his gaze falling on an obese man with three burger meals. No one sat next to or across from him.

Possibility number one.

A well-dressed woman, head high, marched past. Trailing behind her was a young woman burdened with bags of purchases. Possibility number two. The woman snapped her fingers, sat at an empty table, and motioned for the girl to get her some sushi.

A third possibility was a woman whose thighs hung over the edge of the chair she sat in. She had several servings of Chinese food filling her table.

The most interesting was the well-dressed woman. Not a glutton for food, but for things. The other two were sad souls searching for solace. This woman simply wanted to collect and possess. Now, how to let Lucy know.

While the woman studied her phone, he snapped a photo of her and sent it to Lucy. Within seconds, she replied that she would be at the mall in five minutes.

Sure enough, she entered through the doors, dressed in her dowdy clothes and wearing a short, curly, gray wig. "Hello, dear." She kissed his cheek and took a seat at a table.

Playing along, he sat across from her. "How will you do it?"

She grinned. "Is she ordering food?"

He nodded. "I believe it's her assistant getting it for her."

She pulled a small vial from her pocket. "I'm a clumsy old woman, dear. This won't be hard. When we leave, we simply go by her table, I stumble, dumping this into her food, you help me right myself, I mumble an apology, and we waltz out the door. She'll be dead in minutes."

"Marvelous." He'd get to watch her at work.

~

By the time Harper and Liam arrived at the station to question Robert's followers, the rain had stopped. She couldn't believe neither of them had pulled the trigger when the woman approached the jeep. Shaking her head, she marched to the interrogation room and asked for the first man to be brought in.

Liam followed her and stood at one end of the table. He smiled when she glanced his way.

A warm flush rose up her neck. So much for not getting involved with someone during an active investigation. She'd enjoyed his kiss, very much, and wanted a lot more of them. His phone buzzed, and he glanced at the screen. "My guy hacked into

James's laptop. He'll meet us when we're done here."

"Great." She made her face impassive as the man Liam had questioned at the club was brought in. "Please, have a seat. Can we get you anything? Coffee? Water?"

"Nothing." He glared at them as he sat.

"Do you mind if we record our conversation?" Without waiting for a reply, Harper pressed the button on the recorder. "State your name."

He glowered. "Not until you tell me why I'm being detained."

She folded her hands on the table and speared him with her sternest gaze. "Sir, we're asking you to assist in a murder investigation by answering our questions. We're questioning every one that was at the country club today." Not a complete lie. Everyone had been questioned, just not at the station.

"Fine. Steven Maysup."

"Do you know this man?" She slid a photo of Robert across the table.

His gaze flicked down, then up. "Nope."

Liam cleared his throat. "Take another look. Name is Robert Thompson."

The man paled. "No, I don't know him."

"I'm afraid we don't believe you." Liam planted both hands flat on the table and stared the man in the eyes. "We saw you in a meeting a few days back with him. At the country club."

The man's eyes widened.

"How could you attend a meeting with no more than ten people and not know the man speaking?" Harper sat back and crossed her arms.

Maysup pretended to study the photo in great detail, then nodded. "Yes, I know him. Not personally, mind you. He's a motivational speaker on finances."

She pursed her lips. "Really?" She leaned forward again. "What are your views on ridding the world of sinners?"

He glanced from her to Liam. "What's this about?"

"I'm pretty sure Detective Scranton's question was clear."

A sneer curled his lips. "I'm all for it, Agent McConnell."

"Surely, you're guilty of sin, Mr. Maysup." Harper tilted her head. "None of us are free from sin. This man, in fact," she tapped the photo. "Has the sin of anger roaring through him. How can you follow someone who is doing the very things he's killing others for?"

"I haven't killed anyone."

"But you would, wouldn't you?" Liam leaned even closer. "If this man were to ask you?"

~

Liam now leaned so close to the man, he could smell the onions he'd had with his lunch. "Mr. Maysup?"

Shaking his head, he moved as far away as he could without leaving his seat. "No. I have a family. A wife and kids."

"What did Mr. Thompson talk about during that meeting?"

The man clenched his hands together hard enough to turn his knuckles white. "Do you know what happens to those who talk? You've signed my death warrant by bringing me here."

"If you help us, we can provide you and your family with protection."

"There's no way to protect me."

"Then you might as well talk." Liam didn't enjoy playing the bad cop.

Harper stood. "We'll give you a few minutes to compose yourself, Mr. Maysup." She jerked her head toward the door.

Liam straightened and left the room. They stood on the other side of the one-way mirror.

"Do you think he'll talk?" Harper exhaled heavily.

"Absolutely."

"What about the other two?"

He shrugged. "Hopefully. We know that Maysup was at that meeting. I'm not sure about the other two. If they weren't, we can't prove they know Thompson."

She nodded. "How long do we let this one stew?"

"Long enough to have a cup of coffee." He smiled and led her to the breakroom. "Are we going to tell the chief about today?"

"What? And tell him we sat there and did nothing?"

"I wanted to see what she would do. It isn't time for her to kill us."

"No, but now we have to look over our shoulder every minute for the next time she pops up." She poured a cup of coffee and added cream and sugar.

Liam chose his black. "I'll start worrying when we're on the last sin."

When they'd finished, they returned to Mr. Maysup. Harper sat without speaking. Liam stood against the wall and remained silent. After a few minutes, the man started to squirm.

"All he did was talk about the sins and for us to keep our eyes open and let him know if we knew of someone committing one of them that he could take care of." He hung his head. "I've not given him a single name."

"Why not?" Liam cocked his head.

"I agree in making the world a better place, but not by killing people. I think we can teach people to be better."

"How good of you." Harper smirked. "You're still backing a killer. You knew of his crimes and did nothing. That makes you an accomplice."

"Are you going to arrest me?"

"I'm sure we can make a deal. Know where Thompson is?"

The man shook his head. "He's disappeared. No one has heard from him since his identity as the killer was made known."

Liam believed the man. He pulled a business card from his pocket. "We'll let you go, Mr. Maysup, but we need you to call if you hear from him. Got it? If we find out you don't, we will put you behind bars."

"What about protection?"

"We'll get that taken care of. Wait in the waiting room while we discuss this with the other agents." Liam opened the door for him.

Maysup couldn't get out fast enough, banging his shoulder on the door frame on his way.

Making the man wait, they interviewed the two other men. As Liam had suspected, neither had attended the meeting, and neither knew Thompson's whereabouts. Like Maysup, they approved of cleansing the world. One of them didn't care that Thompson's method was murder. Liam really wanted to arrest the man but had no grounds.

"We need a man and his family put under protection," he told Macey and Harris. "Can you take care of it. He's in the waiting room. Name is Steven Maysup."

"Yeah." Macey nodded. "Get anything out of him?"

"Nothing to help us." He told him about the assassin, the spikes, and the text.

"You and Scranton watch your backs. I don't like this."

Neither did Liam, but he'd do almost anything to put a stop to Thompson's game. "We'll be careful."

He joined Harper in the bullpen and started writing his report. He glanced over to where Harper typed. Neither one of them would have a very long report. They'd left before the scene at the club was fully cased.

He added meeting the assassin in the rain. The chief's head would explode when he read about it, but since there wasn't anything they could do, he'd have to get over it. If he or Harper had shot the woman, they'd have a less chance of finding Thompson.

Kill his assassin and he'd simply hire another one.

His phone buzzed at the same time as Harper's. "Got a murder at the Harrington Mall. Food court."

Chapter Three

Harper stared down at a young girl no more than twenty-five-years-old while she sobbed out her story. A crowd had gathered that Annie, Macey, Harris, and finally, some loaned officers from other towns were having a hard time corralling. Either folks wanted to press close to hear better or they wanted to bolt from the mall. "What's your name, ma'am and how do you know the victim?" She spoke in as soothing a voice as she could and still be heard over the crowd.

"Susan Washburn. I'm…was…Mrs. Chandler's assistant." She raised red-rimmed blue eyes. "I'd just brought her the Asian salad she wanted and a bowl of Miso soup."

"Did you see anyone near her?"

"An older couple. The woman stumbled against the table, and the old man helped keep her from falling. Mrs. Chandler cursed. I think some of the soup might have spilled on her dress. I'm not sure what happened." She covered her face with her hands. "I'd stepped away to get my own lunch when I heard her fall."

Harper eyed the bags around the table. "These purchases all hers?"

Susan nodded. "She got bored easy. Mr. Chandler is gone a lot, so she shops to fill her time."

"Don't leave yet. I may have more questions." Harper stood beside the deceased who had toppled from her chair and now lay among the purchases she might have gotten a bit of joy from if she'd had the time.

A bit of lettuce hung from the plastic fork beside the Styrofoam box. A cardboard bowl of soup, the spoon on the edge of the table, had been spilled across the table. If Harper was to make an assumption, she'd guess poison. It wouldn't take long for the lab to find out.

She glanced at the entrance door as the crime scene techs rushed in, then joined Liam doing crowd control. "The assistant mentioned an old woman stumbling against the table. Wanna bet it was our assassin? The old man with her most likely Robert. I think they slipped poison in the victim's lunch."

"It doesn't look as if the woman eats too much. She could've stood to gain a few pounds."

"Maybe it's the abundance of packages that drew their attention to her."

"Do you know her?"

Harper shook her head. "I might have seen something in the papers, some charity event or something, but the name Chandler doesn't mean anything to me." She turned to the crowd. "Anyone here see anything?"

"I did." A older woman's voice boomed out in direct contrast with her tiny bird-like frame. "I was sitting next to the couple that bumped into her table."

"Please, ma'am, come with me." Harper led the woman to a table away from the crowd. "Tell me what you heard or so."

"Plenty, I'll tell you that." Back ramrod straight, she folded her hands on the table. "My name is Ethel Lynne. I heard them talking about bumping into her table after they mentioned her purchases. Then," she tilted her head. "The woman pulled out what looked like a sample of perfume. You know, like one of those tiny vials? Anyway, I filmed the whole thing." She fished in a giant purse the color of eggplant and pulled out a cell phone. "I'm not sure if you can see her dump anything in the woman's food, but I did follow them to try and get a better look. In today's world, it's best to be prepared for anything, you know?"

Harper bit her lip to keep from smiling. This woman might be the gold mine they needed. "I'd like to see it." She waved Liam over.

Mrs. Lynne turned her phone so they could see the screen and pressed play.

A gray-haired man and woman, leaning heavily on each other, shuffled toward the victim's table. Harper couldn't clearly see their faces, but she felt certain she saw enough of the woman's profile to peg her as the assassin. The woman stumbled. Her hand hovered over the bowl of soup before the man righted her. Then, they rushed toward the doors like young people.

"Ah, you can see the vial." Mrs. Lynne tapped the screen. "Isn't it coincidental that they could suddenly move very quickly? When my sweet Hobart was alive, we watched crime shows and unsolved mysteries all the time. I learned a thing or two. I always film people who act a bit strange. Then, when I get home, I watched the video to determine whether I should alert the authorities."

She wanted to tell her she shouldn't be recording people without their knowledge, but it happened all the time. Instead, Harper thanked her and exchanged an amused glance with Liam before returning her attention to the elderly woman. "Here's my cell phone number. Please forward that video to me."

"It's helpful, isn't it?" The woman seemed very proud of herself.

"Yes, ma'am. Very helpful." Once the video had been transferred, Harper and Liam returned to the crowd. No one else seemed to have paid the old couple or the victim any attention.

"At least we're pretty certain of what happened." Several hours later, Liam returned with her to the jeep. "We'll give the chief a copy of the recording, then take a look at James's laptop."

"Sounds good." She liked knowing what their next step would be. Waiting to hear from Robert or his assassin made her stir crazy.

~

"That was fun." Robert tossed his wing on Lucy's table.

"Don't get used to it. I prefer to work alone." She headed for the bedroom.

He scowled after her. He paid her the big bucks and deserved to tag along if he desired to. The woman needed to learn some respect. He shed the sweater he wore and poured himself some whiskey before settling in front of the television. Their little adventure would be on the news soon.

He didn't have to wait long before some talking head stood in front of the mall. The cameraman followed her inside the mall, focusing on the crowd converging around the crime scene and blocking the view of the body. Pity. He drained his drink and refilled his glass. The news was more entertaining than a blockbuster movie.

"Why are you watching that? We lived it." Lucy breezed past. "There's nothing to be gained in gloating. Isn't that a sin of pride?"

Was it? He set his glass down and turned off the TV. He couldn't commit the very sins he was cleansing the world of. What kind of example did that leave?

"Oh, don't look so sad. You aren't perfect." Lucy handed him another drink. "Drown your sorrows and do better." She sat across from him and crossed her legs.

"Very well." She was right. Maybe him slipping up a bit would make him more humble. Isn't that what was needed? A humble man was what the world needed to lead it to becoming a better place. "Thank you." He raised his glass in his toast.

She shrugged. "I told you everyone sins. What amazes me is that somebody is concerned about sinning. Why fight something you're going to do anyway?"

"Because it affects others."

"Oh, and murder doesn't it?" She arched a brow. "Make up your mind as to which side you're on, Robert."

His fingers curled around the glass. He fought the urge to throw it at her, bouncing it off her head, shoving the shards into her skull. Someday, when he no longer needed her. She'd be the first person he killed with his own hands.

~

Liam booted up the laptop his IT guy had dropped off. Rather than go through it at the station, he and Harper took it to her place. They still didn't know who the mole was and weren't taking any chances.

"We got one break today, let's hope we get another." Harper peered over his shoulder.

"Today's break confirmed Mrs. Chandler's killer, it didn't help us find them. I'm hoping James was a wise man. Or a neurotic one." He scanned the files listed.

So far, nothing out of the ordinary. Bills, photos, insurance information. This wouldn't be as fast as he'd hoped. Still, for the first time since the first pride murder, he felt as if they were moving forward with the case.

"Ah ha."

"What?"

"A file named Things I Want to Remember. I found it in miscellaneous." He clicked on the folder. "Wow." A list of names, the place Robert normally holds his meetings when too many people want to attend and won't fit into the country club conference room. He made notes in parenthesis.

"This is a great score." She placed a hand on his shoulder. "James didn't trust Robert one iota."

"It doesn't appear that way." Liam straightened. "But why rebel and try to kill us?"

"Keep digging. Maybe you'll find out. Look for a ledger or diary of some sort. I'll order a pizza." She stepped away, leaving him to keep digging.

By the time the pizza arrived thirty minutes later, he'd found a document where James listed everything that was spoken about at Robert's meetings. From the notes, it was obvious James wasn't comfortable with the escalating deaths and feared for his life if he said anything to the authorities. Hence the reason he tried to kill him and Harper.

His failure got him killed.

Liam straightened in his chair as Harper set a plate with three slices of mega-meat pizza in front of him. "Here's the answer to one question at least."

She glanced at the screen. "He actually thought if he killed us, no one would know? Robert has eyes everywhere. James had to know that."

"The man was too scared to think straight. He'd also been pilfering evidence. I think the guilt became too much."

"Then why not do a murder/suicide?" She bit into a slice. "It doesn't make sense to me."

"Let me keep looking." He turned his attention back to the laptop.

By the time he found what he was looking for, his eyes burned, and his mind spun. The man intended on getting Liam and Harper out of the picture so he could confront Robert himself. It wasn't guilt at all that spurred the man on, but greed. "He wanted to be a partner and was going to blackmail Robert."

"Idiot." Harper shook her head. "I would've never pegged

him for such a person. He'd always seemed so nice."

"Money can motivate some people to do despicable things." Unfortunately. He stretched his arms over his head, then got to his feet. "Tomorrow, we round up the people on this list."

"Do you think we'll find Robert?"

"Nope. I doubt any of them know where he is. Maysup said he hasn't been in contact since the news plastered his name and face everywhere. Other than the mall, the man stays out of sight." They would find him. Liam wouldn't stop until they did.

He met Harper's gaze. Neither would she.

With the two of them, the other two agents, and five borrowed officers, it would be a big task bringing them all in. "We should go to bed. We've got a big day ahead of us tomorrow."

She nodded, her gaze still locked with his. As if they were drawn together by an invisible thread pulling them together, they moved toward each other.

He knew they shouldn't get involved. It wasn't a wise thing to do during a murder investigation, but he couldn't help himself.

Wrapping his fingers in the long, silky strands of her dark hair, he pulled her close, his gaze landing on her lips. He told himself again that they were making a mistake right before he claimed her lips in a kiss.

Chapter Four

Harper rushed into the large ranch house, following close on Liam's heels. "Police!"

A man bolted from the kitchen and out the back door. The other two agents gave chase.

Harper continued through the house checking each room. Hiding in the walk-in closet was a woman and two grade school children. She put her gun away. "Ma'am, you'll need to come with me. Is there someone you can call to care for the children?"

She nodded, eyes wide in a pale face. "Where's my husband?"

"Being detained." Harper motioned for the woman to leave the closet and watched as she called someone from a bedside phone.

After making the call, the woman took the two children to the kitchen to wait. Harper hated scaring the family, but she seriously doubted that the wives were ignorant of what their husbands were involved in. At least most of them, anyway.

They had ten people to round up, and this was only the first house. If they weren't taken quick, the others would be alerted and flee. She cast a look at Liam, then toward the door.

"We need to move faster."

He nodded. "The chief has help. Don't worry. We'll get them all. Once they're all rounded up, you and me are to question the wives, then the husbands. The chief wants the husbands squirming a bit."

It was all taking too long. "The others can handle this. Let's move to the next house." They'd been assigned this one, but she wanted to be involved in the rounding up of every man in each house. One of them could tell her where Robert hid. The man wasn't a phantom.

"If you're willing to risk the chief's lecture, then I am, too." He followed her to the car and stared at her over the hood.

"What?"

"Don't let this consume you, Harper. Don't become obsessed to the point of running yourself into the ground."

She narrowed her eyes. "We have a psycho killing people. Have you forgotten?"

"Kind of hard to forget." He opened the door and slid inside.

She got in the driver's seat. "Then, there is no slowing down."

"Once, I worked a serial killer case. One that involved the death of children."

She pulled away from the curb and headed toward the next address. "I'm listening."

"I became consumed. Got sick. I couldn't do anything, then, and someone else had to step in."

"Did they catch the guy?"

"Woman. And, yes, she was caught. She kidnapped children, thinking they could replace a child she lost. When they couldn't, she killed them and took another."

Harper could see shutting out everything else to stop a woman like that. "This is different. I want Robert caught before we get to the last sin. That's when he comes after us." She cut him a sharp glance. "The assassin is very good. We won't see her coming." A trickle of ice water coursed down her spine.

"Sure, we will." He grinned. "When the time comes, I plan on drawing her into the open."

"What's your idea?"

"Still working on it. We've got some time."

How did he do it? Instead of a sense of urgency, which Harper had, Liam coasted. He did the job, and did it well, but while Harper's nerves twanged every waking minute of the day, Liam treated this exactly like it was…a job.

Maybe someday, she'd be able to compartmentalize her life, but not then. Way too many things occupied her mind. The case, Liam, the impending feeling of doom…

When they pulled up in front of the next house, the place

looked deserted. She took a deep breath and exited the jeep. Two officers paused in the middle of the driveway.

"Thought we were doing this alone," one of them said.

"We're here to help." Harper studied the house. "What do we have?"

"Looks like the residents skipped, but we haven't checked the place. You want to take the house and we'll take the backyard?"

"Sure." Liam stepped to her side. "It looks deserted, but it doesn't feel deserted. Know what I mean?"

She did. The hair on her arms stood at attention. Elephants stampeded through her stomach.

Rather than try the front door first, she peered through the garage window. "Car inside." Was it running? "Liam!" Using the butt of her gun, she broke the glass. The stench of carbon monoxide hit her in the face.

She counted two heads in the front seat. She broke another pane of glass. "I can't reach the handle."

"Automatic door opener." He sprinted for the front door. With a well-placed kick, it broke open.

Harper gave chase, catching up to him as he fumbled with a deadbolt. "Someone locked them in."

"Looks that way." He got the door unlocked. Pulling his shirt over his nose, he led the way into the garage, pressing a lever on the wall to open the garage door.

The driver's side door was locked, resulting in another broken window so Liam could reach in and open the door. He grabbed a man by the shoulders. Harper repeated his actions on the other side.

As she pulled the woman free, she spotted two heads in the backseat. Her heart sank. "Kids in the back."

~

From her vantage point in the house across the street, Lucy watched the drama unfold in the garage. How convenient that this house happened to be up for sale? She did like to watch the repercussions of her work.

While she enjoyed killing, she didn't relish murdering children. So, she hoped she'd done enough to spare their lives.

It hadn't been difficult to subdue the parents as they tried to flee. Then, she'd locked them all inside and turned on the car. Maybe not exactly what Robert meant when he'd told her to make things harder for the agent and the detective, but Lucy knew different. The attempted murder of two small children would mess with the detective's head.

She'd make mistakes. Thus, making it easier for Robert to get his revenge when the time came. Lucy lifted the binoculars to her eyes in order to get a close-up look.

The agent removed one child, the detective the other. They pulled the N-95 masks from the children's faces, both leaning over for signs of life. The detective pulled a radio from her belt as she nodded at her partner.

Good. At least one child lived.

~

Thank God, the children were alive. Unfortunately, the killer hadn't taken the same care with the parents. Liam lifted one of the little girls in his arms and carried her to the grassy lawn where she could breathe the fresh air until the ambulance arrived.

Harper lay the other girl next to her sister. "Why kill the parents and save the children?"

"Maybe our assassin has a bit of a conscience." He knew in his gut who was responsible. The back of his neck prickled. They were being watched.

He stepped closer to Harper, hoping to shield her if danger came. His gaze fell on a for sale sign. Curtains over the front window twitched. She stayed behind to watch.

"Stay here with the girls." He darted across the street and around back where he thought the woman would flee.

Shots out front pulled him back to the street. The roar of a motorcycle engine faded.

Harper stood in the street, gun aimed, the other two officers on each side of her. "She got away. She started firing, I ducked, and she got on the bike." Shoulders slumped, she returned to the girls.

"You okay?" He ran his gaze over her, relieved not to see blood.

"She wasn't trying to shoot me, just provide a way out." She stared down the street as sirens wailed. "Do you think she'll do this at another of the addresses we're headed to?"

"I hope not." What did these deaths have to do with glutton? Or were they simply to keep him and Harper running from one place to the next?

"Once the ambulance is here," one of the officers said. "You two go. We can handle things here."

"You sure?" Liam clapped him on the shoulder.

"Absolutely. Go stop this creep."

The ambulance pulled into the driveway. Paramedics rushed toward the children, shooting glances at the garage. After explaining what they knew about the children's condition, Liam and Harper rushed to the jeep and sped away.

Which house had the woman gone to? He and Harper had them lined up so they wouldn't have to go far, then back. Was the woman going to do the same thing? Either way, she'd gotten a big head start.

At the next house, seeing officers already bringing a man out, they barely slowed before racing to the next address. Neither spoke, the tension in the vehicle thick as swamp mud. Harper's knuckles were white as she gripped the steering wheel.

As they neared their next destination, Liam rolled down his window. The roar of a motorcycle sounded in the distance. Were they too late?

Not this time. The couple in the garage hadn't been in there long enough to succumb to the toxic fumes.

"She's going to keep doing this?" Harper dragged the woman from the garage.

"Yes." After depositing the man next to his wife, he called the chief. "We need to make sure officers are at every one of the remaining addresses.

"I'll have to find some more."

"Make it fast, Chief or we won't have very many followers to question." Not at the rate the woman killed. "With me and Harper having to wait for first responders at each place, we can't catch up to her."

"I'm getting helicopters in the air. We'll get her."

~

Robert listened to the man on the other end of the line blather on about the police arresting them all. He whirled as Lucy barged into the house. He narrowed his eyes at the sight of her wearing skintight leather. "You look like a cat burglar." He returned his attention to the phone.

"Run. Do not let them catch you. If they do, and you're released, you know the consequences." His world was rapidly dissolving. What kind of a leader would he be without followers? He'd have to start all over once the agent and detective were disposed of.

"I've been busy. I'm hitting the shower. I'll fill you in when I'm done."

Robert barely listened. His mind whirled. "Call the others and get out of town. Leave your family behind if you have to. They're safer without you." His blood chilled as the man continued to talk.

"They're already dying! Someone is going around locking people in their garages with the car running. Where am I supposed to go?"

"The church. Tell the others. There is food and water for weeks." He hung up and barged into the bathroom.

The room felt like a sauna from the hot water. Robert's hands curled into fists. He should've brought a gun or a knife. He could end the woman's disobedience right here.

She shoved aside the curtain, mindless of her nudity, and smiled. "You told me to make things hard on them. Don't be upset because it's not the way you would have done things." She reached on a shelf above the shower and removed a gun. "If you approach, I will shoot you. I can always get another job."

"Stop making decisions without me. You're killing my people." He stepped back, his gaze on the barrel of the gun.

"If they were taken to the police station and interrogated, you'd have me kill them anyway." She pulled the curtain closed again. "Go away and let me shower in peace."

One of these days, Robert would stand over her dead body and laugh.

Chapter Five

Robert sat glued to the television set as a camera recorded six of his followers and their wives being ushered into the police station. Six. All that was left after Lucy took matters into her own hands. Hopefully, a couple had managed to escape. There was no mention of any deaths. "From now on, terrorize the agent and detective without killing off my people. Or anyone I don't tell you to. Not everyone deserves to die."

"Of course, they do. Even us." She handed him a box of takeout Chinese. "Haven't you ever been to church? Heard the Bible stories?"

"Don't tell me you believe the fantasies." He dug into his chow mein, desperately wishing for a fine dining experience again.

"I didn't say that." She refused to elaborate further.

Let her keep her silly thoughts to herself. As long as she obeyed him, carried out his will until he was done with her, he'd put up with her moods.

He returned his attention back to the television. Questioning his people would most likely take all day. Then, he had some serious decisions to make. Did it really matter at this point whether his people talk? No one knew where he was. No, it wouldn't solve anything to have Lucy kill them for talking.

"Why don't you stop sulking and tell me what you would like my next move to be?" Using chopsticks, Lucy lifted noodles to her mouth.

He thought for a minute, his hand holding chopsticks halting halfway to his mouth. What did he want her to do? He was supposed to be ridding the world of people committing the sin of gluttony, but here he sat, feeling worthless and bored.

"I need to go hunting."

"Sounds like a marvelous plan."

~

Stupid man. Lucy tossed her empty container in the garbage. Would he ever realize one man couldn't rid the world of sin? She shrugged. As long as he thought so, he'd continue to need her services. Her bank account continued to grow. Soon, she'd have more than enough money to retire in Europe in style.

Maybe she'd get married, start a family. Raise the next generation of assassins. She smiled and grabbed the bag to carry outside.

"Hello."

Lucy glanced over to see a middle-aged woman with rollers in her hair peering over the hedge. "Hey."

"I see you've got a man living with you. I saw him leaving the other day. Your father?"

Nosy old broad. "Old family friend."

She nodded. "I saw a man about my age, then an older one. Lucky gal." She grinned and bustled back into her house.

Lucy heaved a sigh. Nosiness got a person killed.

She climbed the steps to the woman's porch and picked up the pruning shears the woman had set on a small wicker table. Then, she raised her hand to knock.

~

Harper stared at the woman in front of her until the woman squirmed. She folded her hands on the table and leaned forward. "You mean to tell me that you've never asked questions when your husband goes somewhere?"

She shook her head. "It's not a wife's place to ask questions."

For crying out loud. Harper fought not to show how she felt about women living under a man's thumb. "Did your husband ever mention a Carl Landry or Robert Thompson?"

She glanced at her chest. "I've used Doctor Landry for a…" She waved her hand in front of her. "Was contemplating a nose job but couldn't justify the expense. There's really nothing wrong with my nose other than a slight flair."

They'd gotten horribly off topic. Harper glanced at Liam.

He cleared his throat. "Did the doctor ever say anything alarming? In regard to sin, perhaps?"

She shrugged. "He mumbled something about pride once, but I didn't think anything of it. Why would a plastic surgeon have a problem with his job?"

Good question. Harper believed it was so he could find his victims easier. "You're free to go ma'am. We aren't finished questioning your husband."

Liam opened the door for the woman, then turned back to Harper. "This isn't going anywhere."

"We still need to question the wives, just in case. We have one more, then can start with the husbands." She doubted any of them would give any worthwhile information.

"I'll get us some coffee." Liam left her alone.

Covering a yawn, she glanced at the mirror. Seconds later, Chief Donnelly entered the room. "I agree with you, Detective. We can't skip over anyone. If the men won't talk, we'll keep them in holding overnight. Let them stew about their future."

"Yes, sir." She glanced past him as Annie escorted the man's husband into the room. Right behind her was Liam with the coffee. "Would you like anything Mr. Washington?"

He shook his head. "You have no right to retain me."

The chief scowled and marched from the room.

"Have a seat, sir." Liam put a hand on the man's shoulder. "We're only asking you a few questions."

"I want a lawyer."

Harper sighed and pushed a table phone to him. "We'll wait." She sipped her coffee and Liam leaned against the wall as Mr. Washington placed the call. Then, they waited half an hour, in silence as thick as Arkansas clay, until the man's lawyer arrived.

"Why is Mr. Washington being questioned?" The lawyer took a seat next to his client.

"Because we strongly believe he's an accomplice to murder." Harper gave a cold smile.

"What? No! I would never…" Mr. Washington glanced from her to Liam to his lawyer.

"But you were aware of Mr. Thompson's beliefs, correct?" She arched a brow. "How he wanted to make the world a better place?"

"Of course. I believe the same, but I've never killed anyone."

"But you knew he did."

"No." His eyes widened.

"My client has nothing more to say without an arrest warrant." The lawyer stood and looked down his nose at them. "These are preposterous claims against Mr. Washington. Come Lawrence. They cannot legally keep you."

"Leaving, Mr. Washington, will be looked at as an admission of guilt." Not really, but Harper was grasping at straws.

~

Tired of standing to the side, Liam approached the table. "You may go, sir, but we will be watching you. Without speaking to us, we have no reason to offer you protection. You do know what happens to Mr. Thompson's followers when they talk to us, don't you?"

"Enough." The lawyer gripped Washington's arm.

"Wait." He yanked free. "My wife and I need protection."

"Are you willing to talk?" Liam smiled.

"Yes." Against the lawyer's protests, his client dismissed him and resumed his seat. "What do you want to know?"

Liam sat next to Harper, pressing his knee against hers in a congratulatory way. "Where did Mr. Thompson hold his meetings other than the country club?"

The man rattled off an address. "It's a converted warehouse."

"How often were the meetings held?"

"Bi-weekly at first, but since all this started happening, they got sporadic. The last meeting was at the country club. There hasn't been any since Mr. Thompson's face was plastered on the news."

"During the meetings, did Mr. Thompson ever mention his methods of making the world a better place?"

"No. He only spoke about the need." The man shrugged. "Got boring sometimes, but we all agreed the world needed help."

They weren't getting anywhere. "Were you aware some of the followers had no qualms about doing Mr. Thompson's bidding?"

He swallowed hard. A look of panic crossed his face. "He did, on occasion, ask us how much we were willing to do for the cause. A few said anything."

"You?"

"I committed to donations of my money, not to kill."

"So, you were aware?"

He hung his head. "We all were."

"I'm going to need a list of those willing to do anything."

Harper left and returned with a pad of paper and a pen. She flashed Liam a grin and slid the pad across the table.

They soon had five names that matched a couple of those waiting to be questioned, and others that matched men dead that day. Waiting was a Mr. Preston and a Mr. Carter. He rubbed his hands together. "Let's talk to Mr. Carter first." Finally, they were getting somewhere.

The man met their gazes with a stony one of his own. He plopped in the chair across from them and crossed his arms.

Harper showed him her phone. *Gluttony is not a secret vice – Orson Wells.*

Liam understood the quote, but how did it pertain to their case? What person had Robert targeted? It sounded like someone who would be well known. He forced his mind to focus on the man in front of him.

"We've been told, sir, that you were willing to do anything for Mr. Thompson. Did that involve killing someone?"

His face darkened. "Not yet."

Harper's mouth fell open. She snapped it shut. "Are you saying you would've been willing to commit murder if Mr. Thompson told you to?"

"I believe in the cause that much."

Liam's jaw hurt from clenching his teeth. "Who did?"

The name he gave matched one of the deceased. "Now, my life is in danger. What are you going to do about it?"

"Unfortunately, nothing. You made your bed, Mr. Carter. Now lay in it." Liam waved at the mirror for the man to be removed and Mr. Preston brought in.

Before they could question him, the chief entered the room and told them they had a homicide. He slapped an address in front of them. "Mr. Preston will have to wait."

"My family? Are they dead?" His gaze whipped back and forth.

"No. It isn't your family." He spun and left.

Harper followed, Liam on her heels. Lights flashing and sirens blaring, they sped to where police had a residential street blocked off.

Harper parked beside a squad car. Liam and she ducked under the crime scene tape and marched toward a red brick house with black shutters.

Annie met them on the porch. "It isn't pretty." She handed them gloves and slippers. "Victim's name is Gloria Bomber. Age fifty-five. A neighbor walked by and saw the door open, but no sign of Ms. Bomber. Thinking her to be inside, a…" she flipped through a couple of notes. "Mrs. Young went in and found her right inside the entrance."

"The neighbor here?" Liam glanced around.

"The woman leaning against my car. I told her you'd want to speak with her."

"Thanks, Annie." Harper moved past Liam as he snapped his last glove into place.

The victim lay on a mosaic-tiled floor with a pair of garden shears poking from her chest. Her eyes had been cut from her face and put in a glass with a daisy.

"This isn't because of a supposed sin." He glanced into a living room, then a dining room. "This is something else."

"Considering the eyes were removed, I'm guessing she saw something she shouldn't." Harper hunkered next to the body. "This is only a guess, but what if she was pruning her bushes and saw something?"

"Which means she would've seen something close." Liam darted outside. "No one leaves this street! Absolutely no one."

He marched to Mrs. Young. Her story matched what Annie had told her.

"Which house is yours, Mrs. Young?"

"That one." She pointed across the street. "My husband and I are newlyweds. We're renting. Ms. Bomber was so nice to us."

"Do you know the rest of the neighbors?"

"No. I'm normally at work. The only reason I know Ms. Bomber is because she brought us a plant when we moved in. The other neighbors seem to stick to themselves. Can I go now? I'm about to fall to pieces."

Liam released her with an order not to leave town or the street until she received permission. He studied each of the houses, all red brick. An assorted array of colors for shutters. Some doors had a window, some didn't. Every yard landscaped differently. A beautiful, non-cookie cutter neighborhood.

One where either Robert, the assassin, or both were staying.

Chapter Six

Robert, wearing his best disguise ever, sipped a tea at the park across the street from the country club and tossed bird seed to the myriad of feathered friends that hopped at his feet. Who would expect a little old lady with bird pooh on her shoes to be searching for the next person who needed to pay?

Having lived among the country club set, he knew the right person would attract his attention. A person who had so much and thirsted for more.

The roar of a car engine drew his attention to the Mustang convertible that pulled into the parking lot. Three teenage girls climbed out, all leaving a heated kiss on the boy driving before practically skipping into the country club. The boy stayed until they were inside, then turned the car around and parked at the park.

Robert ducked his head, pretending to stir his tea with his finger. Not a gross practice he would actually do, but it allowed him to watch the young man. He recognized him as he strolled closer. The mayor's son, Reynold Sharpe.

He sat at a concrete picnic table and pulled something from his pocket. Two other boys, clearly not the country club type dressed in baggy jeans and hoodies, emerged from the tree line and sat across from Reynold. One slapped money on the table, pocketed the small bag of white powder Reynold and placed on the table, then got up and left without a word.

A smile spread across Reynold's face. So, the mayor's clean-cut, All-American boy dealt drugs.

An entertaining idea took root in his mind. He pulled a syringe from his pocket and slumped over, calling for help.

Reynold glanced over his shoulder, then lunged to his feet. "Ma'am." He rushed to Robert's side only to receive a needle in his neck for his kindness.

"The escape room would be child play compared to what I have planned for you." Robert laughed and slung the boy's arm around his shoulders. Now to meet Lucy at their new hiding place.

~

"Door-to-door?" Harper glanced up and down the street, dreading the task. Already, folks stepped onto porches, curious to know what had happened at their neighbor's house. There'd been no time for law enforcement to keep things under wraps and folks in their homes until questioned.

Time enough for Robert and his lady killer to run.

"That seems our best course of action." Liam put a hand on the small of her back. "We can move faster if we split up. I'll have the other two agents take the other side of the street, and we'll canvas this one."

She nodded. It didn't matter to her. Robert was no longer here. All they could hope for was that someone would've seen him leave. Saw the woman. Noted the type of vehicle. Taking a deep breath, more out of frustration rather than needing oxygen, she headed down the sidewalk with Liam at her side.

The first door they knocked on no one answered. Harper tried peering through the blinds to see whether anyone was home and ignoring them or if, strange as it seemed with the excitement on the street, the residents had actually left to go on about their daily routine.

"Let's check the back before moving on." Liam pushed open a wood and iron gate that led to a yard high with weeds. "Guess they don't care about the back as much as the front."

"Or the neighbors complain if the front yard gets like this." Harper climbed three steps to a deck stained barn red. "Back door is open a bit."

"Like the residents left in a hurry?"

She nodded. "That's what it looks like."

"Excuse me." A pair of dark eyes peered over the fence. "Can you tell me what's going on over there?" Her gaze jerked to the crime scene.

"A murder, ma'am. You should stay in your house." Harper

reached for the door.

"Those folks aren't home. Left with packed suitcases a couple of hours ago."

"They?" Liam approached the fence. "A man and a woman? Can you give us a description?"

"Well, I didn't know her much, even though she's owned this home for a bit. The man is new. Quite a few years older than her, too, but that's none of my business. They came and went at odd hours, rarely together. I thought he might be her father."

"A description?" While gossip often provided needed details, what they really needed was confirmation that Robert and his assassin had been here and what they left in. "Did you see what kind of car they drove?"

"That's easy. Lucy always drives a silver Mercedes."

Lucy? Harper arched a brow at Liam. Did they finally have part of a name? "Do you know her last name?"

"No, I'm afraid we rarely spoke. She was a bit…stuck up, if you know what I mean. Lucy has dark hair, dark eyes. Sometimes she looks quite fancy, other times as if she's wearing my grandmother's clothes. The man is bald and starting to get a spare tire around his waist." She lowered her voice. "I think something wrong was going on over there. Drugs maybe. All kinds of people came and went."

Robert and Lucy in disguise would be Harper's guess. She took down the woman's name, thanked her for her help, and entered the house. They didn't have more information per se, but they did have confirmation about this house. Enough confirmation to suit Harper anyway.

She withdrew her weapon and held it at the ready even though she didn't expect to see anyone inside. The scuff of his shoe signaled Liam right behind her.

Wow. She glanced around the state-of-the-art kitchen. A fridge big enough to hold two people inside, a black granite countertop that sparkled in the morning sun streaming through custom blinds. She moved to a stylish living room with a television that took up one wall.

A sideboard took up another with an array of crystal decanters, glasses, and very expensive Scotch. The assassin business obviously paid very well.

On a glass side table sat a half empty glass of amber liquid. A wine glass rested on the matching coffee table.

Harper turned and headed down the hallway, pausing in front of the first bedroom. A man's room from the style of clothing left behind. Articles on the floor and across the bed. Robert's room.

The master bedroom was clearly a woman's with a white canopy four-poster bed. The open closet showed a few articles of clothing from thrift store to glamour. Same with a few pairs of shoes. Yes, these two had left in a hurry.

She peered at a pair of white sneakers. Rust-colored dots marred the right toe. "Liam."

~

"Want to bet that blood matches our latest victim?" Liam studied the drops on the shoe.

"I'm going with that." Harper turned. "I doubt they left anything behind that would identify them, but let's search anyway."

He nodded. "I was about to search the home office when you yelled. Bag those shoes, please." He headed back the way he'd come and stepped into a minimalistic office. Glass and metal desk, metal filing cabinet, oil paintings of ocean scenes on the walls.

A desk plotter occupied the spot where an empty laptop stand stood. He ran his fingers lightly over the paper. He didn't feel any indents to signify note taking or appointments. The office didn't look as if it were used much.

He tried to open the top drawer of the filing cabinet only to find it locked. He doubted this Lucy woman would have anything in there to identify her anyway. No, she'd hide anything with her name on it, if, and it was a big if, she had bills to this house under her real name. Which Liam doubted.

Still, they had a first name and an address. They'd be able to get something. He sent the little info they had to the IT guy he trusted at the agency. If anyone could find out Lucy's surname, it would be his guy.

"I think we're done here." Harper glanced into the room. "Nothing out here."

"Give me a minute, okay?" He sat in the leather office chair and felt for a latch, a button, anything that would open a secret drawer. Most expensive desks had them and…a faint click let him know he wasn't wrong.

The bottom drawer which seemed to be deep enough to hold files wasn't as deep as it seemed. The bottom lifted up to reveal several Manilla envelopes. He grinned up at Harper. "Want to bet this is good stuff?"

She laughed. "You're always wanting to bet when you know I'm going to agree with you."

Standing, he tucked the envelopes under his arm, tempted to leave them. If they were important, Lucy would be back for them. He paused. "We need to find more of these envelopes and paper to put in them. I don't want her to know right off if she comes back that we took these."

"You want to set a trap?"

"Absolutely. Then, we'll ask more questions of the neighbors, just in case someone saw something." Anything. "Maybe Macey and Harris found out something."

"I doubt it. We got lucky." Harper led the way back through the kitchen and around the house to the street.

The medical examiner's van sat parked in front of the victim's house. Two men wheeled a gurney from the house with the victim's body in a black bag.

Harper stowed the bag with the bloody shoes in the back of her jeep as Macey and Harris joined them. "Find anything?"

"We've questioned everyone on this street. Not a difficult task when they're all out here watching the show," Macey said. "But all we've got is some vague descriptions and the fact that the occupants of that house," He jerked his head toward Lucy's. "Weren't very friendly but had lots of company coming and going." His gaze landed on the envelopes Liam held. "Looks like you did, though."

"Maybe." Liam put them with the shoes, then closed the back of the jeep. "We'll know more when we can go through what's in them."

"We could take them off your hands." Harris gave a slight smile. "Give you more time to pound the pavement."

"I appreciate the offer, but I'd rather go through them myself." Especially since he didn't know who he could trust completely other than Harper, the chief, and his IT guy. "I'm hoping they'll reveal something that can send the two of you on a hot trail."

The phone in his pocket buzzed. He reached for his at the same time Harper reached for hers. This usually meant one of two things. Robert or the chief.

He read the text. "*Remember how much fun the escape room was? Let's try something even better. Even bigger. In two minutes, I'm going to begin a video. This video is live and the link will be posted on every news channel. In this video, a young man, Reynold Sharpe to be exact, will be put through several dangerous trials. Trials that could end his life. Not a great loss, considering he's a glutton of drugs and sex, but I digress.*

"*You cannot interfere outside of what I command you to do. If Reynold succeeds in this chain of events, I will release him to his father in one piece. If the two of you don't follow my orders, I'll send the son to the father in pieces. Wait for the next instruction.*"

Liam's gaze speared Harper's. "Who is Reynold Sharpe?"

"The mayor's son."

Chapter Seven

It was only seconds later that a link to watch Reynold live came through. Soon, the entire state would be watching a poor teenage boy play games for his life. Harper wanted more than ever to see Robert Thompson in the scope of her gun.

Her screen flickered to life after she pressed the link. Reynold, eyes wide over his gagged mouth, stared straight into the camera. The room looked as if it were made from cement blocks. His hands were bound with zip ties. She hoped the boy watched a lot of movies. Zip ties were one of the easier things to get out of.

From off to the side, Robert spoke. "Reynold has one hour to free himself and complete the task. A simple task, really. He must get to the tree by the lake in Oakdale that had been struck by lightning last year. Under that tree is a bag. An empty bag." He laughed. "Reynold, along with Agent McConnell and Detective Scranton, must put their hands on the bag at exactly the same time. One o'clock this afternoon. If not, my assassin will shoot Reynold."

The teen bounced in his chair, screams emanating from his gag.

Harper glanced at the time on her phone, then at Liam. "It's exactly noon." She set the timer on her phone.

A muscle ticked in his jaw. "Let's pray the boy makes it."

"He'll never make it on foot. This is all a ploy to keep us from searching that warehouse."

He nodded. "We'll have to find the time. I see a lot of sleepless nights in our future."

So, did she. She turned her attention back to her phone screen.

Reynold had watched television or at least videos. He made short work of using his shoestrings to saw through the zip tie before yanking the gag from his mouth. "Help me! That freak isn't here right now."

A horn blared, then Robert's voice boomed over a loudspeaker. "Better get going. You're wasting time. Now, put that camera set around your neck."

Reynold slapped his hands over his ears, then raced out of the camera's view. A minute later, the screen showed not only Reynold's viewpoint, but his terrified face.

He ran through a patch of trees and burst onto the highway, waving his arms. A semi-truck swerved, then slowly came to a stop.

Reynold raced toward it. "I need a ride to Oakdale."

"What's that around your neck?" The bearded driver frowned.

"College initiation."

"The boy's quick thinking. He didn't alert the driver to possible danger." Liam breathed sharply through his nose. "Let's hope he keeps his wits about him."

"Okay, college kid, where to?"

"Oakdale lake or as close as you can get me." Reynold stared out the passenger side window.

The fear in his eyes ripped at Harper's heart. If he didn't keep thinking straight, keep doing what Robert told him to for however long it entertained the man, the boy would die by a sniper's bullet. Simple as that. She wanted so much to put a stop to the terror the boy endured.

"How long will it take for us to get to the lake?"

She tore her gaze from the screen as Mayor Sharpe rushed toward them. "Ten minutes. Here comes the frantic father."

The mayor, tall and fit, with light brown hair swept away from a strong forehead stopped in front of them. "I want to know what you're doing to help my son, Detective."

"Agent McConnell and I are going to do our best to follow this man's orders until an opportunity to grab Reynold presents itself. Otherwise, your son will die." She met his angry stare with a stern one of her own. Realizing how frightened the mayor must be, she softened her tone. "We will do everything in our power,

Mayor Sharpe. I promise."

His nostrils flared. "Make sure you do. What kind of a madman makes a young man run for his life live on every social media and news station around?"

"You said it, sir. A madman." She glanced back at her phone as the truck driver let Reynold out in the parking lot of the lake. "Time to go, Liam." She didn't want the boy out there alone if she could help it. "Mayor, why don't you go over there where the chief is? You'll be kept up on anything that happens." Without waiting for an answer, she marched to her jeep.

"How much time do we have?" Liam asked, sliding into the driver's seat.

"Fifteen minutes and twenty seconds."

~

Robert rubbed his hands together and sat back in the leather chair of the country cabin that remained in Lucy's family despite everyone being dead but her. Until they discovered her real last name, which even he didn't know, they should be safe there. Plus, the house had a basement perfect for the games. His phone rang. Lucy.

"How do you expect to get the boy back her for the night?"

"It's all part of the game." He rolled his eyes. "I'll simply have him go somewhere, and you pick him up. Law enforcement won't follow if I tell them not to. They won't risk the boy's life."

"I'm not so sure about that. They might consider him collateral damage if it means getting to us. Don't be naïve." She hung up.

He reached for the glass of Scotch on the side table next to the chair. His fingers curled around it, pretending to close around Lucy's throat.

Robert wasn't stupid. He knew the risks involved in his latest game, but until he got through all the sins, proving to the world the dangers of such sins, he needed to stave off boredom.

Sending the two people he most wanted to punish running in circles, prohibited from helping Reynold provided the most entertainment of all. He paid Lucy to do what he told her. If she stopped, he'd rid the world of her and hire someone else.

He straightened; his gaze locked on the television as Reynold reached the path that circled the lake.

~

Liam climbed from the vehicle. Reynold spotted them and froze.

"Help me." He folded his hands as if in prayer. "Please."

"We can't." Liam's heart dropped. "We'd best hurry if we're going to make it to that bag."

"Less than five minutes." Harper took off running. "Come on, Reynold."

Three pairs of feet pounded the dirt path as they raced against time.

"There's the bag." Reynold darted forward.

"Not yet!" Liam gripped his arm. "How much time, Harper?"

"Fifty-three seconds. We can't touch the bag until exactly one o'clock."

Liam prayed Robert had the same time they did. He watched the countdown on Harper's phone. When it started down from ten, he reached out, not touching the bag until the buzzer sounded at zero. Simultaneously, they all three touched the bag.

"Now what?" Reynold glanced from Harper to Liam.

"We wait to hear something." Were they supposed to keep their hands on the bags until Robert contacted them? He hadn't said anything about releasing the bag, and Liam didn't dare assume anything.

His phone buzzed. He glanced at his screen the same time Harper did hers.

"This is too funny. You may release the bag. I never intended you to stay hunched over indefinitely. Now, for our next task..."

Liam waited for a full minute before Robert continued.

"We've time before nightfall to play some more. You three have thirty minutes to row across the lake to the other side. First, you need to find a way across. Enjoy. If you succeed, Reynold will be given instructions on returning to me until tomorrow. Let him know this is what happens when you are a glutton."

His shoulders sagged as he stared across the expanse of water. "Any idea where we can get a boat?"

"There are canoes stored not too far away. They're free for anyone to use." She set another time on her phone and led them down the path to where three canoes were piled on top of each other. "If we all three row, we might be able to do this."

"You can't let me go back." Reynold shook his head. "I can't."

"We don't have a choice at this point." Liam grabbed an oar from the ground and thrust it into the boy's hands. "He won't harm you. Not while we're playing the game. We stop doing what he says, and you're dead. Come on. This isn't going to be easy."

He slid a canoe into the water. Harper, you take the front. Reynold, center, and I'll be in back. We'll be stroking long and hard to get across. We'll need to be in unison. Either of you ever rowed before?"

Reynold nodded, while Harper shook her head. "Nothing more than a kayak," she said.

"Any of those around?"

"No."

"Let's go then."

"Dig deep. Right. Left." Liam chanted the order.

Soon, the canoe sailed across the smooth surface of the water.

"Fifteen minutes." Harper glanced over her shoulder. "We're not even halfway across."

"Paddle harder." His arms burned from the repetitive motion.

Reynold grunted with each dip of his oar into the water. "My arms are going to fall off."

"Keep paddling."

They'd found their rhythm by now and cut through the water like an ice skater on ice. They were going to make it. He knew they would.

"Five minutes." Harper hunched over and dipped her oar in the water. "Do we have to be out of the boat?"

"I don't know. He only said to reach the other side." Liam studied the tree line.

Something glinted from the dam. The scope of a sniper rifle? The idea spurred him to chanting faster. "Right. Left. Right."

"One minute."

The boat scraped against the opposite shore. The three of them toppled out, lying on the bank like stranded fish.

"What did this man mean by me being a glutton?" Tears streamed down Reynold's cheeks.

"You must have too much of something." Liam's breath slowly returned to normal. "What were you doing when you were taken?"

"Dealing drugs." He choked on the words.

"Before that?"

"Dropping girls off at the club. I kissed all three of them."

Liam fought to keep a smile at bay. "I'm sure your kidnapper believes you're a glutton for girls."

"He'd be right, then." Reynold sat up and hugged his knees. "With this stupid camera setup around my neck, everyone knows now. My dad is going to kill me."

Liam felt pretty sure the boy's father would be too happy to see him alive. He glanced at his phone again as it buzzed. "He wants you to go stand in the parking lot. Someone will pick you up. The detective and I are to stay here. He didn't give a time limit, but I don't think you should dawdle." He met Harper's stricken gaze.

"I don't want to leave you." Reynold shook his head hard enough to flop his hair across his face.

"We'll see you again when the game resumes tomorrow." Liam put a hand on the boy's shoulder. "Keep doing what the man says. You'll be okay. Now go. Don't keep him waiting. Can you do this?"

Reynold stood. "I don't have a choice." He took off running down the path that would circle the lake.

It took all Liam's willpower not to follow. Not to take down whoever arrived to give the boy a ride.

He faced Harper. "Looks like we have the night off. Let's go to where Robert held his meetings."

Chapter Eight

Harper stared out the front windshield at what Robert's man had called a warehouse, but in fact was nothing more than a strip mall. A simple metal sign over double doors simply stated Enlightened. "Sounds more like a spa than a cult."

"Not a spa I'd go to." Liam got out of the jeep and straightened his jacket. "Looks deserted."

"No meetings now that Robert is in hiding." She eyed her phone screen where Reynold, attached to a bolt in the wall by a long chain, sat at a folding table and ate a fast-food burger meal.

So far, the number of people watching around the world had reached over a million. The kid would be more famous than he'd ever dreamed of being. Or ever wanted to be.

Harper tore her gaze away from her phone and followed Liam to the front doors. They opened easily at his touch, prompting both of them to pull their weapons. Liam held a finger to his lips.

She narrowed her eyes. Of course, she knew to be quiet. She hadn't made detective by being stupid.

Flashing her an apologetic grin, Liam entered the dimly lit building. Nightlights guided them through an atrium and down a hall. On each side were restrooms labeled Men and Women. What looked like classrooms were past those. If she didn't know any better, she'd think it nothing more than a contemporary-style church.

Their shoes tapped against the tiled floor, signaling their presence to anyone listening. Liam slowly pushed open a set of swinging double doors that led to what must be the sanctuary if Robert called it that. Rows of about thirty chairs led to a raised podium. A whimper came from Harper's right.

She froze, then motioned to Liam to circle around the other direction. He nodded and followed her directions, the multi-colored indoor/outdoor carpet muffling his footsteps. Harper circled around the opposite direction.

Huddled under one of the chairs was a young girl around six-years-old. Harper knelt beside her. "Are you here by yourself?" She held out her hand. "Come out. I won't hurt you."

"Don't touch her." A woman, hair dripping on the towel around her shoulders, burst into the room. "Elena, come here."

The child scampered out and wrapped her arms around the woman's legs.

Not wanting to frighten them further, Harper got slowly to her feet. "I'm Detective Scranton. This is Special Agent McConnell. We aren't here to hurt you."

"I know who you are." The woman's lip curled. "You're the reason my husband is gone, and my daughter and I are hiding."

"May I ask your husband's name?"

"Maysup."

Harper nodded. "It's for your protection that he's gone, ma'am. Please, have a seat. We'd like to ask you a few questions."

"I don't know what I can tell you."

Harper waved to a seat.

"Only if you promise to take us somewhere safe. This is nowhere for us to live."

"We'll do our best." She glanced at Liam who nodded.

The woman took a seat and pulled her daughter onto her lap. "Ask your questions. If you want to know where my husband is, I don't know."

"We'v already spoke to him." To appear less intimidating, Harper turned a chair around and had a seat while Liam watched the doors. "Is there anyone else here with you?"

The woman swallowed, her eyes darting from one corner of the room to the other.

"Mrs. Maysup?"

She sighed. "There are two other families. Women and children only. None of us knew where else to go. Here, we have running water and a roof over our heads."

"I see the reasoning in that." If they looked on the place as their church, it would be a true sanctuary for them. "Have you heard from or seen Robert Thompson?"

"No. I heard he's on the run. That he's been killing people." Her eyes shimmered. "That wasn't supposed to be the vision. Sinners should be punished, yes, but not killed. Not like that."

"I can't agree more. Please call the other families. We'll get a vehicle here to take you to the station. From there, we'll find somewhere else for you to stay." She stood as the woman and child left the room.

Maybe they'd come back, maybe they wouldn't, but Harper wanted to help get them somewhere more comfortable. She turned to Liam. "We will be able to find them a place, won't we? Not a woman's shelter?"

"I'll make some calls." He smiled.

Harper called for the station to send a van, then turned on the live feed showing Reynold stretched out on a cot, an army blanket over him. Somewhere cool, then. Most likely a basement considering the block walls. The late summer weather outside wouldn't warrant such a blanket.

She made another call to Annie requesting a list of all homes in Oakdale and surrounding rural areas that had a basement. Reynold couldn't have been far considering he reached the tree at the lake on time.

"How's the boy?"

"Sleeping." She leaned against the back of the chair. "It's ten o'clock. Early for a teen."

"He's had a rough day." Liam leaned against the wall. "Ah. I hear the women and children. I thought maybe they weren't coming."

"I thought the same thing." She pasted on a smile as three women and five children joined them.

~

Robert should have thought of something to do during the night rather than let the boy sleep. No show on TV could entertain as much as watching the local law enforcement chase after a boy they couldn't save.

"I'm getting antsy." Lucy swung her foot over the arm of a chair.

"You're getting paid to be here." He stared at her swaying

foot. So white and delicate. Would he have been attracted to her under different circumstances? When she looked like herself and not the dowdy version, yes. But she'd never be as submissive as he liked which meant he'd soon have walked away.

"Why are you looking at me like that?" Her forehead furrowed.

"Like what?"

"As if I'm a slice of prime rib."

He shook his head and turned his attention back to the screen. Reynold had turned onto his back, mouth open in a snore. How exciting.

"I'm simply as bored as you are."

"I'm sure all the viewers are on the edge of their seats." She studied her nails. "I could take a knife in there. Let people think I'm going to start cutting pieces off him."

"No. He won't stand a chance if he's exhausted."

She stared his way. "You haven't seemed to care in the past."

"These is a boy we're dealing with. He's young enough that this experience can change him. He isn't as set in his sin as an adult."

She started to laugh. A head back, mouth wide laugh that burst from her gut. "You're a nutcase."

Again, the urge to choke the life from her almost overwhelmed him. So strong was the urge that he marched from the room before he could act.

~

After a van from the station arrived to drive the women and children to the station where they'd later be picked up by someone in the agency who knew of a safe house, they could finally go home.

Home. The same place Harper laid her head. At least for now.

He woke at sunup the next morning and reached for his phone. Reynold still slept, and he hadn't received a text from Robert. They could start the day without urgency. Wanting to try and catch more sleep but knowing his mind would only whirl with details of the case, he climbed out of bed. He'd need to be ready to go at a moment's notice.

The door down the hall closed. Harper had beat him to the bathroom. Okay, then, he could start the coffee.

By the time she joined him, dressed in her usual dark pants and white blouse, he'd almost finished his first cup. "Sorry. I couldn't seem to move faster than a sloth." She poured herself a cup.

"Not a problem." He gave her a soft kiss on the forehead and went to shower.

"He's awake." Harper held up her phone when he came back to the kitchen. "Breakfast time."

"At least he's getting fed." Another fast-food meal, this one pancakes. "Either Robert or Lucy leave to get this food or they have it ordered. Do all the fast-food places deliver?"

She grinned. "No, and those that do won't drive past a certain distance. We're going to narrow down where Reynold is." She darted from the room and returned with her laptop. "We can start calling right now. Someone delivered those pancakes. Hopefully, they'll remember the address."

A few minutes later, she had five numbers. The first one she called hadn't made a pancake delivery that morning, the next delivered a breakfast, but not pancakes. On the third, she scored and put the phone on speaker.

"Yeah, we had several pancake deliveries today."

"Do you know whether one of those customers also had a burger order around five o'clock yesterday?"

"Hold on. That'll take a minute." She set the phone down with a clank.

Harper held up crossed fingers. "We really need something good here, Liam."

"I can't agree more." He gave her shoulder a gentle squeeze. "One step for us." He hoped.

Muffled voices came through the phone line. He pulled a chair close to Harper and sat. The woman on the other end hadn't lied about it being a bit. It had already been five minutes.

Harper rested her chin in her hands and stared off into space. "This better not be for nothing. And why haven't we received a text?"

Liam glanced at his phone. "It looks like Reynold just finished eating. We should receive one soon…No wait. Someone dragged in a water hose. He isn't shackled anymore." From the slighter build, he guessed the person to be Lucy.

She sat the hose on the ground. "Strip to your underwear."

"What?" Reynold's eyes widened.

"You can't run around all day in wet clothes. Strip. I'll count to three. You won't like it if I say three. One."

Reynold started stripping. He'd learned quick not to mess with this woman. "Are you really going to shower me with a hose?"

"Yes. Here's a bar of soap." She tossed a green square at him. "You'll smell all fresh. Brace yourself. Bet the water's cold."

The world watched as she kept a steady spray of water on the boy. Using the soap, he washed his hair and every other exposed part of his body. When he'd done, he dropped the soap and gave Lucy a belligerent sneer.

"Enjoy that?"

She laughed. "You wish. There's a towel on the hook. Dry off and get ready for a whole new day." She made him kissy noises, then the slam of a door.

Reynold flipped a bird in her direction, then started to dress.

"He's getting defiant." Harper shook her head. "Defiant teens often don't follow orders. That won't be good."

"He seems to be a smart kid. He'll realize that not following orders will get him hurt." If not killed.

Harper held up a finger as the fast-food clerk picked up her phone. "Ok, Detective. We had two houses that ordered burgers for supper and pancakes for breakfast. How do I know you're who you say you are?"

"Are you watching the news? Do you know about the kidnapped boy being recorded?"

She yelled out to someone about a kidnapped boy, then returned. "What's the detective's name on the case?"

"Harper Scranton. I'm with Agent Liam McConnell."

"Okay, but anyone watching the news would know your names. Give me your phone number and I'll text you the addresses."

Liam gave her his number. Two minutes later, he had the addresses. He smiled at Harper. "Let's go get em'."

Chapter Nine

Lucy slammed her phone on the table. "Get the kid. We gotta go. Now."

"What? Why?" Robert jumped to his feet, sloshing a bit of his drink on his hand.

"The detective's tracker shows them headed this way. They found us somehow." She started tossing things into a duffel bag. "We have ten minutes. I've got to use part of that to set this place on fire. Now go!"

Robert tossed a few things of his own in a bag, grabbed the filming equipment, and stashed it all in the trunk of Lucy's Mercedes. Then, he thundered downstairs to the basement and turned off Reynold's camera.

"Are you letting me go?" Hope leaped in the boy's eyes.

"No. We're moving locations." He gripped Reynold's arm and dragged him to the car where he gagged and bound him before shoving him into the backseat.

Lucy threw things in the trunk, slammed it closed, and climbed into the driver's seat. "I've got one more hiding place, Robert. You better start moving through the rest of those sins fast before we run out of options."

She drove them up the mountain to a secluded cabin that had seen better days. A sagging porch, rotted wooden steps, and boarded up windows. "No luxury here, I'm afraid. No heating and air. Water comes from a well. Here's to roughing it." She opened her door and stepped into knee high weeds.

Robert's mouth hung open. He couldn't live like this. "We'll go to a hotel."

"Can't risk it with the boy." She marched toward the cabin.

With a groan, Robert exited the vehicle and pulled Reynold from the back. "Think of it as camping."

"I've never camped a day in my life unless you count resorts." His eyes widened.

"I have, and I hated every minute of it. Let's go. We've a game to set up."

~

"They went off air." Harper restarted her phone. "Why would they go off air?"

"I don't know, but I don't like it." He pressed his foot harder on the accelerator as Harper turned on the whirling red light to signal other drivers to move over.

It didn't seem like Robert to stop his game in the middle, but if he had started to unravel, who knew what he would do? She called the station and asked Macey and Harris to meet them at the address they were headed to.

Despite Liam keeping the car at 80 mph, it seemed as if they crawled to their destination. Fear threatened to choke her. What if Reynold had been overly defiant? Would Robert have had him killed?

Wouldn't they have seen the boy's behavior on camera? She shook her head in an attempt to stop the questions spinning out of control.

"Is that smoke?" She peered through the front windshield.

"Yep."

A fire truck, sirens blaring, sped past them.

Harper's mouth dried. "It's got to be Lucy's house." She felt it in her bones.

When they reached their destination, Harper darted toward the fire engulfed house. "Did anyone check the basement? There was a teenager in there." She raced around to the back despite orders from the firemen to stay back.

Liam grabbed her around the waist and lifted her off her feet. "Stop. Let the firemen do their job. You aren't close enough to help Reynold."

"Let go of me." She kicked backward, connecting with his shin. "Don't you dare manhandle me ever again." She whirled to face him. "How can you stand there and do nothing?"

"Because the roof is about to fall in." As if his words were the only thing holding back the collapse, the roof caved in with a groan. Burning embers floated into the sky, bright orange against an azure blue.

"Reynold." They'd failed him. She buried her face in Liam's chest, not caring that she didn't look like the tough detective she tried to be.

His arms wrapped around her, providing a small element of comfort. "Stay strong. We don't know that he's under there. There is no sign of Robert and Lucy. Maybe they took him with them."

"How would they know we were coming?" His jacket muffled her question.

"I've been thinking about that. Come on." He led her back to the jeep. "I called my IT guy last night and gave him both of our numbers. I think we're being tracked."

"My phone hasn't been where someone can snatch it." She pulled her phone from her pocket.

"If a person is good enough, they can put a tracker connected to your phone number. They don't need your phone in their possession."

"New phones?"

"Most likely. It's just a theory, though."

"Makes sense to me." She turned to where the firemen gained entrance to what was left of the garage. It didn't appear as if a car had been inside. Hopefully, Liam was right, and Reynold had been taken away. A glimmer of hope grew.

Macey and Harris stopped behind her jeep. "Anyone inside?" Macey asked, hurrying toward them.

"No." Harper shook her head. "We don't know about the basement yet."

"So, they got away again." He sighed.

Liam explained his theory about the trackers. "I want to get new phones, but that would prevent Robert from being able to contact us. I'm not ready to end the texts. They're the only lead we have."

As much as she hated the idea of being tracked, Harper agreed with him. They couldn't sever the only contact they had with Robert.

A fireman shoveled hot ashes and debris aside until he revealed the gaping hole leading to the basement. "Doesn't look as if anyone is down there."

The tension fell from Harper's shoulders.

~

"We're back." Liam showed Harper the screen of his phone. "Looks like a cabin."

Reynold had been shackled at the ankle to the pipe of a wood stove. No gag, so they were somewhere noise didn't matter. Misty Mountain?

"If they're on the mountain, it'll take a year to find them." Harper glanced at the mountain rising in the distance. "There are a lot of secluded cabins up there. Some of the people shoot first and ask questions later."

"We'll get a copter in the air. Maybe someone will spot the Mercedes." Macey stepped away, putting his phone to his ear.

Nothing was that easy. Liam leaned against the car. "We can head back to the office and go through what I found in Lucy's drawer."

"Okay. At least until we receive the next part of the game." Harper got in the jeep, her gaze remaining on her phone. "We'll never stop them. They always know where we are, and we can't do anything about it."

"I'm working on that." He drove back to the office.

He did have an idea formulating in his mind, but it would be risky. "We could get the new phones for when we're heading somewhere we don't want them to know. That will put us in the dark for a while in regard to Robert. We won't know what he's doing." He cut her a sideways glance.

"Do we have a choice?"

"We always have a choice."

"I think we should get the new phones. They might be our only chance, albeit slim, to catching Robert and Lucy."

"Agree." He pulled in front of the station and headed to his desk.

He pulled several pages from each envelope. "Wow. We have everything we need to lock Lucy up for years if we can prove these belong to her."

Harper leaned over his desk. "What are they?"

"Lists of hits, the amount of money made, bank account numbers, aliases…everything but her real name. There's even passports." Thank you, God. The passports prove all the information in front of him pertained to the same woman. Once caught, she'd spend the rest of her life behind bars.

"Any Lucy?"

"No."

He opened each passport. Some revealed a pretty woman, others a dowdy middle-aged, all with different disguises and names. "She's been everywhere."

"She's also got more money than she can spend in a lifetime." Harper sat back in her chair. "Why hasn't she gone overseas where US law enforcement wouldn't reach?"

"She's involved with whatever Robert thinks he's doing. I doubt she has the same beliefs. Maybe she doesn't like to leave a job unfinished." He shrugged. "This is the biggest thing we've found so far after learning Robert's true identity."

He returned the items to the envelopes and sent in a request for them to go to the evidence room. A woman now overlooked the things that would be stored there. Fireproof walls and door had been installed to prevent a fire again.

Finished with that, he placed a call and ordered two simple smart phones. They would slowly gain on the ones they sought, and he didn't intend to lose any of the ground they'd gained.

Chapter Ten

Lucy emptied the rushed packing of the duffel bag she'd brought, removing the important envelopes she'd shoved in. Now that she wasn't in a hurry, the envelopes felt too thin.

She slid the papers out. Blank! She'd been discovered. Her hand shook as she dropped the pages onto the board that served as a kitchen counter. They now knew everything about her. She tossed a quick glance to where Robert paced the tiny living room.

Was it time for her to move on? This gig paid more than any other she'd ever had, but she never hung around in one spot this long. The blank pages proved how dangerous letting weeds grow around your feet could be.

"What's wrong?" Robert froze, his gaze locking on hers.

"Nothing." She shoved the empty envelopes into her bag and the papers into the fireplace. "Everything is great." Far from it.

They were staying in a mountain cabin that could fall down around them at any moment, filming a boy sent on ridiculous quests, and all the authorities didn't know was her real last name. Who was she kidding? She had no passports and if she didn't act fast, her accounts would be frozen. The authorities had the numbers and a different name on each account. Things were about to get ugly.

She gripped the countertop hard enough to make her knuckles ache. "What's the next quest? We need this to end." She had some killing to do. Three in fact. Robert, the detective, and the handsome agent.

"It's going to be harder all the way up here, but I'll manage." Robert pulled a bandanna from his pocket and tied it around the boy's eyes. "We need a ride. Can't do anything close to our hideout."

She rolled her eyes. Did he think she was stupid? Of course, they had to take the boy somewhere else.

~

Why hadn't Robert contacted them? The day was almost over. The last thing she wanted to do was follow Reynold in the dark.

Her new cell phone lay on her desk unopened. She reached for the item and started plugging in important phone numbers. Anything to stay busy and help keep her mind occupied.

She and Liam had decided the new phones would be used for everything except receiving texts from Robert. When they wanted to be incognito, they'd leave the old ones behind. But not for too long or he'd grow suspicious.

The phone on her desk buzzed. "Liam?"

"Yeah, I got one. Live feed is back, too."

Reynold stood blindfolded in the middle of the Interstate median. Horns honked as cars and semis sped past.

The text read, *"In ten minutes, I'm going to tell the boy to start walking. His hands are tied, so removing the blindfold will be difficult. It's up to you to get to him before he's struck by a vehicle."*

"Which direction? East or West?" Her blood chilled.

"Macey and Harris are in the air. I'll have them follow the Interstate and give us a mile marker." Liam got to his feet and made the call.

Five minutes after Reynold started shuffling down the median, they got the call that he was at mile marker 108. Another five minutes away.

Lights flashing, they zoomed in that direction. Liam weaved the jeep in and out of traffic.

Harper's heart dropped. "A semi stopped on the shoulder. The driver is trying to make his way to Reynold."

Liam jerked to face her. "That's suicide."

"He obviously doesn't know about the game." As she watched, a shot rang out and the man fell in the right lane of the interstate. A car struck him, went on two wheels, and overturned.

Reynold had frozen in place, drawing in on himself. After

several seconds, he moved forward again.

Harper made a call to the local EMTs to meet them at the scene of the accident. By now, several more vehicles had been rearended or did the rearending. Traffic had stalled.

Her second phone rang. "Detective Harper here."

"Why in the heck aren't you at the scene?" The chief blasted through the phone. "Speed it up before more people die."

"We're driving ninety, sir."

"Don't give me excuses, just get there." He hung up.

They were doing the very best they could. Short of flying…she peered up at the helicopter hovering over the median…they went as fast as possible.

Liam pulled the car onto the median about ten feet in front of Reynold. "Let's get him."

The boy flinched when she put her hands on his shoulders. "I'm going to remove the blindfold. You're okay." She pulled the dirty bandanna away from his face.

"What now?" He blinked against the sudden sunlight.

"We wait until he tells us. Have a seat. I've got to help take care of any wounded. Do not go anywhere."

"I won't. My legs are shaking so bad, I don't think I could anyway."

She patted his head and joined Liam who already strolled among the cars, ducking in windows, on his way to the flipped vehicle. By now, they were joined by Annie and one of the borrowed officers.

"We'll move to the body to the median." Annie grabbed the dead man's legs. That way, we can clear at least one lane of traffic." The other officer grabbed the shoulders. Soon, Annie directed cars slowly down the one lane.

"You folks okay?" She bent and peered into the flipped car.

"Thank goodness we wore our seatbelts." A middle-aged woman turned to the kids in the back. The youngest, maybe eight-years-old, screeched at the top of her lungs. "Ashley, we're all fine. You can stop screaming." The woman covered her face with her hands. "Tell me the man was dead before I ran over him."

"He was."

"I threw up." The crying child sputtered.

"Oh." The woman fumbled with her seatbelt. "I'm coming."

"Ma'am, I don't think the doors will open without the fire department's help. We'll get them here as soon as they arrive." Harper tapped the vehicle's hood, her attention already on the next car.

~

Except for the dead semi driver, injuries weren't serious. Liam helped where he could. He helped a trembling woman to the shoulder. "Wait here until someone comes to clean the scrape on your head."

She nodded, a hand over the bleeding spot where her forehead had slammed into the steering wheel. "My dog? It's a dachshund."

"I'll find it." He searched the van, finding the dog cowering behind the middle seat. Grasping it by the collar, he pulled it toward himself, then carried it to its owner.

A few of the smaller cars would need the occupants cut out of them, but no one would die from their injuries. Since Harper always kept bottled water in the back of her jeep, he grabbed what was left of the case and started distributing. Thankfully, the heat of the day had gone as the sun began its descent.

The chief pulled up and marched toward them. "The boy is asleep in the grass."

Liam glanced over to see the toes of Reynold's gym shoes showing over the wildflowers. "Better he sleeps than sit there terrified while we tend to others."

"Tell that to his father." He jerked his head toward the red-faced mayor marching toward them.

The man glanced at his phone, then veered toward his son. He bent and picked up something from the ground. One of Reynold's shoes. He waved it over his head.

Liam pulled up the live feed on his phone. An empty shoe lay on the ground where the boy had laid. He whirled, searching in every direction.

Reynold was nowhere in sight.

DEADLY ENVY

Cynthia Hickey

Chapter One

Robert paced the living room of the house he was quickly starting to hate. Too small and outdated. It's only redeeming quality was the basement where they now kept Reynold. "How many houses do you own, anyway?" He glared at Lucy.

"One more after this one." She glanced up from her phone. "I bought a house with my first assignment. Then, as I made more money, I upgraded. I've kept all the houses for a time like this one."

"Great. That means the last house is worse than this one."

"Yep." She returned to her phone. "Reynold is trying to gnaw through his ties."

"Didn't you zip-tie him?"

"No, because of a video on the internet, he knew how to use his shoelaces to get free." She cursed and got to her feet. "How long are we going to play this game?"

"I don't know. I've got to work on envy, which is difficult when it's too dangerous for me to go anywhere." How could he choose his next target?

"Social media." She rolled her eyes. "You'll find someone coveting something on there. Just use a fake name."

"I'm not an idiot." He frowned.

"That's debatable." She marched to the door leading to the basement.

He snarled at her back and reached for his phone.

~

"Exodus 20:17. *Thou shalt not covet thy neighbour's house, thou shalt not covet thy neighbour's wife, nor his manservant, nor his maidservant, nor his ox, nor his ass, nor any thing that is thy neighbour's."* The text Harper received read.

She sighed and set her phone on her desk. She'd hoped that after Robert or Lucy had taken Reynold from the Interstate, they'd give everyone a rest. It didn't appear so. She picked up her phone again and turned to the live feed.

"Anything?" Liam glanced up from his computer.

"Just turned it on. Lucy entered the basement. Reynold stopped chewing on the cord around his wrists. He looks unwashed and skinny. Same as yesterday." The boy didn't deserve this kind of treatment just because he's a politician's son. The mayor's to be exact. Why couldn't Robert have gone after the father and left the son alone? Because he was a horny teenage boy? The poor kid probably wouldn't look at a girl for months.

Lucy slapped him, then retied his hands behind his back. Harper didn't understand the typing up since he had a chain around his ankle, unless Reynold had disobeyed in some way when the camera wasn't running.

She waited for the sound to come on. They'd left it off for two days, the feed only showing Reynold in the basement. While she was glad for the boring video feed, she really wanted the whole thing to be over with no more death.

Liam came over and massaged her shoulders, his strong fingers kneading away the tension. "We'll save him."

"Hmmm." She closed her eyes and leaned her head forward. "I hate sitting around, waiting for Robert's next move."

"I'm with you there." He kissed the top of her head and watched the video over her shoulder. "The FBI has agents knocking on the door of every house with a basement in a thirty-mile radius."

"That'll take forever." Besides, Robert and Lucy always seemed to know when it was time to flee.

"But it is doing something." He kissed her again and returned to his desk. "Let me know if there's anything happening on the video feed. I'm on Google satellite marking off houses without basements and those the agents have already visited. Tedious."

She wasn't sure whether she preferred watching the video or if she'd rather do what Liam did? Neither were interesting.

She'd stick to the video of Reynold and pray she didn't watch his murder at some point.

Reynold spit at Lucy and received another slap, this one hard enough to push his head to the side. If looks could kill, the assassin would be on the floor and things would look a lot brighter.

~

Robert couldn't believe how rampant the sin of envy was on social media. Everywhere he looked, someone would post a "look what I got" or "I just got this" and people would say "I want that" or "I'm jealous". How would he ever choose?

He sent the detective a quick text that said, "How does one choose the one who should be punished when there are so many?"

Folding his hands behind his head, he stared at the phone in its holder. Where could he find a group of people envying each other behind fake smiles? Somewhere he could get rid of a few at a time?

"Careful or you'll hurt yourself." Lucy plopped onto the cracked leather sofa.

He knew just the place, and he knew the right person for the job. He still had a few followers not in hiding. He made the call. "I want it done right around one o'clock this afternoon."

"Got it." The man hung up.

"You've hired someone else?" Lucy's eyes flashed. "Why?"

"Because I need a skilled bomber for this job, not an assassin."

"How do you know I'm not one?" She arched a brow.

"Are you?"

"No, I prefer other methods."

"Well, there you go. You're concern right now is Reynold." An idea formed in his head. "Let's make it look like the boy was forced to set the bomb."

She grinned and clapped her hands. "What fun! Imagine the embarrassment his father will feel. I'll go down there right now and tell the boy to do a good job of acting or we'll go ahead and kill him."

Robert nodded. The boy's cooperation was the reason he still drew breath. If he refused, he could be replaced easily enough.

~

"Liam." Harper lunged to her feet and turned her phone to where he could see. "No sound, but Reynold is skulking around in an alley with what looks like several pipe bombs."

"Do we know where?"

She shook her head. "There are too many to count. We won't know anything until he's done whatever they're making him do now."

Liam's phone rang. "Special Agent McConnell."

"This is Mayor Sharpe. You have got to stop whatever they have my son doing."

"We don't know his location, sir."

"Find it! This will ruin me." The mayor hung up.

Liam sighed. The man seemed more concerned about his reputation than he did his son.

"Look." Harper regained his attention.

Reynold pulled back his hand and threw a pipe. The screen went black.

"Explosion at the Cut 'n Curl on Oak Street." Annie popped in long enough to give them the information.

Liam grabbed his gun and jacket and left the office on the run with Harper close behind. He climbed into the driver's seat and held out his hand for the keys. "My turn."

She dropped them in his palm and clicked his seatbelt into place. "Let's go."

He followed Annie's squad car. The salon burned hotter than he thought a pipe bomb could do. He shoved his door open and approached the fire chief. "Anyone inside?"

"We were told four hair stylists, four customers, then the nail tech. No one knows whether she had a client or not, and one customer waiting. No way anyone survived that."

Ten or eleven women going about their life and getting pampered. Gone in an instant. "This the only fire? The only explosion?"

The chief frowned. "You expecting more?"

"Would pipe bombs do this?"

"No. This was a big boom, not small explosions converging together to burn this hot. A gas leak could do this."

Harper moved to Liam's side. "Witnesses say no one made it out. One minute the building was there, the next…boom."

"No one felt a thing," the chief said. "Small consolation, though."

"Reynold couldn't have done this. Not with what we saw him with." Liam studied the cars in front of the building. Not a single one had any windows left, nor did nearby cars and businesses. Nothing burned except the salon.

"Why the salon?" He glanced at Harper.

"Going by the latest text, Robert wanted to take out a few at a time. Women gossip, they talk when getting their hair and nails done. I guess they might envy each other in some ways." She pressed her lips together. "Let's hope he gets through the rest of these sins, so the killings stop."

She marched back to the jeep and stared at her phone as her shoulders slumped.

If Harper started to lose hope, they might never find Reynold. Robert and Lucy could finish the macabre game, and then disappear.

He leaned against the jeep next to her and bumped her with his shoulder. "You okay?"

"Watching Reynold."

Liam glanced at the screen. "He's got a bandage on his hand."

"Trying to convince the watchers that he got burned while blowing up this business?"

"That's my guess."

She stared at him, her face set in grave lines. "Are we going to stop him, Liam? You do know the assassin will be coming for us with sin seven. That one is anger. Robert blames our relatives for the death of his father, and we have to pay the price.

"Neither one of us can outrun a sniper's bullet."

"That means he won't have need of Reynold past envy and sloth." His blood chilled. If they didn't find Reynold soon, they'd be finding his body.

Chapter Two

Harper's eyes widened. Her heart skipped a beat as she peered closer at her phone screen. "Liam." She never took her eyes off the screen as he came to her side.

Reynold stood on the edge of a playground. For anyone with a discerning eye, it wasn't hard to see he didn't want to be there. Pale face, wide eyes, trembling hands.

"Let me get an officer in route. Where is this?"

"There's only one park in this small town and that's off Main Street."

Reynold stepped onto the rubber ground below the play equipment and glanced to where a dark-haired woman typed on her phone. Then, he approached a little girl building a sandcastle, a stuffed animal on the ground next to her. He knelt and said something to her. The child slipped her hand in his and grabbed the toy with the other.

Reynold led her away. The whole thing took less than two minutes.

"Why would Robert have him kidnap a child?" What could a little girl have to do with envy?

"Annie is enroute. Let's meet her there." Liam rushed from the room.

As they sped toward the park, Harper received a text. "Thou shalt not covet thy neighbor's wife can also prove true as in Thou shalt not covet thy neighbor's child."

Liam slammed his hand on the steering wheel. "First a bunch of women in a salon and now a child. Robert is losing control."

"Which makes me very worried." She stared out the

window. The death rate would escalate the more his mind spiraled downward. The fact he used one child to take another made her hands tremble. She clutched them tightly in her lap.

When they arrived at the playground, Liam rushed to her side and opened her door. "Hold it together, sweetheart. There's a frantic mother who needs our help right now."

A mother who had been so busy on her phone, that she hadn't noticed a boy snatch her daughter. Harper took a deep breath through her nose, squared her shoulders, and marched to where the mother cried into her hands.

"Ma'am, I'm Detective Scranton and this is Special Agent McConnell. We'd like to ask you a few questions, starting with your name."

"Rebecca Long." She glanced up at them and blinked. "You're the ones on TV. The ones after that…guy. Does he have my baby?"

She must be one of the few who wasn't watching the live feed of Reynold. "We believe so."

Her wails increased.

With a sigh, Harper sat on the bench next to the woman. "We believe that a young man under orders from the suspect has taken your child. Do you have any idea why?"

"No. Becky is autistic. Why would this man want her?"

"If you know who this man is, then you know that he is targeting the seven deadly sins. He's on envy right now. Do you know why you've been targeted for that sin?" She hated the shadow that crossed the woman's eyes. Whatever she'd done, purposely or not, had gotten her child taken. "What were you doing when Becky was taken?"

"Updating my social media. I only looked away for a minute. I have no idea."

The man had targeted her for a reason. He'd found her someway. "May I look through your recent posts." Harper motioned to the woman's phone.

"Of course." She handed the phone over. "I'm not sure what you'll find. My posts are pretty boring. Even the messaging I do with my friends isn't very interesting. We mostly vent to each other over life."

Harper nodded and started scrolling. Posts of meals, an

achievement her child had done, nothing that could be construed as envy. She opened the private messages. Ah. A simple statement made on a stressful day. "This." She pointed to the message that read, "Somedays, I wish I had your child instead of Becky."

Mrs. Long shrieked. "I didn't mean that! I'd had a bad day. How…Oh." She grabbed the phone. "I originally put it on my friend's page when she bragged about her child's grades in kindergarten, but I thought I'd deleted it before doing a private message instead."

A man sprinted toward them. Harper and Liam stood in front of Mrs. Long.

"It's okay. That's my husband." She launched herself into his arms.

He glanced at Harper and Liam over his wife's shoulders. "Well?"

"All we know is who took her, sir." She hated filling him in on why his child was taken.

He listened stoically as she did, then narrowed his eyes at his wife. "I told you that social media was a bad thing."

"If not for your wife's social media, we wouldn't know why your child was targeted." Not that they could drop in and save the child. Harper pulled up the live feed that had gone black after Reynold took the girl.

She sat in the same basement room as Reynold did. While Lucy rechained him, she left the girl untied. Becky sat in the corner and rocked, her arms wrapped around a stuffed rabbit.

"Everyone can see this?" Mr. Long stared at her phone. "What's the link?"

"Are you sure you want to see Becky like this?" Liam shook his head. "I doubt they'll hurt her, it's the boy they order around, but it's got to be tough."

"I'm positive." He lifted his chin. "We can at least see her until you find her."

Harper told him the link. Mrs. Long immediately pulled up the live feed on her phone. "She's upset." Her words broke off on a sob. "Soon, she'd going to explode."

"No, she's got Bugsy. She'll be fine." Her husband patted her shoulder as he watched the screen. "Heaven help them if they take that dirty thing away from her. No one throws a fit like my baby girl."

More like heaven help the child if they do. Harper doubted Lucy would have much patience with a special needs child.

~

Lucy frowned down at the little girl. "What's wrong with you?"

The child started a low hum much like the sound a bee made.

"I asked you a question, child." She couldn't tolerate rude children. In fact, she didn't like children at all.

"Leave her alone." Reynold glared her way. "I think she's on the spectrum. You guys made me kidnap a child with special needs." He crossed his arms.

"Really?" The corners of her mouth drew down. "Do I do anything special with her?"

"Try not to stress her out. Otherwise, she might throw a fit." He shrugged. "At least that's what my cousin does."

She cursed.

The little girl looked up. "That's a bad word. You're a bad woman." She started rocking again.

"I'm a very wealthy, bad woman." Lucy whirled and marched up the basement steps, refusing to get into an argument with a child on camera.

"Great job, Robert." She fell onto the sofa. "You took a special needs kid."

"What?" The hand holding a glass shook.

"Autism or something according to the boy."

"We can't keep her." He paced the living room. "I didn't see anything on the woman's feed that referred to her child being special. This is not my fault."

"Figure out how to return her." Idiot. She pulled up the live feed. The child still rocked and hummed. "I'll find out the woman's address. Reynold can drop her off tonight when it's dark."

"Good idea. Guess that's why I pay you the big bucks, because it sure isn't because you have a great personality."

"How you wound me." She rolled her eyes. "Just do your homework better next time."

"Why don't you find the person for the envy sin, then? The

salon was good, the child could've been sensational. These are the types of things that will get people to watch the live feed. It won't be long until I have a whole new group of people willing to follow me." He downed the whiskey in the glass.

The man was nuttier than peanut brittle. "I'll have a target by tonight. When Reynold is returning the child, I'll take her replacement."

~

The chief set an eight o'clock curfew in place. The only time anyone would be allowed out after that time is if they were headed to or from work. Liam agreed to an extent, but most of Robert's crimes took place in broad daylight.

A glance at the clock in the bull pen showed way past quitting time. If he had a normal job. One where he wasn't trying to catch a mad man.

Harper jingled her keys in front of him. "I'm going to drive around town before heading home. Want to join me?"

He'd like nothing better. "Are we out looking for curfew breakers?"

"Just looking." She smiled. "Giving the other officers a bit of help."

He took the keys and led her to the jeep. She didn't have to ask him twice to spend time with her. Sure, he stayed at her house, but the night hours were long with her in another room. Each morning, he bounded out of bed like a puppy whose human had just come home.

Two squad cars pulled out of the parking lot ahead of them, ready to patrol the streets. They'd waited until eight thirty to allow people time to remember a curfew was in place.

Liam stopped the vehicle next to an elderly woman walking a poodle. He rolled down the passenger side window. "Ma'am, are you aware of the eight o'clock curfew?"

"A curfew? No."

"A special announcement was made on the news."

"I don't have a television, son. We'll head home right away."

"She shouldn't be out so late alone anyway," Harper said. "Not while Robert is working his way through the sins, anyway." She rolled the window back up. "I'm going to check the feed."

"Let me know anything important."

"You tell me if this classifies as important. Reynold is walking down a sidewalk with Becky."

"Yeah, that's important. Any idea where?"

"I haven't seen a streetlight yet. At least, I think it's Reynold. It's a camera on someone's fore…yeah, it's him. I recognize the shoes."

"Lucy or Robert had filmed him at the park. They could have been right behind the mother, and no one suspected a thing." He tightened his hands on the wheel, turning the knuckles white.

Harper let the station receptionist know so the other officers on patrol could be on the lookout. She then kept her attention glued to the video and tried to make out a landmark or catch a glimpse of a street sign.

Reynold was being very careful not to look at any signs. Still keeping his head down, he led the child up a set of steps, rang the doorbell, and ran.

"He took her home! Quick, turn around."

Liam whipped the wheel and increased his speed as Harper called out directions. Come on, Reynold. Let us see you.

"There." She pointed out her window. "Don't let it look as if we took him easily or Lucy might come after him at a later time."

"Got it." They bolted from the vehicle, guns drawn.

"Stop, Reynold. Hands up."

The boy complied.

"Are you alone?"

"Yes."

Liam ripped the beanie with the camera attached to it from his head. He turned off the camera and tossed the hat in the car. "Let's get you home."

He glanced both ways and opened the back door. Inside the jeep, he turned to face the boy. "I suppose they didn't let you see the location of the house?"

"No, they kept me blindfolded until we were far enough away." He heaved a big sigh.

"Why did they let you go?" Robert would've known that having the boy return the little girl would alert the authorities to his location.

"When they found out they'd had me take a special needs kid, they both flipped." He sniffed. "Lucy, that's the woman's name, is out looking for someone to replace me right now. She's here in town somewhere."

Everything in him wanted to search for her. Harper's expression looked like she felt the same way. "We need to get you to the safety of the station. We'll call your father from there."

"She'll get away!" He kicked the back of the seat.

"If we go after her, she might kill you." He put the jeep in drive. "Is that a risk you're willing to take?"

"No." He plopped back against the seat.

At the station, they escorted him to the interview room. Harper left, returning with a sandwich and soda from the vending machine. "Your father is being called. In the meantime, we'd like to ask you some questions."

"I heard very little and saw nothing, but I'll do whatever I can." He grabbed the sandwich like a starving man. "All I ever saw was the basement. They led me into it through an outside door. You could see for yourself that they chained me up like a dog.

"I'd like nothing better than for you to find them and shoot them."

Liam understood.

Chapter Three

Lucy stood in the shadows on the side of a convenience store. Amazing how many people needed to grab some little something before heading home. At least ten were in the store, breaking curfew.

"I told you, Maggie, that if I had your closet, I'd never want to leave it. I'm so jealous." The woman laughed. "Maybe then I'd have enough room to hang more than yoga pants and tops."

"Your closet is perfectly fine." Margie smiled.

"Yours is as big as my master closet!"

Lucy pulled her weapon from the waistband of her pants and approached the women. "You." She motioned to the blond with a ponytail. "

"Me?" She put a hand to her chest, then glanced at Margie.

"Make it fast or Margie dies. Come on."

"Don't go, Stephanie. She's bluffing."

"Really?" Lucy pulled the trigger. The brunette dropped.

People peered from the store. Lucy shook her head. If this fool didn't come with her right now, she'd have to kill her, too. "Well?"

"Okay." She practically ran to where Lucy told her the car was parked.

Inside, she cried big gulping sobs. "You didn't have to kill her."

"I don't know whether I did or not. All I know is that I shot her." She pulled away from the building as sirens rose in the distance.

"Why me? Where are you taking me?"

"There's a hood on the seat. Put it on. You've committed

the sin of envy and must pay." She kind of liked stepping into Robert's shoes.

"What? Just let me go. Please. I have a family."

"Good for you. Now shut up. I'm not a person you want to disobey."

At the house, she took Stephanie to the basement and locked the chain around her ankle. "Robert, she's all yours."

The woman glanced up wide-eyed.

Robert folded his hands behind his back. "Your life here will be recorded and on a live feed so anyone in the world can see what happens when they envy. You will be assigned tasks that you must accomplish or you will die. If you do what we say, the way we tell you to do it, then you will live. Just like the boy we released this evening." He turned on the camera. "Good night."

~

"Shooting at the convenience store." Harper jumped to her feet and slipped her shoes on. What did she get? Fifteen minutes to sit down? She'd barely taken a sip of her wine.

"Fatal?" Liam opened the front door.

"Didn't say." She glanced at her phone. "Robert has a woman replacing Reynold." Thankfully, no more kids. "Wanna wager the shooting was involved with her abduction?"

"That's one we'd both win because I'm not going against you. You're right, so I'd lose. I don't like losing."

When they arrived at the convenience store, Annie had people held in the store to be questioned. "So much for a curfew, huh?"

"Body?" Harper peered around her.

"Still breathing. Ambulance is on its way. The victim is sitting behind the counter." Annie opened the store door.

All chatter stopped when Harper entered the store. She cast a look at those who should've been safe at home before rounding the counter.

A woman in yoga pants with a matching jacket sat against the wall and pressed napkins against a wound in her side.

Harper introduced herself and Liam. "Can you tell us what happened?"

"My friend and I stopped in here to grab something we'd forgotten earlier, I needed coffee for tomorrow, anyway…" She waved a dismissive hand. "This woman stepped around the corner outside and told Stephanie to get in her car. When she refused, the woman shot me."

"Was it this woman?" Harper pulled up the composite drawings on Lucy.

"Yes."

Sirens wailed outside, then stopped. Seconds later, two paramedics rushed into the store. "Excuse us, Detective."

"Wait." Margie held up a hand to stop them, her gaze still on Harper. "Is Stephanie going to die?"

"Not if she does everything she's told." Harper turned and moved away so the medics could work.

"Find out anything?" Liam asked.

"Lucy took the friend. Shot the victim when the friend, Stephanie West, refused to go with her. Did you get anything out of this lot?"

"I've only interviewed one. He said the same thing the victim did. I assumed it was Lucy."

"Let's split up and get through this. I'll take this side of the room." Liam headed to the men by the beer, leaving Harper to a handful of women, two who swore they didn't know about the curfew. The rest only needed to stop for one little thing.

"Curfews are set for a reason. That woman wouldn't have been shot if she'd heeded the curfew." And, Harper would have to write them all a ticket. Ignorance was no excuse for breaking the law, and there was no way the chief wouldn't know about these people because of the report. "Let's start with your names."

Between each interview, Harper would check the live

feed. Stephanie Long sat, shoulders slumped, on the very cot Reynold had spent so many nights on. She couldn't help but wonder whether the woman had a husband, a family, people watching the feed with dread. All questions which might be answered when Harper returned to the office.

She glanced over at Liam. He wasn't the only one who didn't like losing, and there hadn't been a lot of winning lately. Except for Reynold and Becky. They were safe. Not because Harper and Liam found them, but because Robert and Lucy still had some heart in their cold chests for children.

After getting as much information from the witnesses she questioned, which wasn't much more than the victim, Harper waited by the front door for Liam. His easy-going manner, kind, but firm, had most people more than willing to talk to him. Add in good looks and you had the whole package. An FBI agent people liked. She gave a short laugh.

What would it be like to be his? Kissing, waking up next to him, not barely getting any sleep before being called out again. Did she really know him outside of the job? Maybe not, but she really wanted to.

Movement caught her eye outside. Two men in hoodies were trying to pry open a car door. She stepped outside. "Hey. Drop the crow bars." She flashed her badge.

"What's a woman cop going to do against both of us?" One of them sneered and took a step forward.

Harper tied her hair into a ponytail. "I'm not alone, but I'm pretty sure I could take you." She smiled, ready for a fight. Something she could actually see end with these two behind bars. All he had to do was hit her, and she'd have him on assaulting a police officer.

Not wanting to make the first move, Harper stood still, smiling, and waited for the young men to approach. Her hands curled into fists. She had a lot of anxious energy to work off. Still, she was a good detective and needed to at least try to talk them out of hitting her.

She opened her mouth to speak as the man who'd spoken threw the first punch.

~

Liam turned from the man he'd questioned in time to see a street thug connect a strong right hook to Harper's jaw. He darted out the door and to her side, throwing a punch of his own that knocked the young man to the ground.

Hauling him up by the collar of his shirt, Liam spun him around, slammed him against the wall of the store and cuffed him. He then motioned to the other guy who shook his head and ran. "Watch him," Liam ordered Harper before taking off after the one trying to flee.

He wasn't hard to catch. Soon, both thugs were cuffed.

Liam gripped Harper's arm and pulled her to the side. "Mind telling me what was going on?" His gaze fell on a bruise forming on her chin. The hit had cut her lip. "Are you okay?"

"He sucker-punched me." She dabbed at her lip with the back of her hand.

"Here." Liam handed her a napkin he'd stuffed in his jacket pocket at some time.

"Thanks. I spotted them trying to break into a car. The one in the navy hoodie threatened me. I accepted the challenge."

"Are you crazy?" He frowned. "You were outnumbered."

"Don't be silly. I can take two." She leaned against the jeep. "We should call Annie to pick these guys up. I don't want them in my automobile."

He continued to stare at her.

"What?" She shrugged. "I had some things I needed to work through. Fighting a couple of jerks seemed like a good way to do so."

"How about going to the gym and punching a bag?"

She narrowed her eyes. "You tell me when. We weren't home a half hour before leaving again."

Home. Warmth filled him. He liked that word. Especially when it involved Harper. "The chief isn't going to be happy about you fighting."

"They started it." She grinned, then winced. "No smiling for a while."

After Officer Young picked up the thugs, Liam drove them to the office so Harper could process the young men. Any other reports could wait until morning. He glanced at the clock. Later. It was already past midnight.

The chief took one look at Harper's face as they escorted to the young men to the holding cell and shook his head. "I don't want to know. Mr. Long is in the conference room. Once you take care of those two, give him a couple of minutes. The man is understandably distraught."

Liam nodded. He wasn't a fan of trying to soothe grieving spouses, but it was part of the job. Since Harper's face was turning a nice eggplant color, Liam would speak to Mr. Long alone.

"Go on. I can handle these two." Harper waved him away.

Liam nodded and entered the conference room. Mr. Long, a man approaching forty, sat with his hands wrapped around a Styrofoam cup. His gaze was glued to the cell phone on the table. He jumped to his feet when Liam entered. "Anything?"

"Please have a seat." Liam sat across from him and folded his hands. "As sad as this sounds, it appears your wife was taken because she envied her friend's closet."

The man blinked like someone blinded by a light. "The fifth deadly sin."

"You don't seem surprised." Liam straightened.

"I've been closely following this Seven Deadly Sins

Killer. I want to be a writer, and this is all very interesting. Until he took Stephanie." He glanced back at his phone. "What is he going to do to her?"

"Hopefully nothing, but we can safely assume he'll assign her tasks the same as he did Reynold Sharpe who is safely with his parents tonight."

"The killer released him?" He gave a long exhale. "Then there is hope for Stephanie."

"Yes." Liam wasn't as positive that Robert would release an adult. Not alive, at least. "Do you have someone who can stay with you during this time?"

"I'll call my mother. She can help with our two children." Mr. Long stood. "I'm not sure what I came here for tonight. Maybe just to hear that there's hope."

Liam stretched out his hand. "Don't hesitate to call if you have questions."

When he and Harper could finally head home to end a very long day, he crashed, not waking until a couple of hours past sunup.

Chapter Four

Robert stared at the phone in his hand, the one used only by his followers, then lifted it back to his ear. "Joe?"

"Yeah, boss. I've been here working at the ranch. It's ready for occupancy. Fence is secured. Security system in place. I'm sorry it took so long, but since the feds rounded up most of our guys, there's only been five of us working."

Five. He still had five followers. He grinned. "Make sure my room is ready and the second-best room. We'll be there within an hour." He glanced at Lucy. "We've got a secure place to go. Grab the woman."

"Where?" She tilted her head.

"A ranch I bought. Quite a way from town, secluded. One way in and out." He pulled a suitcase from the closet. Not that he'd been able to escape with much, but he wanted to keep what little he had.

"Did you forget about this place?" Her voice rose. "We could've been there this whole time instead of hiding in this poverty level community."

"I didn't think it got finished. I wasn't aware I had any followers left. Pack your stuff." He placed folded pants and shirts into the suitcase. "No filming until the woman is secure in a vacant room. No one can know where this place is." He didn't even want Lucy to know, but since he wasn't finished with her services, he couldn't think of a way to keep the location from her. Maybe she'd end up converted.

While Lucy retrieved the woman, he strolled through the house making sure he hadn't forgotten anything. He didn't want Lucy to know, but his mind seemed to drift away on occasion.

More than he'd like.

Lucy shoved the woman into a chair, then went to pack.

"Who's there?" The woman lifted her head, trying to see under the blindfold.

"Your Master." It felt good to say those words again.

"Where are you taking me? What are you going to do to me?"

"All in good time." He zipped the suitcase closed. "All in good time." He planned on her attending every meeting. Those watching the live feed would hear his message. Many would convert. He could now continue his rise to power.

~

That wasn't the same place. Harper stared at painted walls instead of concrete block. Stephanie's ankle was now tied to a bed instead of a ring in the wall. The room looked like almost any bedroom in America. Definitely a step up from the basement.

The woman stared straight at the camera and blinked. "Liam, I think she's doing Morse code."

He peered over her shoulder. "It's been a while but get a pencil. First word is dirt. Second is road, and third is country."

"Okay, she's telling us they're on a dirt road in the country. Do you know how many of dirt roads are in this county alone?" They needed a lot more information.

"Patience. She's heard five different men's voices outside of the man and woman who took her. She's heard chickens and cows."

Again, a lot of places. "We could send a chopper up. Get addresses of all the farms in the area." At least, the ones they knew of. "Recent purchases of land. It's something."

Stephanie fell over on the bed and closed her eyes. The door opened and a man Harper didn't know entered the room. He set a plate with a glass of water and a sandwich on the nightstand, cut a quick glance at the camera, then left. All without saying a word.

A faint glimmer of hope rose in Harper. Lucy had abducted a very smart woman. Unless Robert and Lucy stayed as glued to the live feed as a lot of people in the world, they wouldn't have seen her signaling. Please God, don't let them find out. Stephanie could be the very one who brings them down.

"Gutsy woman." Liam perched on the corner of Harper's

desk. "We can safely assume that Robert has moved from his prior location."

"Yes. I wish he'd send a text." No word from him made her nervous.

"He's got something up his sleeve. We have to wait and see what it is, as hard as that will be." He twisted a strand of her hair around his finger. "I've…got to go."

"Okay. I'll see you later."

"No, I'm being called back to the office. There's a case they need me for."

"We need you here!" She pulled back.

"It's only for a consultation. A day or two at the most. I have to leave now. They're going to send someone to take my place during that time. I'm sorry. There's nothing I can do."

"If Robert finds out we aren't together, he'll blow."

"I'll be as quick as I can." He placed a tender kiss on her cheek. "Stay safe, sweetheart."

She gripped his hand. "You, too." She felt too vulnerable when he wasn't at her side.

What if Robert grew angry enough to focus on the seventh sin? He'd told them to stay together. If the man did explode, neither of them would have the other for backup.

Robert might kill Liam and not Harper, leaving her to suffer his death the rest of her life. Her mind whirled with horrible what-ifs."

"I'll be okay. Nothing will keep me from coming back." Another kiss to the top of her head, and he marched from the room.

A tall, thin woman with auburn hair entered. "I'm Agent Susan Warren. I'm here to help you until Agent McConnell returns." She thrust out her hand. "Fill me in."

Harper stifled a sigh. It would take the rest of the day to fill her in. "Welcome to Oakdale, Agent."

~

Liam sat in the backseat of a black SUV. He didn't want to be heading to the office. He needed to be with Harper. Not being able to get out of consultation, he'd have to do his best to wrap things up quickly.

With the time it was taking to bring Robert down, his boss had said they would need to pull him from the field on occasion.

He grunted and stared out the window.

When he arrived at the office, he went straight to the case board. No wonder he'd been pulled. They didn't have enough manpower to stop a serial killer targeting women joggers. Five so far, all their bodies dumped in whatever body of water was closest.

"Sexual assault?"

"We assume so." Agent Preston crossed his arms. "Some were in the water for a few days."

They had more on their guy than he'd thought. A physical description of a suspect. DNA, but the guy wasn't in the system. Since all the women had been taken within a ten-mile radius, it was safe to say he lived in the area. "Have you closed the jogging trails?"

"Yep. Three happened at the same one. Care to take a drive?"

"Let's go." He grabbed his duffel bag off the desk. If they'd be walking, he'd need comfortable shoes.

The jogging trail had three different lengths. A mile, a mile and a half, or a three-mile. Most of the dump spots were closest to the three-mile. He changed shoes and followed the other agent.

"Watch out for the alligator when we reach Black Water pond. He got a dog a couple of years back." Agent Young grinned his way. "My parents saw him once and gave him a wide berth."

"Smart people." Liam shifted his gaze from side-to-side. "Victims missing body parts?"

"The one dumped in the pond was missing a leg. The others were dumped in creeks or the frog pond. Too far for Draco to roam, I guess."

The town had named the gator? Liam shook his head, hoping he didn't see the creature and shoot it. That didn't sound like a way to make friends.

"Found one here." Agent Preston pointed to a thick patch of tall grasses near the water's edge. "We think she might've been the first. She had the most water damage."

Liam squatted near the place where yellow crime scene tape still fluttered. He studied a footprint embedded in the mud, preserved when the ground hardened.

"We took an imprint but got nothing."

"This pattern looks like the shoe skateboarders like." He

straightened. "I think you're looking for someone in their early-to-mid-twenties."

"Not much older than a kid."

"It'll be someone who takes these trails on a regular basis. How long has the track been closed?"

"Over a week. Why?"

"Because there's someone across the pond." Liam unsnapped his weapon's holster.

Preston did the same while slowly stepping behind a tree to take cover.

Liam did the same, then called out. "FBI. These trails are closed at this time."

Nothing. Not even the twitter of birds.

"Show yourself."

A bullet rang out, knocking bark from the tree he hid behind. Liam pulled his weapon, unable to see exactly where the shot had come from. "Anything?"

"Not yet. Why would he be here when there's no joggers?"

"I think he's homeless and lives here." They'd invaded his home.

"Then, let's get him so you can get back to that sicko you're hunting. I'll see if I can draw him out." Preston fired.

Another shot rang out from the other side. Liam's handgun wouldn't shoot that far. The other man had to have a rifle. "Keep his attention on you. I'm going to try and get closer."

Staying low, not an easy thing to do with most of the brush cleared from the area to prevent fires. He darted from tree to tree while Preston let off two shots every minute or so.

Pine needles muffled his footsteps. As he rounded the pond, he spotted the shooter hunkered down behind a log, rifle aimed in Preston's direction.

The man pulled the trigger.

Preston fell.

The man whirled and fired again, his shot grazing Liam's left arm.

He raised his right hand and shot the man through the arm holding the gun, then through the leg. He lunged forward and kicked the rifle out of reach before cuffing the guy to a tree. Secure that he couldn't escape, he hurried back to Preston.

"How bad is it?" He looked for blood.

"Not too bad." He sat up, holding his side. "I'm wearing a vest. Going to have some bruises, maybe a cracked rib or two, but I'm alive. You're bleeding."

"Just a graze."

"Him?"

"Shot twice and hooked to a tree."

"Go get him. I'll call for an ambulance."

Liam nodded and rushed back to the shooter. "Let's go."

"They were all guilty of vanity!"

Liam's blood grew cold. "What are you talking about?"

"The man running the live feed." The young man grinned. "I'm picking up his cause. Those women jogged in clothes that hugged every curve of their bodies. They got what they were asking for."

Liam wanted to shoot him again. "Stop talking." He hauled him to his feet and picked up the rifle.

"I can't walk. You shot me in the leg."

"Then limp." How many more idiots were out there taking up Robert's cause? He glanced at the guy's shoes. Same pattern as by the pond. At least they'd gotten one killer taken care of. He half-dragged, half-helped the wounded shooter to the path where Preston waited.

"Ambulance will be here in five. He say anything?" The other agent jerked his head toward the shooter.

"Confessed. Your guy idolizes my guy. Wants to be just like him." Liam dropped the man beside a tree. "Isn't that great?"

"We've got more of them?" The agent's eyes widened.

"I'd say most likely we do." He glanced in the direction of Oakdale. How many followers still lived in Oakdale? Were they lying in wait for a command from Robert before acting or were they gone except for crazies like the man lying on the ground at his feet?

Chapter Five

Robert strolled around the compound feeling very much like a king. He might not have a lot of followers at the moment, but he did have a handful of very faithful ones. The future looked very bright indeed.

"Look at this." Lucy hurried toward him and pulled up a newsfeed on her phone. "You've got fans."

He watched as a reporter told about a shooting in a park and how the young man continued the work Robert hadn't been able to after going into hiding. He grinned. If there was one out there, there was more. What great news!

"I'm also as bored as a person can get. Either give me a job or I search for one."

"You can't leave now that you're here."

She rolled her eyes. "Don't be stupid. Someone can drive me out, blindfolded, then I'll call you from…never mind." She laughed. "I tracked this location on my phone. It hasn't been a secret to me since we arrived." She flipped her fingers against his head. "Guess who's smarter?"

He'd never wanted to strangle her more than at that moment. "You've jeopardized our location."

"Seriously?" She arched a brow. "I haven't survived this long by not being smart. No one knew who I was until I got mixed up with you. In fact, I think I'm finished. It's time for me to head overseas and continue my work there."

"At least wait until I've disposed of the detective and the agent."

"I can do that for you today."

"No!" She couldn't veer from the plan. "It isn't time. I'll

have a job for you by the end of the day."

"You'd better." She marched back toward the main house.

He could've let her go, the woman was a nuisance, but once he'd completed his quest, he had no intentions of her leaving. When he no longer needed Lucy, he'd dispose of her. Right now, he had more important things to worry about. What to do with the woman they'd taken?

The compound didn't provide many opportunities to use her to keep law enforcement on their toes. He studied the grounds and the buildings. They needed money. He had money. Lots of it, but he couldn't get to it. He sent someone to fetch Lucy.

~

"Detective Scranton?"

Harper looked up from the messages on her desk to see a man in a dark suit standing in the doorway of her office. "Yes."

"Agent Black." He grinned and thrust out his hand. "Yes, I know it's cliché, but I assure you I'm legit."

She stood and returned his handshake. "Welcome. Let me show you the case board. Any idea when Agent McConnell will return?" One day and she missed him more than she should.

"Not long. I doubt I'll be of much use unless they allow me to stay and help the two of you. A couple of days isn't enough time to stop a man like Robert Thompson."

What made him think he could do what she and Liam had failed to? "Maybe you'll see something we're missing."

He followed her to the conference room where he stood with his hands folded behind his back as he studied the case board. "Did you watch the news this morning?"

"Not yet." She leaned against the oval table.

"Agent McConnell was involved in a shooting."

"Was he…?" Her heart dropped.

"Minor. A young man was killing women joggers. Said he was doing Thompson's work."

"Did they get him?"

"Yes. He's in the hospital where, I assume, McConnell will question him when he's able."

Harper turned on the television in the room and turned to the local news where the live feed of Stephanie played. Harper's blood chilled.

The woman wore a head cam and marched into the bank. People screamed and rushed for the door. A female teller backed away from the counter.

"Nobody leaves this bank! Step away from the doors. I need to withdraw as much money from this account as possible right now." Stephanie handed the woman a slip of paper.

The woman's hand shook as she took it, then typed on her keyboard. "This account has been frozen."

"Please." Stephanie sobbed. "If you don't, this bomb strapped to me will detonate."

"I…" the woman glanced to someone on her right. "I don't know what to do."

Harper stared at the stoic face of Agent Black. Were they going to watch this woman and those around her get blown to bits?

Annie and the other two officers they had thundered past the conference room. No doubt they were headed to the bank.

Harper grabbed her jacket. "Let's go. I'll keep the feed on my phone." And pray very hard that the bomb didn't go off. As she passed the receptionist, she told her to call the bomb squad which, unfortunately, wouldn't arrive any sooner than half an hour.

Since the bank wasn't far from the office, they arrived within minutes. Using her jeep as cover, Harper stared at her phone screen as the bank manager rushed from teller to teller filling a bag of money.

He thrust it at Stephanie. "This is all we got. Everything we can readily get our hands on. It's about ten thousand. Will it be enough?"

"I don't know." Stephanie grabbed the bag. "I'm being told to wait."

"For what?"

"I don't know." The last word came as a wail.

Harper's heart ached for the woman. A bomb strapped to her chest as she coerced a bank to give her money wasn't likely to have been on her list of things she wanted to do in her lifetime.

"Did you expect anything like this?" Black peered over her shoulder.

"No, but Robert isn't predictable." She took a step to the side. He stood too close to her. Took up too much of her personal bubble. Plus, he wasn't Liam.

The chief called her over and handed her his phone. "Thompson wants to talk to you."

She cleared her throat. "Hello?"

"Why is there another agent with you instead of McConnell?"

"Hello, Robert." She put the phone on speaker.

"Answer my question!"

"He was called away. It's only temporary." How did he know? She turned and studied the crowd who stood much too close for safety if the bomb went off. She motioned to Black to Annie to move them back.

"My orders explicitly said that you and McConnell were to work together."

"I understand, but his boss needed him. Turns out you have a fan."

He laughed. "I'm sure I have several. Here's what I want you to do, Detective."

"Yes?"

"I want you to leave your phone in your jeep, give the chief back his, and be inside that bank within twenty minutes. Understand?"

"Why?"

"Leverage, Detective. Your time starts now."

Harper's heart leaped into her throat as she handed the chief his phone.

"Let's get you wired. Quickly. Inside the van so whoever is watching won't know what we're doing. I also want you wearing a vest." The chief marched to the police van and motioned her inside. "We don't have much time."

~

Bandage wrapped around his arm, Liam stood at the hospital bed of the jogging killer. "Mind asking a few questions?"

"Sure. I'm not ashamed of what I did. Those women asked for it, dressing all skimpy, everything bouncing. I'd do it again."

"You won't get the opportunity." Liam would make sure the man was locked up for a very long time.

"When my leader finds out what I did for him, he'll send someone to free me." He crossed his arms, then winced. "Stupid

IV."

"Don't count on Thompson sending anyone for you. Until the news, he didn't know you existed. How long have you been following him?"

"Since you identified him as the one behind the seven deadly sins killing. What a brilliant way to fix this broken world."

The guy was as delusional as Thompson. How many other psychos were wandering around out there.

"Hey, a bomber at the bank in Oakdale."

Liam whirled in time to see Harper wearing a Kevlar vest march between parked cars, across the parking lot, and into the bank. The camera then switched to a very frightened bank teller.

The view now was from Stephanie's head cam. Who took the video of Harper entering the bank?

Liam stepped into the hall and phoned his boss, Director Spelling. "I need to head back."

"No can do. We've got a sniper on the roof of an apartment building. You're trained in negotiations. We need you. The detective will have to make do with Black."

Black? "He's new to the force. She needs someone with experience backing her up."

"I'm sorry. I'm texting you the address."

Liam's fingers tightened around his phone as a text came through, then another. The first was not from his boss. "Get back to Oakdale or I blow up the detective and innocent people right along with her. You have until nightfall."

He'd never disobeyed orders before. He stared at the text, knowing Thompson would make good on his threat. Or would he? He hadn't reached the sin of anger yet. Would he jump ahead, leaving Liam to face him without Harper? It wasn't a chance he was willing to take.

Ugh. He had to stop the sniper first. Hang on, Harper. I'll be there soon. He had time. It was only noon. Seven hours.

He raced from the hospital and to the address his boss had texted him.

"Glad you made it." His boss's mouth quirked.

"Under duress." He showed him the text from Thompson. "If things go our way, I have time to do both. Who is the shooter targeting?"

"People wearing green. It's another fanatic. You know…green is the color of envy. No one has been shot, although he fired a few times before we cleared the street."

Liam glanced at the empty street. Not a soul in sight, although he caught a couple of curtains moving in windows and fingers pulling apart blinds. "How many?"

"Two. He called from this number." He handed Liam a slip of paper. "That's how we knew about the color green. He doesn't seem very motivated. He hasn't taken a single shot at any of us."

"You aren't wearing green." Liam punched the number into his phone.

"Yeah?"

"This is Special Agent McConnell. What do you need from us?"

"Hey, you're the one that's after my leader."

"Is Thompson aware that he's your leader?" Liam frowned.

"He will now."

A shot rang out.

Liam dove to the ground.

The shot flattened one of the boss's tires. Thank goodness, the perp was a bad shot.

He scooted with his back against his rental car and put the phone back to his ear. "Just doing my job. Is there something you want? I'm sure we can work together."

"I want my master to let me into his inner circle."

Right. The man didn't want much. "Thompson is so incredible that we have no idea where he's hiding."

"There are news reporters here. He'll see me and contact you. All we have to do is wait."

Harper didn't have time for Liam to wait for hours. Neither did those in the bank with her. He glanced at the Director. "You get me for two more hours, then I'm defying orders and heading back."

"You could lose your job."

"I could." He'd deal with the consequences. "I do my best to remain professional, sir, but if I'm not back in time, not only Detective Scranton will die. There are people in that bank. This man," he motioned to the rooftop. "Is not shooting anyone. He only wants the recognition of Thompson."

The Director nodded. "You're right. I'll call and have the jet ready for you. Good luck, Agent."

Liam didn't need to be told twice. He sprinted for his car.

Chapter Six

Look at all those wanting to help. Robert rubbed his hands together. The poor fool on top of the apartment building would be there for a long time.

He couldn't hear what had been said to Agent McConnell, but he read lips fairly well and got the gist of his conversation with the Director. The man on the building wanted acknowledgement. Something Robert couldn't give him.

Giving the man the address to the compound was a definite no. Sending him somewhere else to be picked up was also a negative. The feds would be waiting, and he didn't have enough followers to lose any at that time. This particular fool would lose patience and get himself killed.

A real pity. He could use followers as determined as the last two.

His phone rang. "Yeah."

"It's getting hot around here. How long do you want me to record the parking lot?"

"Until the agent arrives. The reporters will take it from there. At that time, you find a place to hide out until we figure out what to do with the woman."

"Detonation?"

"I haven't decided. She's doing exactly what we're asking her to. I think she could be convinced to join us if we give her time." He wasn't averse to brainwashing if it got him the results he needed. What he needed was women added to his compound before the men got restless.

~

Lucy cursed and kept the camera on the tripod aimed at the parking lot. Police officers, SWAT team, and reporters milled around like ants. Her finger itched to press the detonation button. Not only would those inside be blown to bits, but several of those outside. It would be a sight for sure.

What was taking the agent so long? Didn't he care about his partner inside?

She called Robert. "Where is the agent?"

"He has until nightfall. Be patient."

"That's hours away." Her stomach growled and she reached for the almost empty water bottle nearby. "You aren't paying me enough."

"Sure, I am."

"Considering you can't get to the majority of your money, no, you aren't."

"I pay you from my offshore accounts. Don't get greedy, Lucy. It won't end pretty."

For him, anyway. She hung up and leaned against the air conditioning unit on the roof of the building she sat on. She moved the camera around a bit so those down below couldn't easily determine where the filming came from, but that ploy wouldn't work much longer.

Sooner or later, someone would figure it out. Most likely the handsome agent.

Ah. Finally.

A car stopped on this side of the barrier. The agent flung his door open and darted to the chief's side. For now, Lucy was finished.

She gathered up the camera and tripod and climbed down the fire escape into the alley behind the bank. She propped the tripod on her shoulder, tugged the baseball cap she wore firmly on her head, and strolled whistling to where she'd left her car. After stowing the things in the trunk, she headed for the coffee shop where she could safely watch the day's excitement without worrying about the blast. For a while, at least. Then she'd move somewhere else. She didn't want to attract too much attention by staying in one place for too long, and the coffee shop wasn't as close to the action as she'd like.

~

After entering the bank, Harper had given a head count. Ten inside, not counting her and Stephanie. "Anyone in the restroom?"

"We don't know." A thin man approached her. "I'm the manager, Bill Cox. What's the plan?"

She didn't have the heart to tell them she didn't have one. All she had was the intense desire to keep any of them from dying that day. Her phone rang. She glanced at the screen to see Liam's face on the screen. "Hey."

"Tell me you're okay."

"I'm okay." She glanced out the window.

He stood on the other side of the chief's car. For the first time since strapping on the wire and vest she had hope they'd all get out of this just fine.

"What's going on in there?"

"Nothing, really." She shot a quick glance to where Stephanie sat slumped in a chair, the bag of money at her feet. "I think we're waiting for orders. Did you get your business taken care of?"

"Not completely. I had to come back." He cleared his throat. "There are two fans of Robert's that we know of. I left one in a standoff with the FBI on top of an apartment complex."

"There will be more." She fell into a hard plastic chair. "There's no way of getting them in one spot with the hopes of Robert being there, is there? Is it feasible to put something on the news they'd believe?"

"Let me talk to the man of his we have locked up. Find out some more details about this group. Right now, you're the main concern."

"No." She shook her head. "Stopping Robert and his misguided followers is top priority. Otherwise, people keep dying."

"I'll never want what someone else has again." Tears poured down Stephanie's cheeks as she lifted her gaze to meet Harper's. "Am I ever going to see my family again?"

"Gotta go, Liam." She hung up wanting to tell him so much, but now wasn't the time. She pulled her chair in front of Stephanie's and took the woman's hands in hers.

"I'm not going to lie and say we'll get out of here. I don't know that for certain. What I do know is that I will do everything in my power to reunite you with your husband and children." She gave her hands a light squeeze.

"He says you'll fail."

She moved the woman's hair. What looked like a hearing aid nestled in her ear. "He's speaking to you?"

She nodded. "He hears everything I say." Her eyes flashed through her tears. "I don't care anymore. I just want to go home, but he won't stop talking. Oh, it's not always him. Unless he wants me to do something, it's a recording reciting the seven sins over and over until I think I'll go insane."

Mental warfare. "Stand strong, Stephanie." She wanted to call Robert a coward. A man who used women to do his dirty work. But, if she said what she really felt, he might press the trigger and blow them all up.

She stood and studied the layout of the bank. Manager's office to the right of the tellers. A couple of cubbies for other bank staff. A small hall that led to restrooms and an exit door. If not for the camera, she could sneak people out the back door. Better her and Stephanie perish than all of them. She had some heavy thinking to do.

She moved to the front window and stared into the growing dusk to where Liam stood, offering support simply by being there.

Behind him, the bomb squad arrived.

~

Every ounce of his being wanted to storm the bank and get Harper out of there. Liam paced the area behind the cars. They'd offer some protection should the bomb strapped to Stephanie be detonated. Should the worse happen, there was small consolation in the fact those inside wouldn't feel a thing.

"Stop that pacing." The chief crossed his arms. "You're making us all nervous."

"You should be nervous because of the situation." Liam spotted movement in the building next to the bank. "Didn't you clear the other buildings?"

"Absolutely." The chief narrowed his eyes. "No one should be in that drugstore."

"Somebody didn't follow orders. I'll get them out." Skirting around the cars, Liam approached the pharmacy from the back.

He turned the knob on the door leading to the alley. Locked. He banged with his fist. When no one answered, he shot the lock. No secrecy for him. Not when the situation was this dire.

"FBI. Come on out." Gun at the ready, he stepped into the pharmacy. "This building should be evacuated."

Silence. The hair on his arms stood at attention as he moved through the part of the store where they filled prescriptions. A fluorescent light flickered overhead.

He could only think of two people who wouldn't announce themselves when he'd called out. Robert or Lucy. He guessed one of them hunkered down in the drugstore to watch the day unfold.

Moving as quietly as possible, he opened the door that led to the customer side of the store. Five aisles of product gave a few places for a body to hide.

The squeak of a gym shoe on the tile floor led him to turn left. He paused and pulled his phone from his pocket.

Lucy, Robert's personal assassin, had her back to Liam as she peered around the corner of a display of greeting cards. Attached to her belt was what looked like a detonator. She held a gun in her right hand.

He pulled back and sent Harper a text. If he could keep Lucy's attention on him, Harper, hopefully, could get the people out of the bank.

Text sent, he knocked over a display of toilet paper and dove out of sight.

"Clumsy move, Agent."

Staying low, he moved another aisle over.

"I've been wanting to meet you. Come out and we'll talk a while. Come out, come out wherever you are." She laughed. "Oh, this is going to be more fun than I've had in a long time. Working for Robert has grown very boring."

Keep talking so I know exactly where you are. Liam moved to the next aisle in hopes of coming at her from the other side.

"What the…?" Lucy cursed.

Liam leaped from hiding and fired. His first shot took her in the shoulder and spun her like a carnival ride. Her gun slid across the floor. The second shot dropped her next to the overturned toilet paper.

"Not good," she muttered as she reached for the detonator.

Liam lunged forward and stepped on her hand. While he had her pinned, he removed the detonator from her belt and set it high on the top shelf of a shelf before letting the chief know that he had her in custody and to send backup.

"I'll kill you for this." Lucy spit.

"You can try. Right now, I have the upper hand." He helped her to a sitting position and cuffed her hands. The woman seemed surprised that she'd lost the fight.

Harper was one of the backups. He'd never been happier to see anyone walk through a door before. "You okay?" She glanced from Lucy to him.

"For once, I'm not the one shot."

"The bandage on your arm says otherwise." She smiled and stepped aside as two paramedics helped the bleeding Lucy onto a gurney.

"Happened before I got here." He stepped forward and pulled her into his arms. "Knowing you were in that bank with Stephanie aged me fifteen years."

"I think I aged a bit, too." She gazed into his face. "Bomb squad is with her now. This part at least is over."

He watched over her head as the medics wheeled Lucy away and lifted her into the ambulance. His shots didn't seem to be fatal. She'd face a jury someday and spend the rest of her life in prison. A small part of him wished he had killed her. One less black heart in the world.

"Let's go home." He slipped his arm around her waist and led her to the chief.

"Do you have to go back?"

"I'll check with the Director." Night had fallen an hour ago. What he really wanted was to sleep.

He called his director who said the man had given up with shouted promises to return to the rooftop in the morning. FBI agents swarmed the complex and arrested him when they found the man entering an apartment on the first floor.

Two of Robert's people off the streets. He smiled and joined Harper in the jeep. In the morning, they'd come up with a way of bringing Robert's fans to one place.

Chapter Seven

Harper stared at Steven Maysup across the table in the prison visiting room. "Don't toy with me. There has to be a place and a phrase that only zealots would recognize as a code to come."

"I'm already in prison, why help you?" He frowned.

"I could negotiate a shorter sentence."

The man scoffed. "No, you can't."

She could try. "Sir, you were one of Thompson's main guys. You had your head on straight." Debatable. "These new people are crazed. They're killing under misguided intentions. We need your help to stop them."

He stared at his folded hands. "You got any change on you? I could use a candy bar."

"Sure thing." Keeping an eye on him, although he couldn't run with two guards in the room, she bought him a Snickers bar from the vending machine and dropped it in front of him. "Now talk."

He sighed and ripped off the paper, taking a huge bite. "Oh, that's good." He closed his eyes and took another bite.

Harper waited until he'd wolfed down the bar before asking again. "Well?"

"I don't know how fans will know this phrase, but Robert used to put an advertisement in the classifieds when he called a meeting. Most of the time, the message was geared to men only, and we'd meet at the club. At other times, it was more like a call to church and aimed at everyone."

"I'd like the everyone, please." She opened her phone to a writing app.

"If this doesn't get me killed, then I'm going to live a very long time." He clenched his hands together. "Wanted: People who yearn to be enlightened and change the world. If you're one of these types of people, there will be a meeting at, insert address, signed the man with a quest to better our world."

She stared at him to see whether he told the truth. Since he met her gaze straight on, she seemed pretty certain he told the truth. What did the man have to lose, after all? Locked up, he'd already lost everything. She thanked him for his help and bought him another candy bar before leaving.

At the office, she met Liam in the conference room where he talked with Black. "They're leaving you on the case?"

"For the time being." Black smiled. "I'm hoping I can help."

She told them about the ad in the classifieds. "I'm going to get that in the paper straight away. What we need is a place for these people to show up at and the manpower to bring them all in."

"I'll look for an empty warehouse set a bit from the busy side of town." Black reached for the laptop on the table.

"I'll handle the manpower." Liam picked up his phone. "Have you run this by the chief?"

"Darn. I'll be right back." She rushed to the chief's office and filled him in.

"Good work, Detective. Let's hope we can trust this guy."

"If he's lying, all we're out is the cost of the ad and a few minutes of work now." She returned to the conference room. "He's good with it all."

"Here's an address. Used to be a church in a store front closed down." Black handed her a sheet of paper. "It's big enough for about fifty people. Heaven help us if there are more."

"Thanks." Trusting Liam to find the manpower they would need, she moved to her desk and typed up the ad, then sent it to the Oakdale and Langley papers with a meeting for Friday night at nine. *Help us out here, God.*

Hope, anticipation, a trickle of fear all swirled through her in a maelstrom of emotion. With Lucy out of the picture, if they were successful in taking Robert's "fans" off the street, they'll have succeeded in keeping a lot of people from being killed.

They were nearing the end of Robert's crimes. She couldn't wait. A vacation on the beach sounded wonderful. Hopefully,

Liam would be able to go with her before returning to his home base. Oakdale would never be the same without him.

What if she followed him? She could transfer to another city easy enough. Could she leave being a small-town detective for a larger city? She shook her head. Now was not the time to think about the future. Until Robert was caught, a future might not happen.

She had to remember that her and Liam would be the targets when the man got on the sin of anger. She turned off her laptop and rejoined the men in the conference room.

~

Friday morning, Lucy pulled the IV from her hand. From her hospital bed, she could see the man guarding her room. A stupid rent-a-cop or hospital guard couldn't keep her there.

She padded to the small restroom attached to her room and searched for a weapon. Anything she could use to get her out of there. Where were her clothes? Blood spattered or not, they were better than a hospital gown.

Not finding her clothes, she removed the toilet paper from the holder on the wall, then used the holder spring to break the bathroom mirror.

"Hey, what are you doing in there?" Rent-a-Cop pounded on the bathroom door.

"Be right out." She grinned and yanked open the door. "I'm escaping." She slit his throat with a shard of glass from the mirror, then did the same to a nurse that rushed into the room. Messy, but needed doing.

The other nurses watched in horror as she held the shard in front of her and shuffled to the elevator. Inside, she demanded the nurse arriving for her shift to strip and give Lucy her scrubs. When she did, Lucy bashed her head into the elevator wall, then waltzed into the hospital lobby and out the sliding entrance doors.

She chose an older model car from those in the parking lot and hotwired it. With a huge grin on her face, she sped toward Robert's compound. The man would not be happy to see her. It was more likely he'd breathed a sigh of relief to hear about her arrest.

Unfortunately, she wasn't returning with the woman he'd hoped to convert. No problem. Once Lucy was healed from her wounds, she'd simply kidnap him another one.

First thing she did upon arriving was visit Robert in his office. She laughed at the startled look on his face when she walked in.

"How did you get out?"

"Dear Robert. Nothing can keep me where I don't want to be." She slowly lowered herself into a chair opposite him, groaning as the stitches in her side pulled. "At least pretend you're glad to see me."

"You're useless in your condition." He poured a glass of whiskey and handed her one before pouring another for himself. "The woman?"

"Free." She shrugged. "Give me a week and you'll have another one."

"I can't wait a week. Things need to speed up."

"Fine. Give me three days." She downed the liquor, then pushed to her feet. "Find your target by then. I'll be ready."

~

Liam wished for an old-fashioned phone with a hand receiver so he could slam it back into place. "Lucy escaped the hospital, killing the guard and a nurse."

"What?" Harper frowned. "That's impossible."

"Not if you're willing to make some noise." He ran both hands through his hair. "She broke the bathroom mirror and used the glass as a weapon." He dropped into his chair. "We didn't need this when we're facing a potential sting operation tonight." Add in the fact that he hadn't gotten as many bodies to help as he'd wanted; that meant they'd have a very long night.

His director had sent two more agents. Oakdale PD had four, counting Harper. Langley, since they were busy with the hospital murders, only lent them two more. With him and Black, that gave them eight to bring in how ever many crazy people showed up.

He rubbed his hands up and down his face. "We need to get some rest before tonight."

"I could handle a couple of hours sleep myself. You want the sofa in the conference room or the break room?"

"Conference room if you don't mind. I'm a lighter sleeper than you."

She stood. "You got it. Set your alarm for two o'clock."

Between the time it took to fall asleep and the time his alarm went off, he'd gotten a little under two hours sleep. While he could use a lot more, he felt refreshed enough to face the evening.

Harper had coffee ready when he entered the break room. "Get enough sleep?" She handed him a cup of black coffee.

"Not in the least. You?"

"Could use ten more." Her weary gaze met his over the rim of her cup. "How early do you want all of us in place tonight?"

"At least an hour early in case anyone shows up before nine. We also need to set up the place to actually look as if there will be a meeting." He glanced at the clock. "You and I could go now and take care of setting up."

"Okay." She took two thermoses from a shelf over her head. "As soon as I fill these. We're going to need the caffeine. What about transport?"

"I've got two vans arriving." Hopefully, it would be enough. He had no idea how many people would show up, if any. They really were grasping at straws.

Thermoses filled, Harper headed for the jeep. Liam drove them to the address and parked a building away. The two of them had gone to so many places in her vehicle that he didn't want to take any chances of one of the arrivals to recognize it as theirs.

The former church had left behind twenty folding chairs. Liam set them into rows while Harper set battery-operated lights around the room. A battered podium dragged to the front of the chairs completed the sketchy meeting place.

By the time they finished, the rest of the law enforcement officers had arrived and taken their places in the shadows or rooms off to the sides. They'd all wait until nine-thirty before stepping out and blocking the exit to keep anyone from escaping.

He sat behind a counter that had once been a coffee bar and took Harper's hand. "This is going to be a success."

"What would be a success is if Robert showed up." Her teeth flashed in the dim light. "Unfortunately, he's too smart to think it to be anyone but us setting a trap."

"Yep. But, since he'd need a credit card to place an ad, he can't set one up to refute ours. Anyone following him that's seen the ad will think it's him." He leaned against the counter.

"Sounds too easy."
"Yes, it does."
All they could do now was wait.

Chapter Eight

Harper jerked to attention as the front doors open. She peered over the edge of the counter.

Two men entered. They paused right inside the door before heading for the chairs.

"We must be early," one of them said, looking at the time on his phone.

"No, it's nine exactly." The other one lowered onto a chair. "Most likely, he's waiting for his people to arrive."

His people. Harper scrunched her nose. This man wasn't God. Not even close.

Liam put a finger to his lips as more men arrived. A few minutes later, two women.

After twenty minutes and no more arriving, Harper counted heads. Ten bodies sat waiting for a man to arrive who wouldn't. Ten more minutes later, and all those in law enforcement came out of hiding.

"What is this?" One man jumped to his feet before the others.

"I'm Detective Scranton of Oakdale PD. This is Special Agent McConnell. We're taking the lot of you in for questioning." They had nothing on them, not enough to hold them indefinitely, but every minute…

Those waiting for Robert started throwing punches. Harper grinned. Now, they had something to hold them on. Assaulting law enforcement.

One of the women's right hook caught Harper in the jaw. She lunged forward and twisted the woman's arm behind her back while unhooking her handcuffs. Within minutes she had the woman cuffed and sitting against a wall. "You should've come peaceably. We couldn't have held you longer than a night. Now, you're under arrest." She swiped the back of her hand across her mouth, wiping away the blood from her cut lip.

Liam cuffed the last struggling man and dragged him outside to one of the waiting vans.

"Let's go." Harper pulled the woman she'd fought with to her feet.

The woman struggled but couldn't do a lot with her hands behind her back. By ten p.m., they had them all in the vans and headed to the office.

Harper had no idea where they would put them all. "This night was a success. Ten stupid fans off the streets."

Liam nodded, turning the jeep into the office parking lot. "I'm sure there are more out there, but this is a great start. I think you should do another press release tomorrow. We want Robert to know what we're doing. He's bound to make a mistake at one point."

"And then we'll have him." She grinned, the gesture pulling at her lip. She touched the spot and winced.

"It's not bad. Not too swollen." Liam reached over and squeezed her hand before turning off the jeep. "You're as beautiful as always." He leaned over and gave her a quick kiss.

She widened her eyes, surprised at how natural he'd made it seem. Clearing her throat, she opened her door. "Might as well start booking these folks."

"Okay." He chuckled. "But, one of these days you and I are going to talk about us."

She froze. Us? Did she dare hope there could be something? She'd have to think long and hard about whether she'd leave Oakdale if he asked. This had been her home since childhood.

She glanced over her shoulder. For Liam she would probably uproot herself. Her gaze met his warm one. Quite possibly. She smiled and stepped from the jeep.

After those they'd arrested were fingerprinted and mugshots taken, the task of interviewing them one-by-one stretched in front of her. She'd thought about her and Liam dividing the fans, but decided against it. Two minds were definitely better than one in regard to anything that had to do with Robert Thompson.

She took a seat in the interrogation room across from the woman who had hit her while Liam lounged against the wall. The woman might respond better to Harper rather than an imposing FBI agent. "Let's start with your name."

"Sorry I punched you, but you really shouldn't have lured innocent people to a pretend meeting." The woman crossed her arms. "I reacted out of instinct. You could've been anyone. I didn't see your badge."

Harper slapped her badge on the table. "Your name." She turned on a recorder.

"Susan Wilson." Her gaze dropped to the badge. "Guess that means he's really FBI?"

"Yep. How long have you been following Robert Thompson?"

She shrugged. "Since his first mention on the news, I guess. He really has a great vision."

"Trying to improve the world is a good thing, but killing people in order to do so isn't." Now, law enforcement in two cities and the FBI were trying to make the world a better place while a bunch of fanatics ran around doing harm.

"What did you expect from the meeting?"

"Guidance. I really want him to let me help him."

Hard to do behind bars. "That will have to wait, Ms. Wilson. You'll be locked up until you stand before a judge. Mr. Thompson is in hiding. What made you think he would come out to meet with people he didn't know?"

She leaned forward, a smile on her face. "Because he's a great man with a wonderful vision who needs new workers since you arrested all the other ones."

Harper shot Liam a "she's nuts" kind of look before returning to the interrogation. No question got a different answer from Susan Wilson. She kept saying how wonderful Thompson was, how great his vision, and how if the rest of the world would open their minds and follow him the world would be a better place.

How did someone get so brainwashed when they'd never met their idol?

She waved at the mirror for Annie to take the woman back to holding and bring in the next one. While they waited, she faced Liam. "Are we missing something here? She has never met

Thompson, yet she's willing to do whatever he tells her."

"Happens more than we'd like. Look at Hitler." Liam sat in the chair next to her since the next one they'd question was a man. "Not all of Thompson's followers condoned murder, thankfully."

"No, but his fans seem a bit more fanatical." That scared the hell out of her.

~

Robert's blood boiled at the news scrolling across his cell phone. The two people he sought to destroy had lured followers to a meeting the people thought he'd be at. Then, they'd hauled them all to jail.

He could've used those people! He needed them. There simply weren't enough on the compound to help him achieve his goal.

He vaulted to his feet and paced the small cottage he'd claimed as his. Maybe it was time to step things up. Start a war. The compound had a nice armory. The men here would be well armed.

The idea held merit. The only drawback was that the agent and the detective might get caught in the crossfire. He had other plans for them than to die by someone else's bullet. They would die by his hand alone.

He'd promised his father as he'd stood over his grave that the offspring of those responsible for his death would pay.

His head ached from tension. A sharp pain plagued him from the base of his skull. He reached for the whiskey, the only thing that seemed to dull the pain he'd been experiencing lately.

The time to end it all was quickly approaching. He couldn't do his part if he hurt.

He moved to the window and caught sight of Lucy leading a man into her cottage. What would it be like for her to lead Robert there? It had been a very long time since he'd been with a woman in the physical sense.

Tomorrow, he'd bring the subject to her. Another aspect of their relationship. On second thought, he'd pass. The woman would be more likely to stick a knife between his ribs than be involved with him in any other capacity than hired assassin.

~

Liam rubbed his temples. He'd never met so many blind

people in his life, and they weren't finished with the interrogations. "I'm getting some coffee. Want some?"

"Absolutely." Harper gave a weary smile. "We've two more to go before we can head home. Sleep is definitely not something we get much of lately."

"It sounds like they're all reading off the same script." The chief turned from the coffee pot when Liam entered the break room.

"Yes, it does, but they all swear they've never met before. I'm going to have the bureau dig deeper and see whether Thompson has something on the internet that outlines his beliefs. Something that these crazy people could memorize." He poured two cups of coffee. "He could hide it easily enough under his alias and on his business website. We still have two to question. We might get lucky, and one of them will tell us how they know so much about Thompson." God willing.

"That's a good idea, Agent." The chief followed Liam back to the interrogation room.

He said a silent prayer, opened the door, and rejoined Harper. Before he could hand her the coffee, the door opened again behind him, and Annie escorted a woman in. He took his coffee and stood against the wall.

Harper moved to his side. "You look more intimidating standing over here glowering over your coffee than if you were at the table." She whispered.

"Really?"

"Yes. Her gaze keeps flicking to you. I need her attention."

"One more thing. Did Mrs. Wilson seem to have had plastic surgery to you? None of the men did, not that I could tell, but I'm sure the woman have."

"Her lips looked a little too full, and her forehead didn't wrinkle when she frowned."

"Okay, good, because I've got something I want to ask Mrs. Dudley." He followed her back to the table and took a seat, letting Harper start with the preliminary questions. When she finished, he folded his hands on the table and pasted a smile on his face, hoping it didn't look too much like a grimace.

"Mrs. Dudley do you have a family?"

"I'm a widow with two teenage children."

"I'm guessing that's why you're trying to improve things. To make a better world for them?"

"Yes." She straightened in her chair, hope lighting her face. "That's it exactly."

He widened his smile. "We all want the same thing in the long run, we simply go about it differently."

While hope still shined on her face, a question flickered in her dark eyes. Eyes that had definitely seen some plastic surgery if her perpetual "surprised" look was any indication. "I…suppose so."

"There's one thing that's been bothering me. Did you start following Mr. Thompson when he was Mr. Landry?"

Her gaze turned stoney. "Why would you ask that?"

"Perhaps you were a patient of his? Did he bring up his beliefs to you or did you find something he'd written?"

She breathed sharply through her nose, releasing her breath slowly. "I was a patient of his. He asked me if I wanted to change the world. At first, I laughed, but said that would be nice, wouldn't it? He handed me a printed pamphlet. It spoke to my heart. He's right about the world being riddled with sin."

Liam nodded as if he agreed with her. "Have you read the Bible, ma'am?"

"No, why?"

"I think you'd benefit from the words written in those pages. Words of sin and redemption. Do you know where I can find a copy of that pamphlet?"

She crossed her arms. "Wanting to expand your thinking?"

"Something like that?"

"Go to the about section on his website. Scroll down to the article Betterment. Can I go now?"

Liam stood. "Thank you for your help, ma'am, but since you assaulted an FBI agent tonight, you'll need to stay until your court date." He gave her another nod and waved for Annie to remove the woman.

"Have I ever told you how brilliant you are?" Harper grinned. "What led you to believe there was such a document?"

"I couldn't figure out how people knew about Thompson unless they'd read something, been a patient of his, spread the word to other people. I guarantee you that his patients, the one on board with his insane quest, told everyone they knew."

"Word of mouth is always the best advertising." She pushed to her feet. "Let's head home and try to catch a few hours' sleep. In the morning, I need to go to church even if only for five minutes. I need to release all the garbage I heard tonight."

"I could do with some peace myself." A quiet sanctuary always left him feeling cleansed and ready to tackle another day fighting crime.

He felt deep down that they still had quite a few days of fighting left to go.

Chapter Nine

"I'm tiring of this game, Detective. I feel as if my time is running out."

Harper showed Liam the text the next morning. Do you think he'll skip straight to anger?"

"Who knows? The man is clearly losing it which, in my opinion, makes him even more dangerous."

She leaned into him and closed her eyes as he wrapped his arms around her. "Unless he makes a move, we've nothing. For him to make a move, someone is hurt. It's a toss-up of who is more tired of this game, him or me."

Her phone buzzed again. "I think, my dear detective, that we will speed through our sixth sin of slovenness and race toward anger."

Then again. "I once read a quote that said, a slowness to applaud betrays a cold temper or an envious spirit." Then, "Why do you not applaud my efforts, Detective?"

Harper glanced up at Liam. "Is he accusing me of envy?" Her mouth dried. If Robert laid another sin on her shoulders, he might come after her before the last sin. He'd already accused her and Liam of lust.

"I'm not liking this. He's spiraling down faster than I thought."

"Not as fast as he's texting." She held up her phone to show him another. "I've decided there is no joy in one way texting. I've unblocked my phone. Oh, not so you can track me, you'll never be able to do that. But so that you can respond to me. What's the point to a one-way conversation?"

Harper frowned. "He wants to carry on a conversation? I've

nothing to say to him other than he's nuts."

Liam's brow furrowed. "He'll be expecting a reply."

"Okay." She stared at her phone. "Maybe I should play along with the sin of envy. Draw him out of hiding before he reaches anger."

"As much as I want this to stop, I don't think that's a good idea. It's too dangerous."

"I'll risk my life if it saves the people of this town." Her gaze clashed with his. "That's my job."

His eyes flashed. "Then what will you say to him?" He crossed his arms as if daring her. "That you really do applaud his actions? You have too much integrity to do that."

His phone buzzed. "Guess I'm getting in on the fun now. Robert says since you aren't willing to speak with him, he's going to send us on a quest, a scavenger hunt. If we fail, someone suffers or may die."

"Another one?" Her shoulders slumped. "I'd better hurry and get dressed. I'm sure the first clue is coming soon." She glanced at the clock. A few minutes before eight. Far too early for dangerous games.

"First clue came through. I'm often called an ambulance chaser."

"That's easy. It's a lawyer. No lawyer office is open this time of the morning."

"We have ten minutes."

Harper sped for her room and dressed faster than ever before. In two minutes, she stood in the living room and strapped on her gun. "There's only one lawyer in Oakdale. I'll call him on the way."

Liam snatched the keys off the foyer table and sprinted for the jeep. Harper followed close on his heels.

"The lawyer is on vacation. He said to do whatever we needed to do. He has insurance on the building."

Liam laughed. "I've never had anyone give me permission to break into their place of business before."

"There's always a first time." She stared out the side window. She hated these games so much a fire burned in her belly. It wouldn't surprise her if she ended up with an ulcer when this was all over.

They had five minutes left to find the next clue by the time Liam shot the lock off the back door of the building. "Send the chief a text letting him know what's going on. We don't need anyone showing up and slowing us down."

She sent a quick text. The chief replied with a bunch of symbols. "He's mad." There was no help for it. They were puppets, and Robert pulled the strings.

They found the next clue taped to the women's restroom door. Not hard to find, thankfully. "Ladies use these so as not to spread germs." She pursed her lips. "Antibacterial spray? Kleenex? Oh." Since he hadn't given them a time limit, it had to be close. She opened the door. On the toilet seat cover dispenser hung another note. "How about some Chow Mein?"

"He's making this scarily easy." Liam huffed. "Do we have a Chinese restaurant in town? He's given us thirty minutes."

"We have three. Two restaurants and a buffet. Maybe we'll get lucky and find the right one first." She darted out the way they'd come.

They found the next clue at their second stop with ten minutes to spare. Thankfully, they didn't have to break into the building. Spray painted on the side wall was the words, "The ditch on sixth street is full of trash. You have fifteen minutes to get there and fill a black lawn and leaf bag. It must be full."

"What the heck?" Liam shook his head. "None of this is making any sense!"

Harper agreed. "We don't have a choice." She rushed back to the jeep. "I'd like to know how Robert knows whether we're making our time or not. Neither of us…he's tracking us." Her mouth dropped open. "Do you think?"

"That would explain the time, but not whether we fill an entire black bag with garbage. Do you have one in the back?"

"Yes." She bit her bottom lip. How would Robert know she kept a box in the back just in case? "He's been watching me, maybe both of us, before he started this whole Seven Sins thing. He needed to know everything he could before he got started." An icy fist wrapped around her heart and squeezed.

"We're going to be okay." Liam shot her a glance. "I promise."

That was a promise he might not be able to keep.

~

Robert laughed as he watched the little blue dot on his phone flit from here to there. He had no reason for sending them all over town except for the fact he was bored. Boredom was not something he was used to.

As a successful plastic surgeon, he'd had more work than he could do and often turned patients away. Add to that his quest to make the world a better place, and he'd had little spare time. How long had it been since he'd had a vacation?

Some might consider this idyllic compound a prime vacation spot. He might have to once if there were masseuses, a bar, relaxing and enjoyable things to do. But there wasn't. He couldn't even get new followers without social media. which he didn't…

Why not use an alias? Set up a new account? Anyone who read his online article could catch the clues he'd leave. The tricky part would be getting them to the compound. But he'd find a way. As soon as the agent and the detective found what was waiting for them at the end of the trail of clues.

~

Liam's hand sank into a pile of rotting lettuce and tomato. An animal had eaten the burger and bun and left the vegetables. Disgusted, he wiped the garbage off on the inside of the bag and glanced at the time on his phone. Five minutes left and the bag was only two-thirds full. "We've got to pick up the pace. Grab the biggest pieces."

Harper scooped up an armful of dried leaves. "I doubt he has a camera on us. This should fill the bag."

"Brilliant." He flashed her a grin and reached out to wipe some dirt from her cheek.

She recoiled. "Oh, no, you don't. You've got…stuff on your hand."

"Sorry." He wiped the rest off on his pants. "Have you found the next clue?"

"No."

The bag now full, Liam studied the area. They had two minutes to find the next clue.

"There." Harper pointed to a sheet of paper that had blown under a culvert. "Please don't let there be any snakes." She ducked inside. A second later, she screamed.

Liam slid down the side of the ditch. "You hurt?"

"No, I thought I saw a snake, but it was only a stick." She handed him the paper.

"You must be hungry by now. Head to the fifties-style diner and have lunch with someone named Jordan." Jordan? "You have one hour to find Jordan and to complete your lunch." His stomach growled, reminding him he hadn't eaten breakfast. "Nice of Thompson to think of our hunger."

"I don't know anyone by that name." Harper held out a hand for him to help her out of the ditch. "But I do know where that diner is. It's in Langley which doesn't give us much time."

They made it to the diner in twenty minutes. Liam burst through the door. "Is there a Jordan here?"

A young black man held up his hand. "I'm Jordan."

Liam let Harper in first, then slid into the booth opposite the young man. "We're supposed to have lunch with you."

"I know. This dude came up to me outside, handed me fifty bucks, and said to give you this note." He pulled an index card from his pocket.

"What's the fastest thing to order here?" Harper asked, peering at the card.

"Soup and salad. You'll have it in five minutes."

She motioned the server over. "Two soups and salads, please. A diet soda and a regular."

Liam read the note. "At exactly one hour, go to mile marker 108. You'll find your prize."

"Cool." Jordan grinned. "A scavenger hunt. I've never been a clue before." He started to slide from the booth.

"You can't leave yet. We're supposed to eat with you until our time is up."

"I've already eaten."

"Order a slice of pie and add it to our tab." Liam shoved the note into his pocket. He glanced around the diner for anyone who seemed overly interested in them. "Do you see the man who gave you the fifty dollars?"

"Nah. He didn't come in." He ordered chocolate pie when the server brought the soups and salads. "What do you get for finishing the hunt?"

"It's a surprise." Liam doubted it would be a pleasant one. Thompson hadn't given a time limit to get to mile marker 108 after their hour lunch.

Under different circumstances, the soup might have been delicious. As it was, it was tasteless. Same with the ranch dressing on the salad. But the food stopped his stomach from growling and the soda wet his throat. When they'd finished, he tossed money on the table, shook Jordan's hand, and thanked him for his help.

The young man might be the first person to deal with one of Robert's people and live another day.

He stopped the jeep on the side of the interstate far enough so as not to be hit by a passing vehicle. There wasn't a lot of room before a deep ditch, but enough. "Get out on my side, Harper." If she opened her door, she'd slide down for sure.

"Definitely." She climbed over the middle console. "I'm terrified of what we're going to find."

He had to admit to some nervousness himself. He didn't see anything out of place in the median unless it was in a tree, so stepped to the edge of the ditch.

A woman's body lay at the bottom. Without a second thought, he slid his way down and rolled the woman to her back. Robert's assassin.

"Is she alive?" Harper stared down at them.

Liam felt for a pulse. "Barely. Call for an ambulance." He checked her for fresh injuries. Nothing but the ones he'd given her, but the woman was very flushed. He held the back of his hand to her forehead. She was on fire.

He ripped open her blouse, sending buttons flying and peered under the bandage on her side. It didn't take a doctor to see an infection had set in.

Thompson had sent them on a scavenger hunt in hopes the woman would be dead by the time they reached her. Liam didn't think she'd be escaping the hospital this time.

By the time the ambulance arrived, she was dead.

Had Robert helped the infection along? Poisoned her?

Who would do his dirty work now?

Chapter Ten

As Harper and Liam headed back to the office, she responded for the first time to Robert Thompson. *Why did you kill her?*

I didn't kill her. The agent did. I simply allowed you some time to find her and save her. The two of you failed.

Again, I ask why. Harper shook her head. No way could he lay the woman's death at their feet. He was the one who had dumped her in the ditch like garbage.

She committed the sin of lust.

Harper relayed the text conversation to Liam. "The man really is blind to his own sins." She typed into her phone. *What about the sin of murder? Thy shalt not kill.*

That fantasy book is not what I follow. Ridding the world of sin will make it a better place.

"Wow." She reread the last statement out loud. "What does someone say to someone so delusional? He's a killer. No amount of justification changes that."

What would his next move be? Would he target someone he perceived as lazy or someone who had an uncompleted task? Oakdale was sure to have plenty of both. Most people had the tendency to be lazy at one time or another. When this was all over, she planned on being very lazy for a few days.

She wanted to ask Liam to bring up the conversation he wanted to have with her. She wanted to invite him to spend a few days at the beach with her. Instead, she slipped her phone into her pocket and stifled a sigh.

Liam cast her a questioning look but didn't say anything until they arrived at the station. "Without someone to do his dirty work for him, Robert will make a mistake. That's when we'll get him. He's not a killer. He's only the mind behind the crimes."

"A very dangerous mind." She shoved open her door. After getting out, she glanced at him over the hood of the jeep. "I don't think we're going to win this one." Her heart sank.

"Yes, we will." He rushed to her side and gathered her into a hug, resting his chin on the top of her head. "I've never failed before. I won't now. Together, we got this."

If only she could believe him. She'd worked so hard to become a detective. The first ever female detective in Oakdale. Her first big case involved a mad man who had no value for human life. A man with a grudge who wanted her to pay for something she didn't do.

She stepped back and headed for the building. She couldn't find comfort in Liam's arms. Maybe that's why they hadn't caught Thompson. The distraction of each other could be interfering. She needed to move back and focus. If they survived this, then she'd examine her feelings for Liam.

She stopped on the top step and faced him. "We cannot be anything more than partners until this is over. Something," she wagged her finger between them, "is distracting us. No more cozy nights on the sofa, no more hugs, no more…kisses. Got it?"

Hurt crossed his features. "The way we feel about each other isn't what has kept us from getting Thompson. Not knowing where he's hiding is what prevents us from locking him up."

"I worked hard to reach this level of my career. I can't let anything jeopardize that."

"So, I'm an anything." He gave a definitive nod. "Okay. We're simply partners. I won't move back to the motel, though. It's too dangerous for you to be alone. Especially the closer we get to the last sin." His gaze locked onto hers.

"I agree." Not only for her safety, but for his. She opened the door and stepped into the building.

"The chief wants to see you," the receptionist said. "He isn't happy."

What now? Harper's shoulders slumped as she marched for his office.

"I want this psycho found." The chief crossed his arms, his chair squeaking under him. "I want the two of you in the air looking for where he might be hiding. I seriously doubt Thompson dumped that woman's body, which means he isn't alone. He's got help. There's a lot of acreage around there dotted with cabins and farms. He's on one of them, I guarantee it. Find him. A copter is waiting."

"Now?" Harper tilted her head. They'd only have a few hours of daylight.

"Yes, now. Every day until he's found. Now, go." He waved a hand in dismissal.

With a quick glance at Liam, she marched from the chief's office. Being a small precinct, they didn't have a private helicopter. This was going to be expensive. "We'll have to go to the airport. That's almost an hour away."

"Orders are orders." Liam didn't open her door for her as he usually did, instead heading straight for the driver's seat. "It's going to make for long days traveling back and forth." He looked like he wanted to say something else, but sighed and turned the key in the ignition. "Should we head to your place and pack a bag? We could stay in a motel near the airport for a night or two."

She nodded. "That would save time." Despite it being her idea, she hated the detachment between them. Still, it would be for the best. Rather than try and figure out whether the two of them had a future, she could focus one hundred percent on stopping Robert Thompson.

DEADLY SLOTH

Cynthia Hickey

Chapter One

One minute Robert could care less about where his quest was going, the next nervous energy filled him, propelling him outside to patrol the grounds and get in the way of his workers. Without Lucy, he had no one willing to leave the safety of the compound to mesh out punishment on whomever he chose.

He cursed and threw his glass at the wall. Donald had dumped Lucy; he'd have to do something else for the cause. Just as soon as Robert found his next victim. Sloth didn't just mean laziness. It also stood for someone not finishing a task. That could not be him! He would bring this entire thing to a satisfying end.

Decision made, he marched outside to find Donald, shoving on the branch-covered netting that helped camouflage the buildings. Not only would he want him to bring the next person for law enforcement to try and save, but they had a desperate need for more people. Someone needed to be out there converting. If he sent Donald, then took the risk of going out himself in a disguise, they could manage. They'd have to.

He located Donald in the barn. "I have something else for you to do."

The man shook his head. "What I did before was horrible."

"I'm not asking you to kill anyone. Besides, you know the consequences of disobeying an order." Robert narrowed his eyes. "We need converts. You know where to find them." Every town had downtrodden people eager to find a place to belong. "Bring as many as you can. I'll take care of finding the next person to use as an example."

"If no one comes?"

"Make sure you come back with no less than ten men.

Women will be an extra bonus. One I'll pay you handsomely for. That's an order." He spun and returned to the house where he opened his laptop and researched unfinished projects in the town of Oakdale, doing his best to ignore the sharp pain in his head.

Lately, nothing seemed to help. No amount of pain killer took the ache away. Nothing did except drinking himself into a stupor just to go to sleep. He didn't have time for that. The liquid pain killer would have to wait until the day's work was done.

There! Due to the high price of building materials, a sustainable living community sat unfinished. What a pity. A place like that would help not only people, but the planet.

He grinned and headed to his room to prepare.

~

Harper buckled herself into her seat and gripped the handle above her head. Her heart pounded. Her breath came in short pants.

"You okay?" Liam shot her a look before buckling himself in.

"I don't like flying, much less in a helicopter." In fact, she'd never been in a helicopter.

"Put that on." He grinned and pointed to a headset. "Otherwise, we can't communicate with each other or the pilot."

She nodded and put it on. As soon as the blades started whirling, she hunched over, wrapping her hands around her middle. When the copter lifted from the ground, she yelped and grabbed the handle above her head again.

Liam started to reach for her other hand and pulled back, no doubt remembering her stupid rule about keeping things professional. She could really use his solid grip but didn't want to give him the wrong impression by flip-flopping. So, she held on for dear life and closed her eyes.

"You can't help look for Robert's potential hideout, Darlin', if you're eyes are closed."

"I don't care." She squeezed them closed tighter. "You can look for both of us."

"The view is amazing."

"Still don't care." Her stomach roiled. "I'm going to be sick."

"Not in my copter." The pilot tsked his tongue. "You'll be fine, Detective."

Never again. Please, God, let them find Robert that day so she would never have to go up again. "See anything?"

Liam chuckled. "No. I could really use your help."

"Not going to happen anytime soon."

He patted her shoulder and started talking to the pilot about the weather and what a smooth ride they had. It became apparent that she was the only sane person on board. The copter hit an air pocket and dropped a couple of feet.

Harper shrieked.

The pilot apologized.

Liam laughed.

"What is so funny?" She popped her eyes open, then narrowed them in his direction. "This is definitely not fun." Her gaze landed out the window.

Trees far below and a mountain looming ahead of them. She closed her eyes again so she wouldn't have to watch them all die.

The copter veered to the left, dipping so much it was a miracle she didn't slide to the side. She peeked with one eye. They turned away from the mountain. Taking a deep breath, she willed herself to study the ground under them.

The rise and fall of tree-covered hills and valleys truly was beautiful. Soon, she forgot all about her fear of flying.

~

Liam smiled at the raptured look on Harper's face once she relaxed. A pang pierced his heart remembering her command that he keep his distance. He'd thought they might have something, only to have his hopes dashed. He wouldn't give up. He'd try again once this case was over. Harper was worth waiting for.

He turned his attention out the window. *If I were a psycho cult-leader type where would I hide? Somewhere heavily wooded? Trees covered the whole area. A valley? No, too easily seen. Where are you, Robert?*

"How far do you want to go?" The pilot asked.

"Start out in a large circle, then make each circle smaller as you pass again. The suspect is out here somewhere." Liam kept his gaze on the ground. *If they didn't find Robert from the air, then the man had completely stumped him.*

"We can't keep letting him kill."

"I agree."

He hadn't realized he'd spoken out loud. He faced Harper. "I'm fresh out of ideas."

"I still say setting a trap is what we should do."

"Too risky." He didn't want her in that type of danger.

"It'll come to that eventually, Liam. We're the last sin. There's only one between us and certain confrontation. We need to stop him now."

"We'll get him." He returned to looking outside. The question was not if. It was when and how many more people would die. "I'm calling for more agents to assist." Not easy. His director said the agency was swamped.

He leaned forward at an odd stand of trees. "Can you get us closer?" He pointed.

"Sure." The pilot pointed the craft's nose downward.

Harper took a sharp breath. "Is this necessary?"

"It is if you want to go lower," the pilot said, evening the helicopter out.

Liam watched closely for any signs of human life. Nothing. He motioned for the pilot to continue the circle.

He doubted Thompson would remain alone for long. He'd have people to wait on him. They couldn't stay in a house all day. They'd have to venture out. The odds of them flying over the exact spot at the exact time was practically nil. The man was too smart. When he messed up, and he would, his mistake would be a big one.

They circled the mountain the surrounding valleys twice. "Want to try again tomorrow?" The pilot glanced back.

"Yes." He sat back in his seat. They'd go up every day until the man was found. His phone rang. "McConnell."

"Donnelly. You and Harper need to get back here asap. We've had another kidnapping."

"On our way. Return to the airport." By the time they landed and returned, two hours would've passed. They'd have a lot of ground to make up.

"Who is it?" Harper removed her headset when they landed.

"I didn't say anything about a who." He jumped from the helicopter.

She jogged to his side. "The look on your face did."

"The chief didn't say, but he sounded urgent." He increased

his pace as they crossed the tarmac. "We're on the sin of sloth. Any names jump out at you?"

"Not really. Who isn't lazy from time to time?"

"Could be something unfinished. Not necessarily laziness. Think of someone big." He climbed into the driver's seat of the jeep.

Her lips rounded in an O. "Landon Barker of Barker Construction. There's an unfinished self-sustainable community on the south side of town that hasn't been completed. The job was started five years ago, and it's been stalled for two of those years. Lack of funds."

"Does he have a family?"

"Got married less than a year ago."

He bet they had the identity of the newest victim but wouldn't jump to any conclusions until it could be confirmed by the chief. "What else do you know about them?"

"Big house, lots of property. Barker inherited business and land from his father who got it from his father. Big news when the latest Barker ran out of money. He had a good idea that he couldn't finish." She got in the vehicle. "Wife's name is Amber. She's the perfect little trophy wife and about twenty years younger. Not from around here. He went to New York one day and returned a week later with a new wife."

"Divorced?"

She nodded. "Right when the money ran out. The trip to New York was about getting his hands on some funds, or so rumor has it. None of this will help us catch Robert."

"No, but it gives us motive." He started the jeep and headed back to Oakdale.

They met up with the chief and other agents in the conference room. The identity of the abducted woman was Amber Barker. She'd been taken from the parking lot of a day spa. "Have either of you received any communication from this nut job?"

"No." Which seemed very strange to Liam. Usually, Thompson couldn't wait to fill them in on his latest exploits.

"He wants me to ask him." Harper pulled her phone from her pocket. "We communicate now, remember? It's no longer one-sided."

"Then contact that creep and find out what he wants." The

chief crossed his arms.

Harper typed into her phone. "Now we wait."

The group drank too much coffee, ate too much vending machine food, and dozed at the table during the hour it took for Thompson to respond. Harper jerked to attention when her phone buzzed. She read out loud:

"I have the new wife of Barker. He needs to show confirmation that he can get funding to finish the self-sustained community within twenty-four hours. If not, I mar this pretty smooth skin. You can watch me cut her on the same live feed we've used in the past. Once I have confirmation, he has three days to begin the work or more cutting. Mr. Barker will finish this job or watch his wife be marred so no plastic surgeon can patch her up. Don't forget, I'm skilled."

Liam's mouth went dry. "Let the chief know."

Chapter Two

Before an hour had passed, Mr. Barker had arrived and paced the interrogation room with a cup of coffee in one hand and a cell phone in the other. "I don't care what you have to sell off. Get me the money." He turned stricken eyes on the two of them. "I'm working at getting the money. Your chief told me."

"Please, Mr. Barker, sit." Harper motioned to the chairs. "Can I get you anything? Water or more coffee?"

He glanced at the cup in his hand. "I could use a refresh, I guess." He ran his hands through gray hair that might have been perfectly styled before his wife's abduction. Now, his hair stuck up in disarray. He nodded and took a seat.

Harper sat across from him. "Is what the kidnapper demanding something you can achieve?"

"Maybe. I don't know. My accountant said we're asking for the impossible. Selling the beach house in Malibu might get me the funds, but it'll take longer than three days to get the work to resume." He covered his face with his hands. "He's going to mar my beautiful wife."

She wanted to promise him that she and Liam would prevent that from happening, but without knowing where Robert had taken the woman, they couldn't do more than keep searching. "We're doing everything in our power to stop this man."

"I'll get the coffee." Liam removed the cup from the table and left them alone.

"Why me?" Barker removed his hands.

Harper took a deep breath, then released it slowly. "You're aware he's going through the seven sins?"

"Yes."

"He's on sloth."

"I am far from lazy, Detective Scranton." He crossed his arms.

She explained the word had more than one meeting. "My guess is that he's targeted you because the community you're building is a worthwhile contribution to Oakdale." She folded her hands on the tabletop. "Mr. Thompson doesn't really need a reasonable excuse. It only has to make sense to his addled mind. Have you been following the prior live feeds?"

"Yes. Thank God those people were returned home. It gives me hope that he will let my wife go."

Harper held onto the same hope. If they could keep the community build moving forward, even if slower than Robert would like, she might be able to pacify him enough to be a little lenient. A long stretch, but with the two-way conversation they could now have…maybe.

Liam returned with the man's coffee and cups for both her and him. He handed Mr. Barker his and sat next to Harper.

The man stared at them. "Well?"

"Sir?" Harper frowned.

"What's the next step?"

"When you have the money, I notify the kidnapper." She glanced at her watch. "We have twenty-three hours."

The man paled and reached for his phone. "I'll make some more calls."

With the promise to return in a few minutes, Harper and Liam stepped from the room and watched from the other side of the mirror where the chief waited. "We're going to watch that poor woman get cut." The chief shook his head. "He can't sell a house in a day."

"No, sir, he can't." A muscle ticked in Liam's jaw. "At this point, all we can hope for is that we can pacify Thompson over the three days, so the woman isn't harmed further."

Harper hated that they'd all accepted the inevitable. Amber Barker would be cut and there was nothing they could do to stop it. Except lie. "How will Robert know we don't have the money within the allotted time? If we can find a buyer, someone with cash, we'll have the funding or at least a hefty down payment."

Both men turned to stare before Liam spoke. "She'll be cut

if we don't and cut if Thompson finds out we tried to deceive him. Might as well try. Let's go talk some more with Barker."

This time Barker looked at them with a glimmer of hope in his eyes. "I have a buyer."

"Great." Harper smiled. "Ask for a down payment big enough to purchase some supplies. I'll take a copy of the receipt once the supplies are ordered and send it to your wife's kidnapper." Her idea would work. It had to. "Any evidence of the building proceeding will help your wife."

The man smiled. "That I can do." He dialed his phone again and soon had a promise for fifty-thousand dollars to be wired to him before the twenty-four-hour time limit.

~

"How does a pizza and a movie sound?" Liam pulled from the parking lot. "We could use some downtime."

"That sounds great." She closed her eyes and rested her head against the back of the seat. "Add in a early night and it's perfect."

"Bed by nine." He grinned, keeping his hands tight on the steering wheel. so he didn't reach over to give her hand a gentle squeeze. He had to constantly remind himself of the new boundary.

Soon, soft snores drifted from the passenger seat. He left her sleeping in the jeep when he went inside to order the pizza. Harper still slept when he came out fifteen minutes later.

Seeing how safe she felt around him, safe enough to sleep, warmed his heart. She might want to keep him at an arm's length, for now, but the two of them had a future. He knew it deep down. When this was all over, he'd help her see it too.

"We're home." He gave her a gentle shake as the garage door closed behind them. "Let's eat before the pizza gets cold. You can pick out the movie while I get us plates."

"Who needs plates?" Her eyes fluttered open. "We can eat from the box, but a diet soda sounds good." She opened her door. "Thanks for the short nap."

"No problem. You needed the sleep." He couldn't wait to get to sleep himself. Inside, he set the pizza on the coffee table as Harper curled up on one end. "Be right back with the drinks."

When he returned, she had some silly comedy on the TV and a slice of pizza in her hand. "I thought we could use some laughs."

"Sounds good to me." He sat on the opposite end of the sofa to give her space and reached for the pizza. "You did good today."

She glanced at him in surprise. "The idea came to me in a moment of desperation."

"Whatever works." He chuckled. "Let's pray Thompson is pacified enough. Has the live feed on Amber Barker started yet?"

"No. I think he's waiting to see whether he needs to torture her. That's the only reason he has her. No sending her out on jobs." She reached for another slice of mega-meat as two goofy men rode a scooter through the Colorado mountains.

"I prefer the live feed over the silence. At least then we knew what shape his victims were in." He toed off his shoes. "Dug into the type of cancer his father of died of. Glioblastoma Brain Tumor. Once detected, the patient usually has less than twenty-four months to live. He would've died with or without medical treatment."

"I wonder if Robert was aware of that fact?" She wiped her hands on a napkin. "Grief can change a person. Sometimes in drastic ways. Robert went so far as to change his look in order to move forward with revenge and take up his father's so-called quest. He used his career to get both followers and victims."

"He'll be looking for more. He can't do this without help. Someone abducted Amber Barker, and I doubt it was physically him."

"A new assassin?"

"I sure hope not. We're trying to keep him from getting more people. We should head back into the air tomorrow."

"As much as I don't want to, despite the beauty of the mountain from that height, it's our best way of finding out where Robert is hiding. If he was in town, someone would've spotted him or Lucy before her body was dumped. Theoretically."

"But Thompson is like a ghost. A master of disguise. We could pass him on the street and not know he was there."

She nodded. "That's what makes him so dangerous."

He stretched out a leg and nudged her. "We'll get him."

"Yes. It might not be until he comes for us, but we will get him." Her phone buzzed. "It's a text from Barker. A receipt for lumber." She grinned. "I'll send this to Robert right away."

~

Robert used a cane as he entered a nightclub frequented by country club members. A few of his followers that weren't rounded up might be there. A loyal few who would join him at the compound and temporarily leave their lives of luxury behind.

He approached one who had not been caught by the police. "Are you enlightened?"

"I am." The man never glanced his way.

"Are there others?"

"A handful. It's good to know you are still with us."

Robert dropped a business card on the floor by the man's feet. "Gather them up and come. All are needed. Convert if you can." He walked on by as if they hadn't spoken and took a seat at the opposite end of the bar.

What he wanted to do was stand and preach about the coming new world, but that would send someone straight to the police. He had to stay in the shadows and let his faithful few take the reins. "A glass of your finest whiskey."

"You got money, old man?" The bar tender tilted his head.

"More than I need."

Seconds later, he had a drink in front of him and studied those in the building. These people were too upscale for the work he needed them for. He needed men and women from the seedier side of life. People who would do anything he asked for the promise of something far greater.

He finished his drink quickly and left for a less nice bar. There, he took a seat between two men already deep into their drinks and struck up an innocent conversation at first, slowly weaving in the great vision of the man the authorities were looking for.

"Think about it. A world without sin?"

"No such thing," one of them said.

"What if sin then becomes whatever the enlightened say it is?" Robert crooked a brow. "Does that kind of world entice you?"

"What do you care, old man?" He downed a shot of amber liquid. "Why so interested in what I believe?"

Robert shrugged. "I'm thinking of joining the cause. Time is short. Why not see an improved world before I go?"

"I'm intrigued. Leave me some details to think on."

Robert slid a business card to each man on each side of

him. "Spread the word." He slid from his bar stool and left with a spring in his step.

His phone signaled a text. He pulled it from inside his vest and glanced at the screen. A receipt for lumber.

He really hadn't expected the man to come through so quickly. He'd wanted to use the woman as an example of what happened when his demands weren't met. He sighed heavily and returned to the rusty sedan he'd left in the alley.

Why didn't the fact he'd cured a man of his sin not make him feel better? He'd rid Barker of being a sloth. The community would be a better place now.

Had he really gone so far that he wanted to cause pain to someone tied to a chair?

Chapter Three

Robert stared at the frightened woman in front of him. "Your husband came up with the money."

Tears poured down her cheeks. "I knew he would."

"If he could get it so easily, why didn't he finish the project?"

"Because I wanted the mansion built here. It's our third home." Her sobs increased. "I never thought he'd run out of money."

Too bad they weren't on the sin of greed. This woman would've been at the top of his list. He snarled and marched from the room, turning off the light and plunging her into darkness. Let her think about her sins.

He climbed the stairs leading out of the storm shelter. A van driven by Daniel pulled onto the grounds. Men, women, and children poured out, pulling the hoods from the heads and looking around. Robert clapped. He was building back his empire.

They would all be crowded until more housing was built. Something they couldn't do as long as helicopters circled the mountain every day. They'd manage.

Arms wide, he welcomed the newcomers and ushered them into the house. "Good job, Daniel."

The other man nodded, then headed for the barn. Ah, the barn. A massive structure that could easily be converted into sleeping quarters. The few men who had built the compound would gladly move there. That would leave the main house for the families. He'd give Daniel the order as soon as the newcomers were settled. They would also need a place to meet so he could properly train his new followers.

So much to do, so little time. He wouldn't finish his mission of ridding the world of the agent and detective as soon as he would've liked. But, he had souls to nurture. They must come first.

~

Harper hadn't had a text from Robert in a week. He didn't respond to any she sent him. The man had gone dark. Why?

The federal agents were as stumped as she was. She'd heard rumors that some of them might be called back to their offices of origin. There was further talk that Robert might have been in an accident or died some other way. She didn't think so. The man was up to something.

She'd thought he would've asked about construction on the new community. Since he hadn't, she had to assume he knew work was commencing. That meant someone had told him. She tapped a pencil on her desk.

"Anxious?" Liam glanced over from his desk.

"A bit. The silence from Robert is both confusing and frightening. I don't like not—"

Annie burst into the room. "We have several abandoned vehicles sitting in a farmer's corn field."

"Okay?" Harper frowned. Rusty vehicles showed up in fields all the time.

"Newer models."

Harper glanced at Liam who shrugged. "We'll check it out. It's a slow day." He stood. "You have something better to do?"

"Not at the moment." She followed him outside. While abandoned vehicles weren't very exciting, neither was sitting idle at her desk. At least they'd stopped going up in the helicopter for a few days.

"Want to grab lunch after we pay a visit to the field?" Liam slid into the driver's seat.

"Sounds good."

"Barker called again this morning. He's worried that we've not seen live feed on his wife."

"I don't blame him. It concerns me, too. We have no idea of knowing whether she's alive."

"I'm going with her being alive until we hear otherwise."

Since she'd expressed her desire to keep things

professional, he no longer opened the door for her. It shouldn't bother her, but it did. No matter how much she told herself things were better at an arm's length, her heart called her an idiot. Her decision might be the reason Liam flees Oakdale the second their case was solved.

The field wasn't too far out of town and set off a ways from the main house. A little used dirt road led to where seven vehicles were parked in a perfectly straight line. "Spooky."

"Orderly." Liam opened his door and exited the jeep. He stopped at the edge of the field. "Partiers?"

Harper stared at the thick stand of trees on the other side of the field. "Why be so neat about their parking if they're going to party in the woods?" She marched toward the vehicles.

She stopped a few feet away and studied the ground. A lot of footprints in the dirt around the cars. The footprints led to where another vehicle had been parked, then disappeared. "Someone picked these people up. A day trip?"

"Looks that way, doesn't it?" Liam peered in the window of a Mercedes. "I don't know many people who would be comfortable leaving a luxury car in someone's field."

Neither did she. Her gut told her something wasn't right. It also told her that the case had escalated to a whole new level.

~

Liam checked each vehicle. They were all empty of any personal belongings. Not even a cup in the console. He tried each door handle only to find them locked.

A man in denim coveralls, followed by a large mixed-breed dog, crossed the field and joined them. "Darndest thing I've ever seen. I'm Hank Bridges. I own this field." He thrust out his hand.

"Special Agent McConnell and this is Detective Scranton."

"Wow. I didn't expect the feds to show up."

"Did you see anything Mr. Bridges?"

"Yep. Bo here set up a barking like I've never heard before. I grabbed my rifle and stepped out on the porch." He scratched his nose. "A van with dark windows sat in my field. Wasn't but a couple of minutes later that these other automobiles showed up. Strange how meticulous they was at parking. Made me think they might be aliens until I reminded myself I didn't believe in such nonsense.

"Anyway. Those driving the cars climbed into the van and drove away, leaving their vehicles. That was this morning about six a.m."

Liam glanced at his watch. "Six hours ago?"

"Well, I didn't know if they'd come back now, did I? When they didn't, I called the police."

"Did you see the driver? Get a glimpse of the license plate?"

"All the way from my porch?" He cocked his head.

"I'll get the crime scene techs out here." Harper retrieved a roll of crime scene tape from her jeep. "I can secure the area while we wait."

Liam nodded, then turned back to Bridges. "Thank you for your help, sir. If you could return to your house now, we'd like to keep everyone away from this area."

"How long? I've a farm to run."

Liam glanced at the field of crops. "I'm sure we'll be finished before you need to harvest." The plants barely reached his knee.

"Sounds good." He snapped his fingers for the dog to follow him. When he reached the house, he sat in a rocking chair on the porch and watched Liam and Harper.

"Not much to do out here, I guess." Harper secured one end of the tape to a fence post.

By now, a few curious cows had moseyed up, their big heads over the barbed wire fence surrounding the pasture apposite the corn field. Too bad the animals couldn't talk. They might have been able to describe the driver of the van or get the license plate.

"Do you think this has something to do with Robert?" Harper reached a hand out to a cow. The animal took a few steps back.

"I'm guessing he's got some new followers. He's most likely keeping his hiding place secret except for a handful of people, hence the leaving the vehicles behind." He glanced to the south. "We need to expand our search from the sky."

She put the leftover tape back in her jeep. "I really hate flying."

He chuckled. "I know you do."

The farmer returned with a brown paper sack. "Looks like y'all might be here a while. If you don't mind bologna sandwiches, chocolate-chip cookies, and water, then I've got you lunch."

"Thank you." Liam's stomach growled. "We're much obliged."

"Fried bologna?" Harper peered into the bag.

"With a fried egg and a slice of good ole American cheese." Bridges grinned, then returned to his house.

The sandwich didn't sound appetizing to Liam, but he was hungry enough to eat one of the cows. The sandwich was still warm and surprisingly tasty. The high point of the simple meal was the large cookie.

He'd just finished the cookie when the crime scene techs arrived. They wouldn't find much. Maybe some prints from the door handles which would tell us the names of the owners, but not where they'd gone.

Where was Thompson? Why the silence? Had he already completed the sin of being a sloth by getting work to continue on the new community? Were they now in the last sin? They had a lot of questions and no answers.

The idea they might not find Robert trickled through his mind. It could very well be that the man would come to them, strike without them knowing. His gaze landed on Harper. He might fail to keep her safe.

When the scene had been processed, they headed back to the office and added notes with a big question mark to the case board. They had nothing more than a hunch on which to believe the owners of those cars were now with Thompson.

He perched on the edge of the conference table and crossed his arms. They'd already checked for property owned by both names Thompson had gone by. Nothing other than his house and business came up.

His IT guy had done everything he could to try and trace the man's phone. Someone had put a block on it to prevent that from happening.

He glanced at the others around the table. So many minds for them to all come up empty. Again, the idea that they might have a mole in their midst crossed his mind. He still didn't use the local IT guy, preferring the one his agency used. He didn't think Annie capable of being dirty, but he could be wrong. They also had the chief. They were the only two people in the room other than him and Harper that had been there since the start of it all. Two other officers, the crime scene techs from the nearby city of Rockdale, and IT were all involved in some capacity.

If one of them worked for Robert, it would be difficult to prove. Still, the idea wouldn't go away. He needed to dig deep into each of their lives, their backgrounds.

"What is it?" Harper frowned. "You're going to stare a hole in that board."

"Follow me." He led the way to the breakroom and closed the door.

Surprise shined in her eyes. "Okay, sounds serious."

"I'm still convinced we have a mole among us. Someone working this case."

"Okay." She nodded. "What do you want me to do?"

The fact she didn't question or argue his idea sent a rush of emotion through him. "How about we fill our evenings by digging."

She smiled. "Nothing I'd like better."

Chapter Four

Harper studied the list of names in front of them. All of them people she'd worked with since joining the force. The thought of one of them being dirty sent a knife through her heart. "Add Annie to the list."

"Really?" Liam sent a sharp look her way.

"She's been there from the very first kill. She was the first on the scene." Nausea rolled through her stomach as she opened her laptop and sat at the dining room table. "I'll dig into her background while you start on someone else."

He nodded, his gaze concerned. "I really hope it isn't her."

"Me, too. I'll start on the chief, then move to IT, leaving you to do all three officers."

Leaving her to do those she'd worked side-by-side with for five years as a detective. If she discovered one of them had been keeping pertinent information on the case from them, it would hurt as much as being shot.

As much as it will hurt when Liam leaves.

She read through Annie's files from the academy. Top of her class. The only complaint was her need to prove herself against the men. An act that alienated some of them. That came as a surprise to Harper. Everyone always seemed to really like Annie.

The woman was definitely a work horse. That's why Harper liked her. She couldn't abide lazy people or those with a chip on their shoulder. Annie's sunny disposition and willingness to get the job done made her a favorite. They weren't close friends by any means, Harper didn't have time for nurturing a friendship, but they got along well.

She straightened in her chair, rolling the kinks from her

shoulders before searching Annie's family information.

"The chief is squeaky clean." Liam stood and headed for the refrigerator. "Too clean. Tea?"

"Top shelf, glass pitcher. It's not sweetened."

"Just the way I like it. Want some?"

"Sure, thanks." How had she not known that Annie was the orphan of a pastor and his wife? She didn't talk much about her family. She typed in the name of her father's church.

It had closed at his death. A bit more searching dug up the old-fashioned ideas of women not cutting their hair or wearing pants. Nor could they work outside the home once they had children. Not what "enlightened" people believed, but maybe they could be easily converted.

Except…Annie wore her uniform of tan pants and shirt. She kept her hair cut around her shoulders and up in a bun, so she didn't fit the profile of her father's former church.

Not exactly something that would clear her name in court, but it did ease Harper's mind a bit. She set the woman aside for now. Tomorrow, she'd try asking some subtle questions to see how Annie responded. Next, she typed in their rookie, Lance Birdwell.

Liam set her glass next to her, his arm brushing against hers and sending a bolt of electricity through her. She glanced up to meet his warm gaze. "Thanks."

"You're welcome." A slow, sexy smile crossed his face before he returned to his seat across from her.

Harper, you are truly a fool to push him a way. She gave a sigh and returned to her laptop screen.

Birdwell had a minor as a juvenile, did community service, and entered the police academy right out of high school. Nothing about him hinted that he'd be into something as crazy as what Robert had going.

Neither did Officer Schultz. "I got nothing."

"Annie?" Liam didn't look up from his screen.

"I'm going to ask some questions tomorrow. See whether any spidey senses start tingling." She reached for her tea. "Maybe we're wasting our time."

"We aren't." This time he met her gaze. "Robert was always a step ahead of us. Now, he's gone into hiding. Someone knows where he is or how to get a hold of him. We have to find that someone and get them to talk."

"He's no longer a step ahead of us. Neither of us are heading anywhere."

"We're going to—"

"I know. We're going to get him." Question was when?

~

Robert couldn't be happier. His men had worked extremely hard over the last week converting the barn. Daniel had picked up a few more converts. Robert's informant deserved a reward for finding them. Some were homeless people from the streets, but since they were happy to be included and willing to work around the compound, Robert accepted them with open arms.

The sound of an approaching helicopter sent everyone scurrying. Everyone except a small boy.

"Get him out of sight," Robert ordered. "Discipline can be swift and unpleasant." He didn't care whether child or adult. Breaking the rules would require punishment.

The child's father darted from under the camouflage, scooped his child into his arms, and disappeared into the barn. Good. The area showed no signs of life as the helicopter passed by.

Robert would bring up the rules and responsibilities of parents toward their children at the next meeting. If they couldn't keep their children under control, they'd never be allowed outside to play. Which would be unfortunate. Children needed sunlight to thrive.

He waited until the copter passed out of sight, then gave the all clear. Within seconds, the area again hummed with people going about their individual jobs.

More room was becoming a necessity. Building would require finesse. First, a camouflage, then small cottages.

He pounded his fist on his thigh. Things needed to move more quickly. He had a job to do!

A pounding started behind his eyes and moved to the base of his skull. He pulled a pair of sunglasses from his pocket and headed inside. What he needed now was a stiff drink and a bed.

Then, when the headache stopped, he'd proceed with his plans.

Two hours later, he stumbled down the cellar stairs, turned on the camera, and focused a single spotlight on the woman tied to the chair. Without a word, he left her.

~

When Liam finished the background checks, he had one possible suspect. The IT guy he'd suspected in the beginning. Too much time between relay of information. Misplaced information. These could be because of an overworked schedule, but he put a check by the man's name.

He glanced up and frowned at the worry lines creasing Harper's forehead. "Are you going to be able to do what needs doing if Annie is the mole?"

Her eyes sparked. "Of course, I will. It's my job. I'd turn you in if I suspected you."

"In handcuffs?" He wiggled his brows.

She giggled and hints of pink tinged her cheeks. Exactly the reaction he's hoped for. She didn't have a lot of reasons to smile lately. His suspicions about someone keeping them from finding Robert didn't help.

"Keep it professional, remember?" She wagged at finger at him.

"Using cuffs is part of my profession." He grinned and shut off his computer. "I'm exhausted, and it's making me lose my senses. Let's crash and watch a silly sitcom to unwind." He'd do almost anything to prolong his waking time with her.

"Ok." She closed her laptop and headed for the living room. "I pick."

She glanced up at him with wide eyes. "The news was on when I turned on the television. The live feed has started back up."

He fell heavily onto the sofa. On the screen, Amber Barker sat in the dark except for one light shining on her face. Tear-stained cheeks and ankles rubbed raw from the zip ties. Liam would venture a guess that her hands behind her back were as bad or worse.

"Please help me. Why isn't anyone coming to save me?" She bowed her head, her hair falling forward to hide her face. "Why?"

"Do you think Robert plans on keeping her until the build is complete?" Harper jerked her head toward him.

"I hope not. That could be months. I doubt she'd survive." The woman already looked at her wit's end in less than a week.

Liam's phone rang. "McConnell."

"What are you doing to find my wife!?" Mr. Barker's voice boomed across the air waves.

"Everything we can, sir."

"Any fool can see she's in a cellar. Maybe a root cellar. There are jars on the wall."

Liam peered closer, barely able to make out glass jars on a shelf. The more he peered through the gloom behind the woman, the more he saw. There were a lot of jars. Enough to feed several people for months. "We'll keep you posted, sir." He hung up.

"Robert is somewhere he can be self-sufficient. Either a farm in the lowlands or the mountain. We have to keep copters up there looking."

"We need to be doing more from the ground." Harper's shoulders slumped. What we need is an army."

Unfortunately, Liam had a horrible feeling that's what Thompson was doing. Building an army to take over the world starting with Oakdale. "At least having the live feed going again will keep what agents were sent to help here." It still wasn't enough. They needed patrols on the street, eyes and ears open, trying to find out who was converting the town's people.

Not just in Oakdale, but the surrounding towns. An insurmountable task. An ordinary man or woman simply talking to other people wouldn't raise concern. They wouldn't even notice Thompson in one of his disguises.

He thrust his hands through his hair as Mrs. Barker continued to plead for help. He'd never felt so helpless in his life.

Harper gently shook him. "What happened to Mr. Optimistic?"

"He needs sleep." Without thinking, he lunged to his feet, kissed her forehead, and headed for the guestroom.

Sleep didn't come easy despite his tiredness. Instead, Liam stared at the ceiling through a room lit only by the moon. Mrs. Barker's face hovered in his light of sight.

The woman didn't look as if she'd eaten or drank anything since her capture. Had Lucy been the one taking care of the captured? Was Thompson going to let the woman starve to death?

He couldn't let that happen. Liam needed to think of a way to get Robert to let the woman go.

He bolted from bed and rushed to Harper's. Since her door was partially open, he stepped inside. "I've got an idea."

She leaped from bed, snatching her gun from the nightstand on her way.

"Whoa, it's me, Liam." He held up his hands.

"I could've shot you." She turned on a lamp. "Are you insane?"

"Quite possibly." He grinned. "I have an idea that might help get Thompson to release Mrs. Barker."

"I'm listening." She returned the gun to the end table.

His gaze fell to the long legs stretching from under an oversized tee shirt. He swallowed against a dry throat and wrenched his gaze away from the legs that seemed to go on forever. "I, uh." He cleared his throat. "I think you should do a press conference tomorrow. Ask people with any news of Thompson to come forward and fabricate how the building is going. If Thompson thinks things are moving quickly, maybe he'll let Mrs. Barker go free."

"This could've waited until morning, but okay." She climbed back into bed, pulling a sheet over her. "Close the door on your way out, please. I had just fallen asleep."

"Sorry." He grinned and stepped out of the room, pulling the door closed behind him.

Maybe now, he could sleep since they had a plan for the next day. He left his door open a couple of inches. The soft glow of a nightlight in the hall shined through the crack. He turned on his side, closed his eyes, and slept dreaming of Thompson behind bars.

Chapter Five

Robert stared with disgust at the blubbering woman in front of him. "What is wrong with you?"

"You're treating me like an animal. I'm sitting here in my own filth. I've had nothing to eat or drink. What have I done to you to deserve this?"

"Oh." The woman was right. He'd been extremely neglectful. "I'll send someone to tend to you." He glanced at the camera. Did they see how he wanted to help people? Even this woman whose husband was guilty of sin? He gave the camera a nod before leaving.

The first woman he came to had small children. While she would know how to clean someone up, he didn't think her children needed to be subjected to what was in the cellar. Besides, the young mother couldn't keep her children in line if she worked. He found a woman around the age of fifty.

"Clean her up, give her a clean gown, food and water. Do not look at the camera. Wear a hat if you need to." He didn't want anyone knowing the identities of his new followers. Secrecy was key to his winning.

"Yes, sir." She bustled away, a spark of fear in her eyes.

Good. Fear made people follow orders. Following orders would allow them to win the coming fight. And win the fight they must.

~

Harper watched as a woman wearing a hat pulled low cleaned and changed Amber before attaching a chain around her ankle. Then, she handed the woman a tray with a bowl of something and a bottle of water.

Amber attacked the food and drink like a ravenous animal. "Thank you," she mumbled through a mouthful of what looked like oatmeal.

With a sigh, Harper clicked off the live feed and donned her suit jacket. Time to try and convince a mad man to let the poor woman return to her husband.

A crowd of news reporters and civilians filled the parking lot in front of the station. Taking a deep breath, Harper opened the door and stepped outside where Liam waited with an encouraging smile on his face.

She squared her shoulders and approached the microphone as flashbulbs exploded in her face. After a few seconds to allow the reporters to settle down, she began speaking.

"I'm Detective Scranton. I've come to you today to ask for anyone who has information on the man we seek to step forward. It's quite possible that he has approached you with information about being enlightened. If he, or one of his followers, have approached you, please contact our office using the number on the bottom of your television screen." Her gaze roamed the crowd looking for Robert, hoping she'd recognize him if he showed up.

"In addition, we'd like to inform the community that the build on the self-sustained living community is moving forward much quicker than we'd anticipated." She forced a smile to her face. "Barker Construction has worked a miracle while not sacrificing quality and superb workmanship." She bit her tongue to keep from calling Robert out. "Chief Donnelly will take a few questions." She stepped back, keeping her face toward the camera.

The chief took her place. Reporters peppered him with questions. He raised his hands. "I'll tell you what we know." When they quieted, he continued, "Robert Thompson has gone into hiding. His latest victim, Mrs. Barker appears to be cared for. We do not know where he is, which is why we are asking all citizens to keep their eyes and ears open and to let us know if he is spotted. As the detective said, we want to know of anyone having contact with this cman or one of his people. If we work together, we can bring an end to this mad man's endeavors. That is all."

He turned and entered the building as the reporters resumed shouting questions. When he didn't stop or turn around, they directed their questions at Harper.

"No further comment." She rushed into the building. Her phone buzzed with a text from Robert. "Liam." She jerked her head toward the breakroom.

"Right behind you." The moment he stepped inside, he closed the door.

"Text from Robert that asks if the building project is really moving as far along as I said." It had been a while since the man had made contact.

"How will you respond?" He leaned against the counter.

"I'm going to say yes," she started typing, "and tell him to fulfill his part of the bargain by releasing Amber Barker."

"What if he sends someone to the construction site?"

"Unless he has people working for the city, he won't know how far along permits are. Want to run along and see for ourselves?" She slid her phone into her pocket. "It won't hurt to know exactly what's been done in case he asks more questions."

"Sure."

Twenty cute little houses lined up on both sides of a grassy square. Off to one end, a rubber ground had been laid in preparation for playground equipment. A pond sparkled from a hundred yards away, and an area had been cleared for a community garden.

"Wow. I almost want to live here." Harper headed down the grassy patch and peered into a house already drywalled. It was very unfortunate the building had been stalled until Robert forced the issue.

"Two bedrooms, one bath, and less than a thousand square feet." Liam read off a sign. "All homes will come equipped with solar panels and well water. Barker thought of everything."

Harper snapped some photos. "I'll send these to Robert. Let him see the progress and send Amber home." She hoped. She sent the photos.

After touring the rest of the tiny community, they returned to the jeep with no response from Robert.

~

Rain splattered the windshield, slowly at first, then a downpour. Liam turned on the windshield wipers to high. A quick glance at the clouds let him know it would be a quick shower.

His phone rang. Annie informed him that someone had come forward by the name of Bill Spooner saying he'd had someone approach him about being enlightened.

"Meet him at the bar on Highway 64."

"On it." He turned the jeep in that direction and tossed Harper a grin. "Your press release might have given us something."

"Your idea." She crossed her fingers. "Here's hoping without putting too much stock in anything."

"Pessimist." He chuckled.

Fifteen minutes later, they pulled in front of a wooden, weather-beaten building with a tin roof. "This place been here a long time?"

"Roy's Bar and Grill is a landmark." Harper shoved her door open and stepped onto the gravel parking lot, then sprinted to the building.

Inside, Liam pushed wet hair out of his face and paused to allow his eyes to adjust to the dim lighting, then called out for Bill Spooner.

"That's me." A middle-aged, balding man waved at them from the other end of the counter. "Let's sit back here." He slid off a stool and led them to a table in the corner. "I don't want anyone butting their noses in where they don't belong." Once he sat, he slapped a business card on the table.

Liam read the words printed there. "Enlightenment awaits you." A phone number had been scrawled under the words. "Did you call the number?"

"No way. I don't believe in that stuff." He twirled his almost empty beer bottle on the table. "This yahoo sat at the bar next to me and started yapping about sin and a better world. He used the word entitlement, so when I hear the detective mention it on the news, I knew I had to call."

"We appreciate it." Harper leaned her elbows on the table. "Can you describe this man?"

"About my age. Dressed in old fashioned clothes that a college professor might have worn. Peaky cap. Spoke well." He finished his beer. "That's about it."

"You didn't see what he drove?" Liam motioned for the man to have another drink.

"Nope. I almost tossed the card in the trash but pocketed it instead. He tried talking to Larry, that's the guy in the overalls, but Larry ignored him."

"I'll see if he'll speak to us." Harper moved to the bar.

The man she approached shook his head, slapped money on the bar, and marched from the building without a backward glance.

Harper returned to her seat. "He's scared. Said he doesn't want that maniac coming after him."

"I ain't scared." Bill frowned. "I haven't committed any of those seven sins. At least not that anyone would notice. I can't ID the man, and I'm sure you'll keep my identity a secret."

"Absolutely." Liam stood. "We'd appreciate you coming down to the station to speak to a sketch artist sometime today."

"Sure. I can do that. I'm off today with nothing better to do."

"Thank you." Liam shook his hand.

In the jeep, he turned to Harper. "We'll most likely never know whether that was Thompson in a disguise or anyone else."

"If we put the sketch on the news, someone might know who he is."

"If we're lucky." They hadn't been that lucky yet, and a big dose of luck was what they needed. "We should've ordered lunch inside."

"We haven't left yet." She got out of the jeep. "You think about food a lot, don't you?"

"I've got a healthy appetite." He nodded at Bill as they entered the building, and he stepped out. They sat at the table they'd vacated, and both ordered mushroom provolone burgers and fries.

"If we don't catch Robert soon, I'm going to get fat." Harper patted her stomach.

"I doubt that." His thoughts returned to the slim legs he'd spotted last night. Even with ten pounds added, she'd be drop dead gorgeous. He had the sudden urge to release her dark tresses from the ponytail, run his thumb across her full bottom lip. Neither thought beneficial to solving the case, thus off limits. Relief flooded through him when their server arrived with the food. Something to do besides dwell on the nonprofessional whirling through his head about Harper.

"Heard from Thompson?"

Her brow furrowed. "You know I'd tell you if I had."

"Surprised he hasn't responded to the photos."

She narrowed her eyes. "What's wrong with you?"

That was a loaded question. "Nothing." He bit into his burger like a man who hadn't eaten in days.

She made a noise in her throat that let him know she didn't believe him and took a much smaller bite than he had. "If I don't hear from him by the end of the day, I'll contact him about something in order to get him to respond. Something that might get him to release Amber. I have to find an idea first."

She dipped a fry in ketchup. "Why America?"

"Huh?"

"Why not Ireland or England law enforcement?"

"My parents brought me here as a senior in high school. I liked America, so I stayed. They're both gone now, so I had no reason to return to Ireland." He shrugged. "Then, I visited the Ozark Mountains on holiday once and knew right then that this was where I wanted to be."

She smiled. "America is very lucky to have you."

"Thanks." He reached across and gave her hand a squeeze, relieved when she didn't immediately pull away.

After they finished eating, Harper leaving half of her burger on the plate, they headed down the highway toward the station. Blue skies had replaced the gray clouds. They'd gone maybe five miles when Liam spotted an older model Chevy truck on the shoulder of the road.

"Let me see whether anyone needs help." He shoved the jeep in park. From there he could see someone sat in the truck's front seat. "I'll be right back." He exited the jeep and jogged to the truck.

Bill Spooner sat behind the wheel, his eyes vacant, a bullet hole between his eyes.

Someone had gotten to him. Liam stared back at the jeep. He strongly suspected the man from the bar who hadn't wanted to speak to them. Although he knew the man was dead, he checked for a pulse anyway. Nothing.

Chapter Six

Harper joined Liam at the truck. Her heart fell. Because they'd questioned him, someone had killed him. They couldn't have help on this case. It had to be her and Liam only. Robert made that very clear.

In a rare fit of showing anger, Liam slapped the side of the dead man's truck. "Any chance of finding out what the man who approached him looked like is gone. Like Thompson. Vanished like a puff of smoke." He paced back and forth, his face dark.

She understood his anger and frustration, she felt them herself, but they couldn't let their emotions gain control. That's the whole reason behind keeping him at arm's length. To keep emotions in check.

What she wanted to do was wrap her arms around him until the tension left his body and the optimistic Liam returned. She started to speak, then stopped. What could she say? She didn't have the answers either. So, she called the homicide in before securing the scene.

She wrapped crime scene tape around the area. At this rate, she'd need a new roll before long. That sounded cold and jaded. She sighed and tossed what was left back in the jeep.

By this time, Liam had stilled, staring into the trees that lined the highway. "What's on the other side of those trees?"

"A railroad track, why?" She followed is gaze but didn't see anything. "One went through not too long ago. I heard it."

"Footprints leading that way. The same footprints stopped there." He pointed to a spot a few feet in front of Spooner's truck.

"The shooter came from the trees, flagged Spooner down, then shot him?"

"That's what I'm thinking." He slid down the ditch and headed for the trees.

Torn between staying at the scene and following Liam, she chose to follow Liam. They'd vowed to have each other's backs. That meant she went where he did.

By the time she reached the bottom of the embankment, her backside was covered in mud. She obviously didn't have the skill Liam did. He didn't have more than mud stuck to his polished shoes.

He moved back and forth, then pointed. "More tracks."

The footprints headed straight for the railroad tracks.

The hair rose on Harper's arms. The feeling of not wanting to know what they'd find filled her. Her hand shook as she placed it on Liam's arm. "I've got a really bad feeling."

"You and me both." He patted her hand, then moved forward.

A shoe lay next to the tracks. A few feet further on, a gun. Most likely the weapon used to kill Spooner. On the other side, Harper spotted an arm parting the weeds. She looked both ways and crossed the tracks.

The man who had refused to speak to her lay dead, his sightless eyes staring upward. Accidental death or suicide?

Liam cursed under his breath, then apologized.

"I've never seen you like this." She didn't like it, either. She'd thought the always optimistic Liam to be annoying on occasion, but this side of him frightened her. The hope he'd always exuded seemed to slide off him in a thin trickle of despair, and she had no idea how to help him.

"Let's get back to the highway. We've two crime scenes now." He turned and marched back the way they'd come, stopping at the steep incline to give her a hand up.

"Thank you." She stepped in front of him and peered up at him. Her gaze swept over his handsome features. She reached up and smoothed his dark, wet hair away from his face.

With a groan, he pulled her to him and claimed her lips in a kiss. Not a soft, exploring one, but a hot kiss that reeked of desperation.

Her first instinct was to pull back, reprimand him, but her body acted on its own. Her arms wrapped around his neck as she returned the kiss with all the emotion she'd kept bottled inside. She could explore what this meant later. Right now, they both needed this. Whatever this was.

When they were both breathless, Liam lifted his head and rested his forehead against hers. "I'm not going to apologize for that."

"Okay." Her word slipped out on a whisper. "Are you okay?"

"For the first time, I feel as if we might not win this. So, I kissed you. What if I didn't and never got the chance?" He stepped back, his gaze piercing hers. "I'll go back to being professional, but I can't guarantee that I won't kiss you again in a moment of desperation."

She gave a slow nod, not sure whether she should be relieved or hurt that he'd kissed her in order to feel alive in the face of death. The crunch of tires alerted her to the fact they were no longer alone and saved her from having to answer.

~

Liam turned to greet the crime scene techs. "We've another body by the tracks. The shooter."

The tech frowned. "It doesn't happen often that someone gets hit by a train, but there isn't a crossing here. I guess he could've stepped in front of it."

"Maybe." He didn't think so. There was a small clearing between the trees and the tracks. The man would've spotted the train unless he really wasn't paying attention. He supposed that could happen if you'd just shot someone in cold blood.

"The detective and I are going to look for the shooter's vehicle. We'll be back to assist you in any way we can." He waved for Harper to follow him.

They turned left at the first railroad crossing, then down a dirt road that ran along the opposite side from Spooner's truck. A maroon sedan sat off to the side of the road. "Let's get the registration and find out who this guy is."

The car had been left unlocked. Using a napkin from the car's console, Liam opened the glove compartment and pulled out the vehicle registration. Mark Beck. He snapped a photo of the registration with his cell phone, then dug through the glove compartment for anything else that might help them. Nothing other than receipts and the car manual.

"Maybe we'll get something when we put his name and the license plate through our system." Harper stepped to the back of the car.

Liam straightened and studied the area. Pastureland stretched to the next rise where he could barely make out the top of a roof. He put the address on the vehicle registration into the GPS on his phone.

Bingo. Mark Beck lived up the hill.

"Let's go visit his house." They didn't have a warrant, but he intended to go inside regardless.

They hurried back to the jeep and drove up the hill to a small white-clapboard mid-century-style home. A black lab lay on the porch, getting to his feet as they stopped, then padded toward them.

Liam rolled down the window. "You friendly, boy?"

The dog sat, thumping its tail.

Willing to catch it, Liam slowly opened his door.

"Brutus." A woman stepped onto the porch and called the dog who obediently went to her side. She glanced up them. "You lost?"

"No ma'am. Is this the Beck household." Liam smiled and moved slowly toward the house.

"It is. I'm Mrs. Beck." She bit the inside of her cheek. "You cops?"

Liam introduced them. How could he tell this woman her husband shot and killed someone, then died on the train tracks? He chose to leave out the murder part. "May we step inside, ma'am?"

Worry creased her face. "This about Mark?" She hitched her chin. "I reckon it is. Come on in."

He shot Harper a look. The woman seemed resigned to whatever they were there to tell her.

"Is my husband in jail?" She motioned for them to have a seat on a striped sofa.

"Is he usually?" Harper asked.

"If he spends enough time at the bar." She folded her hands in her lap. "They don't ever convict him, just let him sleep it off."

"I don't recall ever seeing your husband, ma'am." Harper

frowned.

"That's because he keeps his shenanigans out of Oakdale where folks know him. What was it this time? A fight? Car hit a tree?"

Liam cleared his throat. "I'm afraid your husband is dead, ma'am. On the tracks."

She blinked a few times, glancing from him to Harper and back to him. "Hit by a train?"

"Yes, ma'am. I'm sorry."

"He always did take that crossing too fast." She wiped her sleeve across her eyes.

"He was on foot, just down the hill."

"On foot?" She shook her head. "That doesn't make any sense. My husband isn't one to walk anywhere."

"Has he been acting strange in any way lately?" Liam leaned forward. "Talking about sin or being enlightened?"

"Is this about the serial killer I hear about on the news? Was my Mark pushed?"

"We don't know exactly what happened, ma'am. We're hoping you could clear some things up for us."

She folded and unfolded her hands over and over, wrinkling the dress she wore. "He did say he was thinking about a new church for us to go to. He's gone himself a time or two, wanting to make sure it was for us before taking me."

"Did he tell you which church?" At least they had a mostly confirmed idea that her husband had been one of Thompson's followers. "An address?"

"No." She shook her head. "And I didn't ask. I like the Freewill Baptist in town and didn't want to switch. We fought about it a time or two." She sniffed. "Guess there'll be no arguments now."

"Again, I'm very sorry." Liam got to his feet and handed her a business card. "Please give us a call if you think of anything."

Her eyes widened. "You act as if this is a homicide. Did someone kill my husband, Agent?"

"I cannot comment on that." He'd said more than he should've. Her husband's body most likely still lay near the tracks. "Come in late this afternoon to ID the body, please."

"Is there someone I can call for you?" Harper stood.

"I'll call my sister. She'll come be with me for as long as I need." With a heavy sigh, the woman stood. "I always thought Mark would die of something related to his drinking. Can you see yourselves out? I…need a coffee."

"Well, it wasn't much." Liam stepped onto the porch and pulled the door closed.

"How do you think she'll react if it's determined that her husband killed someone?" Harper marched for the jeep. "I'm sure the bullet that killed Spooner will match the gun we saw near Beck."

"Yep." He slid into the driver's seat and stared at the house. "I don't want to have to be the one to tell her." But he most likely would be. Him and Harper.

Chapter Seven

Robert tapped his index finger against his lips. After Beck's initial call about the other man at the bar talking to the agent and detective, he no longer responded to calls or texts. Which means…he either died in an accident or suicide.

He searched the local news on his phone and found the shooting and the death of the alleged shooter by a train of all things. He didn't have enough people to afford to lose any to accidents caused because of carelessness.

What he needed was another hired hand. Someone smart who would do the job required with no questions. They wouldn't be getting paid to ask questions.

Lucy had been the best and failed. She'd sinned right under his nose. If she had needed physical fulfillment, she should've come to him. They had already had a relationship and not a one-night fling.

Shaking his head, he poured himself an inch of whiskey and sat down to start writing. Time to get things moving along faster. He didn't have time to hire another killer. Things would now be done by his hand alone.

He stopped in the middle of his work and popped a pain killer. When he'd finished, he read over what he had written and carried it downstairs to the woman.

"Read this when I give the signal."

"How about this signal?" She flipped him the middle finger.

"Inappropriate on camera." He scowled.

"I. Don't. Care!" She looked feral, eyes wide, spittle flying from her lips, tangled hair. "The woman taking care of me hasn't been here all day. You're treating me worse than an animal would be treated."

He took a step back. Why hadn't she been taken care of? While he didn't have a problem with killing someone who deserved the punishment of death, he didn't believe in treating the living in such a bad manner. "I'll be back." He set the paper on a table and went in search of the woman he'd told to care for the one in the basement. He didn't care about names. They were all the same to him.

~

Harper plopped down at her desk. A long day and it wasn't over yet. Not until the reports were done.

"Turn on the feed." Annie poked her head into the office. "Amber is sitting in a chair getting ready to read something."

"Thanks." Harper rushed to the conference room where Liam, and the other agents already sat and turned on the television.

Amber Barker, dressed in a flowered dress a couple of sizes too big, sat in a hard-back chair next to a small table. Her hands were tied flat on the arms of the chair, and her ankles crossed. Wet hair rested on her shoulders.

Squaring her shoulders, she began to speak. "I'm here to edu…enlighten you."

"She's reading." Harper sat in one of the padded chairs.

The woman's eyes flicked past the camera, then back. "The world is full of sin and needs to be cleansed. Cleansing starts with enlightenment. Sin, of which there are seven, is an offense against religion or moral law. It is our duty to uphold the moral law before mankind destroys the world." Her brow furrowed, and she glanced away from the camera again. Her hands shook. "We must turn away from these sins. To help you, I will tell you of the seven deadly sins and their meaning.

"The sin of pride is the first sin. It often leads to the commission of other sins in order to feed a person's pride. It is also a rebellion against God. Lucifer fell from heaven because of pride. Adam and Eve commmitted their sin because the serpent appealed to their pride."

"Close but not exactly scripture," Liam said. "I never took Thompson for a religious man, even a misguided one."

"Comes as a surprise to me, too." Harper started taking

notes. "The level of Robert's madness has no ceiling."

"Covetousness is the strong desire of possessions, especially for those that belong to another. It is also the ninth commandment. "Thou shalt not covet thy neighbor's wife" and the tenth commandment, "Thou shalt not covet thy neighbor's goods." Amber seemed to grow paler with each sin. Her shoulders slumped as if she were losing hope.

"The sin of lust is a desire for sexual pleasure that is out of proportion to the good of sexual union or directed at someone whom you have no right to have such a union. A married couple can also have lust for the other if it is for selfish reasons." A tear slid down her cheek at something she could see that they couldn't. "The man who has taken me wants me to let the FBI agent and the detective to know that he has witnessed their lust."

Harper rolled her eyes. "Whatever."

"The sin of gluttony is an excessive desire for…anything. Food, drink, etc. The sin of envy is sadness at the good fortune of another and not being grateful for what you have."

A masked man set a pair of garden shears on the table next to Amber. His eyes glittered behind the mask as he glanced at the camera before leaning against the table and crossing his arms. "Proceed."

Her tears increased. "The sixth sin…of sloth," her words broke on a sob, "the one committed by my husband because of my selfishness, means laziness or sluggishness or letting a necessary task go undone." She closed her eyes. "The seventh sin is anger. The one the agent and detective will have to pay for."

The man Harper assumed was Robert picked up the shears. "This woman will continue reading these sins on live feed over and over and over. If she stops, she loses a finger. I suggest all of you out there pay attention to this woman's sacrifice." He set the shears down and patted Amber's cheek hard enough to leave a red mark. "Continue." He marched out of sight as she started reading again.

Harper's blood chilled. Amber would have to stop at some point. She'd need to eat, drink, sleep, use the restroom, all which she couldn't do while reading.

Liam rubbed his forehead. "That poor woman won't make it out of this. Not unless we save her, and I have no idea how to find her."

~

A sense of helplessness washed over Liam. A sense becoming far too familiar. A sense he hadn't been accustomed to before being assigned this case.

Macey cursed under his breath. "I'm heading back up in the air. She's being held somewhere close enough for Thompson or one of his goons to come to the city."

"Harper and I will continue to canvass the streets." Liam smiled her way.

She shot him a grateful look. "I'm getting a good feel for the way Robert moves. Hopefully, I'll recognize him even if he's wearing a disguise."

"What we need is a vehicle other than your jeep. He'll spot us coming."

"We can use one of the undercover cars in the garage." She got to her feet. "I'll go check one out while you formulate a plan for driving up and down the streets of Oakdale."

Without her actually saying the words, he knew she felt as if they would be wasting their time. She was probably right. It would be a stroke of sheer luck for them to spot Thompson.

"There's a man preaching the very words Amber just read." Annie slapped a piece of paper with an address scrolled across it. "Not sure whether he saw the live and felt compelled to spread the word or if he's been following Thompson for a while."

They had somewhere to go. Someone to question. He grabbed his jacket and went to find Harper.

He found her getting a set of keys from the receptionist. "We've got a man preaching on Elm Street near the park."

"Really?" Her brows rose. "Let's go see if he can enlighten us to a few things."

The drive took less than five minutes. The man they sought stood on a brick wall that came just above Liam's knees and spoke into a megaphone. He didn't look to be over twenty-five. He recited the seven sins over and over adding at the end each time the consequences of being unenlightened. "Judgment day is coming! Only the enlightened will be ushered into the new world. Repent!"

Liam stepped in front of the man and flashed his badge.

The guy leaped from the wall and took off. With a startled glance at Harper, Liam gave chase. He could hear Harper's steps pounding behind him.

The man darted across the park, dodging strollers, dogs, and leaping over benches. On the other side of the park, he entered a gas station.

Liam entered in time to see the man head out a back door. "Harper, go around." He pulled his weapon and continued.

"Stop! Police." A gunshot rang out.

Liam barged out the back door as the man they sought disappeared around the corner. "You exchanged gunfire?"

"Warning shot. I don't think he's armed." Harper took off after him, this time Liam taking up the rear. She could run, he'd give her that. "I'm going to strangle him when we catch him. It's too hot to be running."

Liam agreed and marveled at the fact she could complete full sentences on a flat out run.

The guy tripped over a curb and went sprawling. His megaphone broke into three pieces. He rolled over and held out his hands as if to ward them off.

"Get up." Harper yanked him to his feet. "Sit."

The man sat on the sidewalk. "I didn't do anything wrong."

"Then why did you run?" Liam planted his palms on his knees and slowly regained his breath.

"Because you two are the sin of anger. You're not enlightened. That means you'd stop my preaching."

Liam shook his head. "Thompson is the angry one, although you running off hasn't made me exactly happy. What's your name?"

"Steve."

"You're kind of young, Steve. Where's he hiding?"

He shrugged.

"Do you know Thompson?" Harper crossed her arms.

Steve pressed his lips together.

"What's your last name?"

Still nothing

"Okay." Liam hauled him to his feet. "You can think about your answers at the station." He turned Steve around and cuffed him. Once the man was secure, he searched his pockets and pulled out a wallet. He flipped it open. "Steve Reynolds."

"Hey, I've got rights."

So, Liam read him his rights before marching him across the park and to the car while all the people he'd shoved aside in his haste clapped as they passed.

"I feel sorry for all of you!" Steve's face turned the color of a tomato.

"People don't usually change their minds when someone is yelling at them." Liam opened the back door and helped the man inside the car.

"Mr. Thompson is a great prophet. You'll see."

"Sure, he is." Liam slammed the door closed. It always amazed him at how easily people could be swayed to follow someone with a message no matter how far out there the message might be. Thompson might have a larger cult following than previously thought.

Thankfully the drive back was short, or Steve wouldn't have made it. The fool kept reciting the sins and Thompson's version of punishment until Liam wanted to punch him.

When they arrived, they ushered a still chanting Steve into a holding cell. "He can stay there until he shuts up." Liam locked the door before turning to Harper. "I knew you were fast, but today you blew past me."

"Ran track in high school. Jog when I can. This case hasn't given me much opportunity for jogging." She glanced at her phone screen. "Amber quit talking."

Chapter Eight

Amber's scream and cries of fear resonated through the room. No one spoke. All eyes were on the television screen.

"Please, I'll start reading again. I will. I promise." She jerked against her restraints. "I've almost got it memorized. I needed a drink. Please!"

Robert, at least Harper assumed the masked man was Robert Thompson, stepped into camera view holding the shears. "I told you the consequences."

"They were unreasonable." She tried leaning away from him.

"Unreasonable to you. See…what I'm doing here…what I'm using you for, is to show the world that I mean business. The consequences of sin in the long run are far worse than me cutting off a mere finger. I'll start with the pinky on your left hand. You don't really need that finger unless you're a typist, and you, my dear, don't work at all." He raised her pinky as far as he could while keeping her hand tied to the arm of the chair.

Harper swallowed against the bile rising in her throat. After the first finger, would he order her to keep reading? She'd have to stop again eventually. Would she lose her fingers one-by-one until she had nothing more to give?

Liam rested a hand on her shoulder. She took comfort in his touch, feeling a twinge of guilt that she couldn't give the same to Amber.

With a snip of the shears, Amber's finger fell to the floor. Robert stepped out of sight of the camera. A door slammed. Amber slumped forward.

Mr. Barker barged into the conference room. "Why

haven't you stopped this yet?" He glanced around the room. "There's enough of you here. Why haven't you saved my wife?"

Harper wished more than anything that they had. She got to her feet, feeling as if the weight of the world tried to keep her in the chair. "Sir…"

"Come with me, Mr. Barker." Chief Donnelly swept an arm toward the door. "Let me fill you in on what we've been doing. Would you like a cup of coffee?" The two men left the room.

"Let's go question Reynolds." Liam held the door open for Harper. "Maybe he can tell us something useful."

She doubted it, and from Liam's tone, he felt the same. Still, they had a job to do and needed to give it all they had.

Harper went to the break room to get coffee while Liam went to get Steve. By the time the two men joined her, she had three coffees on the table waiting for them to start their questions. She adopted a stoic expression and folded her hands around her cup.

"Have a seat, Mr. Reynolds."

"I ain't telling you anything." He plopped into a chair and crossed his arms, a belligerent expression on his face. "Us believers need to stand firm."

"You'll be standing behind bars if you don't cooperate." Liam took a seat next to Harper.

"I did nothing wrong. It ain't against the law to preach, you know?"

Harper took a sip of her coffee, then set the cup on the table with slow deliberation. She speared Reynolds with a sharp, silent gaze until the man started to squirm. "You're right, Mr. Reynolds. It isn't against the law to preach, but I had your name run through our system. Know what I found?"

He paled.

"You're a thug and a thief." She tilted her head. "There's a warrant out for your arrest. We have plenty to hold you on. But…" she waited several seconds before continuing. "If you help us, we can lessen your sentence. Maybe get a lesser charge dropped. What do you say? Hmmm? Tell us how Thompson gets information to his followers."

"I can't betray him. I took an oath." He swallowed hard

enough to make his Adam's apple bob.

She leaned closer. "Is that why his people die? He has them killed if they make a mistake? We all make mistakes, Mr. Reynolds."

"No." He shook his head. "The more enlightened we become, the less mistakes we make. People like you and the agent wouldn't understand."

"People like us?" She arched a brow. "You mean unenlightened?"

"Yes."

"If we knew how he makes contact, maybe we could be enlightened. After all, other than the live feed, we haven't heard the message."

Uncertainty crossed his face. "You're part of the quest. You're the final game. It's too late for you."

She didn't like the sound of that at all. "I guess you'll have to spend a very long time in jail then, Mr. Reynolds." She started to stand. "A young man like you will be liked very much in prison. Maybe you can make some converts."

"Why aren't you talking?" He glanced at Liam. "Why are you letting the woman have control?"

Harper frowned. She hadn't realized Thompson's group might be chauvinistic.

"Because she's doing a very good job, and I'm still mad at you for making me chase you and scuff my favorite pair of shoes." Liam smiled. "The Detective is tenacious, Mr. Reynolds. She won't stop questioning you until the iron door of your cell slams shut."

~

Reynolds face fell. "I don't know anything. I'm a follower on the outside." His handcuffs clanked against the table when he rested his hands there. "Mr. Thompson doesn't know I exist. I thought if I did something good for him, he'll tell me where he is."

Liam forced himself not to reveal how frustrated he was. The man had been an entire waste of their time. He planted his palms flat on the table and pushed to his feet. "Looks like we're done here. We'll book you on your warrant."

He led the man from the room and handed him to Annie. With the man's pleas to stop and listen, he had information after all, Liam returned to the conference room and the live feed of Amber Barker.

"A woman came in and bandaged her finger," Agent Harris told him. "Mrs. Barker has stumbled in her reading since you left, but never completely stopped. Get anything from the perp?"

"Nothing. He's a wannabe." Liam fell into a chair as Harper joined them.

"Ready for another needless drive around town?"

"Sure. We could grab something to eat."

"You think about food more than anyone I know." A slight smile teased at her lips. "How do you keep from getting fat?"

He followed her outside. "I keep my girlish figure by staying active."

"Well, this case will sure help, then."

Liam headed for the few streets that made up downtown. He hated stakeouts, but he'd take one over mindless cruising. They picked up burgers and ate in the car.

"This town isn't that big. We're bound to run across a real follower of Thompson's."

Liam cut her a quick glance. "We've switched sides."

"What do you mean?"

"You're now the optimistic one." Having a strong feeling that Amber Barker wouldn't make it out of this alive, had robbed him of his optimism. He eyed those strolling down the sidewalk. One of them could be Thompson. Or the man could have a sniper on a rooftop. He or Harper would be dead before they need it.

She shrugged. "One of us has to be." She wadded up her burger wrapper and shoved it into the sack it had come in. "Eventually, we'll either find a true follower who will talk if the situation is right, or we'll face Thompson. Either way, we'll take him down. If he kills me, you can rest assured that he'll be just as dead."

Brave words.

"I doubt it'll be a sneak attack, Liam." She popped a fry into her mouth. "He wants to torture us a bit for the crimes he believes our family members committed. He'll want to look in our eyes as we die."

Ugly thought. "I'm not the type to wait around, but since we have absolutely no idea what to do next…" He exhaled heavily and grabbed their garbage before exiting the vehicle and tossing it in a nearby trash can.

He nodded at a woman pushing a stroller while talking on her cell phone. A couple of teen boys who should've been in school, loitered near the burger joint. No one resembled Thompson in looks or build.

"Let's drive the mountain roads." He waited for her agreement as he started the car. "Thompson isn't hiding within the city limits. I'd bet on it."

"I agree. We'll need a map. I've lived here for a long time, but there are still places I've never been. City Hall should be able to give us one." She glanced at her phone. "Amber lost another finger. We have to hurry, Liam."

They were doing the best they could. They were able to secure a map of the surrounding area in a thirty-mile radius. There were a lot of roads stitching through the mountain landscape. The clerk had said there were most likely roads not mapped yet. Ones where the landowner had carved one out himself.

When an ink pen Harper had found in the car's console, he marked each road in order of which might provide the best place for a group of people to hide out. If, Thompson resided with what followers he still had. That was big if.

"We've still a couple of hours before sunset. Want to hit the first one?"

Harper nodded. "With time speeding quickly toward the last sin, we need to search as long as possible. I'm thinking Robert would hide as far up the mountain as possible."

"We'll start from the top in the morning when we're fresh. This is a short road. We can be done in an hour." He folded up the map and set it on the dashboard.

A few minutes later they started up the road to a small mountain. The road's switchbacks were so sharp, he felt as if he'd see their own taillights.

~

Robert grew bored with the woman in the cellar. He didn't enjoy cutting off fingers and listening to the sobbing and hysterics every time he got near her. Not to mention, the borderline insubordinate looks the woman who cared for her gave him. Time to dump Mrs. Barker and move to the next step.

Since he seriously doubted the Barkers would repeat their offense, especially after she'd lost not only her left pinkie, but the very finger that had once wore the diamond ring he now twirled around his finger. A ring worth a lot of money. A ring that would help fund the compound for a long while.

All he needed was someone trustworthy enough…no, he'd see to it himself. He'd wear a disguise and go two cities over to pawn the ring before releasing the woman. As soon as she was free and let them know she no longer had her wedding ring, they'd alert every pawnshop in the state.

When he emerged from his closet, not even his father would've recognized him. Well, his father wouldn't have any way since Robert had received plastic surgery before beginning his quest of revenge and cleansing. Instead of a fit man in his early thirties, he now had a middle-age budge, shaggy hair sticking out from under a baseball cap, and a three-day old beard.

He hurried to his car. Time to pawn a ring and find another sinner.

Chapter Nine

Harper leaned as far forward as her seatbelt would allow and peered through the front windshield. A woman, her hand cradled to her chest, stumbled toward them. "Is that Amber Barker?" Had they stumbled upon Robert's hiding place with their first road search?

"Sure looks like her." Liam pulled as far off the road as he could without scraping against the mountain. "I'll have to climb out your side."

Harper shoved open her door and rushed to the woman who had now fallen to her knees. "Mrs. Barker?"

She lifted her head. "Thank God." Her eyes rolled back, and she went limp.

"I've got her." Liam scooped her into his arms and darted for the car where he placed her gently into the backseat. "Further searching will have to wait. She needs a hospital."

"Twenty minutes away." Harper climbed into the backseat and lay the woman's head in her lap. The horrors this poor woman had endured, the pain…unimaginable.

She gave Liam directions to the hospital and roamed her gaze over the woman's tangled hair down to her dirty feet. "I think she's been walking for a while by the looks of her feet." While she couldn't see the bottoms, the tops were scraped, and several toenails were broken.

Liam glanced in the rearview mirror. "Dumped here?"

"That's a good assumption." Which could mean this wasn't the mountain Robert hid on. Hopefully, when Mrs. Barker woke, she could give them some useful information. She called the chief and let him know where they were headed and why.

Liam pulled the car close to the emergency entrance to the hospital and rushed inside to get a wheelchair. When he returned, he slowly helped the waking Amber onto the seat.

A nurse met them right inside the door. "This is the woman from the video."

"Yes. Let's get her out of sight before you start her paperwork." The last thing Amber needed was a lot of attention. Harper glanced around the waiting room as cell phones took pictures. "No pictures. Do not let anyone know she's here." She narrowed her eyes and met as many gazes as she could before following the others through a set of doors.

Her words meant nothing. Before the doors closed behind her, word would be flying across the airwaves. Reporters would arrive. Mr. Barker was going to hear about his wife being freed from someone other than the authorities.

The nurse took over with Amber and slid the curtains to an examination alcove closed. "You may come in when the doctor has looked her over."

Harper shrugged and leaned against the wall. "Going to be hard to ask questions once her husband arrives."

"We'll have to ask in front of him." Liam shook his head. "At least she's alive. I really didn't think she'd make it."

"I don't think Robert Thompson likes to kill. He'd prefer to have someone else do his dirty work." She met his gaze. "That doesn't mean he won't, but I believe that's been his past."

He nodded. "Without the large group he had to call on before, he'll have to step out and do the unpleasant himself. That's how we'll catch him. He won't send anyone for us. He'll come himself."

"Positively."

A doctor slipped into the alcove.

Footsteps thundered toward them. "Where is my wife?" Mr. Barker glanced from them to the curtain.

"The doctor is with her, sir. They'll let us know when we go in."

"When I can go in." He took on a belligerent look.

"We have questions we need to ask." The man might intimate people, but not her. "If you won't cooperate with our ongoing investigation, we'll have to have you stay out here while we question your wife."

He gaped like a fish, then his lip curled. "Have it your way, detective, but if she looks as if it's too much, I will contact your chief."

"That is your prerogative, sir."

Liam took a step forward. "Let's get you something to drink. The doctor might be a few minutes. You need to be calm when you see your wife. She's been through a lot."

The man huffed through his nose, then nodded. "You're right. I need to gain my composure, so I don't upset her. A coffee sounds great, Agent."

How did Liam do it? With a few words, he could diffuse anything, she felt. Here she was, putting on her cop face, and not budging. She could definitely learn social skills from him.

She watched the two of them head down the hall and tried to make out the doctor's mumblings from behind the curtain. She moved out of his way when he joined her.

"Other than her severed fingers, Mrs. Barker suffers from dehydration. I'm sure there's a good bit of mental trauma, as well, but that is not my department. Did I hear her husband?"

"Yes. He'll be back. May I go in?"

He nodded. "Reporters are converging outside, so please keep the curtain closed for her privacy. I will locate Mr. Barker. I'll stall him for a few minutes so you can question her. Make it quick."

"Thank you, doctor." Harper stepped behind the curtain. The nurse nodded and left. "Amber, can you answer a few questions?"

She pressed a button to raise the bed to more of a sitting position. "Yes. I want this mad man locked up." Her eyes flashed.

Good. Harper was happy to see the woman hadn't lost her spunk. "Do you have any idea where you were being held?"

"A cellar. Like a storm or root cellar."

"Near where we found you?"

"No." She took a deep breath. "They blindfolded me, but I could tell we were on a winding road and drove for…I don't know how long. I lost all sense of time in that cellar, but they, a man, let me go on the mountain you found me on."

"One man?"

"That's all I saw. The car stopped. He dragged me from the backseat, yanked off the blindfold, got back in the car, and drove away. I started walking down the mountain." Her eyes widened. "He won't come after me again, will he? I've received my punishment, right?"

"You did nothing to deserve the treatment you got, Mrs. Barker." Harper clenched her teeth as Liam and Mr. Barker entered the room.

~

Mr. Barker almost pushed Liam over in his haste to reach his wife. He fell to his knees beside her bed, cradled her injured hand in his, and sobbed.

Liam jerked his head toward the curtain. "Let's give them a few minutes."

Harper led the way. "She was dropped off on that mountain. Couldn't tell me how long of a drive from where she was held and where she was let go. One man drove her. That's all she could give me."

"That knocks one mountain off our list. We'll head out in the morning. With us searching on the ground, and the other agents in the air, we'll find him." He forced himself to sound optimistic. "Let's head around back and try to avoid the reporters." They were the last people he wanted to deal with.

"I agree. Let's go home."

Home. Strange how quickly her house and Oakdale had come to be home to him. When they finished this case, he'd have to return to his home base. Whether he came back depended on Harper. The only way he could return was if she wanted him to.

A nurse showed them a back way out of the labyrinth of hallways and outside. "If you go right, you can round the building to the parking lot. The emergency room doors are right there."

"Thank you." Liam led Harper at a quick pace. When they reached the corner, he peered around. The path to the car looked clear. If they hurried, they might reach the vehicle before being spotted.

"There they are!" A reporter shouted, then they swarmed toward the borrowed undercover car.

"Quick." Liam sprinted for the vehicle.

He and Harper yanked their doors open in unison, then

slammed them shut. Reporters shouted questions through the windows and held their microphones to the glass.

Liam shook his head and fished the keys from his pocket. Vultures, the whole lot of them. He started the car and slowly drove forward, forcing them to move out of his way. "I feel for the Barkers. They're going to be overwhelmed when they step outside."

"No, they won't. There are two men who looked very much like security guards standing right inside the sliding glass doors."

He glanced in the rearview mirror. Sure enough, two big guys stood like stoic bookends right inside the doors. He chuckled. "Hope they don't scare away the patients." Impulsively, he reached over and took her hand. "Amber Barker lives."

A smile graced her face. "Yes, thank God."

He drove back to her house and pulled into the garage. They had another long day ahead of them tomorrow. Hopefully, tonight they'd both get some much-needed sleep.

After showers, and a short time of watching something mindless on TV, they both went to their rooms. Liam lay on his back, staring at the ceiling. One question hovered over him.

Did the release of Amber Barker mean Thompson had moved on to the last and final sin? Had they finally entered the final countdown?

How much time did they have before they met Thompson face-to-face?

Chapter Ten

A pounding on her door popped her eyes open. Before Harper could sit up, a shirtless Liam stood next to her bed.

She blinked several times unsure whether she still slept. He called her name. "What?"

"Thompson is about to give a speech and wants to make sure we're watching. He's sent both of us several texts. Come on. We'll watch in the living room." He yanked the sheet off her, then marched from her room.

She'd slept so hard she hadn't heard her phone buzzing around on her nightstand. Five texts from Robert all demanding that she respond immediately to let him know she was watching the live feed. She sent a quick reply and padded barefoot to where Liam waited. "Sorry. I was sleeping hard." She fell onto the sofa next to him and stared at the screen.

Robert sat on a plaid sofa. Behind him appeared to be a wall made from logs. "Finally, our sleepy detective has joined us. Listen carefully, all of you.

"The time for games is over. It's time to build my army and proceed with my quest." He folded his hands on a table in front of him and kept his gaze locked on the camera. "For those of you who see my vision, I'm inviting you to come to the parking lot of the empty strip mall on the east side of Harrington tonight at nine p.m. Bring only what will fit in your vehicle. You may pull a trailer if you so desire. Bring what food you may have. Make sure your gas tank is full. We are busy preparing a place for you."

He smiled. "As for our esteemed law enforcement, if any of you show your face at our meeting from either the ground or the air, the consequences to the public will be severe." He leaned closer to the camera. "My dear detective. Agent McConnell. Your time has come. Tomorrow morning ushers in the last and final sin. Anger. The very sin, I've saved for the two of you."

Harper gripped Liam's hand. This was going to finally be over. Her blood turned to ice in her veins. Good or bad, it would be finished. She rested her head on his shoulder wanting so much to tell him of her feelings for him. She couldn't. She had to stick to keeping things on a professional level.

When the danger to them came, neither one of them could afford to be distracted. She straightened and glanced up to see his warm gaze on her. He cupped her face briefly, then scooted a few inches away as if reading her mind.

She sighed and turned her attention back to Robert as he droned on about a new world and how his followers would be held in high esteem. The man really was delusional.

"Our new world will need people of all skills and social class. We're starting fresh with our very own garden of Eden."

More like garden of evil. "If he's preparing to house an army, he needs a lot of space." She shot Liam a glance. "Somewhere without a large, populated city."

"Again, somewhere on the mountain. A valley."

She nodded. "He's managed to camouflage whatever structures have been erected." Hope rose in her. Knowing a little more of what they were looking for gave them an advantage. Robert's arrogance wouldn't allow him to believe they might possibly find him before he could make a move toward them.

"I'll let the other agents know. They'll need to fly lower, study the landscape with fresh eyes. We'll continue our search on the ground." He grinned and stood. "Come what may, the longest case of my career is almost over."

She glanced at the television as the screen went black as Robert told them there would be no more live feeds. A new text from Robert came through to her phone.

This number will now no longer work.

They would be in the dark until he contacted them. Frigid fingers trailed down her spine. He would be coming for them.

Deadly Anger

Cynthia Hickey

"Anger has a way of seeping into every other emotion and planting itself in there."

Chapter One

Harper stared at the camera footage of, at last count, twenty vehicles gather at the place designated by Robert. Most pulled trailers, a few RVs. She'd bet her badge they were all in possession of firearms.

"Doesn't take much to draw out the rednecks." The chief crossed his arms. Most were just waiting for a reason and a cause to shoot somebody."

"Will Robert consider the news reporters as being eyes on the ground?" She glanced up. "He was pretty adamant about us not being there."

"I think he'll want us to see what we're up against. Keep your phone close. He's going to want you and Liam to come out at some point." He marched away, shoulders slumped under the weight of trying to keep a city safe.

Liam passed him, giving Donnelly a concerned look. "He doesn't seem very optimistic." He handed Harper a coffee despite the late afternoon hour.

"I share his sentiment." The clock was ticking, and she had no idea how much time they had left. "I'm tired of waiting for Robert to make all the first moves."

"I'm all ears if you have an idea." He sat in the empty chair opposite her. "More agents are being sent, along with the national guard, in preparation for this so-called war."

"What if he wants Oakdale as his? Like a kingdom? It wouldn't be too difficult. It is a valley. He could fortify himself here once we're gone and start spreading out spreading his web of disillusionment."

"That's a scary thought."

"It would fit with his God complex." Another RV joined the others in the large parking lot. By nightfall, she counted thirty vehicles lining up plus a few motorcycles.

Her phone buzzed with a text. She didn't recognize the number.

"Call off the reporters now, Detective. I will have any copter in the air shot down. I will kill any who try to follow by vehicle. If they aren't in line by now, they cannot join us."

Liam's eyes widened. "I don't think he's bluffing." He reached for his phone and called the local station.

Five minutes later, the video went black, and a reporter started talking about the excitement of those who had arrived. She said the atmosphere had been very much like a rally.

Harper shook her head and headed for her desk. She plucked an ink pen from the bright-colored coffee cup she used as a holder and tapped it on the desk blotter. Law enforcement needed to make the first move. Not easy to do when they had no idea where Robert was.

In the morning, she and Liam would start driving the mountain roads again. It would be too risky tonight. They couldn't be caught.

Liam entered the room and sat at his desk. "What are you thinking?"

"Blank." She sighed. "There's nothing more for us to do tonight. Robert is going to make sure his convoy isn't followed. We still won't know where he is."

He smiled. "Don't be so sure."

"What do you mean?" A flicker of hope sparked.

"We've someone undercover. One of the motorcycle riders is one of our agents. As soon as he can, he'll let us know the location."

"Can he be trusted? What if he's the mole? What if he's a convert?"

"I guess we'll find out. If we don't hear from him within a day or two, we can assume he betrayed us or was killed." He crossed his ankles on his desk. "It's a risk we had to take."

"Why wasn't I informed?" The FBI wasn't the only one that might be betrayed. She felt a bit herself.

"Last minute decision. I only found out a minute ago. My director said the less who knew until the convoy was underway the better." A smile teased at his lips. "You know I wouldn't leave you out of the loop, don't you?"

"Yes." She pushed to her feet. "Let's go home."

"Let's pick up Chinese on the way." He feet banged the floor as he slid them from his desk.

"Okay." The man could eat under any circumstances. Her stomach rolled at the day's events. The city of Oakdale was going to war.

~

Robert laughed with glee and clapped his hands at the long line of vehicles arriving at his compound. Even better with so many RVs. Less buildings to erect. "Get everything into the trees. They'll have copters in the air at daylight."

A few of his men started directing traffic. Motorcycles were sent to the large barn. Cars and trucks were covered with camouflage. The RVs were directed into the thickest part of the woods.

Robert's men had been working fast and furious to build barricades around the compound. Soon, it wouldn't matter if the authorities knew their location. But now was not the time.

When his fort was complete, no one could get to him. All he needed was a few more days.

A droning drew his attention to the sky. A helicopter appeared over the rise. A bright spotlight swept the area.

"Shoot that down!"

"It's the news station, sir." The nearest man glanced up.

"I don't care if it's the president. Shoot it down."

He nodded and sprinted for the storage building. A minute later, he knelt beside Robert, a rocket launcher on his shoulder. As the helicopter turned to leave, he fired.

The copter exploded. Burning pieces of the machine drifted to the ground.

Maybe now, they'd listen when Robert gave an order.

~

Liam's heart dropped. Rice noodles fell from the fork suspended half-way to his mouth as the rocket fired from the ground struck.

Harper gave a small scream and clapped her hand over her mouth. "I thought you said they were told to pull back."

"They were." Before being shot down, they'd managed to show the area where Robert was holed up, but not how to get there. He grabbed his phone and called the station. "Tell me who got the copter's location."

"Not the exact, but a good idea. I'll text the coordinates to you."

Liam's next call was to the chief who told him no one would be back in the air until the national guard could take over.

"I'm not going to have my people, or yours, suffer the same fate as those reporters."

"Harper and I intend to keep searching those mountains in the morning." Nothing could deter him. He'd disobey a direct order if he had to. They were going to stop Robert. Now.

He hung up on the chief's sputterings. "No more copters. He's calling in the national guard."

"For now, it's up to us. I prefer it that way. We're the grand finale anyway. Might as well take the fight to him. Just Robert and us." Despite the weary lines on her face, her features hardened.

"What if the chief orders you not to?"

"Then, I'll lay my badge on his desk. He'll have to arrest me in order to stop me."

"That's my girl." He started to reach for her, to kiss the furrow between her brows, and stopped.

Her eyes widened, then dropped. She started gathering up the cardboard boxes their food had come in, then carried it to the kitchen.

Liam wasn't finished, but his appetite had fled with the bombing of the reporter's helicopter. His phone dinged with the coordinates of the fallen helicopter. He grinned. The compound wasn't hidden any longer. We're coming for you, Thompson. The hardest part would be getting the man away from his followers.

Would he face him and Harper willingly if they contacted him? Maybe they could send a message to the man through one of the men he would have guarding his perimeter.

"A lot more people are going to die." Harper hovered in the doorway. "The National Guard won't back down if fired upon. Those misled people following Robert will die. We can't let that happen. We aren't responsible for what my father and your grandfather allegedly did, but neither are those people."

He nodded. "Are you sure you're ready to face Thompson?"

She gave a nervous laugh. "Absolutely not, but we have to."

One or both of them would most likely not be alive after the confrontation. He had to make sure it wasn't Harper that perished.

"Then, we need a plan."

She sat in the chair across from him and tied her hair into a messy bun. "I say we face him head on. No sneaking up. We park a little bit away from the compound and walk in. We're less likely to get shot that way."

"Not unless we wear our Kevlar."

"I'm definitely fine with that." She tilted her head. "What do we say? We can't very well say "here we are, come kill us", right?"

"No." He stared at the floor between his knees. What would they say to a madman who wanted nothing more than to see them die for crimes they didn't commit?

"Anger is what makes a clear mind seem clouded." – Kazi Shams

Chapter Two

Harper nursed a coffee at the kitchen table the next morning. She'd declined the offer of Liam cooking breakfast, opting instead for a couple of slices of buttered toast. Anything else would sit like a boulder in her stomach.

Today was the day they faced Robert, and she had no idea what to say. They couldn't challenge him. Instead, they needed a way to draw them out so it could be just the three of them. No National Guard, no followers, no law enforcement. Only those three directly involved.

"What do we say?" Liam sat across from her. "I've never not known what to say to someone before."

"Me either." She gave a sarcastic chuckle. "I've talked armed men out of their homes on domestic abuse charges, but I have no idea what to say to a psychotic cult leader. It's not as if we can pretend to want to be enlightened."

"I agree. He set the path of us being punished for the final sin before this all began." He took a sip of his coffee and hissed. "Too hot."

Despite the seriousness of their predicament, she giggled. "You did just pour the cup."

He grinned, sending her stomach flip-flopping. How could she keep a man alive who would be determined to step in front of a bullet for her? The thought of a world without him stabbed at her heart.

She took a deep breath. "We approach Robert and tell him we're ready. We don't have to say what for. He'll know. Then, we tell him to give us a meeting place and time. Just the three of us. If he says no, we retreat and tell him we're sending in the National Guard. If he says yes…we figure out the next step."

"It'll be dangerous."

"Yep." She stared at the dark liquid in her cup. "How far away is he?"

"About an hour."

She exhaled heavily out her nose. "I'll shower and be ready in half an hour." She set her half full cup in the sink and headed to her room.

Twenty-five minutes later, she joined Liam by the front door and hooked cuffs and a radio to the belt around her waist. Her gun holster fit across her. The jacket she wore hid her weapon. "Let's do this."

"No turning back."

"No turning back." She forced a smile to her face that trembled, showing her nervousness as he opened the front door.

They both paused on the porch, studied the area, then marched to the jeep. They had no more reason to hide in a borrowed undercover vehicle. The radio on Harper's belt crackled before she had her seatbelt on.

"Scranton."

"Where the hell are the two of you? We had a meeting scheduled for eight this morning." The chief barked over the air waves.

Ooops. She'd been so deep into the upcoming confrontation, she'd forgotten. So had Liam, obviously. "Sorry, sir, we're out working the case. We're halfway up the mountain."

"Get your rearends back here! I told McConnell last night that we were going to let the National Guard handle bringing Thompson down."

"Sir? You're…break…ing…up." She resorted to the oldest trick in the book.

"I know you can hear me. If you get yourselves killed, I'm locking you up." He hung up.

"I'm going to be in big trouble when we return to the office." She hung the radio back on her belt. It wouldn't surprise her if she ended up suspended. It would all be worth it if they stopped Robert.

"So will I once he informs my director." He reached over and gave her hand a quick squeeze. "Let's worry about that later."

He backed from the drive and headed toward the GPS coordinates he'd put into his phone earlier that morning. Harper stared out the passenger window, working on coming up with the right words to say to Robert.

Hey, wanna meet us at the flagpole in front of the courthouse? Three o'clock? Didn't seem like the right words. This wasn't a playground spat. Confronting Robert would start another war, albeit a smaller one, than what he planned for Oakdale.

She wasn't naïve enough to believe he'd leave the town alone. Once she and Liam were out of the way, he'd swoop in and form his dominion. The man hadn't said so, but she knew it in her gut. He needed a base in order to cleanse the world, and it seemed he'd chosen Oakdale.

As for the exact words she'd say, she would play it by ear.

~

Robert had people every twenty feet or so around the compound's perimeter. Other men strung barbed wire fencing. Two more followed behind with electrical. Anyone touching the fence other than by the gate's entrance would receive a shock.

Things were coming along as planned. Soon, he'd expand into the little town nestled against the foot of the mountain. Whoever didn't convert, didn't see the light, would perish. Sacrifices had to be made for the greater good.

A pain stabbed behind his eyes, and he closed them. The pain had become sharper and more often.

It started to occur to him that he might have the same cancer his father had suffered from. Because of the agent and the detective, he didn't have the choice of seeking medical treatment. Time became a precious commodity. Once he'd finished with them, finished the last sin, he'd be cleansed. Any cancer he may or may not have would be gone. Sickness would never be close to him again. He held onto that fact as he ordered his people to work faster.

He slipped a pair of large sunglasses over his eyes and continued his march around the perimeter. His presence gave the people encouragement. They smiled and nodded, working harder to show their loyalty. He smiled and nodded back. "Well done, my good and faithful servant." His words puffed their chests.

"Sir." His most faithful ran toward him. "We've got company." She pointed toward the main gate.

"Come with me."

She followed without complaint.

~

Seeing no reason to hide, Liam drove and parked close to the main gate. A double-wide gate made of wood. There was enough space between the slates for the barrel of a rifle.

As they exited the jeep, the gate swung open. Thompson and…Annie? The cop's face held an impassive emotion. Gone was the look of friendliness. They'd found their mole.

"Annie?" Harper's steps faltered. "You?"

The other woman hitched her chin but remained silent.

"She has been invaluable to me." Thompson smiled. "She will be greatly rewarded in our new world."

"Why?"

Annie's eyes flashed. "My parents were killed because a drunk driver, a glutton for liquor, got behind the wheel of a semi-truck. I believe in this cause."

Thompson put a hand on her shoulder. "What brings the two of you here? I have not summoned you. It isn't the time yet."

"It is for us." Harper crossed her arms. "It's time for just the three of us, Robert. Time to bring this to an end. We are willing to let you pick the time and place."

He laughed. "Two against one? That won't do at all, Detective."

"We're much better than the National Guard." Liam narrowed his eyes. "That's who you'll see next."

"War is war, Agent McConnell. My people are well fortified as you saw yesterday." He matched Liam's posture. "Let the guard come. It's all part of the plan. I want the world to see how strong faith can make a handful of people."

More than a handful. From what Liam could see inside the gates, the compound was full of people. "Why wait for us to end this?"

"Anger is a great force. If you control it, it can be transmuted into a power which can move the whole world." – William Shenstone." Thompson smiled. "Yes, I'm very aware that I am the one suffering the sin of anger. The only way to rid myself of this sin is to rid the world of those who made me angry. Since the men responsible are no longer with us, I must seal their fate with their offspring."

Perspiration dotted his forehead and he seemed to draw in on himself. After what looked like a difficult action, he straightened. "Good day, Detective, Agent. I'll be in touch." He turned and entered the compound, the gate closing behind him.

Back in the jeep, Liam turned to Harper. "Did he look ill to you?"

"Definitely. He's lost at least twenty pounds since his license photo was taken."

Liam rested his hands on the steering wheel and stared at the gate. "Didn't we determine that the type of cancer his father died from is hereditary?"

"Yes." Her eyes widened. "He's dying."

"The tumor is making him unpredictable. Spurring him to greater evil. What comes next is going to be huge if he isn't stopped." His blood chilled to his toes. "We're running out of time."

"What do we do?"

"Let the National Guard do what they will."

"People will die."

"Collateral damage." He swallowed against a dry throat. "More will die if the compound isn't brought down." Tough decisions were going to have to be made, and he was glad he wasn't the one to make them.

The drive to the office was made in silence. Harper kept her gaze out the passenger window. She'd drawn so close to the door, he thought she'd try melting into it.

"If you have another way, I'm listening." He turned his attention back to driving and pulled into the station's parking lot.

"I don't." She shoved her door open and marched for the building.

He hadn't meant to make her mad, but the whole town would be destroyed if Thompson wasn't stopped. Fifty people or several thousand?

When he entered the building, the first thing he heard was the chief's shouting coming from the conference room. Squaring his shoulders, he joined the others.

"The two of you got your way." He shot Liam an accusing look. "The National Guard is here to protect the town. SWAT and FBI will take down Thompson and his people."

"We said nothing, Sir." Liam stepped next to Harper who didn't glance up. He stifled a sigh. He didn't like that she was still upset that he'd consider collateral damage in order to stop Thompson, but there really wasn't any other way. Hopefully, she'd see reason soon.

"I'll want the two of you there with the other FBI agents," the chief continued. "You know this man better than any of us and have good instincts."

Harper scoffed.

Chief Donnelly narrowed his eyes. "If there is a problem between the two of you, get it worked out. We'll be marching within a few days."

"A few days gives them more time to fortify." Liam stepped away from Harper. "The gate is wood. We can probably burn them out. Maybe save some of them that way."

"Or they can all choose to stay and be burned alive." Harper glared his way.

"Again, I'm open to suggestions."

"We wait until he orders us to come."

"The whole town could collapse by then!" He struggled to bring his voice under control.

"The guard will make sure that doesn't happen." Her face darkened.

The others in the room glanced from him to her and back again, clearly enjoying the show.

"You can't discard people's lives like that. We've sworn to serve and protect." Tears shimmered in her eyes.

His heart dropped. "I'll do my best to make sure there's as little death as possible. Even if it means my life."

Chapter Three

Harper still didn't understand Liam's willingness to have "collateral damage". She couldn't believe the words had fallen from his lips. Yes, people would die. She wasn't foolish enough to think otherwise. But, to have it said in such a matter-of-fact way pained her.

Because of that, she'd avoided Liam as much as possible. Easy when they'd gone home to sleep, not so easy the next morning when he handed her a cup of coffee.

"Agents will be filing in today." His gaze roamed her face.

"That's good." She popped bread into the toaster. "Toast?"

"No, I'll pick up something heartier on the way to the office." He sighed. "I wish I knew what to say to make my words yesterday easier to bear."

"It's me." She took the popped-up toast out of the toaster and slabbed butter and strawberry jam on top. "Every death we haven't been able to prevent is another dagger to my heart. I feel like such a failure." She planted her hands on the countertop and bowed her head. "I think it's time to seek peace in church before going to the office."

She hadn't attended a single service, but sitting in the quiet soothed her, quieted the demons. She'd need that peace more than ever as they worked to prevent Robert's war.

"That sounds like a great idea. I could use some peace, too. Ten minutes?"

She nodded and carried her toast and coffee to her room. She dressed quickly, ate even quicker, and joined Liam in eight minutes. They were due to the office by eight and she didn't want to be late again. The chief would have a coronary, and no one wanted the morning to start with a lecture.

Liam pulled up to the side of the church, and they entered through a side door left unlocked for people seeking solace. Harper sat in the front row, glanced at the wooden cross, then closed her eyes.

As she sat, the weight of the previous weeks slipped from her shoulders. Her strength renewed. Come what may, she'd be ready to face Robert and accept the consequences of whatever action she might have to perform. While she'd do everything possible to keep Liam and as many others as she could safe, she'd be able to stand under the deaths she couldn't prevent.

"Time to go." Liam's soft words broke the silence.

She nodded. "I'm good now."

"Me, too." He smiled and held out his hand.

Without speaking, she slipped her hand in his and let him lead her back to the jeep. God, spare his life, please.

The chief stopped them before they entered the station. "All meetings will now take place in the high school gym. School is canceled until this is over. Folks are leaving town for a while. Get what you need and make it quick." The stress of his job caused deep lines in his face.

"We'll be right there." Good. It relieved some worry to know the town would be emptier of occupants when Robert made his move.

Harper packed up her laptop and accessories, ammo for her gun, and glanced around the bullpen. Her gaze landed on Annie's desk, now clear of anything.

When she'd told the chief about Annie being a mole, he'd paled, a hand to his chest. Said he'd always looked on her as a daughter.

Harper took one last glance around the room she spent so much time in. Would she be back? Refusing to dwell on the possibility she might not, she squared her shoulders and followed Liam back outside.

"Stop." He took her laptop from her and stashed it in the back of the vehicle. "There's something I want to say before this day begins."

Her heart stuttered. "Okay."

"It won't be today, but the day is coming when we'll be

standing in front of Thompson's compound preparing to fight." A shadow crossed his eyes. "There is no one I'd rather be standing strong with than you. Promise me you won't do anything foolish."

Not a promise she could keep. "I'll do my best."

He sighed. "I guess that's all I'm going to get. When this is all over, there's a lot more I want to say." He climbed into the driver's seat.

She had a lot to say too, which included some apologizing. She slid into her seat. "The gym is two blocks over, then turn right. Another half a mile and you'll see it. It's not a small building." She shot him a sharp look. "I don't want you to be a hero either."

"I'll do my best." He tossed her a wink.

Touché.

The drive took five minutes. Already several buses and vans filled the parking lot. "I wonder how many we'll have."

"There were 185 at that fiasco in Waco." He climbed out and retrieved their things from the back. "You're getting ready to enter the biggest bull pen you've ever seen."

He wasn't kidding. The gym had been transformed.

The bleachers were folded along the walls. Battered metal desks were placed around the room. Electrical cords weaved a web across the polished wood floor. Voices echoed to the rafters.

"Looks like the chief is gathering the office in that corner." Liam jerked his chin toward the far, right end.

Harper felt like a foreigner. She might be a detective, a good one at that, but this definitely put her out of her element. The noise alone made her want to flee. The reason they were all gathering squeezed her heart. The saving grace was that it would all be over soon.

~

The noise and commotion wasn't new to Liam, although he'd never been involved in something this large. Harper's wide eyes showed her rising anxiety.

"Breathe. Focus on how you felt in the church."

"Right." She took a deep breath and set her things on an empty desk. "Now what?"

"We wait for orders. Excuse me." He spotted his director near the rear entrance to the building. "Sir?"

Director Payson turned. "McConnell. Darndest thing, isn't

it?"

"Yes. What are we supposed to be doing right now?"

"Once everyone arrives, we'll move to the compound. We're all hoping that Thompson gives up peacefully and no one gets hurt."

Liam's sentiments exactly.

"Let me know if that psycho makes contact with you or Detective Scranton."

"Will do." Liam returned to where Harper set up her laptop. "Nothing yet."

"So, we wait." She sat in a rolling chair with duct tape on the seat and booted up her computer.

"What are you doing?" He peered over her shoulder.

"I grew up here. I'm going to see if there is a back way into that compound now that I know where it is." She pulled up a satellite map. "It beats doing nothing."

He agreed. Sometimes there was a lot of waiting in law enforcement. "Let me know if you find anything."

She murmured something and kept her attention on the computer screen.

How many days until everyone assigned this case would arrive? How long until Thompson fired the first shot? He sat in a chair and propped his feet on the top of the desk, his gaze locked on the door. Would Sheila be one of those arriving?

It could be awkward. No, why should it? He and Harper weren't an item. He wasn't sure what they were, but she'd made it plan to be only professional until Thompson was either dead or behind bars. Liam was starting to think the cancer might kill him before he could be arrested.

What then? Would his followers disband, or would someone step up to take his place?

Liam had never wished anyone dead before, much less from something as horrible as cancer, but Thompson dying could solve a lot of problems. He stiffened when he spotted the top of a head full of red hair. Nope, not her.

"Liam, look." Harper waved him over.

He dropped his feet to the floor with a thump before once again peering over her shoulder. "What am I looking at?"

"Here is the compound. He's not even trying to camouflage

anymore, which tells me the satellite must have gone over within the last few hours." She tapped the screen to zero in. "Here is an old logging road that runs fairly close to the far perimeter. It's overgrown, but four-wheel drive could get in, then it would require maybe half a mile hike. We could surround him. He wouldn't see us coming until we were there."

He grinned. "You're amazing. Ever considered joining the FBI?"

"No, this is my home. All I could think about at the academy was to try and get on to the police department here."

His heart dropped. He'd gotten the answer to one of the questions he wanted to ask her when all that was over. "I'll get the chief and Director Payson. They'll want to see this."

A few minutes later, they all crowded around Harper's laptop. "Good job." The chief grinned. "The SWAT team can sneak right in. We'll get a sniper to take Thompson out." He clapped Harper on the shoulder before returning to those gathering in the center of the gym.

Payson nodded, admiration gleaming in his eyes, and followed the chief.

Liam grinned. "Takes a lot to impress that man."

"It really wasn't that hard. If the chief wasn't so stressed, he would've remembered these mountains are laced with old roads, some mere trails anymore. Is there a printer close by?" She glanced around them. "Oh, there." She hooked to the printer via wifi and printed off the map. "I'll get some copies of these made."

"Hello, Liam."

He pulled his attention from the retreating Harper and met the amused glance of Sheila Turner, his ex. "Hello, Sheila."

"What a surprise to find you here. I thought you'd moved back to Ireland."

"Why? America is my home now." He crossed his arms. "I did wonder if you'd be assigned this case."

"I'm not excited about it." She leaned against Harper's desk. "Nothing worse in my mind than a cult leader waging a war. Who's the pretty woman?"

"Detective Scranton." In case Sheila didn't know, he filled her in on how he and Harper had been drawn together.

"You dating her?"

"No, we're simply working together to stop a madman." He had to fight to keep his gaze from returning to Harper when her laugh rang out.

"Same as when we were searching for a serial killer." A sly smile spread across her face. "That didn't stop us from getting involved."

"A big mistake." Especially since she'd chosen someone else over him. He hadn't known until spotting them hot and heavy in a car outside a restaurant. That had been enough for him to ask for a transfer. "How is Marcus?"

"Oh, we broke up shortly after you left. He was nothing but a fling, Liam." She straightened his tie, stepping too close for comfort. "I've missed you."

He moved a few steps away. "I've barely thought about you." The truth, because after meeting Harper, no other woman ever drifted through his mind.

"Now, you're being cruel." Her smile faded. Her gaze grew cold. "I never took you for a cruel man."

"I never took you for a cheating woman. Now, if you'll excuse me, we all have jobs to do." He turned and bumped into Harper.

Her gaze flicked to Sheila. How much had she heard?"

"Hello, I'm Detective Harper Scranton."

"Special Agent Sheila Head. Liam's ex-fiancé." She held out her hand.

"He never said anything about being engaged before, but then again, the subject never came up." She gave him a look that pierced straight to him, then returned Sheila's handshake. "Welcome to Oakdale. I'm sure the two of you have a lot of catching up to do." She sat a stack of printed maps on the corner of her desk. "Feel free to take one. I've handed out several. Director Payson will let us know soon what the next step is." Without sparing Liam another glance, she marched away.

Liam watched her go, wishing very much that Sheila hadn't been one of those sent to help.

Chapter Four

Wow. A fiancé. Why hadn't Liam ever mentioned he'd been engaged before? She banged a pot on the stove, not really hungry, but knowing she had to eat.

"I've ordered a pizza. Maybe you could take a hot bath while we wait. You've got twenty minutes."

She turned to face Liam. Her gaze roamed from the bedroom eyes to the chiseled jaw. Any hopes she'd had of a future with him now had a crack through them. Get over, Harper. His past was none of your business.

His gaze locked with hers. "Sheila and I have been finished for three years. She doesn't mean anything to me. Nothing more than a nuisance in my mind."

"Things sounded pretty warm on her end."

"But not on mine." He stepped forward and gripped her shoulders. "I know you don't want any commitments while Robert is loose, but when this is over, I'm going to tell you how much I love you."

"No." The word came out in a hoarse whisper. "We can't do this."

"Why?" His gaze intensified. "Why not say I love you? If one or both of us don't make it out of this, I want to die knowing I've told you what you mean to me."

Tears blurred her vision. "You're telling me now."

He gave a sad smile. "No, I'm telling you what I'm going to tell you."

A nervous giggle escaped her. "Sneaky." She wrapped her arms around his waist and rested her cheek against his chest, counting the heart beats. "I won't say it back. Not yet."

He tilted her face to his. "And that is okay." He lowered his head and kissed her. Soft at first, but growing in intensity and heat as if they had a future worth of kisses to put into that one kiss, that one moment of letting go of boundaries and giving into emotion.

Both were breathless when they pulled away.

"I…I'll go take that bath now." Before she did something she couldn't back away from.

He gave a sexy one-sided smile. "Probably a good idea."

Wow. She closed the bathroom door and leaned against it. She'd savor that kiss for as long as she lived.

When the doorbell rang, she stepped from the bubbles still left in the tub, dressed in cotton drawstring pants and a tank top and joined Liam on the sofa. He jabbed a slice of pepperoni pizza toward the TV screen.

"News reporters made it to the gate."

"Brave after what happened the last time." She grabbed a slice of her own and sat cross-legged on the sofa.

"Blowing up the copter was simply a show of strength. Letting us all know that he would follow through on any threats." He finished the slice and reached for another one.

"This looks an awful lot like history is repeating itself." The familiar icy fist gripped her heart. A feeling that rarely left her anymore.

"Yeah." Liam wiped his mouth and hands, then got to his feet. "Right now, Robert and his people are staying behind that gate. Let's hope they stay there until we're ready to move on our end."

Harper closed the box with the few remaining slices and stored it in the refrigerator. "Goodnight." She started to head for her room.

"Not so fast." His arm snaked around her waist, and he pulled her close. "Not without a goodnight kiss."

She was more than happy to oblige.

~

Robert couldn't sleep. The pain in his head had intensified. No amount of prayer or alcohol numbed the pain. Neither did having Annie in his bed. The former cop was more than happy to do anything he asked.

He popped two more pain pills and poured another shot of

whiskey. He wasn't worried about the combination. No one died before their time.

"Is there anything I can do?" Annie ran her hand across his back.

"No." He marched to the window. The spotlight on top of a news van shined through the wood slats of the fence.

"I can make them go away."

"No. They're right where I want them." He wanted the world's attention on him. Wanted its sympathy. He would need as many people on his side as possible when things got rough. People who would follow his commands, stand in front to shield him, follow him to the end.

His gaze moved to the largest outbuilding that housed most of the single men. Not one of them would back down from a fight. Most of the women would most likely be in the thick of things. Underneath the compound, his men had widened the storm cellar to provide a safe place for the mothers and children if the compound was attacked. He had thought of everything.

He downed another shot of whiskey, then left the building. Sometimes, when the pain was at its worst, a walk around what had become the beginnings of his kingdom helped. Pride filled him at every obedient guard at his post. At those who worked under the light of lanterns to complete their assigned tasks.

All nodded without smiling or speaking. All knew the severity and importance of the fight to come. That's why he had them working around the clock in shifts. The protection of the compound needed to be completed before he could make his next move. Once he did, law enforcement would storm the place.

That's when he would bring the agent and the detective to their end while the whole world watched.

~

Liam woke the next morning with a smile on his face. Harper might not have said she loved him back, but he'd seen the emotion in her eyes. God willing, they'd get the chance for him to hear the words slip from her lips.

Would she move to Little Rock with him? She'd said Oakdale was her home. Could he give up his career for the small-town life?

Some of the joy of the day before rolled off him, crashing to the floor like a shattered water glass. Maybe all they had together was right now, this moment.

He sat up. If so, he'd take every second with her he had.

He showered quickly, dressed, then headed for the kitchen. They'd both need a good breakfast for another long day.

How long until they swarmed the compound? Set up camp right outside the gate? No one knew how long Robert and his followers could survive without going into town for supplies. Liam's guess was that the place was well stocked. Thompson wouldn't have let something that important slide. He would know law enforcement would come.

Soon, he had bacon sizzling in a cast iron skillet and whipped eggs in a bowl. "Ever have a French omelet?" He turned and smiled as Harper entered the room.

"No, I don't think I have." She headed straight for the coffee pot. "What is it?"

"Smooth eggs with a cream cheese and herb filling. You'll never want omelets cooked any other way once you've had this."

Cup filled, she leaned back against the counter. "And how did an FBI agent learn to make such a thing?" She arched a brow.

"TV cooking show." His grin widened, then he turned his attention back to the stove.

"My father enjoyed cooking shows. Said it helped relax him after a long day at work. I guess an oncologist would need downtime like a cooking show."

Liam nodded. "I'm sure most medical fields are stressful." As rough as some days of being FBI? His grandfather had never complained about being a general practitioner. When he'd passed, the small church where his service was held had been standing room only.

He sighed. Now, a madman wanted to kill the grandson that had nothing to do with said madman's father's death.

"Why the sigh?"

"All..." he waved the spatula. "This. I'm sure there are people behind bars that would love to see me dead, but I've never actually had one say so."

"Me either." She sat at the table and sipped her coffee. "I'm fairly new to being a detective, and being one in a small town, did not prepare me for something of this magnitude. I feel very incompetent."

"That's only because we don't have a clear path." He set her omelet and three slices of bacon in front of her. "If we did, if we had the authority to enter that compound ourselves and ferret out Thompson, this would be over. One way or the other."

"Thanks." She eyed the food in front of her. "Looks different." She dug her fork in. "What's keeping us from doing exactly that? What's the worse that can happen other than being killed? Losing our badge? I might be willing to risk that in order to save lives." She put the bite of omelet into her mouth. "Oh, wow. This is delicious."

Her idea halted him in his tracks. Could he risk his career that way? His gaze landed on the top of Harper's head as she ate. For her…yes. If they could think of a way to enter the compound and get rid of Thompson without losing Harper, he would do so in a heartbeat. "What do you have in mind."

She straightened, an evil gleam in her eyes. "Robert Thompson isn't the only one who can wear a disguise. We change our appearance, slip inside, and blend in until we locate him."

"It can't be that easy."

"Probably not, but I'm willing to try." She set down her fork and picked up a slice of bacon. "After we lose our jobs, you should take up being a chef."

He laughed. "How about a mall security guard?"

"That's my next career choice." Her smile faded. "I'm just really tired of this. Not of being a detective, dealing with this case. We've been nothing but puppets on Robert's string since the very first text."

He carried his plate to the table, glad she hadn't waited for him. A cold omelet never tasted good. "We'd need wigs."

"There's a thrift store in town. We can run over during our lunchtime. I'll dress as a man—"

"There's no way anyone could mistake you for a man."

"Why not?"

"You are far too gorgeous to be anything but a woman." He winked. "If you can look like one, you'll have my undying admiration."

"Watch me and be amazed." She laughed and carried her plate to the sink. "Some Halloween makeup, a wig, a hat, bind my womanly parts, and I'll be a very realistic thin man. Overalls will help."

He widened his eyes. "You've been thinking about this."

"All night long."

He stood and faced her. "What if I hadn't agreed to go along with your plan?"

"I'd have found a way to go myself." She hitched her chin, giving him a defiant look. "I said I would do everything possible to prevent as many deaths as I can. I meant that."

"That's my goal, too, but I thought we were a team." He crossed his arms. The romantic feelings from the night before flew out the window. Not even a kiss would dispel the pain of knowing she'd go on without him.

"Might as well head to work." He put his half-eaten breakfast in the garbage and set his plate in the sink before marching from the room.

He gathered his gear, made sure his weapon was loaded, slid his badge into his pocket, and then headed for the jeep. Feelings of love or not, he would keep things on a professional level from now on. His heart panged at the thought. He'd really thought the two of them had taken a step forward the night before.

As soon as Harper had gone to bed, she'd started devising a plan without him.

Chapter Five

Why couldn't Harper and Liam stay in the warm fuzzy of new love instead of the pain of perceived betrayal? She wouldn't have done anything without mentioning her plan to him first. She would have gone without him, though. That's what a good detective did, right? Serve and protect? Which meant doing what it took for the good of the people of Oakdale.

They'd stayed silent on the way to the office. Liam avoided her most of the morning, remaining at his desk or conversing with Director Payson. Occasionally, Sheila would drift by, but whatever he'd say to her sent her on her way.

Harper smiled. He'd kept secret the fact he'd once been engaged. Her secret had lasted less than a day. His had been the whole time they'd been here. Ugh. It wasn't his fault. She was the one who said to keep things professional. That most likely cut out any personal backstory.

She shot him a glance. He laughed at something Agent Harris said. She was glad they could laugh now, because she'd hear a rumor circulating that they'd been gathering outside the compound at nightfall. There wouldn't be any joking once that happened.

By lunchtime, she'd had enough of Liam's cold shoulder. Since he was going to infiltrate the compound with her, he had to go to the thrift store with her. At noon, she approached his desk.

"Ready for lunch?"

"Sure." He grabbed his jacket and followed her to the jeep.

This time she drove. If he wasn't going to talk to her, she wasn't going to let him drive her car. "I'm sorry." She shouldn't have kept her idea to herself. "I really would've told you. Did tell you at breakfast. Did you want me to wake you up?"

He glanced at her sideways. "Of course not. I'm being silly." He reached for her hand. "Your plans scare me. Fear makes me grouchy." He smiled.

"Still a team?"

"Still a team." He raised her hand to his lips. "Always."

Feeling a hundred percent better, she parked in front of the local thrift store. "They don't have a lot, so do the best you can. If we are caught once we're in the compound, there's some consolation in the fact we probably won't be shot on sight."

"I agree. Robert will want to kill us himself." Liam thrust his door open. "I'll give you fifty bucks if you wind up looking like a guy."

"Deal." She laughed and followed him into the store where she headed straight for the men's clothing section.

Wasn't hard to find denim overalls. She chose a pair one size too big, a checkered shirt, then went to find a hat. The tricky part would be hiding her long hair…ah. A gray wig that would suffice once she gave it a haircut. In the odds and ends section, she found an open package of Halloween makeup. All that was left was a handlebar moustache that looked as if it were made from horsehair and a bit of glue. It didn't match the hair, but if people didn't look too closely, it might work. Better yet, she'd dye the wig to match the moustache.

She glanced over to see Liam flicking through the clothes, then rushed to the changing room. A few minutes later, the wig still on the long side, but tucked up under a faded baseball hat, she strolled past Liam as if she were looking for something.

Up and down the aisle, even bumping into him at one point and mumbled, "Excuse me," in as deep a voice as she could muster.

Liam glanced up, back at the rack, then back to her with wide eyes. "Guess I owe you fifty bucks. That's good."

She grinned, blew on her fingers, then rubbed them on her shoulder to congratulate herself. "Having any luck?"

"I think I'm going to put on about twenty pounds." He held up a pair of khaki cargo pants that were way too big for him. "This ought to do for a middle-aged man. I didn't shave this morning, so the stubble will be thicker each day. I'll get a pair of eyeglasses and put clear lenses in them. I can get that done at the optometrist office quick enough."

"Sounds perfect. I'll play the part of your son." It would all be fun if not for the reason for the disguises.

Harper changed back into her regular clothes, then paid for her purchases. While Liam ordered glasses with plain glass lenses, she went to the drugstore next door and bought hair dye as close in color as possible to the fake moustache.

They wouldn't be faking their identities for long. Just long enough to get close to Robert. That meant their disguises had to be just enough that they weren't readily recognized.

"We'll have to grab lunch on the run." Liam held out his hand for the keys. "We've been gone long enough as it is."

"Burgers?"

"Sounds good."

They bought lunch and scarfed it down on the way to the office. Since they'd been told they'd be sleeping in shifts in vans during the standoff, they'd taken changes of clothing inside and shoved them under their desks. The bags with their disguises joined the other clothes. All except the wig. Harper took it and the hair dye to the women's restroom.

Unfortunately, she couldn't lock the door to keep others out. She'd have to add the dye to the wig, then stash it somewhere safe until she could rinse it out. With the dye applied, she tucked the wet wig in a plastic bag from the trash bin and stashed it behind one of the toilets.

Thirty minutes later, she retrieved the wig and plunged it under the faucet as the bathroom door opened and Sheila walked in.

She eyed the wad of hair in Harper's hand and the scissors on the side of the sink. "What are you doing?"

"Dying a wig." She put on a "duh" expression.

"Why?"

"I don't want Robert Thompson to recognize me." Best if she kept the conversation as close to the truth as possible.

"I doubt the man will have time to pick you out of the more than a hundred law enforcement officers who will be there, but go ahead and waste your time while the rest of us are making plans to lock up a madman." She opened a stall and stepped inside.

Harper was doing the same thing as all the other officers. Trying to stop a madman.

~

"Why is Detective Scranton dying a wig for a disguise?"

Liam glanced up from his desk. "What?"

She narrowed her eyes. "What are the two of you up to?" She glanced at the bag at his feet. "Those clothes aren't exactly your style. The two of you are planning on going in alone, aren't you?"

"That would be putting my career at risk." He crossed his arms.

"So, you aren't denying it."

"Look, Sheila." He got to his feet, gripped her arm, and pulled her as far away from the crowd as he could. "We're all heading out tonight. Things will get ugly very quickly. Harper and I have a chance to stop this before it escalates."

"I have to tell Payson." She took a step back.

"Please." He reached for her. "This is important. Thompson wants us. We're willing to accept the risk if it saves lives."

She shook her head. "You'll be killed."

"Possibly."

"This was her idea, wasn't it?"

Liam chose not to answer.

"You would never have been willing to risk life and career for me." Her eyes shimmered. "Am I right?"

"At one time, I would have given you the moon. But now, I realize what love truly is. I'll do whatever it takes to try and keep her safe. Even if that means entering the lion's den."

She squared her shoulders. "I'll give you one hour from the time I notice you're gone. Then, I'm telling Payson." She whirled and marched away, not glancing Harper's way as she headed for her desk.

"What's wrong with her?" She shoved the wig into the bag with the other clothes.

"She figured out what we're doing."

"How?" She jerked upright.

"The wig and my bag of clothes. Sheila is not even close to being dumb."

"Is she going to rat us out?"

"She'll give us an hour."

"That's not enough time, Liam. Not nearly enough." She shook her head.

"It will have to be." Once inside, he could make a good guess as to where Thompson stayed. If nothing else, he could ask, but only as a last resort. Every follower who had been there more than a day would know. They couldn't give themselves away by asking too many questions.

"It doesn't matter anyway." Harper stared after Sheila. "Once inside, the chief can't very well force us to leave. We'll get the job done." Her face set in determined lines. "Robert Thompson will be behind bars within a few days."

He really hoped she was right. He'd meant every word he'd said to Sheila. He'd do everything he could to keep Harper safe. Even if that meant taking a bullet for her or making a deal with Thompson that would allow her to go free in exchange for his life.

"What are you thinking?" Her narrowed eyed gaze studied his face.

"Same as you. I'm thinking about tonight when we sneak through the woods and into the compound."

She didn't look convinced. "The tricky part will be changing into our disguises without getting caught."

"We'll have to do that in the woods. It's going to take a while according to the map you handed out. That back road is at least a mile away, then another mile through the woods to the back of the compound. If we try any other way, we'll be seen by our own people." Seen, stopped, and locked up for their own protection.

By late afternoon, the atmosphere in the building changed. The place hummed with nervous energy. Orders were given and bags grabbed. Over a hundred pairs of feet thundered for the front door.

Liam and Harper entered the first van they could find two seats in and settled down for the hour ride. Once the vans started moving, conversation stopped. The solemn atmosphere mirrored everyone's thoughts.

If they were like Liam, they were all wondering whether they were going to repeat that historical time in Waco, Texas. He moved closer on the bench seat so that his thigh pressed against Harper's. Feeling her warmth dispelled some of the chill that had set up residence inside him.

How many law enforcement would die? How many of Thompson's followers? That was the reason he and Harper had to get inside. There couldn't be a repeat of that day in Texas.

He also knew it was quite possible that he and Harper wouldn't make it out alive. Collateral damage as he'd once called Thompson's followers. He knew Payson wouldn't hold back gunfire if it came to that because one of his agents had violated orders and gone out on his own.

Resting his head against the wall of the van, he closed his eyes. It was going to be a long night, and an hour's rest would be beneficial.

When he opened his eyes, the van had stopped. Those inside climbed silently out.

Liam took Harper's hand and stared at the wooden gate. Behind that wall would be the final confrontation. Behind that wall, justice would be served, God willing.

Chapter Six

The night grew late before Harper and Liam could sneak away. Since Robert had yet to make contact with the authorities and vice versa, most of those in front of the compound had taken the time to sleep. Only a few milled around conversing in low tones.

When Liam motioned for her to follow him, she was more than ready. Idleness was never a good thing for her. She hated stakeouts of any kind. She grabbed her bag of thrift store clothes from the van and rushed after Liam.

The moon played peekaboo in an indigo sky, casting the thick woods into almost utter darkness. She paused a few feet in to let her eyes adjust wishing they could chance a flashlight.

Liam waved her forward. "We can't dawdle." His whisper sounded loud in the night.

She picked up her pace, keeping her gaze locked on his back. A few times, her heart leaped into her throat when he stepped into the shadows, and she lost sight of him. She'd never been afraid of the dark before, but that night evil permeated the air with a stench so foul her nose twitched.

She'd never been more frightened than moving through that forest toward a confrontation she might not walk away from. Even worse, she might survive, and Liam perish.

The wind picked up, blowing her hair in her face. She tripped over an exposed tree root and almost went sprawling face first in dry leaves and pine needles.

Liam glanced over his shoulder. "You okay?"

"Yes." She tied her hair into a bun and continued on what seemed like the longest mile she'd ever walked, but she was wrong. The mile from the logging road to the compound would feel longer.

They stopped at the edge of the road. Liam pulled his clothes from his bag. "We change here. If we're caught outside the compound, we'll say we were coming to join them. Let's hope that doesn't happen, though. I'm sure Thompson greets all his newcomers. Our disguises might not be good enough to fool him."

Especially since the man was a master at disguises. She quickly turned around and changed. Stuffing her long hair under the wig, then jamming the cap on top was no easy feat. She should've cut her hair. It would grow back. Nothing she could do then. "I'll need help putting the moustache in the right place without a mirror."

Before gluing the piece above her lip, he lowered his head and kissed her. "Had to do that first. I don't think I'd enjoy kissing someone with a moustache." His teeth flashed. "Let's hurry. I know we have some light here on the road, but that also makes us vulnerable."

She glanced around and nodded, then felt the hair on her lip. Definitely not something she was used to. She transferred her phone and weapon to the pocket of her overalls. "I'm ready." Not really, but there was no turning back. They had to finish this.

She squared her shoulders and stepped back into the woods. Every crunch of a leaf or snap of a twig made her cringe. Robert was bound to have guards set out. They'd hear them coming and shout an alarm.

"We're making too much noise," she whispered.

"We still have a way to go. We'll move slower, being more careful where we put our feet once we see light."

She nodded, although he wasn't facing her and kept moving forward. When they saw the glimmer of light from a window, they stopped. The back of the compound didn't have a tall wall yet.

A barbed-wire fence stretched from rebar to rebar. Another straight wire entwined with the barbed. "It's electric?"

"Yeah, this changes things a bit. Stay here. Let me look around." He slipped away like a wisp of smoke leaving her to hide behind a tree.

Her heart faltered at every sound. Any second, she expected a shout or a gunshot. When had she become such a scaredy-cat?

When she met someone and fell in love, that's when. It was no longer just her she had to worry about.

She peered around the tree as an armed guard marched along the perimeter of the fence. Again, she expected Liam to be seen and an alarm ring out. When none came, she let herself breathe again.

There. Moving silently from tree to tree and coming toward her was who she hoped was Liam. She sagged against the tree when he joined her.

"I found a way in. You okay?"

"I've never been more scared in my life."

"That's surprising. You've always seemed so tough."

She swallowed past her dry throat. "I am. Not knowing when or if we'll be discovered is more frightening than facing an armed lunatic."

He chuckled. "Come on, chicken. I've got you. Stay close and watch where you put your feet."

Watching the placement of her feet made progress slow. The allotted hour given by Sheila before she reported their absence, had to have passed. Would Chief Donnelly send someone after them, or consider them as more collateral damage if it should come to that? Most likely the latter. She and Liam chose their path when they'd left the van.

~

The relief at seeing Harper still standing where he'd left her had almost made him weak in the knees. He'd had a strong fear she would be gone. Taken while he searched for a way in. Finding a place where they could squeeze in between a shed and the end of the fence had taken longer than he would've liked.

When they reached the opening, he put a finger to his lips and pointed to the opening. At her nod, he squeezed through, then waited for her.

They moved through a cluster of RVs and trailers. No lights burned in any of them. One shined from a window in the main house and what looked like a large barn.

A few men stood in the middle of the grounds. It looked to Liam like a shift change of the guards. He pulled Harper into an area light didn't reach. Once the men were gone, they'd head to the barn and try to blend in. Tomorrow, they'd search for

Thompson.

"I want you to enter through the side door of the barn. If anyone asks, you were out taking a leak. Find a spot to wait out the night. I'll follow in five minutes and use the same excuse. I'm Bill Harkins and you're my son, Bobby. We're from up state. Got it?"

She nodded. "Be careful."

When the coast cleared, she sprinted for the door. A boulder lodged in Liam's throat. He didn't like her out of his sight for even a minute and this was the second time that night. But she was a good detective. She could handle herself.

After five minutes, he strolled to the side door and pushed it open. Inside, he peered through the dimness in search of Harper.

She waved at him from a far stall. He headed that way. A man stepped in front of him.

"I ain't seen you around here before."

"Just arrived today." Liam thrust out his hand. Bill Harkins. "That's my boy, Bobby." He did his best to lose the Irish accent and sound Southern.

The man didn't look convinced but shook his hand anyway. "That stall back there belongs to Harold. You can't sleep there. Since we're full up, you'll have to find a spot in the main area." He turned and marched away, then turned back. "Oh, and you ain't allowed outside after ten p.m. even to take a piss. Not unless you're on guard duty. You should know that."

"We haven't been here long enough to know much of anything. Got here right before the shut off time." He had no idea if such a thing existed, but it seemed to appease the man who hadn't given his name.

Liam waved for Harper to join him, then found a vacant corner for them to hunker down in. They should have brought some personal belongings. Showing up empty handed except for their weapons looked too suspicious. They needed a better story.

"We're a couple of homeless men from Rogers. Ex-veterans, both of us. Uncle Sam hasn't taken the care of us we deserve, and we've been looking for a place to belong. This place is it."

"Sounds good to me, Pa." Her lips twitched.

It sounded ridiculous her calling him pa. He tucked his hat lower over his eyes. "Might as well pretend to sleep." He wouldn't be able to sleep for real. "You can get some shut eye. I'll keep watch."

"We'll both keep watch." She mimicked him by pulling her cap brim lower, crossed her arms, and pretended to sleep.

His shoulder pressed against hers, Liam listened to the snores of the men in the building. A few lay beside motorcycles, more slept in horse stalls, a very few slept like him and Harper. Hopefully, that meant they'd blend in just fine. He breathed deep of sweat and motorcycle fumes, then settled in for a long few hours until daybreak.

When the others started to stir, he yawned and stretched his arms, then shook Harper. "Get up, son. Time to work." He marched to where the man he'd shook hands with upon their arrival barked orders. "Where would you like us?"

"Got any skills?"

"I know how to build. So does my boy."

"Good. We've some homes to build. There's one half-finished. You can't miss it. Head over there after breakfast. You get that by knocking on the back door of the big house. The cooks will hand you a plate."

He and Harper followed the line of men to the kitchen door where they were served biscuits and white gravy. "Put the bowls in that tub," a woman told him. "Lunch is at noon."

"I love biscuits and gravy." Harper sat at a wooden picnic table.

"Don't get too comfortable. We've got a job to do." He sat across from her and dug into his breakfast. He glanced around, not seeing any sign of Annie or Thompson. Maybe they ate in the house. All he saw around them was workers.

"Robert Thompson! Time to come out and resolve this." Director Payson's voice bellowed through a bull horn. The battle had begun. "No one needs to get hurt. Send out the women and children first."

No response came from the house. All those eating had paused and resumed when no order came, but the atmosphere had thickened. Tension showed in the lines of their bodies and the speed with which they ate. These men would be ready when Thompson gave the order.

He caught Harper's resigned gaze. When she looked straight

at you, no one would believe her to be a man. Her skin was too smooth, her cheeks too rounded. They needed to find Thompson fast before someone approached her to talk.

"What?"

"Keep your head down or we're in big trouble."

"We're going to be in big trouble soon enough." She finished her breakfast and took both her bowl and his to the tub.

As they joined the men heading to the unfinished building, she asked, "How do we find Robert? We'll have to go in the house if he isn't out soon. I can't think of a reason a couple of worker bees would need to be inside."

"I'll think of something." He bent and grabbed a stack of two-by-fours. "Look busy."

She grabbed a nail gun. "This isn't my first building rodeo." Without a backward glance, she moved away from the crowd and started shooting nails into the wood of the building's frame.

Impressed, Liam grinned and gathered another pile of boards. He added them to the growing pile. The men around him jerked to attention.

Liam turned as the very man they'd come to find approached them.

"Heard we had some new people." Thompson smiled. "Welcome." He thrust out his hand.

Liam returned the handshake and introduced him and Harper with their aliases.

"Wonderful. I insist on interviewing every new member. Please follow me." Thompson turned and headed for the main house. The man obviously expected his orders to be followed immediately.

Liam and Harper fell into step behind him.

Chapter Seven

Harper's heart lodged in her throat. There'd be no hiding in Robert's office. He'd see past her disguise in minutes.

She glanced up at Liam. A muscle ticked in his jaw. He was as nervous as she was.

"Sir." A man jogged toward them, stopping a few feet from Robert. "You need to see this."

"Now?" Robert frowned.

"Yes, sir."

Robert sighed, then pasted on a smile. "I will talk to you, my new friends, later. Excuse me."

Harper almost sagged with relief. "That was close."

"Too close. He'll discover us sooner or later. I'd rather it be later. We need a plan for when we get into his office."

"A plan to take him down." They couldn't very well shoot him. They'd never make it out of the compound alive. Plus, the sound of a gunshot was bound to cause some trigger-happy agent on the other side of the gate to start shooting. People would die.

Another order from the FBI director ordering Robert to come out or release the women and children. Robert laughed and opened a window in the wall. "I cannot do that my good man. Unless you send me Detective Scranton and Agent McConnell. Then, I will consider sending out the women and children." He glanced at the men surrounding him. "Not a chance, my friends. I will not separate the families of my trusted followers. I am simply biding my time." He slammed the window closed.

"Let's go. If he sees us, he'll take us to his office." Harper tugged on Liam's arm. "We need to think of a way to get him away from his people. Until then, we'd be foolish to confront him."

"We still need to get a layout of that house."

"I didn't see any men in the kitchen at breakfast time. Maybe they aren't allowed in the house."

"I'm pretty sure families are, so men with a wife would be." He stared at the second floor. "Ten windows. So, either ten rooms or some rooms have more than one window. One of those has to be Thompson's."

"You planning on grabbing him in his sleep?"

"Better than an open confrontation. Safer for us and for these people."

Harper bit the inside of her lip. "We can try to sneak in once it's dark. I don't see another way." She ducked her head as Annie exited the house and headed for Robert. "We have to get out of sight." If Robert saw them again, he'd be reminded of wanting to get to know them. Annie could very well rat them out.

They headed for the back fence. A couple of men worked on repairs. Harper picked up a tire jack in hopes of looking busy. She really had no idea what to do. Clearly, she was out of her element in overalls and a baseball cap. She needed her suit and gun to feel like herself. This person she masqueraded as had her mind muddled.

"When we take him from his room, I don't want to be in disguise."

Liam stared at her for a moment, then nodded. "Okay. If things go south, I want to finish my life as myself, too. I can fetch our clothes easily enough once it gets dark. I'll slip out the same way we came in. You can wait in the barn, then slip out when you hear a whippoorwill."

She smiled. "Now, we have a plan." They just needed to stay free until then. If they did perish under the hand of Robert, no one could say they didn't give it their all.

When a cowbell rang out at noon, Harper and Liam hid behind a shed. If Robert remembered them at all, he'd look for them at mealtime.

She sighed and leaned her head against the weathered wood of the shed. "I feel like a teenager trying to get back into the house after breaking curfew."

"You broke curfew?" Liam arched a brow.

"Sure."

"I took you for someone who always followed the rules."

She laughed. "Then, you are sorely mistaken. If I didn't, I wouldn't be here with you, would I?"

"Guess not." He flashed a grin and gave her hand a squeeze. "There's no one I'd rather break rules with than you."

"Don't get gushy, Pa. I'm a grown man." She gave him a playful bump of her shoulder.

"Ha ha." He sobered and got to his feet as the sound of men returning to work reached them. "I saw a garden by the kitchen. Maybe we can hide there and pretend to weed for a while."

"This is the weirdest sort of stakeout situation I've ever been in." Why hadn't the chief tried to get through to her? Had he washed his hands of her and Liam so easily or had Sheila not said anything? Either way, they were bound to be missed by now.

~

"Where are the two newcomers?" Robert glanced around the tables at noon.

"Newcomers?" Annie's brow furrowed. "I didn't know we had any. When did they arrive?"

"Last night, according to Harold. I need to speak with them. A middle-aged man and his adult son. Find them."

Sure that his order would be carried out, he marched back to the room he called his office. The place he retired when the headache got unbearable. Everyone knew no one entered his office without an invitation. Even Annie.

There had been something about the way the younger man carried himself that seemed familiar. He'd definitely seen him somewhere before and would like to find out where he came from and why it took him so long to arrive. The location of the place was no longer secret. Anyone that could get past law enforcement…how did the man and his son get inside?

He barked at a passing man to check the fence perimeter. He couldn't blame the two for sneaking in since the front was so heavily guarded, but he did want to know any weaknesses in his fence.

In the quiet of his office, he closed the blinds and lay on the lumpy sofa he'd had brought in upon his arrival. He closed his eyes and let the darkness take him. Once the worst of the pain ebbed, he'd drown the rest with a glass of whiskey. Something he was quickly getting low on. He'd have to make a deal with the authorities outside to get more.

Sometimes, the pain grew so bad, he contemplated putting himself out of his misery. He couldn't, though. Not while the agent and the detective still breathed, and his father didn't. Once they were gone and this town belonged to him, he'd seek medical attention. Until then, he'd do the best he could.

He groaned and pressed a hand to each side of his head and squeezed. Sometimes the pressure helped, but not today. He fought back tears. Tears were a weakness, even when a man's skull was splitting.

Tomorrow, he'd offer the law enforcement outside a trade. It was time to end it all.

~

As the rest of the men broke off and headed to their beds, Liam slipped away and through the hole in the fence. Someone had set another post and wire nearby. Tomorrow, this spot would be closed. There would be no other way to go in or out except the large gate.

He raced through the woods as quick and quiet as he could not wanting to leave Harper alone for too long. His being gone would raise suspicion.

Their clothes were right where they'd left them. He glanced at his watch. He'd been gone for thirty minutes already. Another thirty back. Someone would definitely be wondering where Bill Harkins was.

When he slid back through the fence, Harper waited for him. "They're asking questions. I told them you were assigned guard duty by this hole. I assumed it had been discovered." She glanced at the wire. "I wanted your story to match mine. Anyway, I've got to get back. It doesn't take long to go to the bathroom."

"Good girl." He gave her a quick kiss on the forehead. "I'll set these clothes here and join you in the barn in a few minutes. Then, once everyone is asleep, we'll come back and change."

"Okay." She sprinted back to the barn.

A few heads turned his way when he entered the barn, but no one said anything. Guard duty seemed to be a reasonable reason for him to be gone so long. About thirty minutes later, the building filled with snores.

Liam got slowly to his feet and motioned for Harper to follow him. They stayed in the shadows as much as possible as they made their way to their clothes.

Harper peeled the moustache off her face. "Thank, God. It was very itchy."

"It left a rash." Her upper lip looked red in the moonlight.

"I'll worry about my lip later." She tossed the wig and hat into a nearby trashcan. Her dark locks fell past her shoulders. "Turn around, Liam." She unhooked the overalls.

Right. He turned and started changing back into the fit FBI agent rather than an overweight man. When he turned back around, Harper was again a beautiful woman. She'd tied her hair back, shoved her weapon into the waistband of her pants, and tossed everything else in the garbage.

"I missed me." She flashed a quick grin. "Nice to see you back, too."

"Come on, Detective. Let's get this over with."

"Has the director tried to contact you?"

"No. The chief you?"

"I find that strange. They must be furious." She pulled her phone from her pocket. "No service. I usually have service on this mountain. Do you think there's a blocker around here?"

"I'd bet on it. I'm sure everyone turned over their cell phones. In case someone didn't, Thompson wouldn't want his people contacting the outside." He peered around the corner. "Coast is clear. Let's go."

She kept one hand on his back and followed close enough to step on his heels a time or two. Liam turned the knob on the kitchen door. It turned easily under his touch.

They couldn't risk a light, but the full moon outside made it easy enough to see his way around. Liam checked a door to his right. Storage. He pointed to the ceiling. Robert's room would most likely be upstairs. Finding it without someone seeing them would be difficult. All rooms looked the same from this side of the door, and they couldn't very well knock on each of them.

They passed a door with a sign that said office. Good. They were getting closer. He stopped in the center of the hall and studied the doors on each side. Eenie Meenie Miney Mo.

A baby cried from behind the door on his left. Not that room, then. He strained his ears to hear other sounds that would mark a room off as a possibility.

"A woman's voice in this one," Harper whispered.

Two down, eight more to go. They moved past the first two doors. The next two were quiet. Liam pressed his ear to one, Harper the other. He heard nothing and moved further.

Snores, but he couldn't tell whether they came from a man or a woman or whether whoever made the noise was alone. He slowly turned the knob. Locked. Of course, it would be.

Frustration burned through him. They had Thompson right in front of them and still couldn't find him! He stepped back so he wouldn't slam his fist against the wall.

"Let's check the office." Harper put a hand on his arm.

"Not without me." Annie, gun in hand, stepped from one of the next set of rooms.

"Just the people I wanted to see." Thompson exited the office and aimed a weapon in their direction. "Please, come in. So nice of you to come to me without being asked. The newcomers?" He tilted his head.

"Yep. Right under your nose." He made a move for his gun.

"I wouldn't, Agent, unless you want the detective gunned down in front of you. Annie, please take their weapons." He opened the door further to allow them to precede him.

Liam felt as if he entered an execution chamber.

Chapter Eight

Harper wiped sweaty palms on the legs of her pants and stood rigid in front of Robert's battered metal desk. He'd fallen a long way from being a successful plastic surgeon.

He steepled his fingers under his chin. "I'm going to make a guess that the two of you are the newcomers. That you took a page out of my book and wore a disguise? Very clever. Are you ready for your punishment?"

"The people you blame are dead." Harper crossed her arms. No way was she going to cower before this man. If she was to perish, she'd do so fighting.

"Someone has to pay. It isn't personal." He laughed and waved a hand. "Okay, it is personal. I've had great fun playing with the two of you, but the game is over. I don't have much time and need to find a successor before I go. Annie is a likely candidate. She pulled the hood over your eyes, Detective. The agent's, too."

"Cancer?" Harper arched a brow. "The same kind as your father? We can get you medical help, Robert."

"Do not call me by my first name." His smile faded. "I do not want the kind of medical help you'll give me. My fate is in the hands of God. Take me or spare me, either way my vision will live on."

She doubted it. "So, now what?"

"The two of you will be tied to chairs. The whole world will watch one last video feed. Your deaths will make the headlines for sure."

Liam made a noise deep in his throat. "You won't finish what you've started before this place is stormed by law enforcement."

His lip curled. "But the two of you will be gone when that happens. Don't sell my people short, Agent. They are capable of more than you know. Annie, take them away. Make sure their bindings are secure. We aren't dealing with fools."

"Let's go. Don't make any stupid moves or I will shoot you." She ushered them from the building as Director Payson gave another order for the women and children to be released. He added Harper and Liam to the list this time.

Sheila must have gotten worried by this time. She and Liam couldn't count on being saved. They were on their own. Payson would not jeopardize putting Robert behind bars for a couple of wayward law enforcement. Sure, they'd be sorry to lose an agent and a detective, but they would be collateral damage if they didn't find a way to save themselves.

She cut a glance at Liam. He gave her a soft smile and mouthed the words, "I love you."

For a second, tears stung her eyes, but she blinked them away. She returned the sentiment and refused to lose hope.

Annie led them to a storm shelter. It looked like the very one Amber had been held in. Two chairs had been placed in the center of the room. Wrist shackles were bolted to the far wall. Two men stood at attention. "Sit." Annie turned on the camera and smiled at the lens. The two men tied their arms to the chair armrests and their feet to the legs.

Almost immediately, Harper's hands started tingling from the tight binds. "Now what?"

"You wait for Mr. Thompson. I'm sure he won't be long." She left with the men.

No light pierced the darkness except for a small one placed above the camera to shine on their faces. She shared another glance with Liam, not wanting to say anything personal while being filmed.

Would Robert torture them before killing? Would he kill them slow? She didn't think her death would be quick. Not if he wanted to keep the world watching. She stiffened her shoulders and stared into the camera lens.

A loud battering sounded, muffled, but still audible. The strong gate was being attacked.

"Help is coming." Liam grinned.

"Yep. Hopefully, they'll break through in time. The closer they get, the sooner Robert will come for us." If they kept talking, the chief and the director would get word from the live feed. Maybe, they'd slow the attack and give her and Liam some more time.

Liam nodded and studied the room. "Nothing here for us to use." He jerked against his ties. "Solid. Thompson had definitely turned the storm shelter on the north side of the house into a prison cell. Good thing we found that hole in the fence where they hadn't strung the electric wire. Easy access."

Harper grinned. He gave those on the other side of the fence their exact whereabouts and how to get in. "Right. Finding that hole sure helped put us in a good place. I'm being facetious."

"I could tell. Solid concrete blocks. This cellar can withstand almost anything, I bet. Even fire."

Harper widened her eyes. Fire would burn the house full of women and children. It would be Waco all over again. "No fire."

"If the people are warned first…"

She stared at the camera. "Please, no fire."

"I'm trying to get us out of here."

"Not at the expense of civilians." She narrowed her eyes. "I couldn't." Did Liam have a cruel strength or merely being practical?

"You know I'll do everything in my power to keep the loss of life to zero, but some things may be out of our control. It's best the people are warned."

Less than five minutes later, Payson issued the command that Robert had until sunrise to surrender, or the compound would be set on fire. Any of his followers willing to come out would be given safe passage back to Oakdale.

The war had started.

~

Robert downed the last of his whiskey and laughed. Threats were useless. His people were willing to be martyrs for the cause. They weren't afraid. But, it might be time to move things along. Punishment awaits, and he intended to enjoy what the agent and detective will go through.

He marched to the barn and asked for a volunteer. Someone not afraid to be on camera doing something most people would think vile. A man in his twenties, Bruce Holder and already hardened by life, stepped forward.

"Good. You'll be handsomely rewarded in our new world. Follow me."

Bruce followed without a word. This was the type of follower Robert appreciated. One who volunteered before knowing what the job would entail.

He stopped at a shed and pulled out what he needed before leading Bruce to the cellar. "You may keep your face away from the camera if you'll feel more comfortable."

"I'm not worried about being seen."

"Very good. Are you armed?"

"Yes, sir."

Robert held out his hand. "I would like to borrow your weapon, please. Only until the prisoner is secured."

Bruce handed him a Glock.

Robert opened the cellar door and led the way down the concrete steps. "Hello. Are you ready?"

Both prisoners turned their heads to face him. "After your little invitation to those outside the gate, we need to get a move on. You need to receive your punishment before it's too late."

~

Liam's heart froze at the sight of the whip in the second man's hands. He then met Harper's frightened glance. Gone was the strong determination only to be replaced by sheer terror. After a few seconds of locking gazes with him, she hitched her chin and stared at the camera, resolve coating her features.

Good. She'd need to be strong to endure what was coming. They both would. It didn't seem as if help would arrive in time for them.

Thompson aimed a gun at Harper. "Agent McConnell you will be untied and shackled to the wall. If you resist, I will shoot our lovely detective between the eyes. Understand?"

Liam nodded.

His ropes were cut, and he was secured facing the wall, his back to the camera. With a quick slice of a knife, his shirt and jacket fell open, exposing his skin to the cool air of the cellar.

"No." Harper's cry rang out. "You can't do this. It's barbaric."

"Since I'm the one in charge, Detective, I can do anything I desire."

Liam glanced over his shoulder and met the cold eyes of the man holding the whip. He'd endure the best he could. Taking a deep breath, he faced the wall.

"Let's start with twenty, shall we? I prefer to watch from the comfort of my office. Wait five minutes before you start." Thompson dropped the keys to the shackles on a wooden shelf on the wall. "Annie will come after the lashes are dealt."

The five minutes after Thompson left were the longest five minutes of Liam's life. Harper's pleading for the man not to do this echoed through the concrete room as the man cut away the rest of Liam's shirt and jacket, dropping the pieces to the dirt floor.

Never in his wildest nightmare had Liam thought he'd be whipped on live feed for the world to see. Orders from Payson had ceased. The battering on the gate had stopped. All eyes seemed to be glued on what was about to unfold in that underground room.

The first slash burned like fire along his ribcage.

Harper's scream pierced the air.

The second slash took Liam's breath away. A hiss escaped his lips. He shut off his mind, filling it with an empty darkness and removed himself from the pain. He barely heard Harper's sobs as the lashes came with a painful regularity.

He lost consciousness by lash fifteen.

He woke to Harper calling his name. He opened his eyes and struggled to his feet to take the pressure off his wrists.

"The man is gone," she said. "But said he would return."

"Did he finish?"

"Yes."

So, there would be more. Thompson intended to continue the whipping until Liam stopped breathing. "Payson?"

"We have an hour until daylight. I have no idea what's going on out there. Everything is quiet."

He coughed, then took a deep breath, regretting the movement instantly. Expanding his ribs pulled at his back, or what was left of it. "How bad is it?"

"There's too much blood for me to be sure, but I think it's pretty bad."

The man who had whipped him entered the cellar with a

bucket. He tossed cold water onto Liam's back, the liquid mixing with his blood and soaking the waistband of his pants and the dirt under his feet, turning it to mud. Then, he tossed the bucket in the corner and left.

Liam shivered so hard the chains rattled and his teeth chattered. He'd take the cold over the whipping, though. "Looks like I get a break."

"Maybe something is happening up there after all."

"Promise me something."

"Anything."

He'd hoped she'd say that. "No matter what happens to me, no matter what threat is made to my life, if you can escape, you go. No looking back."

"Liam—"

He leaned his forehead against the concrete wall. "You said anything, Harper. I can endure anything if I know you'll escape if you can."

Maybe, by saying his feelings out loud, letting those watching hear his struggle, his declaration of love, some of the followers' eyes would be opened. Some would see what a monster they followed.

"Oh, Liam."

"You promised."

"I did." Her words broke on a sob. "I will escape if the opportunity shows itself."

"Good." He closed his eyes and breathed through the pain. "You're the best partner anyone could have, Detective Scranton. Don't let anyone tell you otherwise."

Despite making her promise to escape, the worry that she wouldn't be able to, ripped sharper than the whip. What punishment would Thompson do to Harper? Part of it was watching him be whipped. What would he do to kill her?

The door above the stairs opened.

"I love you, Harper."

Chapter Nine

Annie marched down the stairs, casting an expressionless glance at Liam. "Time to move you, Detective."

"To where?" A lump formed in Harper's throat. She didn't want to leave Liam. What if the man with the whip returned? What if he killed him? She couldn't let Liam die alone. She had to fight; do whatever it took to prevent that from happening.

"Since we know that law enforcement is watching, and we also know about the agent basically told them how to bring down this compound, we're going to put you in the house." She grinned. "They won't want to kill the lovely detective, now would they?"

"If it means stopping Robert Thompson by my death, they won't hesitate." She hoped. "What time is it?"

"Nightfall is in half an hour. Let's go." She kept the gun aimed at Liam with her left hand while cutting Harper's ties with her right.

As soon as the last piece of binding fell from her ankles, Harper kicked the gun hand and head-butted Annie. The gun skittered across the hard packed floor and landed near Liam. Harper lunged to her feet.

The cold concrete walls of the cellar echoed with the women's harsh breathing and Annie's curses. They circled each other, their gazes warily on the other.

Without warning, Annie lunged forward, her fist aimed at Harper's face. But she was too quick, darting to the side and delivered a swift kick to the other woman's knee. Annie fell back.

She grunted in pain but refused to back down, charging forward with renewed fury. Harper dodged and weaved, her movements fluid and graceful as she struck back with lightning-fast punches and kicks, putting all her fear and anger into each strike.

They clashed in a flurry of blows, their fists and feet a blur. The sound of their fists and grunts filled the cellar as they battled for dominance.

A sharp upper cut split Harper's lip. Her left eye had started to swell shut, but neither her nor Annie was willing to give up. Harper continued to fight with a fierce determination, her muscles straining with the effort.

Annie kicked her legs out from under her.

Liam shouted her name as she crashed over the chairs, shattering the dry wood, and into the camera, knocking it off its tripod. She rolled as Annie's foot stomped inches from her face.

She leaped to her feet, fists raised. "Give it up, Annie. You won't win this."

"Watch me." Her lip curled.

Harper eyed the gun near Liam. Too far for her to retrieve quickly. Instead, she bent slowly and picked up a broken chair leg. The adrenaline of the fight was starting to wear off. She didn't know how much longer she could fight.

Annie screamed and charged.

Harper lifted the chair leg above her head. She swung it like a bat. The thud of it hitting the other woman's skull vibrated up her arm.

Eyes wide, Annie collapsed, her sightless eyes staring into the camera lens.

The shock of actually killing someone left Harper numb, but she couldn't dwell on those feelings. Not yet. Not until they were safely out of the cellar and away from the compound.

She dropped the chair leg and rushed to snatch the shackle keys from the table Robert Thompson had dropped them on. She retrieved Annie's gun from the floor and tucked it into her waistband, then quickly released Liam.

He sagged against the wall, his breathing as ragged as hers. "Dang girl, you can fight."

"I had no idea. All I knew was that I was fighting for our lives. Can you walk?"

"I'll crawl out of here if I have to." He leaned on her and let her help him up the stairs and outside.

The allotted time had expired during her fight with Annie. Firebombs were flung over the wall, igniting anything made of burnable material. One side of the wooden gate hung open.

People surged from the buildings and were rounded up by FBI and SWAT team members. Harper couldn't see any sign of Robert. "Let's get you some medical help."

"Not until we find Thompson."

"You're too injured to deal with him." She headed for the gate.

Liam's arm slid from her shoulders. "I'm going to finish this, Harper."

She nodded at the determination on his face, feeling the same way. "Okay. Let's check his office." She glanced at the burning building. "We'll have to hurry." Only fools rushed into a burning building with no intention of saving someone.

They had to be quick. Liam's strength wouldn't hold up for long.

She spotted the FBI director. "I'm sorry." She cupped Liam's face and kissed him. "I love you."

"Sorry for what?" He frowned.

"For this." She turned and yelled for the director.

Spotting them, he rushed their way, calling for a medic. As Liam was ushered from the compound, a betrayed look on his face, Harper backed toward the main building. She'd apologize later. With one last look at the man she loved, she darted into the burning building.

Smoke filled the building. Upstairs, she pulled the neckline of her shirt over her nose and headed for Robert's office, pulling her weapon from her waistband.

Robert sat at his desk. A revolver lay next to his right hand. He made no move to pick it up when she entered.

"It's over." She kept her weapon trained on him. "Your people are being rounded up. Annie is dead. Let's not have any more bloodshed."

"I really am impressed at how you and the agent reacted in that cellar. The clues the agent gave. Oh, I know Annie is dead. The sight of her face in the camera will haunt me for the rest of my life. A life that won't be much longer." He twirled a pencil on the desktop. "I had such grand ideas for a new world, Detective.

Now that it's gone, what is left for me?"

She had no answer for him other than the fact he'd spend the rest of his short life behind bars. "Let's go, Robert. This place won't last long." Already the smoke burned her lungs. She coughed.

"No need." Before she could react, he lifted the gun, pointed it at his temple, and pulled the trigger.

Shock reverberated through her. She took in the scene for a second, then whirled to race from the building.

~

Liam woke lying on his stomach in a hospital bed. His back burned under a thick bandage. He turned his head to see Harper slumped over in a chair fast asleep.

A groan escaped him as he moved.

Harper's eyes popped open. "Are you in pain? I can fetch the nurse."

"I'm okay. I don't want to be under the influence of a painkiller while you fill me in. How much time has passed?"

She smiled. "It's the next morning." She scooted the chair closer to the bed and held his hand. "Other than Robert and Annie, no lives were lost. The man who whipped you is being arrested, but most of the people will be released to resume their lives, what they can get back anyway."

"How did Robert die? Fire?"

"He shot himself when I entered his office." A shadow crossed her features. "It was so fast, I couldn't stop him."

"The man was dying anyway. He spared himself a lot of pain."

"That's what I keep telling myself, but after killing Annie…" Her thumb stroked the back of his hand.

"You did what you had to, sweetheart, and saved both of our lives. I'm forever grateful." He reached up to cup her cheek. "Want to talk about us now?" He smiled. "I did promise that we would."

She gave a soft laugh. "You want to be my boyfriend?"

"Absolutely not."

She jerked back, her eyes wide. "What?"

"I want more than that. Let's explore the idea of something more permanent."

"Are you proposing? Because if you are, it's a very strange one."

He laughed. "No, but I will when the time is right. Will you say yes?"

"Maybe." Her smile widened. "If you behave yourself. What then, Liam? Who picks up and moves?"

"Wanna draw straws?" At her frown, he continued, "I'm kidding. I think the city of Oakdale could use another detective, don't you?"

"You'd leave the agency for me?" Tears welled in her eyes.

"Without a second thought. Let's seal the deal with a kiss. You'll have to come to me. I'm not able to bend that way."

She lowered her head and kissed him with a promise of a future together.

The End

Dear Reader,

I hope you've enjoyed reading this series as much as I've enjoyed writing it. You may purchase paperback books signed by the author at my bookstore. Signed books make great gifts for yourself or someone else.

Please visit my website to find your next favorite series.

Cynthia

www.cynthiahickey.com

Cynthia Hickey is a multi-published and best-selling author of cozy mysteries and romantic suspense. She has taught writing at many conferences and small writing retreats. She and her husband run the publishing press, Winged Publications. They live in Arizona and Arkansas, becoming snowbirds with three dogs. They have ten grandchildren who keep them busy and tell everyone they know that "Nana is a writer."

Enjoy other books by Cynthia Hickey

Misty Hollow
Secrets of Misty Hollow
Deceptive Peace
Calm Surface
Lightning Never Strikes Twice
Lethal Inheritance
Bitter Isolation
Say I Don't
Christmas Stalker

The Seven Deadly Sins series
Deadly Pride
Deadly Covet
Deadly Lust
Deadly Glutton
Deadly Envy
Deadly Sloth
Deadly Anger